DARK MASKS

The Vickie Chronicles
Dark Masks
Written by I. Savage

Published by Improvisation News LLC / IN Studios

Copyright © 2022 Israel Savage

ISBN: 978-1-959791-00-3 (Digital)
ISBN: 978-1-959791-01-0 (Paperback)
ISBN: 978-1-959791-02-7 (Hardcover)

Contact company for Library of Congress control number.

Edited by Aime Sund
Cover, chapter and part page design by Katarina Prenda
Author photo by Ismael Fernandez
Blueprints by Oleg Stepanov
All other Illustrations by J. Ferd

First printing edition 2022

Improvisation News, LLC / IN Studios
Suite 5B
New York, NY 10031
https://thesavagebooks.com/

The
VICKIE
CHRONICLES
BOOK 1

DARK
MASKS

I. SAVAGE

BOOK TWO

Be the first to read the second book in this six-book series, *Dark Chains*, available for order now on Amazon.

DEDICATION

To Lisa, my childhood best friend,

To Rose, Aunt Hilda, David, Todd, Veronica, Peyton, Toren,

and Gitana, the most ardent story lovers in my family,

To Grandma Thomas, the steel-trap-minded keeper of our

ancestral lore,

To Wilbur, whose riveting, made-up tales were the last thing

I heard each night as a child—I continue that nightly tradition

with my own children,

And, finally,

To childhood best friends and story lovers everywhere,

I wrote *The Vickie Chronicles* series with all of you at the

forefront of my mind.

ABOUT THIS BOOK

Aside from the characters and story, there are several things that make *The Vickie Chronicles* unique.

Birthed During the Pandemic - The series wouldn't have been born had it not been for the focus and stirred emotions the pandemic of 2020 brought. Perhaps this book might serve as a silver lining to that experience.

Began as a Script - The first few drafts of all my books are written as screenplays or TV pilots. I find it's the most efficient way to refine story, characters, and dialogue. I'm also a visual thinker and see the story in front of my eyes like a movie, so I might as well write it down that way. Once I have a solid script, I know a solid novel is inevitable and just a matter of time.

Developed Using Improvisation - I love improvisation. Rather than sit alone in my room with my computer, I prefer to get a group of my actor friends together and improvise different potential character choices.

Incorporating Video Technology - As far as I know, we're among the first, if not the first, young adult book series to incorporate video into our pages. I'm enjoying the experiment. As mentioned, I think visually and hope this added element enhances your connection to the world of the series.

Resonance with Readers - Most importantly, so much focused energy infuses the pages of this series, that I'm certain, like the banging of a gong, it will call all those who resonate. Hopefully, you will be among those who feel the creative energy behind this project and answer the resounding echo.

JOIN OUR MAILING LIST

I love presents! I like to get them, but I especially like to give them. If this story resonates with you, take a moment to join our mailing list. You'll be the first to hear about the release of new books and you'll receive exclusive goodies.

Like what, you may ask? Well, if I told you, that would spoil the surprise.

Join Our Mailing List Here:

https://bit.ly/TheSavageBooksNews

Or

Scan the Code Below:

READ THIS FIRST

Don't you love a good mystery? You're embarking on a unique, often surprising, sometimes thrilling adventure, and, *Dark Masks,* is just the beginning of this six-book series! Before you get started, I'd like to point out a few things that will enhance your experience:

Hidden Treasures - To unlock some of the bonus features of this book, simply point the camera on your phone at the QR codes appearing throughout the novel and tap.

Sensitive Topics and Triggers - If this book were a movie, it would be rated PG-13, however, please keep in mind the story centers around a home for troubled teens. Although the novel is filled with humor, hope, and resilience; identity, eating disorders, abandonment, suicide, kidnapping, potential homicide, and violence are some of the topics with which these brave teens wrestle.

If you or someone you know needs mental health assistance visit the following site for resources:

https://bit.ly/InternationalMentalHelplines

Pass it On - If, *Dark Masks,* resonates with you, please consider writing a review on Amazon or telling a friend about it the old-fashioned way. I'm looking for a tribe of readers who love these characters as much as I do. I'm hoping you'll be one such reader. But there's only one way to find out.

So, without further ado, *let the journey begin!*

WELCOME TO

Blueberry Hill

HOME FOR TROUBLED YOUTH

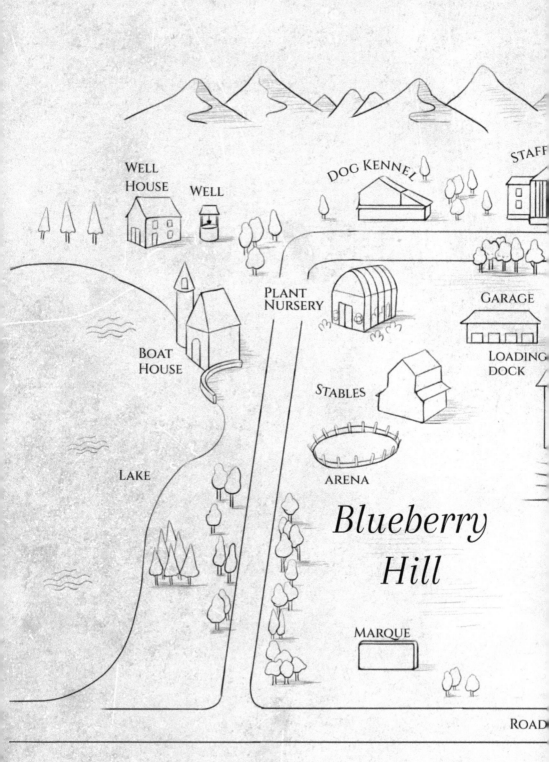

WELL HOUSE

WELL

DOG KENNEL

STAFF

PLANT NURSERY

GARAGE

BOAT HOUSE

LOADING DOCK

STABLES

LAKE

ARENA

Blueberry Hill

MARQUE

ROAD

NOT TO SCALE

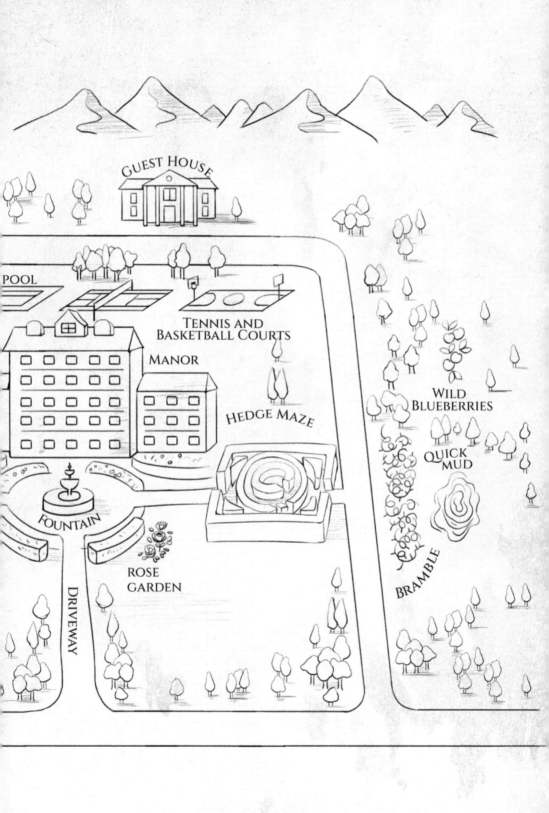

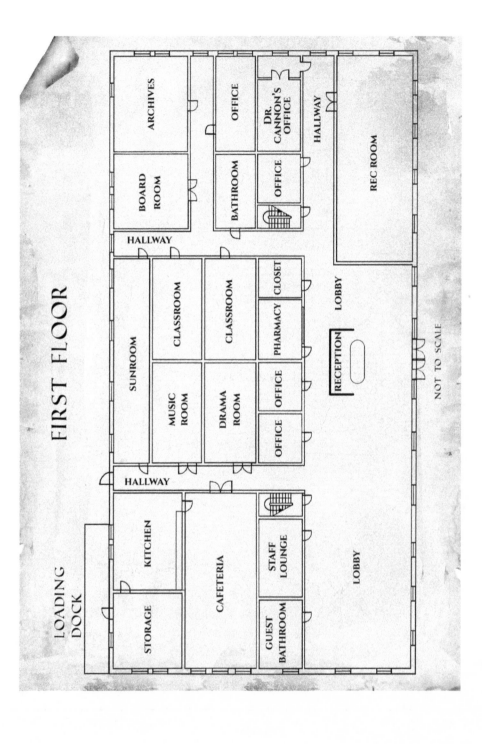

SIXTH FLOOR

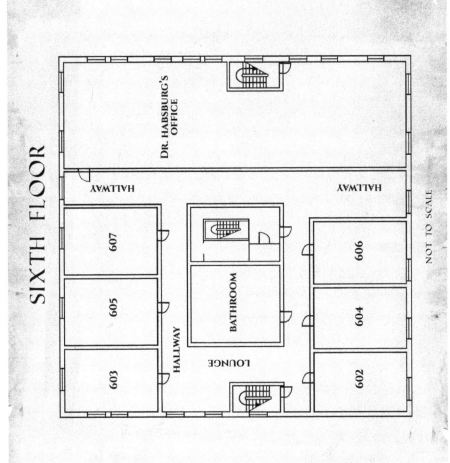

DR. HABSBURG'S OFFICE

HALLWAY

HALLWAY

607

605

603

HALLWAY

BATHROOM

LOUNGE

606

604

602

NOT TO SCALE

Assessment and Plan

Provider: Blueberry Hill Home for Troubled Youth, LLC **Client Name:** Linda Rossi
Group Assignment: Pod #1 **Session Number:** #1

Diagnosis: Anorexia Nervosa, Mild Depression

Treatment

Intake Protocol: Clinical Assessment **Medications:** Olanzapine 0.625 mg/day,
        Medical History   Fluoxetine 20 mg/day,
        Labs, weight, BMI   *as per* Dr. Mariska Habsburg, M.D.

Long-Term Goals (3 Months):

1. Restore healthy eating patterns and weight maintenance.
2. Demonstrate healthy cognitive beliefs about self that lead to positive identity.
3. Develop healthy interpersonal relationships that help prevent relapse of the eating disorder.
4. Stabilize current foster family situation and resolve housing insecurity.
5. Develop coping strategies (i.e., assertiveness).

Session Notes

Body Language, Facial Patterns: Downcast, glazed eyes. Shoulders slumped. Monotone speech.

Summary:

1. Client presents as mildly depressed. Instability of foster placement may be a contributing factor.
2. Expressed loneliness and isolation.
3. Client restricts her food intake to feel some sense of control, given housing insecurity and disconnection from biological family.

Other Observations/Comments:

- Follow-up with housing security questionnaire for caregivers.

Client Signature: *Linda Rossi* **Primary Caregiver 1:** *Deena Evans*
(Age 14 and up)   Linda Rossi   Deena Evans
                                          (Caseworker)

Primary Caregiver 2: _____ **Therapist Signature:** *Ara Cannon*
            N/A   Dr. Ara Cannon, Ph.D.

PROLOGUE

The Fourth Floor
11:52 p.m.

It was the kind of darkness you could get lost in, or find yourself in, or both. But Linda didn't need the light to see. She had memorized every inch of room 402.

Not that there was much to memorize. The furnishings were simple: three creaky iron beds, each with a matching bedside table; a shared chest of drawers; a tiny sink; a simple desk; and her two roommates, who couldn't be more different from each other.

From the partially open fourth-floor window, she could hear the lull of the wood frogs and field crickets as they hummed in perfect unison to the *tap, tap, tapping* of the treetop branches on the windowpanes. The scent of wet evergreens and dark earth fluttered inside, permeating the room.

Lying in her bed, she tilted her head ever so slightly to the right, catching the whisper of Annie's sleepy giggles in her fairy-and-gumdrop-dusted dreams. Turning her head to the left, Linda found the light snores coming from her other roommate even more comforting. She smiled at the irony of the image in her mind, picturing Vickie as an almost cuddly, docile bulldog slurping bits of air through her open mouth.

Finally, Linda focused on the ceiling above her, aware of the faint, rhythmic tick of the nearby hallway clock. She breathed in this dark place, this moment, these two friends, for what might be one of the last times.

Still glued to her bed like a fly stuck to a hanging sticky tape, Linda frowned, thinking of what the morning had in store for her. But first, she needed to bid farewell to someone she felt more connected with than either of her trusted sleeping companions.

She exhaled as she slid the pressed white sheet off her body, inch by inch, until she uncovered her ankles, making the liberation of her feet as effortless as two flurried kicks. The metal bed frame of the single bed creaked with each emancipated foot she placed on the cool tile floor.

This wasn't the first time she had snuck out of bed to meet him; finding her way in the dark had become routine. She felt her way to the end of the mattress, one hand over the other, stepping into her slippers. Then, after twelve paces toward the door, holding her hands out as guides in front of her, Linda groped until she felt the jiggle of the old, metal doorknob and turned it slowly. Despite her caution, the door whined like a disagreeable old cat as she opened it, making her laugh softly.

As the dim light from the sconces that lined the hallway spilled into the room, she looked back over her shoulder and saw Annie and Vickie still fast asleep. The corners of her mouth stretched into a contented smile, faltering when the notes of a distinctive melody overtook the stillness of the moment.

The sounds seemed to come from everywhere and nowhere. In the faint, tinny dings of what sounded like a toy xylophone, she recognized the tune . . .

The more we get together, together, together,
The more we get together, the happier we'll be.

Stationary, half in and half out of the room, Linda tucked a strand of her long, dirty-blonde hair behind her right ear, furrowing her brow in concentration.

Odd.

She had heard the familiar childhood tune at some point during her stay at the manor, but couldn't remember when. Maybe it was in a dream?

The last three months seemed surreal. She never expected to make a best friend or find — him. Her cheeks plumped, lifted by her grin.

Am I actually going to miss this place? She snickered at the thought.

Slowly, her mind wandered back to the song that tickled the air. She was uncertain if the tune was simply stuck in her head, or if she was truly hearing it echo through the resting halls. The notes trailed off and evaporated into the darkness so swiftly, she couldn't be sure.

A mystery for another time. She had an appointment to keep. A rendezvous.

Linda crossed the threshold into the hallway and closed the door to room 402. The finality of the soft, dull sound as its lock set latched made her shiver.

"Someone just walked over my grave," she whispered to herself.

Vickie would have made fun of that silly saying. Her roommate and best friend didn't believe in superstition or anything she couldn't see, touch, taste, smell, or hear.

Linda had only taken a couple of steps when a clang sounded behind her at the far end of the long, shadowy corridor, causing her to freeze in place.

Have I been caught? Her breathing quickened. *Or maybe it's him?*

"Hello?" she whispered, turning toward the noise. "Is that you?" Her muscles contracted and her eyes sparkled in the barely adequate yellow light at the possibility the latter might be the case. Awaiting a response on the tips of her toes, she poised motionless, as if someone had pressed pause.

Only silence answered.

It's probably just the old pipes complaining.

Her posture relaxed, and she continued walking with purposeful caution, her eyes aimed forward and her heart quickening with each measured step.

Anyway, even if I am caught sneaking out to meet him, what can they do to me this late in the game?

Both hands of the five-foot-high, nineteenth-century grandmother clock were nearing twelve. There were grandmother clocks on every floor of the manor, standing guard, keeping time, reminding all who resided there of the moments they were losing during their stay. She halted to touch the glass covering its face.

Linda knew the difference between a grandmother and grandfather clock, corrected once by her very precise and rigid English foster mother. Both were freestanding, with a swinging pendulum, but grandmother clocks were a foot shorter.

Linda passed in front of the clock, another tiny laugh of mischievous delight escaping her lips at the thought of him waiting for her, as she continued forward and down the stairwell.

In her absence, there was a stillness in the hallway once again, save the unrelenting swinging of the pendulums as they *tick-tocked*.

⁕ ⁕ ⁕ ⁕ ⁕

Seconds became minutes; minutes became hours.

The long hand revolved three times around the clock face before there was any notable sound or movement.

Then, the sound of a young girl's voice dreamily humming the same tune as before pierced the quiet. It echoed from the upper floors through the stairwell door.

Linda.

Descending the steps from the upper floors to the bottom, she bounced from wall to wall like a ball in slow motion.

The more we get together . . .

It had been a harmless tune when she first heard it, but like dripping water drilling into the cavern floor, over time, it pounded deep into Linda's bone and marrow. Snared by the sound of it for a moment too long, she now paid the price, entranced as it carved its way into her.

She descended the staircase past the fourth floor until the door at the bottom of the first-floor stairwell creaked open. If Linda's English foster mother were here, she should would have insisted, "It's called the ground floor, dear." Linda's humming continued to hang in the air. She lingered for a moment, putting her hands on the inside of the door frame to steady herself.

Linda noticed her distorted reflection on the slippery-clean tiled floors and couldn't help but stare at it for a moment. She liked this shifting version of herself more than what she saw in mirrors. Linda avoided mirrors most of the time.

On the stairs, she had felt like a toy slinky propelled downward by her own momentum, one headlong step at a time, but she had made it all the way down without stumbling. Somehow, walking down the first-floor hallway that stretched in front of her seemed like it might be harder to manage. In fact, peering down the endless corridor, the journey seemed insurmountable.

The entire manor appeared to sway like it had set sail on a turbulent sea. Yet Linda felt a steadiness inside her, a resoluteness. Her head spun, and she felt nauseous, but knew somehow if she could just get a gulp of the fresh night air, it would revive her.

The light from the antique light fixtures lining the hallway danced on the dingy wallpaper, positioned on both sides of the corridor every twelve feet, brighter and more comforting than she remembered. She moved toward the first pool of light on the right-hand side, cocking her head to the side to balance herself.

After a cautious first step forward, her feet glided toward the light until she gently bumped the wall and ricocheted across to the next glowing space. Before long, her body moved from wall to wall down the corridor.

Present reality evaporated as she continued onward like an untethered balloon, a ghostly apparition—free, yet held tight in the warm grip of the propelling force.

Losing herself, if only for a moment, enthralled her. It was one thing to listen to the symphony and quite another to conduct, no, to be the symphony.

Linda hummed, and it was as if the entire world swayed along. The night air wafted through cracked windows, unable to resist joining the game, gently blowing the hanging plants in the lobby to the haunting tune. Even the lanky night janitor mopping the floor kept time with the music, swabbing right, then left, stepping backward, swabbing right, then left again, in an awkward reverse box-step of a dance.

At another time, Linda would have hidden from the janitor for fear of being caught out of her room past curfew, but emboldened by the exhilaration of the moment and the wooziness, she didn't hide from anyone or anything.

In fact, Linda felt gloriously numb and electric, teetering on the edge of something unknown. Her heart expanded and enveloped everything with its warmth. Possibility hung heavy in the air around her as she watched the gangly young man, his dark hair spilling from under his cap, continuing mopping, finally disappearing around the corner without having noticed her.

The tune she carried inside her now beat along with her heart, moving her with a determined grace. She meandered past the vacant, first-floor reception desk, admiring how the moonlight played on the tiled floor and the polished desk surfaces.

Her flowing white nightgown glowed in the moonlight that poured through the glass of the french doors as she placed her hands on both handles and effortlessly pulled the doors open, exiting the building. As if it were a portal into a new realm, she breathed in so deeply her eyes closed involuntarily, then she released it into the expectant night. Behind her, the grandmother clocks on each floor chimed 3:00 a.m.

Goose bumps peppered her arms.

The darkness was like icy water lapping against her entire body. Even in the summer, the Maine night air was exhilaratingly chilly, but not enough to rouse her from her trance.

She moved through the garden and caught the scent of Nurse Lilly's exquisite roses infusing the air, humming all the while.

The lake that bordered the property, large and foreboding, separated the residents of Blueberry Hill from outside influence. It was expansive enough that the water in the distance caressed the horizon. Linda heard the tiny little waves kiss the shore one after the other as she flowed past. Their rhythm nudged her forward and down the hill into a clearing.

Transfixed, focused but unfocused, she walked with intention, though not at all certain where she was going. She passed a large stone marquee tangled in the lush ivy. Words cut out from mahogany read, "Blueberry Hill," then underneath in smaller letters, "Home for Troubled Youth."

She drifted through the grass, dampened by the night air, and onto the nearby deserted road. There she found a stillness, a welcoming acceptance that embraced her as she closed her eyes and soaked it all in. Gently, she released the rest of her mind over to the hypnotic tune in her head. She wrapped her arms around herself, enraptured by the moment.

Linda's dress and body glowed in the beam of the comforting, approaching light. She bathed in it, eyes shut, rocking side to side with her hips, as if wading into water. The words from the tune escaped through her lips in a whisper, ". . . the happier we'll be—"

Crash.

Pain.

There should be pain.

But there was only darkness; so abrupt, it was as if someone had flipped a light switch to the off position.

Was it the beginning, the middle, or the end? Did it matter?

At that moment, amid the beauty of the night, Linda's sweet but brief life ended as an old, red pickup truck collided with her and passed over her limp body without regard, the impact sudden and the effect immediate.

The truck paused just a few hundred feet down the road, engine idling as a pool of crimson blood pulled Linda's white dress into it, her eyes wide-open, empty. Her body lay sprawled in the middle of the road as her life leaked from her, eyes glazing, now truly free.

The time of her death was 3:33 a.m.

Like a bull after charging, snorting engine fumes and puttering ponderously, the truck drove away until the light was no more.

Only darkness remained.

PART ONE

*Your Friends
Are My Friends*

Assessment and Plan

Provider: Blueberry Hill Home for Troubled Youth, LLC   **Client Name: Vickie Bartolucci**
Group Assignment: Pod #1   **Session Number:** #1

Diagnosis: Symptoms of Oppositional Defiant Disorder (ODD), though not chronic.

Treatment

Intake Protocol: Clinical Assessment   **Medications:** Fluoxetine 20 mg/day,
                  Habsburg, M.D.   *as per* Dr. Mariska

Short-Term Goals for Client (2 Weeks):
1. Keep a journal identifying triggers for anger.
2. Introduce CBT coping strategies (e.g., breathing, visualizing a safe place).
3. Discuss client's feelings before, during, and after stealing. Identify patterns that led to the behavior and substitute adaptive coping strategies or rewards.

Long-Term Goals (3 Months):
1. Explore identity with client, cultivating the ability to discuss client's Korean heritage while maintaining positive or neutral affect.
2. Consistency with applying coping strategies for anger and implementing adaptive rewards that replace the dopamine hit from stealing.
3. Participate in group discussions and form trusting relationships with other pod members.

Session Notes

Body Language, Facial Patterns: Client refused to break eye contact. Wiggled fingers involuntarily, possibly a form of cricketing to soothe nervousness. Crossed arms when discussing mother. Voice elevated when asked about her father or Korean heritage.

Summary:
1. Client asked to take a seat, responded with, "Don't tell me what to do." Remained standing for the majority of the session.
2. Client seemed agitated when staff took the sandwich she brought from home. Relaxed when told she could eat the sandwich while in my office.
3. Topics that seem to bring distress: her mother, father, Korean heritage.
4. When asked why she steals, client responded, "Because I'm good at it."

Other Observations/Comments:
- ODD symptoms may be the result of a chaotic home life. Inconsistent discipline by parents, as well as being exposed to abuse, neglect, or trauma at an early age can lead to the onset of ODD symptoms.
- Client lives in a single-parent home and shows signs of being a parentified child, assuming the role of her absent father and sometimes parenting her mother.
- Difficulty managing anger, history of stealing, including multiple arrests.

Client Signature: *Vickie Bartolucci*   **Primary Caregiver 1:** *Renaldo Bartolucci*
(Age 14 and up)   Vickie Bartolucci   Renaldo Bartolucci
                                (Power of Attorney for Rosemary Bartolucci)

Primary Caregiver 2: ———————— **Therapist Signature:** *Ara Cannon*
             N/A   Dr. Ara Cannon, Ph.D.

CHAPTER 1
Pod 1

DAY 45 for Vickie

The Rec Room

8:00 a.m.

19 Hours, 33 Minutes Until Linda's Death

Vickie owned the rec room the moment she entered. Scanning from one wall to the other, she visually gathered Dr. Cannon and the other members of her pod like playing cards, assessing their relative positions to one another and the most direct path to the metal chairs that leaned against the window like a pile of orphans waiting to be claimed.

The spacious room easily accommodated a pool table and a Ping-Pong table behind the designated meeting area. A locked glass case held the pool sticks. Residents could only remove and use the sticks with adult supervision, which made little sense to Vickie. The Ping-Pong paddles, however, were always available, and given the choice, she'd much rather use one of those to pummel someone than a cumbersome pool stick.

Vickie shifted her weight from side to side as she walked toward the clump of metal chairs by the window, shoulders back, chest out with the swagger that came from spending her formative years in Queens, New York. It was a power of sorts.

Visible flushes of pink colored her light brown face, and her dark,

3

straight hair, thick and unkempt, barely moved as she picked up speed with each step. She wore a button-down sweater with a large *V* embroidered over the bottom left-hand pocket. It fit her snugly, making her look even more formidable.

Teenagers parted like the Red Sea as Vickie approached. After all, when a truck was coming toward you, you got out of the way, and she wasn't slowing down. The last person to play a game of chicken with her had regretted it.

Creak, thump, creak, thump.

In a fit of flurried activity, each teenage attendee placed a folding chair in a circle.

Vickie was the only person who grabbed two chairs, carrying one under each arm. The other teens left space for Vickie's two usual spots in the mostly formed circle of seats.

No sooner were Vickie's chairs unfolded than Squirt slipped into one of them and grinned. Looking up at her with wide eyes, his loose blond curls framed his tiny face. Squirt was always looking up at Vickie, whether seated or standing. The height difference between them was more than noticeable and bordered on comical. Despite that, getting close to Vickie remained the primary goal of his teenage existence. She might have found it charming if he wasn't . . . well, Squirt.

"Move." Vickie snapped her fingers and growled a warning snarl.

Squirt beamed, eager for more interaction. Any attention from Vickie was better than no attention from her. There's no fun in being ignored, even though he was used to being overlooked because of his size and his accommodating nature.

Still grinning, Squirt relented, shimmying over to his abandoned chair.

The last to enter, Linda dashed in, her wiry body heaving with quick breaths, her face glowing with perspiration. She headed directly toward the circle, dropping into her usual saved seat beside Vickie.

This time it was Vickie who beamed, staring at her best friend and roommate.

Even though the powers that be had prearranged the roommate assignments, their decision to become friends was of their own choosing. Linda's consistency and kindness had attracted Vickie like a magnet, inspiring a mutual trust both girls craved, and Vickie protected fiercely. When Vickie allowed someone to be her friend, it was deliberate and solidified a bond that couldn't be easily broken. Real friendship meant a loyalty and commitment that lasted forever.

Dr. Cannon's dark hair, always pulled back in a tight bun, made her look more serious than she was. "Moduleul hwan-yeonghabnida," she said, welcoming everyone in Korean, her words heavily laced with a posh French accent. The combination was mind-bending for Vickie.

Vickie looked directly at her, making eye contact, unrelenting, like a pit bull clenched down on an opponent's limb.

Vickie didn't like Korean, even with a French accent. She had her reasons. And she hated ulterior motives, bristling when people tried to make her do things she didn't want to, like speak her father's language. At least, she assumed that was his language. She never knew her father, only a handful of details about him that she pretended not to be interested in when her mother would share them.

Just say what you mean and mean what you say. That was Vickie's motto.

Her uncle Aldo had taught her that, repeating it whenever he suspected someone was being evasive.

Knowing Vickie was half Italian and half Korean, she suspected that Dr. Cannon, a French Korean woman herself, wanted her to embrace their shared Asian heritage.

It wasn't working.

The squeaking of the chairs slowly subsided. As the group settled, Dr. Cannon began again, in English this time, still coated with her throaty French accent.

5

"Why don't we start by having everyone share what's on their mind?"

Dr. Cannon slowly scanned the circle of teens. First, she looked at Squirt, then Linda, lighting for a moment on Vickie, before moving to Eagen, Annie, and finally, Tracy.

Of all the group therapy pods, theirs was the most eclectic in terms of personalities and, overall, theirs was the wealthiest. All members, except for Vickie, were from some of the most affluent and influential families in Maine. Even Linda's foster parents were well-off.

A tense silence wrapped around them as the group fidgeted and looked off into the distance.

Dr. Cannon offered a nudge. "Tracy?"

Vickie's eyes brightened, and she sat up a little straighter when Tracy's name was called. She wasn't sure where Tracy was from originally, but he sounded like one of the Beatles, a band her mother and her uncle Aldo liked. Tracy's flowing dark locks spilled over his ears and onto his neck. She was sure his mane made teenage girls swoon and middle-aged balding men writhe with envy.

"Nothing's on my mind," Tracy answered in his outrageously cute accent.

Eagen interjected, "Except that nest you call hair."

Tracy caught a strand of his hair in his teeth, like a dog biting for a treat, then cocked his head, squinting at Eagen and flashing a sideways grin.

Vickie couldn't help but jump to Tracy's defense.

Even though, as far as she could tell, Tracy barely knew she existed, he was still kind to people, and that made him worth protecting. She fired a jab at Eagen. "You're just jealous his hair color is natural, and yours comes from a Walgreens."

All the teens in the circle laughed, except Eagen, who hung his head, his ink-black hair covering his eyes as he doodled on his notepad. Vickie imagined he was sketching ways he might murder her. She didn't mind.

She considered his anger her badge of honor.

He shouldn't have started it, she thought, justifying her action to no one but herself.

Eagen wore black jeans, a hoodie, had black nails and, as Vickie pointed out, jet-black hair, which was not his natural color. He was attractive in his own way, though he did everything he could to hide it.

"Back to our question. What's on everyone's mind?" Dr. Cannon asked.

"Technically, it's minds," Squirt interjected. His voice cracked as he spoke. "'Cause we don't all share a brain." Squirt continued under his breath, "Thank goodness."

"Well, they *do* call this a 'pod,'" Eagen said. "Which is just a step away from—"

"*Invasion of the Body Snatchers,*" Eagen and Linda said simultaneously.

Linda laughed. "We're pod people."

Vickie cut her eyes toward Linda and then glared at Eagen. "You're so weird," she said to him, her upper lip curling in a snarl.

"How do you feel about pods? This one, pod number 1, in particular?" Dr. Cannon asked.

"I like it," Squirt said, quickly eyeing the group. "I mean, it's not so bad."

"I wish the kid with Tourette's was in our group," Tracy quipped. "He curses like a sailor."

"He's in pod 3, I think. Yeah, that would be cool." Squirt gazed at Tracy like a puppy deferring to the alpha dog.

Dr. Cannon probed, "Why is it you think we have pods? What might their purpose be?"

"To control us," Eagen responded.

"Oh, we don't need pods for that. That's what the microchips we implant while you sleep are for," Dr. Cannon said, expressionless.

A moment of sustained silence passed among them. Tracy was the one to break it with a snicker, and the others joined in.

"All joking aside —" Dr. Cannon began before Eagen cut in.

"That was a joke? You obviously never studied comedy when you were an actress."

Dr. Cannon's eyes twinkled.

Vickie knitted her eyebrows, frowning, staring at Dr. Cannon.

Dr. Cannon was a master of facial expression. Her formal training, both as an actor and as a drama therapist, equipped her for these moments.

Each of the teens had relaxed into their chairs and the fidgeting had decreased significantly. It was time to cut to the chase.

"I know it's been an unusual couple of weeks for everyone here at Blueberry Hill. I'm just wondering how you are feeling?" Dr. Cannon asked.

"You mean because of —"

Before Squirt could finish, Tracy said, "I say good for them."

"That's heartless," Linda said.

Tracy shrugged and explained his rationale. "They got out. They're free."

"Did they?" Eagen blurted.

Dr. Cannon studied Eagen. "What do you mean?"

"They could be lying in a ditch somewhere. Waiting for someone to rescue them," Linda said.

"Or who's to say there wasn't a suicide pact," Eagen said, with even less expression than Dr. Cannon had used earlier.

"Someone would tell us if that's what happened," Squirt said. "Right? As soon as they found them?"

"Dead or alive," Eagen added.

"They'd tell us. Right, Dr. Cannon?" Squirt asked. His eyes were wide, matching the urgency in his voice.

Dr. Cannon smoothed the folds in the sleeve of the colorful smock she wore. "The truth is, we may never know what happened," Dr. Cannon said.

"What's weird is, all four of them were from different pods," Linda said.

"What's weird about that?" Tracy asked.

Linda continued, "How did they know each other well enough to coordinate an escape? I mean, I don't even know their names. No one's names really, except for all of you."

"People are coming and going every other day here," Vickie said.

Dr. Cannon added, "The goal isn't to stay here forever, is it?"

"No, staying is not the goal," Vickie said.

"Neither is a suicide pact," Squirt said, grimacing.

"I'm just saying there are like 1,000 people here. I'm surprised anyone even knew they were missing," Tracy said.

"Good point. Maybe we *should* chip you," Dr. Cannon said. "For tracking purposes."

"Like pets," Squirt said. "We chipped our bulldog, Frank. Of course, we think he drowned. But we don't know. Chips don't work in the water. They should tell you that. In a disclaimer."

"Trust me, we know when someone goes missing. It matters. There are thirteen pods. Currently, ninety-nine of you," Dr. Cannon said.

"Sarah. Justin. Tika. Nathalie," Annie said.

Everyone sat in stunned silence. Annie rarely spoke during group discussions, but clearly, she paid attention. Her frenetic curls seemed to shoot out from her sincere brown eyes.

"Yes, those were their names. I knew each of them and feel their absence acutely," Dr. Cannon said.

The teens shifted uncomfortably in their seats as the tone of the conversation became more somber. Eagen broke the momentary silence.

"Knew? Past tense. Sounds like you do believe they're dead after all."

"They're not dead, Eagen," Annie said, agitated, but offering a gentle smile.

"Of course they are. The doctor just told us as much," Eagen said.

Annie's lip quivered and her eyebrows wriggled upward.

"Eagen!" Linda admonished, seeing the effect Eagen's words had on Annie.

Dr. Cannon exhaled before speaking. "Eagen—"

"What's your problem, mate?" Tracy asked, his muscles tensing in response to Annie nervously shifting in her seat.

"You, Ringo!" Eagen said.

Vickie watched as Eagen reached under the bottom of his hoodie, fidgeting with his belt.

"Of all the Beatles, Ringo? Really?" Tracy grinned, reveling in the effect his rebuff of the insult had on Eagen.

"Such a phony," Eagen said.

Tracy picked up something from the floor and handed it to Eagen. A black Lee press-on nail.

"I believe this is your *fake* nail?" Tracy said.

Eagen reddened as a scowl melted onto his face. He adjusted his belt again. Vickie saw something near Eagen's waistline reflect in the light, and she glared at him.

"As I said, we may never know what happened, but what I do know is that we are all here right now, sharing this moment," Dr. Cannon said, tapping her pen lightly on the clipboard. "Is running away something any of you have considered?"

"From Blueberry Hill?" Tracy asked.

"And go where?" Annie asked.

"I like it here," Squirt said. "What?" He searched his peers' faces for reassurance that he hadn't been too vulnerable. "I like you guys . . ." Squirt's words trailed off as if he swallowed them.

"I've thought about it. If I'm being honest," Tracy said.

"You have?" Vickie asked, her eyes widening.

"Sure. But like Annie said, and go where?" Tracy replied.

"Well, I'm still hopeful for a safe return for all four missing kids.

10

Running away—"

"Escaping," Eagen corrected Dr. Cannon.

"Let's just call it leaving prematurely. Even though running away from problems can seem like an attractive option at times, one thing I've learned is that you always take yourself with you. That's something to think about."

Conversation continued over the next thirty-nine and a half minutes in much the same way, until at last the teens heard the auditory cue for which they had been waiting: a hollow-sounding bell that echoed through the intercom system.

"And that's our time. Have a good morning, everyone," Dr. Cannon said.

Each of the teens stood, then folded and returned their chairs to the stack against the wall, readying the multipurpose space for however it might be utilized next.

Creak, clank, creak, clank.

"Good chat, as always, Doc," Tracy said, folding his chair and exiting ahead of Annie.

As Dr. Cannon moved toward the door, she whispered to Linda, "You're making progress, Linda. Keep it up."

Linda met her comment with a soft smile.

Vickie waved as Dr. Cannon left the room. "Bye, Dr. Cannon," she said eagerly.

Dr. Cannon offered a tiny wave in return.

Vickie stood still, frozen to the spot, waiting for the door to the room to close. Time slowed to a halting crawl, until finally, the latch snapped into place.

Linda, Eagen, and Vickie were now alone in the room.

Vickie's head pivoted from the door to Eagen.

Her throat closed, and her chest tightened as she curled her fingers into fists. The world around her collapsed into a tunnel from where she stood to where Eagen casually chatted with *her* friend Linda.

Vickie drew one deep breath, then propelled herself forward, the clopping of her charging feet interrupting the stillness of the room.

Thud. Thud. Thud. Thud.

She slammed into Eagen's tall, slender frame, knocking the air from his body. She would have pushed through him if she could, but the wall behind him stopped his backward momentum, her arm coming to rest against his throat.

"Vickie!" Linda said, her voice unusually high, trembling with panic.

"Someone's jealous," Eagen said, struggling to breathe, perspiring from the effort.

"Where is it?" Vickie said, a growl tinting her voice.

"What?"

"Stop it, Vickie!" Linda shouted.

Vickie leaned in harder with her forearm, feeling Eagen's Adam's apple cave in just a little under the pressure.

"Fine," Eagen croaked.

Vickie relaxed her grip as Eagen reached under the bottom of his hoodie, fumbling with his belt, his hands shaking as he handed Vickie a sharp piece of metal he'd fashioned into a crude knife.

"I wasn't going to use it."

"Do you know what they'd do to you if they found this? To our whole pod?" Vickie tossed the knife out the open first-floor window and into the tall hedges below.

"I'm sorry," Eagen said to Linda, defiantly not acknowledging Vickie. Linda's lips tightened and she nodded her head, not looking at Eagen or Vickie, but off in the distance.

Vickie strode toward the door, scorn clouding her face. "Coming?"

Linda followed Vickie out, dazed, leaving Eagen standing alone in the rec room, massaging his throat and wheezing.

CHAPTER 2
Karma

```
The Lobby
8:40 a.m.
18 Hours, 43 Minutes Until Linda's Death
```

Vickie and Linda sat in prolonged silence in the lobby on the only two wingback chairs. These were their usual seats at this time of day, and no one dared challenge her for them. Vickie liked the way the tall, salmon-colored chair wrapped around her, like a hug from royalty. She felt fancy and cozy at the same time.

The lobby, which functioned as a sort of library and congregation area for the teens, was the perfect vantage point from which to see most everything. Seated there, she could observe the door to the staff lounge, the circular nurse's reception desk, the medication dispensary—also known as the sunshine room—and the doors to some administration offices. The primary hallways were also visible, leading to the cafeteria, drama, music, and rec rooms.

There was a lot to take in, but like a hawk perched in her nest, Vickie was more than capable of following most of the important happenings. A hodgepodge of other less formal seating, including other chairs, sofas, and love seats, filled the rest of the open room. The furnishings, by some miracle, all complemented each other in a way that was tasteful despite them representing various time periods during the last century.

But the best feature of the lobby could only be found by looking up. There was always something new to notice in the fourteen-foot-high deco ceiling. Its intricately painted floral designs had hues that shifted between bright and shadowy depending upon the ambient light. The colors, still vibrant with an added depth only time could bring, floated soothingly in a sea of heavenly perfect sky blue.

She indulged the impulse to look up every time she sat in her favorite lobby throne, as if she were at the planetarium on a school trip. But instead of stars, flowers hung in the air, suspended amid lush green ivy, so realistically depicted that Vickie wished she could change the laws of gravity and fall up, splashing into the vivid palette.

Vickie leaned back, resting her head against the dobby-striped fabric, counting the petals of one of the flowers painted right above her head. Five petals, plus one disconnected from the flower disc as if blowing away on a whispered breeze.

"Sorry," Linda whispered, calling Vickie back to the moment.

Vickie's gaze dipped to Linda's eyes.

"For what?"

"I should have trusted you."

"Well, yeah."

"Eagen's not all bad, you know?"

Vickie raised an eyebrow and twitched her lips to one side.

"I mean, he might be right. Maybe the missing four didn't run away."

"You think they killed themselves?" Vickie stared at Linda.

"If you kill yourself, you don't usually hide your own body," Linda said.

"Good point." Vickie shrugged. "But they could've jumped off a bridge or something." Her eyes wandered to the porch and lingered there. The inner french doors were opened to the inside, and the breeze gently blew a strand of her near-shoulder-length hair into her eyes. Only a pair of screen doors separated her from the world outside.

Angelo stood on the porch, feet wide in a protective stance. His folded, muscled arms were barely contained by the tight white sleeves of his uniform.

Vickie didn't recognize the older man with disheveled clothes with whom he was speaking. The man didn't make eye contact with Angelo as they spoke.

When Angelo walked inside, the man immediately began nosing around, touching the sides of the building, the door frame, even kicking the front steps a couple of times, like you'd kick the tire of a car to make sure there was no leak. He appeared to be sizing the place up.

Vickie continued watching the stranger, who was much more interesting to her than Angelo. His old suit looked slept in, and his hair was greasy. She surveyed his actions until Angelo neared Linda and her, and the old man teetered off to the side of the door, out of her field of vision.

As Angelo passed, he smiled at the pair of girls. Now that he was closer, Vickie was reminded first-hand that the white uniform definitely fit him differently than the other male employees. In his case, the uniform didn't make the man; the man made the uniform.

Angelo approached the staff lounge located to the side of the reception desk. His broad back framed Vickie's view of the lounge door from diagonally behind him. She leaned a little farther out of her chair to watch, but not enough to be noticed, intent on hearing his words.

He knocked on the door of the lounge. When it opened, conversation fluttered out in murmurs like manic moths.

Arching her neck, Vickie could see Nurse Lilly, the happy one, Nurse Dorothy, the flirty one, Nurse Fran, the stern one, and the clearly outnumbered Mr. Fitch, the shy music teacher.

Linda leaned across the space between her chair and Vickie's. "Vickie, there's something I want to . . ."

"Shhhh." Vickie tucked her hair behind her ear, trying to hear the sounds coming from the staff lounge more clearly, tuning into them like a radio.

Nurse Lilly's distinctive giggle leaked unmistakably through the now partially open door.

"Sorry to interrupt your break, ladies . . . and gentleman," Angelo said.

Dorothy, the youngest of the three nurses, batted her false eyelashes and smoothed her auburn hair. "Oh, it's all right, Angelo." She said his name like it was a sentence all by itself. Judging by his body language, he didn't seem bothered by her eager attention.

An expectant silence followed.

Speaking directly to Nurse Lilly, Angelo continued, "It's that reporter."

"Tell him to go away. I'm in a 'conference,'" Nurse Lilly said, giggling.

The three ladies and Mr. Fitch snacked on muffins smothered in a thick, dark jam. They looked delicious, even from a distance.

That is my kind of conference, Vickie thought, licking her lips.

"Nurse Lilly's trying to get the secret ingredient in my blueberry jam, Angelo. And it ain't gonna happen," Nurse Fran said emphatically over the rim of her glasses. Nurse Fran laughed heartily, from the back of her throat, without opening her mouth. Nurse Dorothy followed with her own breathy laugh.

It was unclear to Vickie, from the glimpses she could catch, if handsome, young Angelo made flirty Nurse Dorothy nervous, or if she really found Nurse Fran amusing. From the way Nurse Dorothy's voice quivered, and given the exaggerated laugh, probably the former.

"I told him you were in a conference the last time and the time before," Angelo said. The hint of amusement in his voice seemed to put them all at ease.

Angelo fit right in with the rest, yet there was something different about him. He was younger, not much older than the residents. But he

16

also seemed happy to be at his job. Maybe that was because he was new?

"What am I supposed to tell that nosy man?" Nurse Lilly asked.

"You can't blame him for looking for a story. That's his job," Nurse Fran said.

Nurse Lilly scrunched her nose. "He smells like bourbon and mothballs."

"That's his business," Nurse Fran responded with an emphatic sharpness to her tone.

"Yes, but his intrusions disrupt the children."

"Disrupt the children?" Nurse Fran looked at Nurse Lilly over the rim of her glasses once again.

"OK, so I just don't like him!" Nurse Lilly confessed.

"Mmmm-hmmmm," Nurse Fran grunted, her posture more at ease now that she had dislodged the truth.

"Fine, I'll get rid of him." Nurse Lilly turned her back to Nurse Fran. "I was so close to getting that secret ingredient," she mumbled.

"No, you weren't," Nurse Fran said as Nurse Lilly headed for the door, Angelo stepping aside so she could exit with ease.

Over her shoulder, Nurse Lilly said, "I'll be right back. And save some jam for me."

Angelo closed the door and left, continuing down the hallway, while Nurse Lilly joined the older gentleman on the steps outside.

It was time for Vickie to recap what she had overheard.

"That guy on the steps is a reporter," Vickie said, relaying the intel for Linda's benefit.

"You think they found the missing four?" Linda asked. "I wish they would let us have a TV, so we'd know what's going on. At least the news."

Vickie shushed her again.

"Why do you get to talk when you want to, but I have to shush?"

Vickie waved a dismissive hand. Her reconnaissance mission wasn't over yet; there was more eavesdropping to do. Her attention now focused back on the porch. She strained to hear what Nurse Lilly and the reporter were discussing. When the reporter made eye contact with Vickie through the screen doors, she held his gaze. Something about him reminded her of the sad drunk that had lived next door to her in her old neighborhood in Queens.

Mr. Fitch exited the staff lounge with his coffee cup in hand. He walked as if one leg were shorter than the other, teetering back and forth. His clothes resembled the sort of attire faculty might have worn at an Ivy League school forty years ago. His two-sizes-too-big, brown tweed jacket made his yellow bowtie seem clownish.

There is something sad about Mr. Fitch, too, Vickie thought.

Sheets of music and various papers stuck out of an old-fashioned briefcase that Mr. Fitch had latched too quickly. He carried a folded newspaper under his arm, bumbling his way around the reception desk and past Vickie and Linda, presumably toward one of the offices on the same floor.

Vickie glimpsed some guys from pod 2 lingering at the far end of the lobby. She felt her chest tighten and her teeth clench. Pods 1 and 2 were often in the lobby at the same time. Although the pods interacted little, Vickie had observed enough to know that this all-male pod was full of troublemakers, which was saying a lot in a home for troubled youth.

Linda watched as Vickie focused intently on the group of boys. "Wasn't one of the missing four from pod 2?"

"Yeah. James," Vickie said.

"You mean Justin."

"Yeah," Vickie said, not taking her eyes off Tim, the apparent leader of the pack, who stuck his foot out just as Mr. Fitch approached. Vickie didn't have time to warn poor Mr. Fitch before he took a nasty spill, his coffee cup flying and its contents soaking into the Persian carpet that blanketed much of the seating area.

In a flash, Vickie was up on her feet, rushing toward the hapless man to help him gather his belongings.

Dog-eared sheet music and lesson plans scattered from the tattered leather briefcase, some bearing the stains of previous coffee spills.

Some of Tim's fellow pod members snickered and slapped Tim's shoulder in approval.

Vickie and Mr. Fitch clumsily worked together on their hands and knees to gather the loose items like mother hens corralling their chicks. Vickie was close enough to the music teacher to hear the breath wheezing in and out of his skinny chest. And she noticed for the first time how the flower pattern in the carpet subtly mirrored the ceiling, soaking up the dark liquid until the stain looked like part of the design.

She sympathetically handed Mr. Fitch his half-empty, extra-large coffee cup, the handle now broken off. He held up the two pieces, showing Vickie the saying imprinted inside a big sun: "Off to a Great Start!"

"Ironic," he said.

Vickie smiled.

"Thank you, Vickie." Mr. Fitch looked directly into Vickie's eyes, emphasizing the sincerity of his gratitude. His mouth resumed its loose downturn. "I'm such a klutz."

Vickie fixed her eyes on Tim with a glare full of daggers. It was enough to make Tim look away and pretend not to be bothered.

"It could have happened to anyone," Vickie said, returning her attention to Mr. Fitch.

Mr. Fitch thanked her again and hobbled away.

Vickie strode over to Tim and stood next to him, her arms folded across her chest. The other boys continued to laugh, though a little less boldly now.

"What? What did I do?" Tim said, half laughing.

"Ever heard of karma?"

Tim looked down at Vickie's monogrammed sweater and then back up at her, staring directly into her eyes.

Vickie spun around in disgust, walking back to rejoin Linda.

"What does that *V* stand for, anyway? Venereal?" he called after her.

The boys high-fived each other.

"Venereal disease," one boy said.

"Vickie's got crabs," another said. They chuckled.

Vickie rolled her eyes and reclaimed her seat next to Linda. "What a bunch of jerks," Vickie said, loud enough for them to hear.

"Yeah, Mr. Fitch is so nice," Linda added. "My lessons with him keep me sane."

Vickie looked over her left shoulder, then her right, before winking at Linda.

"What? What's that wink for--"

Vickie pulled Mr. Fitch's folded newspaper from under her sweater.

"How—" Linda asked.

"It's what I do," Vickie said. "Let's see what's in here." The two girls divided up the paper and rearranged themselves in their seats to read. The front-page headline drew their attention, "Mayor Johnson Launches Re-election Campaign," with a photo of the middle-aged Korean American mayor underneath. His perfect hair and lopsided smile made Vickie's lip curl.

Vickie and Linda continued digging through the articles and scanning each page, searching for news of their missing compatriots or anything about Blueberry Hill.

"Have you found something?" Vickie asked.

"Nothing."

"How could there be nothing?" Vickie exhaled. "Oh, wait. Here it is. In the back after 'Advocate Seeks New Moose Crossing Sign.'"

"Wow. The moose have an advocate, but four missing teenagers don't?" Linda said.

"Unbelievable."

"What does it say?" Linda asked.

"The police have suspended the search. Two weeks and that's it!"

Out of the corner of her eye, Vickie spied Tim and his cohorts walking away from their chairs and toward her. Her lips tightened into a thin line.

Just as he was about to pass, Vickie casually stuck her foot out. Tim tripped, catching himself before completing a full face-plant, but not before his buddies burst into laughter again.

Tim shot Vickie a death stare.

"What do you know? Karma *is* a bitch," Vickie said as she flashed a fake, toothy metal grin, her braces glistening in the morning light like a gangster's grill.

They held each other's stare.

Tim feigned a grin of his own, his bottom lip quivering.

He looked away first.

No one ever won in a game of chicken with Vickie. No one.

CHAPTER 3
The Secret

The Rose Garden
9:00 a.m.
18 Hours, 33 Minutes Until Linda's Death

Gentle breezes licked the foliage, lapping up the leftover morning dew from each of the petals on the colorful blossoms punctuating the green backdrop of the rose garden.

A cacophony of scents escaped the blooms, mingling into a seasonal bouquet: lilies, phlox, honeysuckle, gardenia, echinacea, fresh-cut grass and, of course, the roses.

Vickie loved walking around the grounds, letting her nose lead the way. It reminded her of the numerous bakeries in her old neighborhood, where the smells made you feel something down deep, a comforting and delicious sensory delight.

As Vickie opened the screen doors, crossed the stone porch, and stepped onto the Blueberry Hill lawn, she felt the damp, pillowy grass under her feet. The soft ground yielded to her sneakers, leaving an imprint for the sun to erase.

So much wide-open space!

It called to her, yet made her uncomfortable. Growing up in Queens, Vickie only found enormous expanses of grass in carefully planned parks.

Grass in such abundance epitomized luxury for her. Even her tiny yard in Maine was mostly gravel and concrete.

She had liked Queens. The tall buildings felt like a weighted blanket to her, familiar and calming. And the bars on the first-floor windows and gates on the walkways meant people had boundaries. She liked boundaries, mainly because she often found them lacking in her own home.

One by one, the teens in her pod emerged from the manor and trickled down the stone steps to join her. Their reactions to the great outdoors varied.

"Gross," Eagen said, squinting his eyes at the bright morning light and doing his best to keep the damp grass off his chunky, black platform shoes, or worse, from touching his ankles!

Quiet little Annie, in contrast, perked up in the sun like one of the garden plants. Even her hair shone bright in the light, as if the sun ignited a spark in her that dimmed within the confines of the manor. She had tossed her shoes to the side the second the sun hit her face. She was in her element, immediately spinning round and round until she was dizzy and almost fell over.

"What was that?" Squirt jumped, swatting frantically at the air. "Was that a bee?"

"I believe it was a murder hornet," Tracy said with a straight face, his eyes twinkling as a look of horror washed over Squirt.

Squirt gasped as a white moth flew past his face and landed on his shoulder.

"Get it off. Get it off!"

"It's a butterfly," Annie said.

Tracy clasped his hands around the winged insect. "It's a murder moth."

Tracy opened his hands.

Annie watched wide-eyed, mouth open, as the bug flitted away. She

23

gasped, then chased it onto the grounds from flower to flower, her bare feet gliding across the grass.

"All right, let's get to work," Nurse Lilly said as she traipsed toward them. "This garden won't weed itself."

"Mr. Phang, would you distribute the trowels, please?" she asked the elderly gardener, who was bent over a miniature rose bush. He straightened and shuffled forward to claim the box of tools.

Nurse Lilly handed each of them a basket with a pair of colorful gloves and a real garden hat made of woven straw with a wide brim, some with sashes that tied under the neck.

They took the hats, shoulders slumped forward, their frequent sighs punctuated with the occasional eye roll. Thankfully, only Nurse Lilly, Mr. Phang, and their own pod were out there to see them in these get-ups. Vickie presumed all residents had to dress like this at some point, so at least the embarrassment was equally distributed.

Mr. Phang bowed his head in a sign of respect as he handed each teen their trowel. Linda returned the bow with a smile, and Vickie gave him a quick nod and an awkward grin.

Vickie whispered to Linda, "That guy's definitely a serial killer."

"That sweet old man?"

"It's his name."

"Phang? Because he's named after teeth?"

"Because he spells it with a *Ph*. That's just unnecessary. Never trust anyone with extra letters in their name."

"That's ridiculous."

Ever met a Jason with a *y*? Jay-y-y-yson? So extra."

"I have not."

Vickie tilted her head down, staring directly at Linda. "Trust me, you don't want to. Extra letters are the mark of the beast."

"Wait, aren't you Vickie with an *i-e*?"

"Exactly. Never trust anything I say. I'm a troubled youth."

Linda laughed.

Vickie's eyes gleamed, and her face softened. Linda's laugh was like a ray of sunshine through a cloudy sky. Vickie breathed in deeply and then exhaled. Her heart warmed in her chest as her face beamed with a sense of pride that she had contributed to Linda's smile.

Besides the usual garden tools, Nurse Lilly placed a leather pouch on a nearby bench. She took her time gently running her fingers down the edge. The worn brown leather was so thick it flapped as she unfurled each side. She paused, savoring the moment until her eyes widened so much they invaded her whole face.

Vickie and Linda stood nearby, slipping on their gloves and hats, curious what was inside the pouch after Nurse Lilly had given it such a ceremonial unwrapping.

Nurse Lilly approached the two girls, holding out a pair of sharpened, golden garden shears as if they were the holy grail, waiting for Linda to take them.

Nurse Lilly didn't trust everyone with the usual garden shears. Even Vickie wasn't given a pair, especially a pair as special as these appeared to be. But for the first time, Nurse Lilly gave Linda the honor.

"I was hoping you could gather a pleasant arrangement for Dr. Habsburg's office," Nurse Lilly said, her eyes reflecting the golden color of the shears.

"Why me?" Linda asked.

"Can't you make Squirt do it?" Vickie added.

Nurse Lilly's lips quivered. Clearly, she was more excited about this rite of passage than Linda was in receiving the shears.

"Because I think you have an eye, Linda. And you've earned it. We've got just enough time. Roses are most hydrated and have the highest respiration before 10:30 a.m. Never, and I repeat, never cut the roses during the middle of the day." Nurse Lilly made the comment with an unusual amount of emphasis, letting it hang in the air.

"Uhhhh. OK." Linda took the shears, turning them over, feeling their weight in her frail hands. "Thanks."

"Look for roses whose outer petals have just opened. That means that the rose is in the late bud stage. The exterior petals must have unfurled, without the entire flower being completely exposed. When you trim" — Nurse Lilly used her fingers to mime scissors since Linda now held the shears — "trim the stems at a 45-degree angle, close to the base of the leaf on the stem."

Nurse Lilly grabbed a waiting pail of cool water and handed it to Vickie. "Put the stems in here right away."

"Any special instructions for me with the bucket?" Vickie asked.

"Just put the flowers in the bucket, Vickie," Nurse Lilly said.

"Roger that."

Just a few minutes later, everyone was busy with their various assigned tasks: some were pruning, some planting, some unenthusiastically weeding.

The flowering plants and sculpted evergreen shrubs in the garden ranged from one to six feet in height and formed complex designs that looked good from a distance, but appeared haphazard up close.

Fortunately for them, the placements left plenty of places for the reluctant gardeners to relax unnoticed, if only for a moment. Nurse Lilly would sometimes watch the teens work from the porch steps presumably for that very reason, but for now, she was nowhere in sight.

Linda approached a tall, solitary rose, staring at it, shears open, but Nurse Lilly stopped her, gently grabbing her arm.

Linda jumped.

"Geez. Where'd you come from?" Linda asked.

The cobblestone walkways usually announced someone's approach, but not this time.

"It's those nurse shoes. Stealth," Vickie whispered.

Nurse Lilly smiled. Vickie ran her tongue over the metal wiring that filled her own mouth, mesmerized by the whiteness of the nurse's teeth. They looked like tiny pearls, like jewelry in Nurse Lilly's mouth. Beautiful.

There was even an elegance in the way Nurse Lilly stood, her weight shifting slightly to one side, her posture always perfect, and her neck rising out of her shoulders like a sunflower. Vickie couldn't help but admire her.

Nurse Lilly spoke. "It's not time yet to take this one. It's almost ready, but not yet."

"It's pretty," Linda said.

It kinda is, Vickie silently agreed.

The rose was a gorgeous, velvety blood-red and emitted a strong fragrance.

"Seventeen petals, three and three-quarter inches in diameter. It offers blooms throughout the season," Nurse Lilly added, entranced by the flower.

This woman actually measures her flowers? And we're the troubled ones? Vickie thought.

This particular bush was tall, spreading, and well-branched with large, glossy, dark green foliage.

"I nurtured it from a seedling and here it is yielding gorgeous blooms! It's called the 'Flawless Rose.' Have you ever heard a name more appropriate?"

"Sounds like a lot of pressure . . . to put on a rose," Vickie said. Sometimes Vickie said the quiet part aloud.

Nurse Lilly's gaze shot to Vickie. "She can take it," she said, gently cupping the rose in her palm. "One of the seed parents was a deep red, miniature rose created in a 1994 breeding program. This one almost died several times. In fact, Mr. Phang was ready to dig it up and mulch it when I intervened. And this is my reward, its sweet, enveloping smell. Perfection!" Nurse Lilly deeply inhaled the rose's scent.

"You really love your roses," Vickie said. It was true. In fact, she had noticed Nurse Lilly loved all living things.

"How much longer?" Squirt asked, frantically swatting at something. Nurse Lilly sighed, staring at him. Well, Nurse Lilly loved most living things, most days.

Nurse Fran appeared on the steps and placed her hands around her mouth, using them as a megaphone as she shouted to Nurse Lilly, "Nurse Lilly! Your meeting with Dr. Habsburg!"

"Oh my. I forgot. I'll be back to check on everyone. You're all doing fantastic work! Linda, be mindful of those shears. They're not a toy."

With that, Nurse Lilly headed back inside the mansion. She walked with such pep in her step she could have been skipping. Vickie hated skipping.

"We've got another hour of this crap," Vickie said, stone-faced.

"Cheery thought," Squirt said, followed by a loud sneeze.

Vickie moved from Queens to Maine when she was eleven to be closer to her extended family, who had moved years earlier when Uncle Aldo got a job with the Maine police department.

She was unaccustomed to yardwork, because she didn't have a yard in Queens and their tiny backyard in Maine didn't require it. "It's 'horticulture,'" Nurse Lilly would say, correcting Vickie when she called it yardwork. Fancy labels did not fool Vickie, though. She recognized yardwork when she saw it.

Vickie glanced at Linda and noticed a gleeful shimmer in her eyes like she was choking back a belly laugh. "What? What's wrong with you?" Vickie asked.

Before she could spit out her words, Linda grabbed Vickie by the hand and yanked her away. They scampered past the other teens, who were too busy wallowing in their own angst to notice. Linda's bony fingers felt like a fist full of twigs in Vickie's strong palm.

Linda moved so quickly Vickie could barely keep up. As light on her feet as Linda was, Vickie, in contrast, had the grace of an untrained Clydesdale. She didn't mind, though. Her feet got her where she wanted to go. No frills. In fact, if she were to design a T-shirt, that's the slogan she would use to sum herself up best—No Frills.

Attempting to keep up with Linda's quick legs, Vickie still clasped Linda's hand as though she held on for dear life when they breezed through the hedge maze on the side of the manor, about one hundred yards from the front rose garden.

The hedges stood ten feet in height and were well-manicured. The thorns bristling among the foliage made them impossible to climb. Linda had navigated the maze with ease for as long as Vickie had known her. More than likely, she had figured it out through trial and error in the weeks before Vickie arrived.

Vickie normally enjoyed being in control, but felt comfortable enough to submit to Linda's guidance, though her muscles still tensed going through the maze. She held her breath for most of it. As someone who liked predictability and routine, the unexpected twists and turns of the hedge tunnels made Vickie's chest constrict and her teeth clench.

Turn after turn, Vickie followed Linda's lead until they made it through to the other side.

The kids were told when they arrived that Blueberry Hill sat on thirty acres, or in kid-friendly terms, about twenty-two-and-a-half football fields. Three of those finely manicured acres included the house and grounds. That left twenty-seven acres of bramble—trees and bushes that grew because they wanted to, not because contractors and landscapers ordained it that way.

Sometimes the resident teens took guided nature walks with their pods. But since the missing four had "run away," the administration forbade exploration.

The girls slowed their pace as they entered the edge of the woods, which were so overgrown it was difficult to find an entry point.

"Where is it?" Linda scanned the dense brush, ever-changing amid new summer growth. Her eyes landed on two trees that had twisted together halfway up their trunks. "There."

"Beautiful," Linda said as they crawled through a sort of tunnel.

As difficult as it was to do in that moment, Vickie refrained from saying her thoughts aloud.

Creepy.

She didn't want to yuck Linda's yum.

Once past the nature-made gate, the two girls walked through the thicket until they came to a series of slender boards laid over a muddy area. Linda made it across quickly. Vickie took a little longer, and just when she thought she was home free, she lost her balance and stepped directly into the mud.

"Crap!" She tried pulling her foot out to no avail, and before she knew it, her leg had sunk knee-deep.

"What the . . . quicksand? In Maine?" Vickie exclaimed.

Linda, fast as a gazelle, hopped back over to Vickie and offered her hand, hoisting her up before Vickie could blink.

This girl is stronger than she looks, Vickie thought.

"It's more like quick mud! Are you all right?" Linda asked.

"Yeah, but my shoe's not." Vickie dug down deep in the mud with her right hand; the cool goo suctioned around her arm. She felt something hard. Hoping for the best, she pulled her hand up in a reverse thrust to reveal her shoe in her palm.

"I hate nature," Vickie said, dead-faced.

"You love nature. You hate tripping into quick mud. Come on! We'll rinse your shoe in the stream." Linda pulled Vickie to her feet.

"Has anyone looked for the missing four in this sludge?" Vickie grumbled.

Vickie and Linda continued moving briskly, venturing deeper into the woods. Leaves and twigs crunched under their feet. Vickie chose to put her muddied shoe on rather than encounter the occasional sharp rock or briar with her bare foot.

Moments later, they both sat on rocks in an open field.

Vickie's heart still raced, happy to have a moment to recover her breath. Looking around, she noticed green bushes speckled with dots of blue all around. A sea of wild blueberries surrounded them.

Linda had already picked two handfuls by the time Vickie caught up to the moment and realized what they were. Linda gently placed a handful of blueberries, warmed by the morning sun, into Vickie's hand.

"You brought me here for blueberries? We got those back at the crazy house."

"Not the same."

"They look a lot like these, I gotta tell ya." Vickie held one of them up between her fingers like pincers.

"These are wild."

"Do we need to wash them before we eat them?"

"Nope. The rain and morning dew take care of that."

Vickie bit into a berry and it burst in her mouth with blue liquid delight, reminding her of the popping boba balls she had tasted at fancy frozen yogurt joints Uncle Aldo would sometimes treat her to back in the city.

Apparently, Linda had more treats to offer.

Vickie's eyes widened when Linda pulled out a pack of American Spirit cigarettes, offering one to Vickie.

"Anyway, we couldn't do *this* at the manor."

"You're smoking now?" Vickie's posture straightened. "Who *are* you?"

"I'm . . . *making progress!*" Linda said, imitating Dr. Cannon's voice.

"All change is not progress. Smoking is not progressing. In fact, smoking cigarettes with a guy wearing a culturally appropriated tribal headdress on the package is just wrong."

"I'm moving at least. Does it matter what direction?" The playfulness in Linda's voice and the coy smirk spread across her face were enough to disarm Vickie.

"Yes! Yes, it does. And where did you get these?"

"Somewhere. Come on, explore the wild side of life a little with me."

Linda offered the cigarette a second time. Vickie took it, relenting. "Hold on. Before I contaminate my body, a few more antioxidants."

Vickie threw a berry up in the air and caught it in her mouth.

Linda giggled, her eyes wide in admiration. She lit both of their cigarettes. They inhaled and immediately coughed. Simultaneously, both of them spat, "Yuck." Vickie had never been interested in trying cigarettes or alcohol. If she was going to pollute her body, she preferred Twizzlers and Slurpees.

"Maybe it gets better?" Linda sputtered. They puffed again and coughed even harder.

"Nope."

"That's pretty bad," Linda said.

"So bad," Vickie agreed, still coughing.

They both threw down their cigarettes and stomped them out.

"Make sure that's out all the way. Forest fires," Vickie said.

"You're more of a mom than all my moms put together," Linda said

"Yeah, well. You're welcome. And why are you suddenly so peppy?"

"What?"

"What?" Once again, Vickie threw a berry in the air, catching it in her mouth. "A mother's instinct. Something's up."

Linda leaned in closer, the morning light catching her long hair in silhouette. "I was going to tell you earlier. I wanted to tell you, but I can't. I shouldn't. I promised. It's a secret."

"Enough already. You can't do that. You can't say you've got a secret, but you're not telling me."

"What do you want me to say? You want me to lie?" Linda asked.

"Say nothing. Don't bring it up," Vickie said with a wave of her hand, as if she were wiping a chalkboard clean.

"I didn't. You did. I'm going to tell you soon, though. Very soon. "

Vickie's posture relaxed. "Well, I already know. It's a boy. Right?"

Linda blushed.

"It's a boy. I knew it," Vickie continued.

"I'll tell you. Soon."

"Whatever." Vickie threw a blueberry, hitting Linda squarely in the forehead.

Linda gasped.

An epic battle ensued over the next five minutes. Blueberries were their bullets, stray boulders and bushes their shields.

And soon, both laughing, they found themselves collapsed on the ground with their backs against the same large rock.

Linda stared at Vickie, still looking forward. A wistfulness washed over her face as the gentlest of breezes rustled her hair. "I'm glad I met you."

Vickie's heart swelled in her chest like a tire pumped to capacity, until finally she relieved the warm pressure. "What is this, a Hallmark movie?" Vickie jabbed Linda lovingly in the arm.

They exchanged a silent moment akin to having a milkshake with two straws, and then, without a word, Vickie gathered up their things — the cigarettes, lighter, and a handful of the succulent blueberries. Even though she didn't wear a watch, she had a good internal sense of time and knew they should head back.

They plucked a couple of wildflowers from the edge of the thicket as they journeyed back to the formal gardens. That would be their cover story if questioned, they decided. Linda knew them all by name. One of her foster mothers loved gardening and had taught her. White and red baneberry, silverweed, marsh marigold, and a few others that were too different sounding to remember.

On the walk back, Vickie's face flooded with color, and her eyes smiled.

This time she was extra careful walking over the quick mud. She tried to never make the same mistake twice. Dragging her foot through a tiny stream, she even managed to clean off most of the incriminating dirt.

When they arrived at the rose garden, there was still no sign of Nurse Lilly. Everyone seemed to be carrying on just as they had left them.

"Phew," Linda said under her breath.

Eagen plucked the grass off his shoes strand by strand, Squirt swatted at bugs, Annie twirled, and Tracy hummed to himself as he weeded the flower bed.

Tracy took his straw hat off to wipe the sweat from his brow, sliding his forearm and then his fist across the top of his head.

Vickie watched him, her mouth slightly open.

Tracy saw her looking at him and smiled his crooked smile at her, his lips cocked to the left. She smiled back, her lips cocked to the right, her heart still racing from her sprint.

Linda snatched the wildflowers from Vickie's hands.

"You're drooling on the flowers," Linda said, her words unable to break Vickie's trance. Linda exhaled, suppressing a giggle.

And then out of nowhere, "Linda!" Nurse Lilly said.

Linda jumped.

Vickie whispered to Linda, "I've got to get a pair of those nurse shoes. So stealth." She turned away from Nurse Lilly to hide the heat in her cheeks and her quick breaths, aftereffects of her run and from watching Tracy.

Vickie, convinced they were both busted, waited to hear the reprimand that was sure to follow.

"Yes?" Linda responded angelically.

"Come with me. Dr. Habsburg would like to see you."

"Me?"

"Yes. You *are* our only Linda."

A chorus of "Ooooooh, you're in trouble" came from the rest of the pod as they gathered their gardening gear.

Vickie fidgeted, her eyes darting to her fellow pod members and back, while her mind worked through all the plausible scenarios of what Dr. Habsburg wanted with Linda.

Should I take the blame for us both? Tell them it was my idea to explore the forest and not Linda's?

"Does Dr. Habsburg want to see me too?" Vickie asked.

"Just Linda," Nurse Lilly said.

Maybe Dr. Habsburg wants to see Linda about something else. A visit to her office isn't always bad.

Even so, she couldn't shake the ominous feeling she had.

"What's it about?" Vickie asked.

"That's not really your concern. It won't take long." Nurse Lilly turned to Linda. "Bring the bouquet. It's always good to come bearing gifts. And my shears."

"Oh no," Linda said, her eyes darting around from rose bush to rose bush.

"Linda." Nurse Lilly's expression fell, and her lips constricted. A momentary cloud of disappointment passed over her sun-shiny face.

Nurse Lilly sighed and forced a smile, her left eye twitching just a little. "It's all right. Accidents happen. They will turn up. I'll have Mr. Phang look for them. Let's not let it ruin our beautiful day."

Nurse Lilly put her arm around Linda, who now carried the bouquet loosely. The two of them led the way back toward the manor, with everyone else trailing behind, including Vickie.

Linda, like a stray dog being loaded into a dark van by the dogcatcher, glanced back at Vickie.

"Finally," Squirt said, "we can leave. I hate bugs!"

CHAPTER 4
Crown of Thorns

The Sixth Floor
10:00 a.m.
17 Hours, 33 Minutes Until Linda's Death

Vickie ran her hand along the cold mahogany wood that paneled the hallways of the sixth floor. Her fingers glided with ease across the smooth, waxy surface. She smelled her palm, detecting no trace of the trees the walls used to be. Instead, the scent of stale furniture polish tickled her nose and almost made her sneeze. The fragrance reminded her of the odor that always clung to the pews of her local Catholic church growing up.

She had attended Catholic school on scholarship when she lived in Queens thanks to a well-meaning neighborhood nun, Sister Murphy. The sister once told Vickie that she saw "nun potential" in her. Vickie wasn't sure if that was a compliment or an insult, regardless of how it was meant.

She welcomed the chance at a fresh start at St. Hilda's School for Girls, but her scholarship was revoked a year later. The administration cited lack of funding, but Vickie knew it was because she asked too many questions.

She still remembered watching the portly priest squirm in his throne of a chair when she raised her hand during theology class to ask things such as, "If everything in the Bible is literal, and it says Jesus was a vine and a door, was he really a vine? Was he really a door?"

She brushed her hand down her thigh in one swift stroke to wipe off the waxy coating, and perhaps the memory. For a moment, she could taste the dry but filling communion wafers she used to binge on when no one was looking. Her stomach growled, bringing her back to the task at hand.

The windows were fewer and smaller up here, but the cascading crystal chandeliers made up for it. Not just one, but a trifecta of illumination drooped from the ceiling like big, fancy, upside-down wedding cakes, providing more than ample light down the center of the corridor. Dazzling twinkles appeared on the floor as the delicate crystal droplets danced in the draft seeping through the ceiling cracks, looking like daytime stars waltzing across the wood.

This was the first time Vickie had been on the sixth floor, for a few reasons. First, there were only a few residence rooms on this floor, and they were only assigned to boys. She wondered if that reflected the amount of supervision those specific individuals required or some other reason. Second, climbing six floors unnecessarily could rarely be justified, and third, not least of all, the proximity to Dr. Habsburg's office made an excursion to the sixth floor seem like torture for Vickie.

But the biggest deterrent was that Eagen's room was here. A wry smile wriggled across her face at the thought of him. She blew a stray sprig of hair out of her face with one quick puff, conveniently clearing the thought of Eagen along with it.

Vickie had waited downstairs for as long as she could stand it—all of five minutes. She wanted to be as close as possible in case Linda needed her; she was still ready to take the blame for any and everything if it meant Linda could avoid punishment. According to the daily schedule, at 10:00 a.m. her fellow pod members alternated between assigned morning jobs, a dressed-up way to say chores, and a choice between music lessons or extra journaling. Only Tracy and Linda opted for the private half-hour music lessons. Since there was only one music teacher, one or the other of them was usually excused from morning jobs once a week for private lessons.

Of the three options available during that time slot, Vickie preferred jobs, so she ignored the rotation. She found sorting and cleaning, or whatever task they were assigned, more gratifying. It made her feel useful and responsible for something. Journaling didn't make sense to her because you had nothing but words to show for your effort and the time expended.

Even though this was her first time on the floor, she knew where she was going. The expansive sixth-floor lounge area right off the stairwell beckoned to one place, down the main hallway and to the left. Once she neared Dr. Habsburg's office, she approached more cautiously, gingerly stepping one foot at a time.

The old wood floor relieved itself in sharp creaks that froze Vickie midstep.

She breathed slowly and steadily and waited.

When no one came to investigate the noise, she straightened up and continued onward. She repeated this halting step-dance several times until she made it to the last turn toward Dr. Habsburg's office.

As Vickie rounded the corner, the blue, red, and yellow light that beamed from a giant stained-glass window surprised her. The black bird designed into the colorful glass wore a crown of thorns. Vickie moved closer, touching the window and the thorny halo, then holding her hand up in front of her face to watch the colored light slide across her palm.

The doorknob to Dr. Habsburg's office jiggled, and the door creaked open, leaving her less time to watch the lights than she would have liked. Vickie quick-stepped her way back around the corner, breathing rapidly, her heart beating loud in her chest. She pressed her back against the wall, closing her eyes tight, bracing herself, until she heard the door click shut again.

When, after a few moments, nothing disastrous happened, she unclenched her eyes and peeked around the corner once more to find

Linda standing in the corridor alone, colored sparkles sliding over her pale face.

Phew!

During the few seconds before she noticed Vickie, Linda's unguarded emotions spilled out. It looked as if Linda's whole body was sinking, her eyes, her cheeks, her shoulders, as if the flesh might drip right off her bones.

Seeing her friend suffering for something she could have taken the blame for herself made every organ in Vickie's body shrivel and ache. She shifted her weight intentionally, making the floor crackle to alert Linda of her presence.

Linda heard the noise and looked upon her friend, her face returning to its usual pleasant configuration.

"So? Are they going to throw you to the hounds?" Vickie asked dryly.

"Kind of. Good news is I'll be leaving soon," Linda answered.

"Leaving?"

"Blueberry Hill."

Vickie struggled for breath but put on a brave face. "When?"

"Tomorrow."

"What?" Vickie's heart raced all over again. Now it was her own face that dropped. She took a step back backward, considering whether to run away or toward Linda. She swallowed so hard she choked on the air and saliva. "That's fantastic." She spoke before her emotions caught up with her words, making them ring false and hollow in the silence of the hallway.

"Is it?"

"Of course it is. You're getting out of this place. That means they really do think you're making progress."

The two girls stared at one another for a moment as if they were swimming underwater, seeing who could hold their breath the longest.

"Congratulations, you fooled everybody!" Vickie said, lightening the mood.

Linda laughed. "I'll miss you, Vickie."

"I'll miss you too."

"I don't know if I can do this without you," Linda said.

"Do what?"

"Life."

"That doesn't sound like a girl making progress. What did I do?"

"You've made me laugh on a daily basis, for one. And you were a good friend."

"Were? Are you trying to tell me something?"

Linda laughed again, sounding a bit forced this time.

"Are you divorcing me?" Vickie joked.

Linda laughed sadness and unease into the air between them.

"I'll visit you," Vickie said.

"It's not that easy," Linda said.

"Sure it is. I'll get a monthly bus pass. Student discount. Twenty bucks."

"You don't understand." Linda's lips tightened as she hyperventilated just a little and held her breath at the same time. Vickie surmised she was holding more than her breath inside, but didn't want to push Linda where she might not want to go.

Instead, Vickie smiled, hoping to reassure her friend. Even though she wanted to move from this spot, leave this painful, clumsy moment, she knew they had more to say to each other. "We'll still see each other. I'm going to get out of this place, too, you know? They can't keep me here forever. Trust me. They don't want to keep me forever," Vickie said with a twist of her mouth.

"This is true."

Another moment of awkward silence stretched between them as Vickie watched the shifting light patterns from the stained glass on the floor, avoiding Linda's eyes.

"I wish I could come with you," Vickie said, hanging her head, a lump rising in her throat.

"No, you don't. Trust me."

"Your foster parents can't be that bad. Can't be worse than here."

"How would you know?"

"True. I only know what you tell me. And you don't really talk about them. And I'm not one to pry."

Linda chuckled. "Heavens, no. Not you." Linda attempted to hide her unrest, but she wasn't doing a great job of it. Silence stretched between them.

Finally, Vickie spoke. "I just want them to be good people. 'Cause you deserve that. So . . . " Vickie kicked at the floor as if it were made of dirt, looking down at it. "Well, how do you want to spend your last day?"

"Oh. I'm not sure." Linda turned her face away, her eyes glistening with moisture.

"Come on, let's get some Jell-O," Vickie said.

Linda's lips parted in a half smile, and she nodded. "I have my music lesson first."

"I'll walk you."

They continued down the hallway, passing the residences.

Linda stopped in front of a door. Vickie stopped as well, her eyebrows crinkling.

"Linda?" The timbre in Vickie's voice deepened.

"What? I'm going to see Eagen. Just for a second. He usually journals in his room," Linda said.

"Eagen? Won't that spoil your appetite?"

"Vickie." Linda rolled her eyes at her friend. "I'll catch up with you later."

Linda knocked on room 602, and a warning scream penetrated through the door from inside. "Go away!" Eagen said.

"That means come in. I speak his language," Linda said to Vickie, breathing in, raising her shoulders then dropping them in preparation.

"You want me to stay here just in case?"

"That's not necessary."

"I just found a knife on him," Vickie said, folding her arms over her chest and glaring at the door.

"Exactly. I'll be even safer now that he's disarmed. Save some Jell-O for me. I'll see you after my music lesson. Right after. Promise."

Vickie left, casting glances behind her as the distance between her friend and herself grew.

Assessment and Plan

Provider: Blueberry Hill Home for Troubled Youth, LLC   **Client Name:** **Eagen Dresden**
Group Assignment: Pod #1   **Session Number:** #1

Diagnosis: Conduct Disorder, Mild Depression

Treatment

Intake Protocol: Clinical Assessment   **Medications:** Fluoxetine 20 mg/day,
                      Self-report Mood Questionnaire   *as per* Dr. Mariska Habsburg, M.D.

Short-Term Goals for Client (2 Weeks):
1. Understand contributing factors to own low self-esteem.
2. Articulate relationship between cognitive distortions and low self-esteem.
3. Journal thoughts daily.
4. Participate in group discussions, generating positivity around peers and peer relationships.

Long-Term Goals (3 Months):
1. Identify and address issues of denial and trust.
2. Increase awareness of defensive behavior by providing examples and encouraging client to identify similar behaviors in his life.
3. Address issues of defensiveness and counterproductive behavior in dealing with authority figures.
4. Use new vocabulary to support expression of thoughts and feelings.
5. Identify specific feelings and issues and more appropriate ways of coping with them.
6. Better management of anger. Reduce potential for violence.

Session Notes

Body Language, Facial Patterns: Oppositional eye contact and posturing at points, contrasted with long periods of silence and staring into the distance.

Summary:
1. Client vacillated between sketching in his pad during session and prolonged periods of silence and aggressive posturing.
2. When shown the violent drawings provided by his parents depicting the gruesome deaths of his classmates and asked what he thought of the drawings, he responded, "Not my best work."
3. Client reports he no longer sketches the deaths of others, but sketches their fears instead.

Other Observations/Comments:
- Parents provided drawings depicting violent acts involving weaponry perpetrated against classmates.
- Parents also reported client verbally threatened sibling and is fascinated with the death and dying of others.
- Also of note, according to school transcripts, client has a tested IQ of 198.

Client Signature: *Eagen Dresden*   **Primary Caregiver 1:** *Anthony Dresden*
(Age 14 and up)   Eagen Dresden   Anthony Dresden
                                                                       (Father)
Primary Caregiver 2: *W. Dresden*   **Therapist Signature:** *Ara Cannon*
                      Wilhelmina Dresden   Dr. Ara Cannon, Ph.D.
                      (Mother)

CHAPTER 5
Introverts

Room 602

10:13 a.m.

17 Hours, 20 Minutes Until Linda's Death

On the other side of the door, Linda found Eagen alone, reclining on his bed, sketching. The vigorous strokes of his pencil scratched across the textured page loud enough to hear. She entered and closed the door softly behind her before taking three tentative steps forward and pausing.

Both hands behind her back, she held her pointer finger for comfort, swinging slowly from side to side, staring down at the hardwood floors.

"Sorry about the way I left this morning. But you shouldn't have done that," Linda said, lifting her head, seeking out Eagen's eyes.

Eagen shrugged his shoulders, not looking up at her.

"What are you drawing?" she asked, changing the topic to something that might put him at ease.

"Same thing I always draw. Fear."

Linda almost giggled. "Fear? What does fear look like?"

"It's different for every person," Eagen said, still not giving her his gaze.

"So . . . you draw what people are afraid of? How do you know?"

"People aren't as good at hiding things as they think they are, especially when you know where to look."

Linda stiffened, standing up straighter to brace herself, suddenly apprehensive Eagen could see right through her. "What am I afraid of, then?" she asked.

Eagen tore a piece of paper from his pad and handed it to Linda. She examined it, turning it over to look at both sides. "It's blank? What is this supposed to mean? That I'm not afraid of anything?"

Eagen offered her a half smile, his eyes narrowing. Linda looked back at the paper, uncomfortable with the added weight of his words now that his eyes rested on her. She willed herself not to look away.

"You're afraid of being invisible," Eagen said, his pupils like black-rimmed pits that bore into hers.

Linda's eyebrows raised unsteadily, her body quivering until it shook her voice out of her. "Invisible?"

"Yeah. Like a ghost. Here but not here. Seeing everything, but you're powerless to stop it or change it. Seeing others, but they can't truly see you."

She chuckled uncomfortably, masking the effect his words had on her. "You think so?"

"I don't need you to tell me I'm right to know I'm right. If there's one thing I know, it's fear," Eagen said. "It's my genius."

"Well. People are more than their fears. And people can change." Linda folded the blank paper in half and then tore it in two, throwing the scraps in a nearby wastebasket. "Just because you are afraid of something doesn't mean it has to control you."

"Why are you here, Linda?" His voice dropped an octave.

"I have something to tell you." A rustle on the other side of the door broke her focus. She smirked. "Just a moment."

Linda walked toward the door and opened it.

No one in sight.

She took one quick breath and put her hand on her hip. "Vickie?

45

Vickie? I know you're there," Linda said.

A voice replied from farther down the hall and around the corner.

"What?" Vickie said. "I was admiring all the . . ." Vickie turned to examine a couple of creepy portraits of long-dead men in Union soldier uniforms and dour-faced women in lace-encrusted dresses. "Beautiful artwork."

"I'd like some privacy, please? I'll see you in the cafeteria after my lesson."

Vickie turned and walked away, saluting the artwork as she left. "As you were."

Linda closed the door, amused, sad, and shaken all at the same time. "Sorry 'bout that."

"Not as sorry as I am," Eagen said, his face tightening. "So, go on. You wanted to tell me something."

Ten minutes later, Linda emerged from Eagen's room, pausing for a moment after she closed the door behind her to wipe the moisture from her eyes with her bare hand, then she continued to her music lesson.

The Music Room
11:00 a.m.
16 Hours, 33 Minutes Until Linda's Death

The music room was small, but big enough. Mr. Fitch kept a variety of instruments in a closet off to one side. There were music stands that never found their way back to their corner, stacks of sheet music on the windowsills, and an old piano that invariably went out of tune every couple of weeks.

Tucked away in the corner was a Hammond organ that still functioned but had needed replacement parts since the manufacturer went out of business in 1985.

"Great work today," Mr. Fitch said, rising from his seat at the piano next to Linda.

"Mind if I stick around for a bit?" Linda asked.

"Not at all. I have thirty minutes until my next student."

Linda's fingers perched lightly on the keys, taking in the coolness of the ivory. Unsure of what she might play, she allowed her fingers to guide her as she struck a few somber notes. Mr. Fitch bustled about in his version of tidying the room, which somehow just made it look more untidy.

"Whatever you play, put your heart into it," he advised. His warm smile sunk into Linda's heart.

She plucked out a few nonsensical chords until something familiar seemed to bleed through her fingers. Linda played a slow and haunting version of "The More We Get Together" that sounded more like a funeral dirge than a happy childhood tune.

Mr. Fitch paused from the rearranging of his piles of papers, staring into space for a moment. "What's that?"

"Just a little something I have stuck in my head," Linda said.

Mr. Fitch pursed his mouth, puzzled.

"What? I put my heart into it like you said."

"That's supposed to be a happy song. It's in the lyrics. *The happier we'll be.*" Mr. Fitch sang the last part.

Linda's eyebrows raised at the lightness singing brought to Mr. Fitch's face. She stared at her fingers. "I can't put happy into the music if it's not in my heart."

Mr. Fitch set the music stand he was holding down in its new position, giving Linda his full attention. His eyes fluttered as if he was searching for the right response.

"Saying goodbye can be tough."

"You heard?" Linda asked.

Mr. Fitch moved back over to the piano and stood next to her. "Yes."

"Who told you?"

"Before email or the phone or telegrams, there was the teacher's lounge. I may not say a lot, but I listen. I observe."

"Well, I guess you're going to tell me how strong I am. And everything is going to be OK."

"No."

"No?" Linda took her hands off the piano, looking more intently at him.

"Like I said, I see things and I hear things and I feel things. Like you. Even if the words aren't said . . . Beware of us introverts. We're different. Better, if you ask me." Mr. Fitch winked at her conspiratorially.

Linda laughed. She liked Mr. Fitch and appreciated his unassuming disposition. She was a shy kid, an introvert like he said, who felt forced to be more outgoing and social than was natural for her. All foster kids learned quickly that the extroverts got adopted first. Prospective parents assumed there was something wrong with the quiet ones. Or they couldn't be bothered with trying to get to know them. "They're too much work," the couples would say, and they'd wait for a more outgoing child to become available.

"You're lucky to be leaving, Linda."

"But you know I'm going to—"

"Trust me. You're still better off. No matter where you are going. Something's not right here. At Blueberry Hill." Linda leaned in closer as Mr. Fitch explained further. "Remember, we introverts feel things. I'll bet you feel it too?"

Linda offered something more than a smile. It was the kind of expression she knew Mr. Fitch would understand. The kind that said, 'Thank you, Mr. Fitch, for hearing me, for seeing me. Thank you for not pressuring me to be something I'm not.'

"Well, I'd better go. I'm meeting Vickie."

"She's not an introvert."

"No. Definitely not. But she is a good friend," Linda said, pushing her stool away from the piano and heading toward the door.

"Linda," Mr. Fitch called.

Linda turned back to face him, surprised by the concern that had spread over his face.

"Be careful."

They exchanged knowing looks, communicating volumes in a way that only introverts could.

CHAPTER 6
At Your Own Risk

The Cafeteria
8:33 p.m.
7 Hours Until Linda's Death

Pod 1 busied themselves with their assigned kitchen duties. Vickie and Tracy shared a mop bucket, each of them with their own mop, while Eagen wrote the menu for the next day's breakfast on a chalkboard. Squirt carried a dishpan full of suds, sloshing pine-scented water over the sides as he walked.

"Hey! I just mopped there!" Vickie said.

"Sorry. It's heavy," Squirt replied.

"I'll help," Linda offered.

"No. It's your last day. I've got it," Squirt said, heaving the pan onto the table, splashing more water onto the floor.

"What the—" Vickie yelled, rushing over with her mop to clean up the mess. "Squirt!"

Linda moved toward the soapy water.

"I told you, I'll take care of it," Squirt said.

"That's sweet. But it'll take my mind off things to do something productive."

Eagen shot a look at Linda, which she promptly ignored.

Linda and Squirt both reached for the sponges at the same time, their hands touching briefly in the water. Squirt blushed, and before he could take his hand away, Linda squeezed his hand firmly.

"Thank you."

"For what?"

"You've always been kind to me. Kind to everyone."

Squirt reddened more and exhaled nervously.

"Hey, what's going on over there?" Tracy kidded as he slid chairs out of the way so he could mop under one of the tables in the back.

"Nothing," Squirt said, his face still flushed with color.

As Squirt and Linda wiped the same table, she asked, "How'd you end up here, Squirt?"

Always listening, Vickie chimed in, mopping under the table next to him. "He probably did something pervy."

"I did not!" Squirt looked earnestly at Linda.

Linda reassured him. "I know."

"I'm here for the same reason as you, Vickie. I like to take things. But I use my computer to do it."

"And you, Eagen?" Tracy asked.

Eagen still drew on the chalkboard as he answered. "Why do you think I'm here?"

"I couldn't even begin to guess," Linda said.

"So many dark possibilities," Tracy said.

"Come on, you can tell me. I'm leaving tomorrow," Linda pleaded.

Eagen stopped writing, but still stared at the chalkboard.

"I told the truth. Parents say they want the truth, but they only want the rainbows and not the rain," Eagen said.

There was a moment of considered quiet before Linda looked at Tracy. Vickie's mopping slowed as she listened.

"The real reason or the fake reason?" Tracy asked.

"Real," Linda said.

"My mom and I were close. After she died, I didn't really get along with my dad and his new girlfriend. So, they both agreed it would be better if they sent me off."

"What was the fake reason?" Squirt asked.

"The reason that made them feel better about themselves, you mean? I got into a car accident."

"What's wrong with that?" Vickie asked.

"I don't have a license. And it wasn't my car. And I ran over my father's girlfriend's chihuahua. Twice."

Vickie's mouth fell open.

"I didn't mean to. I was aiming for the girlfriend. But I'm a terrible driver."

Annie's face contorted into fifty shades of horror.

"Relax. The dog lived. And regrettably, so did the girlfriend."

"I thought I had demons," Eagen said.

"No, I *have* demons. You *are* a demon," Tracy said.

They all laughed. Even Eagen smirked, which was his version of a belly laugh.

"All right, all done mopping," Vickie said.

"Me too," Tracy added.

"Tables are done," Squirt said.

"Eagen, how about you?" Linda asked.

Eagen hung the chalkboard he drew upon onto the nail in the wall. Written on the chalkboard in beautiful lettering were tomorrow's breakfast items: Ham and Eggs, Cinnamon Toast, Oatmeal, Cantaloupe, Milk. Next to the handwritten menu was a chalk sketch of a skull and crossbones and the words EAT AT YOUR OWN RISK.

"The lunch ladies aren't going to like that," Linda said.

"That's what they get for selecting me for this task. They know my work."

"Let's get out of here," Vickie said.

52

The First Floor
10:00 p.m.
5 Hours, 33 Minutes Until Linda's Death

An eerie quiet permeated the manor as Angelo exited the staff lounge.

The building's residents were required to be in their rooms by 9:30 p.m., with lights out at 10:00. Part of Angelo's job was to be sure they complied. Only nineteen himself, he felt that 10:00 p.m. was an unrealistic bedtime. However, the days started early at Blueberry Hill, and many of the teens were on medication that required they sleep a little more. Walking toward the first-floor rec room to check and make sure it was empty, he heard soft voices and the rustling of papers.

As he rounded the reception desk, Nurse Dorothy sat in front of an outdated computer, wrapping a colorful scarf around her neck several times as Nurse Fran attended to some filing.

"It's freezing in here all of a sudden," she said to Nurse Fran. "Don't you think?"

"Same as always," Nurse Fran answered.

"Well, luckily, I get off soon, so I can go outside and warm up," Nurse Dorothy replied, her words carried in spurts by her breathy laugh.

Angelo's hand rested on the flashlight holstered by his side. The top button of his white uniform was purposefully undone, which didn't go unnoticed by Nurse Dorothy. Angelo glimpsed her staring at him out of the corner of his eye and saw Nurse Fran shoot a reprimanding glare in her direction. He couldn't help but chuckle to himself.

"Night checks?" Nurse Dorothy asked.

"Yep. Chilly, huh?" Angelo asked.

"Yep."

"Want my jacket? It's in the lounge."

"No. I'm warming up." Nurse Dorothy smiled, sending him a look that could melt butter.

Angelo nodded his head, which was his modern-day version of the gentlemanly tipping of the hat. He continued down the hallway, barely controlling the grin that threatened to escape.

Nurse Dorothy exhaled deeply and dreamily. "It should be illegal to be that hunky."

Nurse Fran rolled her eyes.

"Criminal. Just criminal," Nurse Dorothy said, biting her lower lip.

"Don't you have a boyfriend?" Nurse Fran reminded her.

"No. A fiancé. And there's no harm in window shopping."

"Well, he's not a window, and you're not here to shop."

"Killjoy!" Nurse Dorothy said.

"You're at work. There's no joy in that." Nurse Fran returned to her filing, her face cast in a disapproving scowl.

After confirming the rec room was empty, Angelo climbed three flights with little effort, sometimes taking a few steps at a time just for fun. He worked his way down the floor, room by room, eventually tapping lightly on the door of room 402. Technically, he didn't have to knock, but he wanted to avoid embarrassment for both the teens and himself, lest he walk in on something he shouldn't. They were teenagers, after all. Privacy was valuable to them. He paused a moment to listen for a reply, then opened the door only wide enough to peer inside.

He only had to shine the flashlight on each of the beds, if the overhead lights were off as they were supposed to be, to check that there was an occupant present. However, the rules allowed lamplight for reading or urgent late-night conversations.

In general, Angelo preferred not to speak to the residents so he could get through checks as quickly and as easily as possible. Of course, if they spoke to him, he spoke back. The entire process was awkward and, if he was honest, was one of his least favorite tasks as an orderly.

When it came to room 402, however, he was always eager to speak, but he still let the residents lead — one resident in particular.

"Night checks," Angelo said in a firm yet quiet voice, poking his head inside the room.

Annie was already fast asleep, a contented smile spread across her face, and Vickie and Linda faced each other in their own beds, talking.

A small bedside lamp beside Linda illuminated the room; a book lay open in her lap.

Angelo lingered for a moment. As he closed the door, a voice stopped him, like a forceful tap on the shoulder.

"Thanks, Angelo." Linda smiled at him in a way that was pure and genuine. Vickie raised one eyebrow and pursed her lips, looking at Linda, then Angelo.

Angelo blushed. *Does Vickie suspect?* He couldn't imagine how she would.

He looked down before smiling back, nodding slightly. "See you tomorrow." Angelo allowed the door to close softly and slowly exhaled.

Room 402
10:13 p.m.
5 Hours, 20 Minutes Until Linda's Death

The Masque of the Red Death was the title of the short story Linda had read and reread over the past couple of nights. A part of a collection of works by Edgar Allan Poe, bound in an ebony cover with chipped golden embroidery, the pen and ink illustrations found within captivated Linda almost as much as the words themselves. She ran her fingers over the rough, thick pages, touching each detail in the sketch of death incarnate. Linda felt the deep blood-red, the only color on the page, seep into her heart. She was afraid to touch it for fear she might melt into the crimson mask and cloak of the bony figure.

Inspired by the story, she had painted the papier-mâché mask Dr. Cannon forced them to create in drama class red. After three coats, it still wasn't red enough, not as red as the mask worn by Poe's Death.

Maybe I have time for one more coat, she thought. *But when?* Time was running out.

Stuck between the frayed and yellowed pages, the piece of paper marking her place in the book drew her attention. She stared at it, motionless for more than a moment.

Peering at Linda from her own bed, Vickie interrupted Linda's lucid wandering. "What's that?"

Linda paused for another moment, still lost to the present. She inhaled deeply before lifting the tiny paper and handing it to Vickie over the arms-length expanse between their two beds.

Vickie held the wallet-size photo of Linda and two adults with care, looking at the image then back at Linda. She waited, resting in the expectant moment until Linda chose to fill it.

"My foster parents," Linda explained.

"Oh." Vickie looked back at the photo.

Linda was usually tight-lipped about her home life and appreciated the space Vickie gave her to share as much or as little as she wanted. "They gave me a photo of themselves to settle me. To make me feel better. How vain is that?"

Vickie shifted the photo from side to side as if it were a 3D image that she could somehow peek around. "So, these are the evil Endlethorps. They don't look smart enough to be evil. Being bad takes some degree of intelligence."

Linda's laugh bubbled up from deep inside her, catching her off guard. "They're rich. They don't have to be smart."

"Well, they took in a teenage foster kid. That takes some balls. And they chose you, so that was a pretty smart choice." Vickie smiled, a warm feeling enveloping her like a blanket.

"I'm sure it just made them look good to their friends. Real saintly taking in a kid. The wife's Catholic."

Vickie nodded her head in acknowledgment. "Ohhhh. I know the type."

"But having a kid, even a foster kid, who doesn't eat doesn't fit their pretty picture."

Vickie examined the photo again.

"And what are you wearing here?"

Linda put her head in her hands, shaking it. "The wife loved buying me clothes. She always wanted a daughter."

"I take it back. She might be a little evil. That dress!"

"It wasn't so bad in the beginning. They took that photo before everything started. There are no pictures of me when things got bad enough for people to see. I disappeared from their photos and then from their house. A living ghost."

"Why do you still have this?"

Linda's posture stiffened. There was none of the usual brightness in her words as she spoke. "It makes a good bookmark," she deadpanned. They both giggled at the unapologetic glibness in her tone, muffling the sounds with their hands so as not to wake Annie.

"Now who's got jokes?" Vickie turned onto her side and, nuzzling into her pillow, asked, "Did you do everything you wanted on your last day?"

"I wanted to finish my mask. Help me remember to pack it tomorrow morning?"

"Why would you want that thing? It creeps me out."

"I kind of like mine. Makes me feel more like myself when I have it on."

Vickie yawned and snuggled tight with her pillow.

Linda's face relaxed as a maternal feeling washed over her. "Well. Guess we better get some sleep," Linda suggested. "Big day tomorrow."

"Big day," Vickie agreed. "Hey, what about that secret? You gonna tell me now?"

"I'll tell you when you get out of here. I don't want to get anyone in trouble."

"Intriguing. Promise?"

"Promise." Linda looked at Vickie, reaching out to her with her words. "Thanks for helping me get through this."

"You'll be okay."

"Promise?" Linda asked.

"Promise. And Vickie Bartolucci does not lie. To my friends, at least. Not without good reason. See, I can't even lie about never telling a lie. Capisce?"

"Capisce."

"Well, there's only one thing left to do." Vickie reached over into the nightstand and pulled out two charcoal pencils, handing one to Linda.

At the head of their mattresses on the wall behind each of their beds were a series of hash marks.

"This is the last time you'll do this."

"Day ninety-one," Linda said as she etched a mark onto the wall.

"Show-off. Day forty-five for me."

Linda offered the pencil back to Vickie.

Vickie waved her hand. "Keep it. As a souvenir."

"Are you sure?"

"I stole them from Eagen. He's got a million more," Vickie confessed.

Linda chuckled, then lay the pencil by her book on the nightstand.

They smiled at one another. "You'll be all right." Vickie said, turning toward the wall. "Night."

"Nigh . . ." Before Linda could finish the word, Vickie was snoring.

A warm, nostalgic smile spread across Linda's face. "You're a good friend, Vickie Bartolucci," she whispered.

Linda glanced at the book still on the nightstand and ran her hand across it.

The Masque of the Red Death.

She flicked off the lamp. The afterglow of the bulb blinded her for a moment before her eyes accepted the lack of light. Outside her window, clouds already covered the moon, plunging the entire house into darkness.

CHAPTER 7
Lost and Found

DAY 46 for Vickie

Room 402

2:22 a.m.

1 Hour, 11 Minutes Until Linda's Death

S hadows played across the walls. The moon was much higher in the sky now and nearly full. Vickie woke up with a start, her heart beating fast, her brow furrowed.

"Linda." The whisper escaped her lips like a last breath.

Vickie glanced over at Annie's side of the room and saw she was still sleeping. She closed her eyes and yawned, saying her best friend's name again.

"Linda?"

Her vision twisted in and out of focus with only moonlight illuminating the room, but she could see enough to notice Linda's bed was empty. She pulled back her own sheets, slid into a pair of house shoes, and smoothed down her rumpled pajamas, shaking out a wedgie as she took her first couple of steps.

Maybe Linda went to the bathroom? Can't hurt to go see in case she's sick again; Linda's nervous about leaving. Vickie could tell.

She tiptoed to the door and quietly pulled it open.

Cr-e-e-e-e-ak.

Vickie pattered down the dimly lit hallway to the communal bathroom, yawning and rubbing her eyes. She placed her hand on the old, heavy wooden door and it opened slowly until it hit the interior wall with a thud.

Vickie entered, her slippers sliding against the freshly cleaned tiles. "Linda?"

The door closed behind her.

Drip, splash.

Drip, splash.

Drip, splash.

The faucet cried into the water pooling in the ceramic basin, one slow drop at a time. Vickie walked over and turned the faucet handle, shutting off the flow. The overhead light flickered with a pulsating electric buzz.

This place is falling apart.

She yawned again and shuffled over to the stall closest to her, pushing open the door with her hand.

Empty.

She repeated this process for the next two stalls, until finally there was only one stall left. Wide awake now, she strained her ears for any sounds indicating she wasn't alone. "Are you in there?"

She put her hands on the handle of the stall door, steadying herself, breathing in and out before opening it.

Vickie had often found Linda hunched over the toilet, vomiting, but that hadn't happened in weeks. Maybe a month? Or days? It was so hard to keep track of time in any traditional way in this place.

Vickie pushed against the stall door, more slowly than the others. It squeaked at her touch. She only had a moment to register that the stall was empty when the door to the entrance of the bathroom banged open. Vickie jumped and fell back against the nearby wall, her hand flying to her heart.

"What the —" Vickie blurted.

Annie wandered in, all smiles, as if she were still in the middle of a never-ending, blissful dream.

"Geez," Vickie added.

"She's not in there," Annie said.

"I can see that. Have you seen her?" Vickie asked.

Annie giggled, looking at her reflection in the mirror, then stuck her mouth under the faucet and slurped two quick sips.

"Why don't you use the water fountain?" Vickie asked.

"It tastes better in here."

"It comes from the same pipes." Her comment didn't seem to register as Annie took in another gulp.

"If you see Linda, tell her I'm looking for her," Vickie continued.

Vickie walked toward the door and slung it open. Just before she exited, she paused, stopped momentarily by the tune Annie hummed.

The more we get together, together, together . . .

Vickie closed the door, wrinkling her eyebrows and clenching her lips. Then, she took a step forward, determined to check all the usual places and then the unusual ones until she found Linda.

Her eyes narrowed, and her throat tightened as she walked, her pace accelerating with each step. She cared less and less about getting caught roaming the halls after night checks with each hiccuping beat of her heart.

As she passed the grandmother clock, it chimed softly, indicating it was half past the hour.

"Shut up," she said out loud.

The hallways were so quiet Vickie could hear her quickening breath. She could have sworn she once again heard the tinny dings of the song Annie was humming.

The more we get together . . .

But she didn't have time to figure all that out. She needed to find Linda and couldn't be bothered with what other residents might be doing in their own rooms with musical contraband they smuggled inside.

Vickie barreled down the staircase, throwing open the door of the first-floor stairwell. She lingered for a moment, putting her hands on the inside of the door frame to steady herself, out of breath.

Briefly, she looked down and saw her own reflection in the tiled floor and couldn't help but stare at it for a moment; but a moment was all she gave herself.

She sensed that time was of the essence.

"Hello? Hello?" she called with an elevated voice.

No one was at the reception desk, but a familiar scent hung in the air. Flowers. It reminded her of Linda and the time they had spent together the day before.

Vickie looked toward the reception desk and spied wildflowers arranged in a clear vase, no doubt emanating the sweet scent that summoned her memories.

Moonlight seeped through the double french doors, casting shadows around the lobby. The window shades clinked against the glass-like wind chimes, rippling in the incessant drafts. Their clipped notes melted into the silence.

A mop bucket full of dirty water propped the door of the janitor's closet open. She craned her neck to see if anyone was around.

Not a soul in sight, as if everyone had vanished.

Vickie always wondered what the night staff did while the teens were all sequestered in their rooms at night. Apparently, nothing! They all went on break.

Scanning the space for any trace of Linda, she noticed the french doors were slightly ajar. Vickie walked over to them and poked her head outside.

That's weird. Why are the doors unlocked? Shouldn't someone have checked the doors?

"Hello? Linda?"

No answer.

Vickie pushed the doors closed with a thud, turning the double bolt. Her heart sank with the turn of the lock.

She spun around and continued her search, walking around the corner, then down the hall, approaching the drama room. A light from behind the door brightened the outside corridor. Vickie inhaled deeply and smiled. "There you are," she said, her shoulders and entire body relaxing as she pushed down the door handle and stepped into the room.

Desks lined in rows filled the room as usual, each with a papier-mâché mask on it in various stages of completion. The masks sat on sticks and were covered individually in shimmery eastern fabrics.

On the desk farthest to the back sat a crimson mask. There was no fabric covering this one, but there should have been.

Linda will be upset if anyone's touched her mask.

Vickie's smile slipped away. "Linda? Are you here?"

Vickie approached the mask slowly.

Just as she reached out to touch it, she felt a hand on her shoulder.

She gasped, fists clenched, her shoulders hardening like steel.

"Vickie? What are you doing here?"

"Angelo? I almost punched you in the face. Don't sneak up on people."

Angelo's arms looked even more jacked in the undulating shadows of the night. Still, Vickie was confident she could take him.

"You aren't supposed to be in here. You're gonna get in trouble."

"No, *Linda* is in trouble."

"What? Why would you say that?"

"I can't find her."

His face fell before he lifted himself up with reassuring words. "She's probably in the bathroom."

"I checked."

"Maybe she's using the bathroom on another floor?" Angelo suggested.

"Why would she do that?" Vickie asked.

Angelo stared at Vickie, tilting his head down and raising his eyebrows as if he were a librarian looking over bifocals.

"I know. And she doesn't do that anymore. She's been eating and keeping things down for a long time now."

Vickie didn't question how Angelo knew so much about Linda's behavior. Even in her 127-unit apartment building in Flushing, Queens, the staff somehow knew all the residents' business.

"I'll check the other floors, just in case. I'm sure she's around. Go back to bed. Or you'll get me in trouble," Angelo said.

Vickie walked out with Angelo, but let him continue on ahead of her.

She didn't think Angelo would rat her out, but several questions leaped forward in her mind: *Why didn't he escort me back to my room? Does he really trust me to go back on my own? Wasn't he supposed to check the front door to make sure it was locked at night?*

They led her to one conclusion, maybe two. Angelo really sucked at his job, and if he was trusting her to return to her room and stay put, he obviously didn't know her very well.

Vickie watched Angelo turn the corner toward the stairs and then bolted toward the other set of stairs at the opposite end of the hallway, continuing up, up, up.

She was out of breath, but would have taken the steps two at a time if her legs allowed it. She pushed onward, gritting her teeth when her body wanted to slow down.

Panting, she flung open the door to the sixth-floor hallway and stopped. Her wide-awake eyes adjusted reluctantly from the brightness of the lit stairwell. This floor also looked quite different at night.

During the day, the light streaming in through the stained glass and from the tiny windows lining the hallway reminded you that there was life outside. This nighttime version was the opposite — menacing and creepy. The dark paneling of the wide corridor sunk into even darker hues, and she couldn't tell where the floor started, and the walls began. It was as if the surfaces closed in all at once, choking the air out, like a shadowy coffin trapping her six feet underground.

Despite the darkness and her fatigue, Vickie walked in as straight a line as possible, still not able to see more than a few paces ahead of her, until finally her feet stopped in front of room 602.

Just hours earlier, she had stood in this same spot, eavesdropping on Linda's conversation with Eagen. And now, she stood here seeking help, not from Eagen, but from someone else.

She closed her eyes and crossed her fingers, hoping the right inhabitant of 602 would answer her knock. She rapped on the door, and just before she could knock again, the door creaked open.

There stood Tracy, groggy, his glorious hair mussed, but still beautiful. Vickie's body relaxed a little, glad that he was the one who came to the door.

"Vickie? What's going on?" Tracy asked, eyes half-open.

"Linda's disappeared. She's in trouble."

"Disappeared? Where?"

"I don't know where. That's what disappeared means. No one's at the front desk. Angelo doesn't believe me—"

Tracy stepped into the hallway, closing the door behind him with focused intention, speaking in a hushed tone.

"Slow down." He put his hand on her shoulder. "Are you sure?"

Vickie felt the heat from his palm penetrate the cotton of her pajamas and into her skin. He stood close to her and spoke with such intimacy that if it were possible, her heart would have beat faster still.

"Trust me. Something's wrong. Why isn't anyone listening to me?"

Tracy paused, looking down at the floor for a moment, then back up, meeting her eyes directly. "We'll make them listen," he said in a voice so steady Vickie felt as if he were carrying her.

Tracy glanced over at the red "break in case of emergency" fire alarm box within arm's reach. Vickie followed his gaze, though it was hard to stop looking at his beautiful face.

"If she's OK, we'll see her on the lawn with everyone else. If not, well, you'll have everyone's attention."

They stared into each other's eyes once again, breathing in sync as Tracy reached out and shattered the glass of the alarm cover with the side of his fist.

Relief washed over Vickie's face and down her arms in a warm prickle. There was so much more she wanted to say to him, but no words came out. The earsplitting alarm broke into their bubble, and she smiled in shy thanks.

Vickie was the first to break eye contact and dash away, the warmth of his breath still lingering on her neck.

Almost immediately, from every corner of the building, confused and annoyed teenagers stumbled out of their rooms and headed for the designated meeting points. Mutterings and protests about fire drills so early in the morning shot through the hallways like a handful of pellet-gun BBs tossed hard enough to sting on impact, but not forceful enough to penetrate flesh.

The Rose Garden
3:32 a.m.
1 Minute Until Linda's Death

The lawn was already damp with the dew the cool Maine summer night brought with it. The chorus of crickets and mating bullfrogs blended with the blare of the alarm that escaped from the cracks, crevices, and flung-open doors of the building.

Vickie was the first to exit the manor, her long, determined strides trotting toward the central circular fountain. She turned back to face the house several times as she ran, making her dizzy as she stepped up onto the fountain's edge, looking around, waiting.

She planted her feet and faced the manor in anticipation. Several strands of her unruly sleep-hair blew into her eyes, obstructing her view. She smoothed it back, only to have it return to the same position.

Goose bumps rose all over her skin, but Vickie wasn't cold. She felt an anticipation different from the exhilaration she felt the day before, when her best friend had whisked her away on a woodland adventure. The moment had her teetering between desperation and hopefulness.

At last, the residents flowed down the stairs onto the lawn in a seething, noisy wave, along with the miscellaneous night staff. Some teens carried stuffed animals, some didn't, some wore jackets, some didn't, but all of them complained. About everything. The damp grass, the unpleasant alarm, the early morning breath of the person next to them. Everything presented a problem for someone.

A couple of unfamiliar night orderlies attempted to gather the kids into their pods, calling out numbers and pointing out locations in barely controlled chaos.

Vickie's posture changed and she hung her head when the last stragglers exited. The rumble of a large, old vehicle up on the highway reverberated under the shrill shriek of the fire alarm loud enough to attract her attention. It paused briefly, then resumed its throaty progress away into the distance.

Sirens wailed from down the road. Within seconds, a fire truck, followed by a couple other vehicles, sped up the drive.

The firefighters entered the building as soon as their truck slowed to a stop. One stout figure broke away and approached the knot of nurses near the fountain. Vickie noticed her pod amid the chaos, gathered in their designated location. Briefly, she locked eyes with Tracy and he nodded. His encouragement was all she needed to remain on task in her mission to find Linda. She scanned the sea of faces one last time, surveying the grounds as far as she could see. Desperately, she turned back to the hedge maze and the clusters of trees and shrubs just beyond, her eyes stopping on the clock tower. It was 3:34 a.m.

Then, as if pulled by an unseen force, she looked toward the dark ribbon of road beyond the sprawling lawn and driveway. Something white shone in the moonlight amid the dark asphalt. She took a few slow steps away from the grumbling crowd. Whatever it was, it didn't move.

She quickened her pace toward the road until she was sprinting. Shouts arose behind her. She thought she heard someone call her name, but she ignored them, focusing instead on the white object in the middle of the highway.

Long before she arrived at the graveled shoulder, her body trembled with dread at what she might find when she reached the road's edge.

Linda.

Before she knew what she was doing, Vickie knelt beside her friend's body, still-warm blood pooling around her, soaking Linda's white nightgown.

"Over here! Over here! Somebody! Help!" Vickie shouted.

The once-tranquil road soon became a noisy blur of shock and uniformed personnel.

The paramedics, police, and a sea of young, morbidly fascinated faces, all for whom this probably wasn't the first tragedy they had witnessed, nor the last, ventured closer. EMTs rushed over with bags and stern words and attempted to resuscitate Linda. Vickie heard her name called again, but it was muffled and fuzzy, like her ears were full of cotton balls.

She clung to Linda's still-warm hand, refusing to let go, even though she knew it was too late. When a paramedic tried to shove Vickie aside, she remained fixed to the spot, steadfast in her dawning grief.

Only a couple of minutes passed before a deep voice pronounced Linda dead.

Her friend was gone.

She had felt it and known it in her core the second she saw the unmoving, white-clad figure in the road. Now, there was nothing she could do for her. At least, there was nothing she could do to bring her back. She inhaled deeply, but couldn't exhale the breath back out right away.

Vickie felt a familiar hand on her shoulder for the second time that day. And it wasn't Tracy.

"You don't want to see this part," Angelo said.

Vickie didn't move, still kneeling by Linda, remaining unconvinced until Angelo said, "Linda wouldn't want you to see her like this."

Vickie nodded, finally exhaling, shifting back from Linda's body slowly. Angelo attempted to help her to her feet, but she pushed his hands away. She really wanted to punch him. Punch somebody, something. She wasn't sure why she didn't.

As the pair approached the police perimeter, Vickie couldn't help but look back over her shoulder one last time. The paramedics and police hadn't moved Linda yet, but she saw them cover her with a tarp.

Flashes from an officer photographing the scene made spots dance in her vision before she turned back around again.

She stumbled down the slope on the side of the road, her feet skidding on the loose gravel and her hands flying into the air. Angelo wrapped an arm around her and steadied her.

She let him help her back to the house; she no longer had the energy or attention to fend him off.

CHAPTER 8
Force of Habit

Room 402
5:00 a.m.

Vickie made her way back to her room, escorted by Nurse Lilly, who had taken over from Angelo once they returned to the house.

Nurse Lilly had found another room for Annie to stay in that night and suggested Vickie do the same, but Vickie wouldn't hear of it. That would be abandoning Linda all over again. She knew it probably made little sense, but didn't care. Linda was dead. Vickie reasoned it was only fair that she not run from the uncomfortableness, from the pain of being in their shared room. It was the least she could do.

Vickie wondered why Nurse Lilly was there to begin with that evening, when she usually only worked the day shifts, but it made sense that it was an all-hands-on-deck kind of night. She had heard there was an employee house somewhere on the grounds. Maybe Nurse Lilly lived there or somewhere else nearby. The night staff must have called for reinforcements.

Nurse Lilly said little, thankfully, but Vickie appreciated her presence and was glad she was there.

Even when she shut her eyes tight, tight enough to see colors, Vickie couldn't get the image of Linda's vacant eyes out of her head. And she didn't want to go to sleep because someone might need her to do something for Linda. Linda wasn't coming back, but what if the police had questions? What if there were details only she knew about Linda that the investigators could use to make this all make sense?

Mostly Vickie avoided sleep because she didn't want to wake up and endure the realization that her best friend was gone forever all over again. And having Nurse Lilly there meant the day wasn't over yet.

So, Vickie sat on her bed instead, watching the light from the window make patterns on the walls. Reds and blues from the sirens spun around the room like an eighth-grade dance until, one by one, they were gone and only moonlight and the yellow illumination from the bedside lamp remained.

Staring at Linda's empty bed, Vickie marveled at how the disheveled white covers resembled cake frosting. She could imagine Linda's slender arms pulling the covers back, the creaks that the bed must have made, the coolness of the floor on her feet as she slipped into the dimly lit hallway from room 402.

And then what? Vickie couldn't see in her mind's eye what came next. *Why did Linda leave the room to begin with?* She pictured the door to the room closing with ease, but the next image was always Linda's dead eyes staring up into the sky.

What happened in between seemed hopelessly inaccessible.

"Take it easy today," Nurse Lilly said.

"Huh?" Vickie responded, still staring blankly at Linda's bed.

Nurse Lilly offered a comforting smile. "I brought you something." She held out a little white cup.

Vickie looked at Nurse Lilly's offering, then back at the bed.

"No pills," Vickie said.

"To help you sleep. You've been up all night. Just this once. I'll leave it here." She placed the cup on the nightstand next to Linda's book, open to the story she was reading, *The Masque of the Red Death.*

Nurse Lilly paused before exiting and turned back to speak over her shoulder.

"I'm so sorry, Vickie."

"It's not your fault."

"It's nobody's fault," Nurse Lilly added.

"No, it's somebody's fault," Vickie said. The door clicked shut behind Nurse Lilly as she exited. Vickie knew Nurse Lilly had lingered outside the door for a couple seconds, because the doorknob jiggled when she finally released it.

Vickie glanced at the pills on the nightstand and frowned. They were a retro shade of blue. The little white paper cup reminded her of the ones the dentist gave her full of some sort of fluoride rinse. She got out of bed and, instead of picking up the tiny cup o' sleep, she moved over to Linda's bed. The covers were just as Linda had left them. She placed her hand on the indention in the pillow where Linda's head had lain.

No warmth remained.

Vickie, lip quivering slightly, stared for a moment at the bed, imagining Linda lying there, smiling up at her. Then she placed her body on the bed exactly as Linda had.

It wasn't long before her eyes got heavy, but they never fully closed.

Room 402
6:30 a.m.

The sun rose as it always did. Vickie followed her normal routine, stretching, then sitting up, and plopped her feet into her slippers, which she had left nearby earlier that morning. They were speckled with dried dirt and grass. She took a quick trip to the communal bathroom down the hall and then back to her room to brush her teeth and splash water on her face.

Climbing into her clothes didn't take more than two minutes. They forbade bringing multiple clothing options, which was just fine with Vickie. Fewer choices.

She almost always wore the same thing every day anyway. Her sweatpants with no drawstring and a frayed T-shirt that Uncle Aldo had loaned her when she stayed over as a kid. It used to fit like a nightgown. Now it was just right. And, last but not least, her sweater with her signature *V* on it.

The only thing unusual about that morning was that Linda wasn't there, which was a very big difference

No one was there to make fun of the way she stretched, or the grunt Vickie made as she plopped her feet on the floor. No one to share the tiny sink with or to fuss at her for squeezing the toothpaste from the middle or forgetting to put the toothpaste cap on.

Vickie had done one thing out of character this morning, however. She made her own bed, knowing Linda would have been proud. Then her eyes landed on Linda's bed, studying the covers, but she decided to leave it unmade.

At that moment, the discomfort of holding her breath became unbearable. She wasn't even sure how long she'd been holding it. When she exhaled, it came out in sharp spurts, and she felt her eyes fill with tears. In one great gulp, she sucked it all back in, then she opened the door, walked into the hallway, and closed it behind her.

The cafeteria was emptier than usual. Not surprising given the events of the early morning. Vickie breezed through the line, hardly registering what she was doing, but getting a scoop of oatmeal in her bowl. Sitting alone. This wasn't unusual. Most of her pod didn't eat breakfast, but grabbed an early morning snack just before Dr. Cannon's session instead, preferring to sleep in.

```
Rec Room
7:55 a.m.
```

Vickie headed in the direction of the rec room and joined the other teens as they filed inside, faces bleary and blank. Each of them grabbed a folding chair and placed it in the circle for themselves before sitting in it as they routinely did, but they moved slower than usual, hardly looking at each other, dazed.

When Vickie entered, Dr. Cannon visually assessed her in one quick glance.

"Vickie? I'm surprised to see you here."

All of pod 1 stared at Vickie, wide-eyed.

"I've got nowhere else to be," Vickie responded, her voice low and a bit hoarse.

Vickie strode to the window, grabbed what she needed, and joined the others, placing two chairs in the circle. The other teens continued watching her, not knowing if she intentionally placed the chairs or if it was a mistake, a force of habit. In any case, everyone knew Linda wouldn't be rushing in to claim her saved seat. Vickie returned their looks, surveying the entire room in stubborn, stony silence.

"Moduleul hwan—" Dr. Cannon began her welcome, her words thrown into a silent abyss.

There was an awkward silence as the teens avoided Vickie's assertive eye contact, each not daring to even fidget under her challenging gaze.

Eventually, "No one's going to say anything about last night?" Squirt asked.

"What is there to say?" Tracy asked.

"It's OK to not say anything," Dr. Cannon added, pursing her lips, staring down at the floor.

Two minutes passed.

Silence.

Vickie resisted the impulse to look sideways for Linda.

A wheezing breath issued from Squirt as he took a hit from his inhaler.

Five minutes passed.

Vickie squared her shoulders, sitting straighter in her seat, preparing herself to face the rest of the session without Linda and their easy banter, which always made time slip into nothing.

Tracy hummed to himself, almost inaudibly, trailing off as quickly as he began.

Fifteen minutes passed.

Vickie stared forward, her eyes glazing over as Eagen doodled on a pad more intentionally than usual. He dug his pencil deeper and still deeper into the paper, finally tearing a hole in it, the utensil unable to bear the weight of all he held inside.

Each teen, too lost in their own thoughts, failed to notice how the silence stretched like uneasy tentacles throughout the entire room, except Annie.

She smiled shyly at Eagen to lift his spirits. But he only continued to focus on his pad, hunching his shoulders into himself, like putting on a cloak that rendered him invisible.

Twenty minutes passed.

Annie whispered quietly, "Sarah, Justin, Tika, Nathalie. Linda."

A single tear rolled down Vickie's cheek. She quickly wiped it away with the back of her hand.

Everyone saw it, including Dr. Cannon, but they all looked down, pretending not to notice. Even Eagen did her that courtesy.

She appreciated it.

Three more minutes passed.

The odd, hollow-sounding bell echoed through the hall, signaling a session change.

The teens folded their chairs and placed them against the window without saying a word.

Vickie carried her two chairs toward the window. Tracy reached out his hand, offering to carry one of the chairs for her, but he quickly withdrew it when Vickie pulled the chairs tighter under each of her arms.

Vickie was the last to leave the room and noticed Dr. Cannon remained seated, alone. She heard the doctor exhale deeply as she clicked the door closed.

Pod 1 filed down the hall still wrapped in their silence and went about their day as usual, defaulting to the comfort in the familiar.

Room 402
10:55 a.m.

Just before lunch, yawning and eyes glazed from lack of sleep, Vickie slowly climbed the steps to her room. Each step landed with a dull thud that echoed hollowly in her chest until she was back to the place that had, out of necessity, become her cocoon over the last forty-six days.

As she opened the door of room 402, she noticed the lights were on.

She had turned them off when she left earlier that morning, she was sure of that. And the covers pulled taut over Linda's bed no longer offered any trace of the wrinkles of use. Someone had been here.

Linda?

Linda always made her own bed, she recalled, smiling wearily, though her face brightened.

Hope flooded her chest, swelling like a balloon while she stared at the bed, and her heart beat faster with excitement, thinking there was only one explanation.

Linda must be back.

Her exhausted and overwrought mind allowed her to believe in the impossible, but only for a moment, until her face fell once more.

No. Linda's not here, and she's never coming back.

Reality strangled her chest, a lump rising in her throat as she looked around the room and saw the emptiness where all of Linda's belongings used to be.

Someone had been here, but it wasn't Linda.

The cleaners.

They swooped in like vultures to pick the bones bare of any trace of a disappeared and disregarded resident.

Out of sight, out of mind.

The cleaners were only engaged under three circumstances: One, after an abrupt, official discharge; two, following a prolonged disappearance; and three, after a death.

The cleaners showed up when there was no hope the resident would ever return.

Vickie's eyes narrowed as she balled her hands into fists, then spun on her heels and flicked the light switch to its off position.

As she exited, she waited for the creaky door to close behind her. Except . . . this time, there was no creak.

This was too much to bear.

Out in the hallway, she ground her teeth, her mind roiling like a storm cloud just before it rained.

Someone had "fixed" things, even though Vickie had liked them just as they were.

Sometimes when you fixed things, you broke them—for good.

Her room no longer felt safe, more like a home felt after a burglary. Violated. Plundered. Changed forever.

Vickie folded her arms, bringing the fabric of Uncle Aldo's gifted T-shirt as close to her body as possible, imagining he was there hugging her.

She'd never be able to embrace herself tight enough to feel safe here again and wondered if she was ever really safe here to begin with.

PART TWO

*The More
We Get Together*

Schedule
Pod 1

6:30 - 7:00	Wake Up / Dress
7:00 - 7:30	Optional Breakfast
7:30 - 8:00	Morning Snack / Med Distribution
8:00 - 8:45	Morning Meeting
9:00 - 9:45	Horticulture / Hiking
10:00 - 10:45	Morning Jobs / Private Music Lesson or Journaling
11:00 - 11:45	Lunch
12:00 - 12:45	Afternoon Jobs / Art or Journaling
1:00 - 2:45	Alternating Outdoor Activities (B-ball, Horseback Riding, Tennis, Swimming, Boating)
3:00 - 3:45	Alternating Art / Music / Drama
4:00 - 4:45	Alternating Science, English, Math
5:00 - 5:45	Dinner
6:00 - 7:45	Alternating Indoor Activities / Med Distribution (Pool, Ping-Pong, Puzzles, Reading, Board Games)
8:00 - 8:45	Alternating Evening Jobs / Study Hall
9:00 - 9:45	Showering
10:00	Lights Out / Night Checks

CHAPTER 9
The Flawless Rose

DAY 60 for Vickie
Two Weeks Later
The First Floor
8:00 a.m.

Vickie arrived right on time as usual, but found a note taped to the door of the rec room:

Morning meeting is moved to 10:00 a.m. today. Please join Nurse Lilly for Horticulture from 8:00 a.m. until 10 a.m. instead.

During all her days here, this had never happened. Vickie's face contorted.

Change.

She didn't like it.

Vickie pivoted on the back of her heels and stomped back toward the lobby.

The Rose Garden
9:10 a.m.

Nurse Lilly, full of sunshine and sugary-sweet happiness, took a deep breath, inhaling the scent of the "Flawless Rose," which was especially fragrant after the rain the previous evening. She waved its core petals so close to her face that she could feel them tickle her skin.

Beautiful.

Succulent.

She wanted to bathe in the flower, clothe herself in its scent, exist in its bloom, but people were watching; worse, teenagers were watching.

Compose yourself, Lillian.

There they were, in their gardening clothes, doing some obligatory pruning of the flower beds. *This is good for them in ways they don't even realize,* Nurse Lilly thought as she watched their little faces contort into all kinds of inhuman grimaces while they grappled with the gardening gear. It was true that she couldn't help Linda now, but she could help the rest of them. Or at least try to bolster them in some small way. These young humans were her charges, entrusted to her the same as this rose seedling had been. She would nurture them and protect them from anything that might wilt them prematurely. And she'd plant seeds in their young, developing brains, watering the distracted residents with nourishing words as they went through the reluctant motions of gardening.

"If you don't soak in the beauty around you, the ugly will seep in. Remember that," she said, her cheeks full of color. A smile spread across her face as she scanned the entire garden, admiring the fruits of her long hours of work both with the residents and the flora and fauna. *There. Firmly planted.*

The leaves of the bush next to her shimmied, though she had not touched it. Upon closer inspection, she glimpsed a long, wriggly creature working its way through the foliage.

Squirt's eyes widened. "Is that a sna —"

Nurse Lilly placed her finger on her lips. "Shhhhh. It's harmless and keeps the rodents away."

Nurse Lilly hadn't always been so relaxed around slithery things. She once had been terrified of snakes. As a youngster, having come across a small, black-and-yellow-striped garter snake, she had screamed. Her mother, usually composed, came running, half-dressed. By the time her mother arrived, the snake had hidden under a leaf.

Her mother had glowered disapprovingly at the unnecessary commotion, but that was OK. Young Lillian was simply relieved the snake was out of sight.

That evening, when Lillian had returned to her room to wash for dinner, she paused at the open door. Her heart quickened and her breath halted, the hairs on her arms standing at attention. Her eyes slowly took in every detail of the familiar space, sensing something amiss.

At first glance, all appeared as it should be — her bed made with not a wrinkle in it, the window left open just enough to allow the breeze inside and keep out any of the nearby nesting birds, and the glass of cool water left by her favorite reading chair — nothing unexpected or out of place.

She forced her eyes to the far side of the room, where the ceramic gilded box holding some of her trinkets now lay, placed atop an end table. A tiny gasp escaped her lips. Her mother didn't like things to be out of place. That box usually sat on her chest of drawers.

Her eyes darted toward the chest of drawers and soon discovered the reason for the change. A small glass tank had replaced the trinket box, and inside was the snake that had caused her such a fright. She later discovered her mother had demanded the gardener retrieve it and place it by her bed.

Forced to care for it, feeding and handling it daily, she hated every minute and every inch of the creature — the smooth, dry skin, the vertically slit, forked tongue, the all-knowing eyes. *Yuck.* Everything about it made her squirm.

But it all came to an abrupt end several days later when her new pet mysteriously disappeared. Reprimanded for leaving the top off the tank, Lillian had made sure to appear unfazed. Her mother made her keep the tank for the rest of the month in case they found the snake, but Lillian knew the snake would never return. She had seen to it.

Young Lillian learned two valuable lessons from that experience, though not the ones her mother intended: Never scream when you're frightened; and you don't always get caught when you do something naughty.

The Rose Garden
9:30 a.m.

Fool me once, shame on you. Fool me twice, shame on me.

Vickie prided herself on not missing much. And when she did overlook something, she made a point of paying even closer attention so as not to repeat her oversights.

She followed Nurse Lilly's gaze up toward the driveway. A large black limousine wound its way around the circle drive, meandering like the black snake she had heard Nurse Lilly and Squirt chatting about earlier. Fancy cars weren't an unusual sight here. The smell of old money dripped from the patients, but the cars that rounded the circular drive often did so to deliver new residents, and that was a subject of profound curiosity.

Blueberry Hill was already filled to near capacity, yet every new addition drew the attention of the current residents. There was something enticing about the new strangers. They still smelled like freedom. It was a scent that was intoxicatingly familiar to all the onlookers, like dreaming the same dream over and over, but not remembering it until you were wrapped in its throes. That sweet aura of the outside world began fading as soon as the feet of the newcomer touched the grounds of Blueberry Hill, so the kids in the garden knew to breathe it in deeply as quick as they could.

The limousine paused in front of the door of the facility, engine purring like a resting kitten. Pod 1 watched from the rose garden as the driver opened the back door for a petite blonde girl. Dressed in soft pastels, her nails finely manicured and makeup subtle and sophisticated, she stepped out one leg at a time, extending her hand without looking, as if anticipating the driver would be there to assist.

Makeup couldn't cover everything. In the morning light, her skin was paler than it should be, and her posture looked as if the Earth's gravity was pulling her down with a force she had to work hard against just to move.

The teens in the garden continued watching from the shrubbery. Three of them were more transfixed than the others.

"Do you think her parents are with her?" Annie asked hopefully.

"I've told you before, parents never come. Too emotional for them," Vickie said.

"Too emotional for them!" Squirt laughed that sort of laugh that hurt a little down deep.

"She's so pretty. Like a princess," Annie said, clasping her grubby hands together and twirling around, her face lit by a day-dreamy smile.

Vickie didn't respond. She couldn't take her eyes off the girl. Had she looked like that when she arrived? So clueless? Of course, she hadn't arrived in a limousine, but instead, had pulled up in a beat-up police car.

Vickie wasn't the only one lost in thought, though.

The other members of her pod were all trapped in that sort of out-of-body haze that clouded the mind when memories were firing rapidly. Perhaps their thoughts were also tracing back to who they used to be before being dumped on the curbside. Back when they were free. Or at least freer.

A sinking ball of unease landed in the bottom of her stomach, bringing with it a lightning rush of truth: *We are all here for different reasons, but we have one thing in common. There is something about us that the adults in our lives can't manage. And if they couldn't handle it, how can we be sure that we can?*

The memory haze and lightning-quick truth infected Vickie as her mind wandered back to her first day at Blueberry Hill.

DAY 01 for Vickie
Uncle Aldo's Car
1:00 p.m.

"*Your Ma woulda come, but —*" *Uncle Aldo said.*

"*I know,*" *Vickie said, cutting him off. Inside the beat-up cop car, Vickie stared forward. Uncle Aldo fiddled with the radio as the stations dipped in and out of static the deeper the roads wound into the countryside.*

"*You got a good head on your shoulders. You're dependable. Reliable. You remind me of me. You'll be all right. My girls could stand to be a little more like you. They're just good at trying to look pretty,*" *Uncle Aldo said. He laughed a little, but it didn't reach his eyes.* "*I pulled a lot of strings to get you in here. Don't waste this opportunity.*"

"*Opportunity? Uncle Aldo, they won't even let you have pants with drawstrings. Sweats are the only kind of pants I got!*"

"*You're worried about drawstrings right now? You could have gone to juvie. Trust me, this is better. You think all these rich people would send their kids to a place that wasn't top-notch?*"

"*I know,*" *Vickie said, acknowledging her uncle was doing his best and was trying to make her feel better in his own way.*

"*When you act like a putz, kid, you pay putz prices. Take responsibility for your life. You got some time now, figure it out. Worry about your goals.*"

You got too many talents to waste like this."

"I'm nothing special," Vickie said.

"If you think you're a nothing, that's what you're going to get — nothing. You're somebody. Sangre. My blood. You think we're a family of nobodies? Do I look like a nobody to you? Huh?"

"No, Uncle Aldo."

"You think the Queen of England didn't wake up in her panties and think she was a nobody sometimes? She got up and did the job she was supposed to do. You don't let that bullshit in your head mix up your feelings."

There was a moment of silence between them, but the silence was full and seemed much longer than it was. "Sorry I let you down, Uncle Aldo," Vickie said.

She saw Uncle Aldo's eyes tear up and his lip quiver as he fought to hold it all back. He was a tough guy, but also a closet crier. Like the time a bird flew into the windshield of his car, and he brought it home to nurse it back to health, only to watch it die later that night, or when his girls were born, or when he won fifty dollars on the scratch-offs. Big things, little things, there was no predicting what would start the waterfall of tears. But Vickie never let Uncle Aldo know she saw them. She knew he prided himself that no one had ever seen him cry; and if they had, he'd deny everything anyway.

"Sorry? What is this, a Hallmark convention?" he asked with a quick sniffle. Waterworks averted.

He was making a joke. That was a good thing. His lightened speech made Vickie think everything was going to be all right. She hoped so, more for Uncle Aldo's sake than for her own. She wanted to believe it was true. More accurately, she wanted him to believe that she believed everything was going to be OK.

"You don't need to apologize to me. This is your life. It starts here." Uncle Aldo tapped the side of his head with his pointer finger, then dragged his finger down to his heart to emphasize his point. "Head and heart. Connected. Capisce?"

"Yeah," Vickie responded quietly.

"What was that?" he asked, holding his hand to his ear.

"Come on! What is this, a Hallmark convention? Capisce!" Vickie said.

"Oh, you do comedy now? Get outta here," he said as the car reached its destination: the Blueberry Hill Home for Troubled Youth. "Hey, you know I'd walk you inside if they'd let me."

Vickie nodded, offering a half smile.

She exited Uncle Aldo's police car, carrying a small bag, including a sandwich she had made for herself for the trip. She hadn't eaten it and knew they'd probably take it from her when she entered. It wasn't on the approved list of items, but she didn't want to give it up. It was her favorite, pastrami, with fancy mustard and cheese. The type of bread didn't matter so much to her. It was the filling that counted most.

She stopped at the bottom of the stairs to take in the enormity and creepiness of the manor house, seven stories and hundreds of years old from the look of things.

A sad-eyed and emaciated girl — Linda, she would later learn — stared at Vickie from the fourth-floor window.

Their eyes locked.

Linda reminded Vickie of a ghost trapped behind that glass. Yet Vickie detected a tiny smile on her face, like a single ray of sunshine breaking through a cloudy life. It was a hopeful, albeit broken, smile.

Vickie smiled back.

A large black bird flew onto the ledge outside Linda's window, breaking their stare.

Linda unlatched the window on the fourth floor just enough for the bird to squeeze inside. Vickie shivered despite the heat of the sun beating down on her shoulders.

She remembered those first few steps toward the manor, while her hold on freedom leaked through her tightened fists. She could never forget Uncle Aldo's quivering voice, the wind on her skin, Linda's gaze, and most of all, *she remembered him.*

There he was, perched on the stone steps, strumming his guitar, with wavy, raven-black hair that seemed to dance with every breath. Tracy.

He seemed so alive that she felt like she was the ghost with a glass between the two of them, observing, separate, until he looked up and winked. At least she thought he was winking — or was it a smile? He had smiling eyes.

"G'morning," he said with his English accent.

"You're my sangre. Remember that. Find the bright spot!" Uncle Aldo shouted from his cop car, interrupting the moment she was sharing with this beautiful creature.

Tracy nodded at Vickie and continued playing a Beatles tune. She recognized it as one of the ones her mother played over and over on their record player, "You're Going to Lose That Girl."

Something in the words echoed how Vickie was feeling. In the pit of her stomach, she felt she was losing something, but wasn't sure what.

Despite the feeling, Vickie's eyes twinkled, looking at Tracy longer than she knew she should. "Think I found my bright spot," Vickie said in response to Uncle Aldo under her breath. She put one foot in front of the other and climbed the Blueberry Hill steps toward the stern-looking nurse who waited for her.

The Rose Garden
9:45 a.m.

The reality fog melted away as Vickie blinked rapidly, shaking free of the memory. She slowly took off her gardening gloves and exhaled. The others had already gathered all the tools and coiled the garden hoses.

"Vickie? Vickie? Are you coming?" Annie asked.

"All right already! Geez," Vickie responded.

Eagen trailed behind the group, walking on his tiptoes to avoid the puddles. As he passed Nurse Lilly's treasured 'Flawless Rose,' he nonchalantly broke off the perfect flower's head, watching it fall to the ground and purposely putting his foot down flat, trampling it under his thick black boot.

Vickie glimpsed Eagen's action over her shoulder. *Good thing Nurse Lilly didn't see that!* Although Vickie was curious to see how she would react.

Just before Vickie left the rose garden behind, she saw something sparkle under the mulch. Now all alone in the garden, she went back for a closer look. She pushed the mulch back with her pointer finger to reveal Nurse Lilly's prized golden garden shears, the ones she had entrusted to . . . Linda!

Vickie's lips and chin tightened, and her heart fluttered like moths waking up inside a jar.

Assessment and Plan

Provider: Blueberry Hill Home for Troubled Youth, LLC   **Client Name:** Julie Maxwell
Group Assignment: Pod #1   **Session Number:** #1

Diagnosis: Suicidal Ideation, Mild Depression

Treatment

Intake Protocol: Clinical Assessment   **Medications:** Fluoxetine 20 mg/day,
as per Dr. Mariska Habsburg, M.D.

Short-Term Goals for Client (2 Weeks):

1. Administer Patient Health Questionnaire. This tool is made up of nine questions about suicidal thoughts and behaviors.
2. Establish a baseline of current affect through self-reporting and clinical observation.

Long-Term Goals (3 Months):

1. Consistently illustrate an optimistic state and self-confidence, the ability to return to a normal level of function measured through self-reporting, and clinical observation of body language and facial cues.
2. Regular time outdoors and exercise, including walks.
3. Form trusting relationships with peers within pod.

Session Notes

Body Language, Facial Patterns: Client sat legs together, hands in lap, back straight for the entirety of session. She mostly looked down and to the left, averting any eye contact.

Summary:

1. Began with welcome and asked if client had any questions, to which she shook her head, indicating that she did not.
2. When asked to describe her mood, her response was, "I don't know. You're the expert, you tell me."
3. A nurse inadvertently dropped a tray just outside the office door and there was no acknowledgment of the disturbance.

Other Observations/Comments:
- Tight and constricted body language may indicate withholding.

Client Signature: _Julie Maxwell_   **Primary Caregiver 1:** _Randolph Maxwell, III_
(Age 14 and up)   Julie Maxwell   Randolph Maxwell, III
                                                              (Father)
Primary Caregiver 2: _B.W. Maxwell_   **Therapist Signature:** _Ara Cannon_
                    Barbara Winthrop Maxwell   Dr. Ara Cannon, Ph.D.
                    (Mother)

93

CHAPTER 10
The Chair

The Rec Room
10:35 a.m.

Over two hours and three orientation videos later, Nurse Fran escorted Julie down the imposing corridor to the rec room. Julie heard the scraping of chairs and chatter from the other side of the nondescript door.

I hate being the new girl, she thought, steeling herself for the stares she knew would come and the inevitable personal questions.

Why are you here? Why are you wearing long sleeves in the summer? Why aren't you as pretty as your mother? Why? Why? Why?

Julie lingered outside the doorway for a moment before placing her hand on the knob. She looked up at Nurse Fran for some sort of reassurance, only to be met with a stone-faced glare. With a flick of Julie's wrist, the door whinnied open. She spied Nurse Fran out of the corner of her eye, already on her way back to reception.

Thanks for the support.

Six out of seven folding chairs placed in a circle were already occupied. Julie's teeth unclenched for a moment at the sight of Dr. Cannon, but immediately tightened again, noticing all the unfamiliar, watchful teenage stares pointed toward her. She would later learn their names, but with a quick scan she knew their type: the heartthrob, the Goth kid, the weird

94

one, the nerd, and — the bully.

"We're wrapping up our morning meeting, but come in, Julie." Dr. Cannon returned her attention to the center of the circle to address the rest of the group. "We have a new friend joining us. I had the pleasure of welcoming her this morning for orientation."

"*She's* why you canceled our time?" Vickie growled.

"Let's relax. Not canceled, rescheduled for just two hours later," Dr. Cannon said.

Julie entered, walking with a cautious swiftness toward the circle, where she finally sat in the empty seat beside the girl with the *V* on her sweater, the bully of the group.

Julie noticed the rest of the teens all stared at the girl she'd sat beside, waiting for something. The now-silent group shifted uncomfortably in their seats. By the looks on everyone's faces, she knew she'd done something wrong.

Annie was the first to speak, her eyes wide and her voice soft. "That's Linda's seat."

Julie deflated like a balloon with a hole in it, then crossed her arms and sat back. "Well, Linda's late, and I'm here."

"I don't think Linda will be coming," Tracy said. His expression fell when he noticed the sad exhalations of Annie and Squirt.

"Then I'm meant to sit here," Julie said.

"She's dead," Eagen said, his face like stone.

Julie noticed the girl in the monogrammed sweater turning redder by the minute.

"Like I said, fate," Julie replied, uncrossing her arms to rest loosely around her midriff. She pretended not to care, not to be curious about this girl who was apparently deceased.

"No such thing as fate," Vickie retorted in a tone that sounded much like a challenge. Julie, who had been feigning indifference by picking her at nails, shifted her eyes to the speaker. This girl looked like a stray dog.

Not the cute kind you wanted to rescue, but the kind that had rabies.

"Get your own chair," Vickie warned.

Julie shifted her weight in her seat. *Should I be worried?* Julie was not a fighter, but she was smart enough to know when she needed to pretend to be. Unfortunately, she also was not an actress. She assumed some could see right through the charade. But, so far, no one had called her on it.

Julie was, in fact, a lover, feeling things more deeply than most. Physical pain didn't bother her nearly as much as the emotional pain of two parents always bickering, treating her like a piece on a chessboard, moving her back and forth between their respective estates.

"Vickie is right. That seat is just closest to the door. So, I don't think it's fate you sat there. It's more like laziness, really," Tracy said. "You didn't want to grab your own folding chair like the rest of us."

"You're sitting in a dead girl's chair," Vickie said, her mouth drawn and her face still full of color.

"You're sitting on a ghost. How does that feel?" Annie inquired with an honest, childlike curiosity and openness.

Julie shifted her weight forward. Her instinct was to get up and get another chair, but she stopped herself, finding different words coming from her lips.

"It feels great," Julie offered.

"That's really disrespectful," Vickie said.

Julie could almost see the heat rising through the collar of the T-shirt Vickie wore as sprinkles of sweat materialized at Vickie's hairline.

"I'm not breaking any laws," Julie said.

Vickie stood. Her folding chair slid back a few inches, making a loud sound that punctuated the aggressive action. "How about I break your face?"

"I'm sooooo scared," Julie said in a sarcastic tone, gripping the sides of the chair to hide her trembling hands. Vickie was bigger than her, most likely stronger than her, and certainly angrier. Julie glanced at the dark-haired boy with the British accent, pleading for intervention.

"Well, this is going swimmingly, Doc. Just ducky," Tracy said.

Julie never appreciated the value of comedy to defuse a situation more than at this moment.

"Reminds me of home," Tracy continued.

She smiled from her eyes, recognizing that Tracy and she shared a common sentiment about their unpleasant home life.

"Let's take a breath. Vickie, have a seat," Dr. Cannon said.

Vickie still shook like a volcano seconds before eruption.

"Vickie!" Dr. Cannon repeated more firmly.

Vickie complied, hooking her leg under her chair, and sliding it in place beneath her, but never taking her eyes off the new girl.

"We lost one of our members suddenly. That was her usual chair," Dr. Cannon said.

Julie had so many questions, like why Dr. Cannon let this confrontation go on for so long? Was it just to see how they'd handle things? But she just wanted this to end. All of it. So, she didn't say a word, just nodded.

Vickie's nostrils flared. "It was always her chair."

"Today, we'll leave another chair out for Linda."

Dr. Cannon rose from her seat and walked over to the window. From the stack, she grabbed a chair. She returned to the circle, sliding her own chair over with one hand, while unfolding the new chair with the other.

"And maybe try a different seating configuration next week as well? All of us. OK?" Dr. Cannon sat. "A new perspective. We'll take note of how perspective changes as our position shifts," Dr. Cannon said.

"I'm not changing seats," Vickie said.

"This is for next week. For now, everyone is fine where they are," Dr. Cannon said.

"I'd like to request to sit next to Vickie. When we switch," Squirt said.

"I'd like to request that he sits as far away as possible. Thank you," Vickie said.

"I'd like to sit in your seat, Dr. Cannon. The throne of power," Annie said, gasping in excitement.

Dr. Cannon nodded before changing the subject. "Julie, would you like to introduce yourself to the group?"

"Do I have to?" she asked.

"No. Maybe our other members would like to introduce themselves?"

"My name is Annie. Julie, first, welcome. I just want to say, there is this white glow around you. I see it. And I think Linda is feeling squished because she is still sitting there under you. Thank you."

Julie wriggled uneasily in Linda's chair, offering an uncertain half smile.

Vickie glared.

Squirt sheepishly raised his hand. "I'll go next. I'm Theodore Kevin Moses."

"His name's Squirt," Tracy clarified.

"Because he's a walking hormone. You figure the rest out," Vickie added.

"Gross," Julie said.

"It's because of my height. I'm a late bloomer. That's why they call me that, not because of anything else." Squirt's words tripped over one another in his haste to explain, and his posture changed as he melted into his seat.

"Eagen?" Dr. Cannon prompted.

"Pass," Eagen blurted without even a breath.

"Anything you'd like to say, Tracy?" Dr. Cannon asked.

"Welcome, and rock and roll, Julie," Tracy said.

"Rock and roll," Julie flirted back. If her words had wings, they would have landed all over him and lingered there like a thousand butterfly kisses.

Tracy winked.

Vickie audibly gagged.

"Vickie? Would you like to--" Vickie's abrupt interjection washed away Dr. Cannon's question. Julie held her breath for what Vickie might say, as if bracing for a punch to the gut.

"I'm Vickie, and why don't you just rock and roll out of here before I throw up, *Julie*, and nobody likes you."

"I do," Annie said.

"Thank you, Annie," Julie replied, looking at her and quickly back at her nails.

"She seems nice," Squirt said to the group.

"Shut up, Squirt," Vickie protested.

"What's up with the monogrammed clothing?" Julie asked, making eye contact with Vickie, then flicking her eyes to the giant *V* across the left pocket of the button-down sweater she was wearing.

Each teen perched on the edge of their seat, waiting for the next shot to be fired. All eyes fixed on Julie, then on Vickie, then back to Julie.

"It's not like anyone would want to steal something that hideous," Julie continued.

Tracy turned his head to the side, scrunching his face, bracing for impact. "Oh noooo," he said, without realizing it.

"Maybe you should mind your own business," Vickie said, balling up her fists. "Guess you'd need a mind to do that, though, huh?"

Dr. Cannon jumped in quickly. "Well, on that note, it's time for ALL of you to rock and roll on out of here."

The tension in the room eased as everyone relaxed a little in their chairs.

"Vickie, would you show Julie around the facility, please?" Dr. Cannon continued.

Vickie coughed, choking on the idea.

"The sooner the two of you get acquainted, the better. You're going to be roommates, after all," Dr. Cannon said, not looking at either girl. Julie was sure she saw Dr. Cannon grin at the idea.

This woman's a masochist, Julie thought.

"What?" Vickie said.

"Oh, sorry, did I spoil the surprise?"

"Are you out of your mind?" Vickie shouted.

"Are you sure you've thought this through, Dr. Cannon?" Squirt added.

"You're killing me!" Julie continued.

"Not the best choice of words in this situation," Tracy teased.

Everyone got up, returned their chairs, and headed toward the exit. Julie followed suit. Vickie grabbed her two chairs as usual, walking them over to the stack by the window.

"Julie, the nurses should be finished checking your luggage this evening. You can collect your things then at the nurses' station. Don't forget."

"It takes all day to check luggage?" Julie remarked, and then under her breath mumbled, "How incompetent can you be?"

"Another session full of warm fuzzies, Doc," Tracy added.

"Glad you had fun," Dr. Cannon replied.

Squirt nervously wrung his hands, while Eagen rolled his eyes in contempt.

"Next time, I'm going to sit in your chair. Don't forget!" Annie enthusiastically reminded Dr. Cannon.

"Oh, I won't."

CHAPTER 11
More Than Meets the Eye

The First Floor
10:46 a.m.

In the corridor, Julie and Vickie stood facing each other as the rest of pod 1 whizzed past them, except for a lingering Eagen.

Julie shrank from the inside out in Vickie's presence. She clutched the two sides of the delicate pink, cashmere cardigan she wore, bringing them together over her chest to warm the chill in her bones.

Eagen stood uncomfortably close to Julie, watching. She didn't make eye contact with him, but out of the corner of her eye, she could see his head angled downward, the dark hair framing his pale face; his unrelenting glare made him look like a *Harry Potter* villain.

"Can I help you, creepface?" Vickie asked.

"I love a good cockfight," Eagen said, with neither his face nor body flinching as he watched the interaction between the two girls.

"We're always fascinated by what we don't have," Vickie said.

"Hmmph," Eagen muttered.

A giggled erupted from Julie, like a drink with bubbles that went down too fast. Vickie ignored Eagen as he made his way down the hallway, pivoting her head toward Julie.

Julie's heart raced inside her chest, but she was determined not to break eye contact with this girl she already didn't trust. She knew better than to let Vickie know she was looking forward to this forced tour, so she did her best to wipe the smile from her face. Despite her trepidation at being within punching distance of Vickie's arms, she wanted to know more about this place, no matter who the source was.

Vickie, on the other hand, made no attempt to mask her authentic emotions about spending time with Julie.

"Well, um—" Julie said, with the sourest face she could muster.

"Let's just get this over with," Vickie interrupted, shoulder-checking Julie as she walked past her.

Julie gasped.

Vickie continued down the main hallway, giving Julie the lay of the land as she saw it. The other residents of Blueberry Hill stole quick glances at Vickie as she marched past leading her charge. Judging from the way the other teens looked at her tour guide, Julie surmised Vickie was like the resident sheriff, or perhaps the resident outlaw. Either way, she had earned some respect among her peers and had a reputation. Julie stood up straighter walking behind her, bolstered by the spillover of deference heaped on Vickie.

Vickie spoke matter-of-factly, like a girl at the fast-food drive-through window near the end of a shift. "We aren't allowed to leave the grounds unaccompanied. There are communal phones down the hall along the wall." Vickie stabbed a finger in the direction of the phone bank. "You get one phone call a week, or no phone calls, depending on your current status. Incoming only, so you have to sign up for a time and have one of the nurses set it up with whomever you want to talk to. The internet is available, but surfing is monitored, tons of sites are blocked, and the computers are ten years old––"

"And you can't bring hardly anything from home!" Julie interrupted.

"Outside items are limited. As you know, no shoes with laces or drawstrings on a hoodie or in your pants. That one was tough for me.

Some people don't even get a toothbrush," Vickie said, softening her tone the slightest bit.

"What?"

"You can stab someone with a toothbrush." Vickie cut right through Julie with her steady gaze. "Not to give you any ideas, princess."

Julie recoiled, horror plastered all over her blush-streaked face. "This place is a prison."

"It's not a prison. Just prison-like."

They continued down a hallway, approaching the reception area on the first floor. "Here's the medicine room where they stuff us up with drugs, so we do what they tell us." Vickie waved a hand at a door of the room. Located just next to reception, it looked like the kind of place you could walk up to and order a fruity tropical drink or a fancy coffee.

"We call it the sunshine room."

Julie scrunched her face in disgust. "I don't take any medication." Julie was quick to correct Vickie's obvious assumptions that she somehow belonged here and was like the other residents.

"You will." Vickie's response was so immediate and filled with so much certainty that Julie paused for a moment to digest everything. The facility she had been in for three weeks before her transfer to Blueberry Hill had been awful, and this was supposed to be better. She began to wonder if indeed it was.

Up ahead, a couple of nurses busied themselves at the resort-like reception desk. Nurse Lilly's much-too-bubbly-sounding voice interrupted their conversation as she waved enthusiastically.

"Hi, Vickie!"

Vickie returned a subdued but polite greeting. "Hi, Nurse Lilly."

"She seems friendly," Julie remarked.

"I never trust anyone that smiles that much, or people named after flowers."

Vickie continued the tour, pointing to a large bulletin board next to the sunshine room. Stapled to the bulletin board were thirteen individual sheets of paper, one for each pod, separated into three rows. "Daily schedules for each pod are posted here. And job assignments."

"Jobs?" Julie blurted.

Vickie rolled her eyes and exhaled.

"Yes, princess. Work."

"Why do you keep calling me that?"

"Because what I really want to call you would get me in trouble."

The pace of the tour accelerated, no doubt keeping step with Vickie's increasing annoyance, until they came to the far end of the lobby, where the room forked right into another hallway. "On your left is the staff lounge, and farther down is the cafeteria. The food is mostly delicious, occasionally disgusting. Our pod's job is in the cafeteria for the next couple of months. So, when you're not eating, you'll be hauling trash and dumping scraps."

"Lovely."

"Somebody's gotta do it." Vickie stood in one spot for a moment, pointing down the long hallway. "On the right there is the drama room. The music and art rooms are farther down.

"Basically, the first floor is co-ed and open to everyone. This is where all the classes happen. And the boys' and girls' rooms are generally on different floors."

"OK," Julie said.

Vickie seemed to be at a stopping point, so Julie drew in a deep breath. They had walked so quickly through the lobby that this was the first time she allowed herself to take in the space. It was fairly large and filled with various vintage chairs and couches that gave off a hip coffee shop vibe. Littered throughout the lobby, teens she recognized from her pod passed the time. The area was pleasant enough and seemed like a natural gathering place.

"This is where everyone hangs out in between activities."

Julie noticed Vickie staring at a small table in between two wingback chairs. A distant glaze passed over Vickie's eyes, and a smile escaped her lips.

Julie wondered if Vickie was thinking about the dead girl again. She considered asking about Linda, but instead she turned her attention to the large fish tank with seven goldfish in it. "Fish!"

Vickie lowered her head and scowled, catapulted back to reality from her daydream.

Julie couldn't explain why she was suddenly so excited by a fish tank. She liked fish, but not as much as her voice indicated.

Maybe because there was something comforting about seeing creatures that were in a worse state of confinement than she. Or maybe she just wanted a break from her encounter with Vickie.

Vickie meandered over to Julie, who pressed a hand against the tank. "They're all new, like you. But don't get too attached. They won't last long. Also like you."

Eagen sketched in his spiral-bound pad, seated in an oversized chair next to the tank, and Annie finger-painted nearby.

Julie giggled at the contrast between Annie, so cheery, next to the dark cloud that was Eagen.

Julie tapped on the glass of the tank, and Vickie scolded her. "Don't you think they can see your big head pressed against the glass?"

"She's right. They're clearly trying to avoid you," Eagen said.

"Tap, tap, tap," Annie said out loud, smiling. "Tell her what happens to the goldfish when they leave the tank," Annie pleaded, sitting on the edge of her seat, her back straight in anticipation.

"What happens?" Julie asked.

"They get flushed," Eagen remarked dryly.

He's funny, Julie thought, but wasn't sure if his humor was intentional. If it was, then he masked his watchfulness and intelligence well. If it wasn't, then he was just a caricature, dressed all in black, moody and distant, saying the quiet, snarky things he thought out loud.

Vickie reluctantly fulfilled Annie's request. "If you release a tiny goldfish into a lake, it grows as big as your arm. It's the tank that keeps it small."

"No!" Julie exclaimed in amazement and disbelief.

"Yes," Annie confirmed.

"*Attack of the Giant Goldfish*, coming to a theater near you this summer. And don't miss *Goldfish Week* on the Discovery Channel," said Tracy, who was quietly strumming a guitar the entire time, lounging in a picturesque window seat close to Eagen. "You know the fundamental difference between a pet and an invasive species?"

Julie shook her head from side to side.

"Freedom," Tracy said.

"That's right. Better to keep us tanked, caged, and locked up like a pet. Controlled. Whenever you reach your full potential, others will always consider you a threat and mark you for destruction," Eagen said.

Julie cocked her head to the side, listening intently. She had felt caged most of her life, but thought it was because something was wrong with her. She never considered it could have been because something was right with her.

There was an undeniably poignant and true ring to Eagen's words. Julie took a step toward Eagen, leaning in without realizing. She determined at that moment that he was definitely smart. Still, she sensed he had already decided that she was as useful as a bag of rocks, so she didn't dare come any closer.

Julie drew her attention to another section of wall lined with copper- and gray-colored stone busts in small, recessed alcoves. Vickie tracked her gaze, both of them now staring at the bodiless statues. Their feet followed their stares until they were close enough to touch the busts. Vickie raised her eyebrows and watched for Julie's reaction from the corner of her eye.

The other teens resumed their independent activities as Vickie and

Julie continued to feel one another out.

"What's up with all the creepy heads?" Julie asked.

"That's everyone who has run this place for the last one hundred years," Vickie said.

Julie scanned the names on the busts. Among the five busts, there was a male with a receding hairline and pronounced jaw named Dr. Habsburg. Immediately following was a female with high cheekbones and a slender neck—another Dr. Habsburg.

"Are they related?" Julie asked.

Vickie shrugged her shoulders and yawned.

Julie stopped in front of the female Dr. Habsburg's stone head. "So, she's in charge now?" Julie asked.

"Yep."

"What's she like?"

"She probably looks like that head, except with a body."

"You've never seen her?"

"And don't want to. Rumor has it when you go to see her, you never come back the same."

Julie ran her fingers over the gold nameplate on the last bust: "Dr. Mariska Habsburg." She spoke as if invoking an evil spirit.

The name sounded powerful, important. She, herself, came from a lengthy line of important-sounding names. Randolph Maxwell III, Barbara Winthrop Maxwell.

And there she was with her name: Julie Maxwell. Just two names and no exotic letters or numbers. Not important sounding at all, which was fitting because she didn't feel especially important most times.

Julie's sweater slid down her forearm toward her elbow as she raised her arm to the female Dr. Habsburg's cheek. She pulled her sleeve up quickly, but not before Vickie saw the marks on her wrists.

"And that's about it. Tour's over," Vickie stated emphatically.

"What do you have against me, anyway? So what, I sat in a chair."

"I know your type."

"I'm a type?"

"Rich girl. With rich-girl problems. Waaaa. Waaaa. Pay attention to me."

"You don't know anything about me," Julie said, looking to the side, trying her best to disappear.

"I saw your wrists. If you really wanted to do it, it's not that hard. Like I said. Looking for attention," Vickie said.

Julie's mouth gaped open involuntarily as she sucked up a silent gulp of air.

In a flash, she remembered how her parents tiptoed around the topic of her wrists for days following the event. And how her mother had bought her lots of thick bracelets, pretending they were all the rage in Paris this year. Meanwhile, Julie knew her mother was just trying to make her hide the scars.

A grin quivered across Julie's face, and her eyes lit up. In her estimation, Vickie's tone indicated she thought Julie was strong enough to handle the truth. Julie didn't always feel strong, but she knew she could be. She hoped she could be strong enough to survive this new type of gilded prison.

Vickie had already walked away from Julie to join Annie back by the fish tank. Julie lingered, still pretending to stare at the wall of busts, her arms folded tightly in front of her. There was something curiously different about Vickie. There had to be more to Vickie than met the eye.

CHAPTER 12
Pipe Dreams

Room 402
9:45 p.m.

The two remaining residents of room 402 shared a companionable silence as night descended on the manor like a spider slowly spiraling downward from a tree branch. Annie sat crisscross applesauce with an enormous box of crayons spilled out and splayed over her covers like a splintered rainbow. On the opposite side of the room, reclining on her own bed, Vickie tossed a baseball in the air and caught it, over and over. The feel of the cool casing, the sound it made as it slid out of her hand, the clicking of the joint on her wrist, all offered a welcome and comforting familiarity. She liked the predictability of the ball's return.

An empty bed remained between the two roommates. Unlike a ball tossed in the air, people didn't always return.

Vickie hadn't used her voice in a few minutes, and so had to clear her throat to get the words out smoothly. "What are you drawing?"

"My new family," Annie said with unquestioning belief. Her adoring gaze breathed life into the paper as crayon people took shape in front of her.

Vickie nodded, eyes on the ball as it flew upward, noticing Annie's contented glow in her peripheral vision. Annie lived in her own world. But whatever reality Annie lived in seemed much better than this one.

Vickie yearned to create a fantasy realm where everything was just as she wanted it to be. But instead, she felt like a child trying to see the menu behind the cashier at a fast-food restaurant. No matter how she tried, she couldn't see above the counter. Vickie couldn't get past what was in front of her, staring her right in the face. Reality. She remembered something Linda had often said, how your greatest strength was also your weakness. Vickie's realistic outlook on life was a strength in her estimation, but she could see how that might also be a weakness as well. Not much changed when you couldn't see past where you were and imagine something different. But Vickie was fine with that. She didn't like lying unless she had to, especially to herself. And she hated change. In part, that's what made her such a great friend. Once Vickie Bartolucci decided to be your friend, you had a friend for life, a friend to the end. Like a bodega cat, you'd have to try hard to get rid of her. Yep, Vickie liked things just the way they were. Change had to sneak up on her, because if she saw it coming, she'd punch it in the face!

Unfortunately, sometimes things changed no matter how hard she fought to keep them the same. Vickie sighed, glancing over at Linda's empty bed, then back at the ball as it flew upward once more.

Change.

The antique metal doorknob of the room jiggled. Vickie maintained one eye on the ball, the other on the door. Julie entered, pausing at the entrance, holding a small bag containing her belongings.

The ball fell to the floor with a thud, rolling over to Julie. Julie stopped it with her foot. There was a tense pause that only lasted a few moments, but it felt like a gut punch. Then, Julie tapped the ball back over to Vickie with her foot in what seemed like a chess move, staring at her.

Julie was the first to break eye contact, moving over to the empty bed and nightstand, cautiously putting down her things. Vickie didn't take her eyes off her.

"I thought you weren't coming," Vickie said.

"You mean, you hoped," Julie replied.

Vickie raised her eyebrows in agreement.

"They just released my things. Can you believe that? And they kept half of what I brought. My nail file. Nail polish. My phone. All my eyebrow pencils."

"You can use my crayons," Annie offered.

"Didn't you read the list of approved items?" Vickie asked.

"I don't see the big deal."

Julie stood next to the bed in the middle of the room as Vickie breathed in, her posture stiffening.

"This was hers, wasn't it?" Julie asked.

Vickie resumed throwing the ball in the air without responding.

"It's okay. Linda doesn't like to sleep here anymore. She lives in the pipes now," Annie said in a whisper.

Julie's eyes widened as she slowly sat on the bed, the coils in the mattress tensing as they rearranged themselves. Vickie monitored her while Julie turned her head slowly from side to side, surveying everything in the sparsely furnished room. Annie stared at Julie, smiling in a way that would have been creepy on anyone but Annie.

There was a knock at the door, but this time it opened so quickly there was no warning jiggle. Julie jumped, startled.

Angelo poked his head inside the room, quickly scanning it. "Night checks," Angelo said.

"You scared me," Julie chastised.

"She's new," Annie added.

"I'm new too. Started three months ago," Angelo said.

Vickie continued to watch without looking in either of their directions.

"How'd you end up, um, here?" Julie asked.

"Strong family ties to this place," Angelo said.

"Angelo!" a nurse shouted from the hallway.

"Got to go." Angelo winked and smiled as he whipped out of the doorway.

Julie's smile lingered after he left.

"He's cute," Julie said.

Annie giggled. Vickie's face dropped into a frown.

"Do you always do that?" Vickie asked Julie. "It's vomit inducing."

"Do what?"

"Whatever." Vickie exhaled with so much force that if she were a lion, it would have been a roar. The rest of the night continued in much of the same way. Julie settled in, Annie smiled, and Vickie snarled until only two of the roommates remained awake.

Room 402
10:30 p.m.

Julie removed her shirt, leaving her pants on, and quickly slipped into an elegant, pink nightgown featuring a classic, feminine cut, made from ultra-soft cotton. The midlength nightdress with the long, butterfly sleeves also covered Julie's arms and wrists. That's why her mother liked it.

Julie liked all the detailing — it was whimsically embroidered, outlined in beautiful eyelet trim, with a simple neckline.

Once her arms were in place and the gown cascaded down her body toward the floor, Julie shimmied out of her pants, folding them, then placing them neatly in the chest of drawers.

"Pretty," Annie whispered, peeking from under her covers.

"Thank you," Julie said, unsure how else to respond.

Annie was weird in Julie's estimation. But she didn't mind weird. She appreciated it. There was something freeing about oddness. *Where has wearing the right lipstick, the right shoes, the right purse gotten me? Right. Here. And here sucks.*

But, if she were being honest, everywhere sucked. Everywhere she went sucked. Lately, she had begun to think she might be the problem.

And then there was Vickie.

Julie needed to keep her eye on her. Vickie was different. At least different from the girls at her high school. And in this case, different might also mean dangerous.

Julie refused to fall asleep before her other two roommates, despite her exhaustion.

She didn't trust this place or her roommates. So, she waited.

All right. This is it. This is my life, so I'd better get used to it, she thought as she climbed into bed and stared at the ceiling.

As soon as her eyes fluttered closed, she heard the sound. The loud, open-mouthed snores coming from across the room.

Julie's eyes sprang open. She tried to cover her ears with the pillow, throwing a rolled-up sock at Vickie's body, wrapping herself under the covers like a burrito with no effect.

Finally, she sat up and screamed.

Footsteps pounded down the hallway. Angelo flung open the door.

"What is it?" Angelo asked.

The snoring stopped. Vickie rustled but didn't wake. Annie bounced upright in her bed.

"Sorry, thought I saw a mouse," Julie said.

"Where is it? Don't hurt him," Annie said.

"False alarm," Julie said. "Just my imagination. Good night."

Angelo nodded, slowly closing the door as Julie nuzzled under the covers, smiling contentedly, her eyes shutting again.

Then, cutting through the silence, Vickie snored again.

Julie's eyes popped open.

Time passed slowly.

Julie tried pretending Vickie's snoring was the sputtering of the ski lift at the resort near the private school in Maine that Julie attended.

That life seemed so far away.

What must her classmates think? The gossip that must have spread as her seat was empty in class for a second month would be devastating.

Pregnant? Kidnapped? Married?

She giggled at all the juicy possibilities, but knew her parents well enough to suspect the story they might conjure. Something like, "The Academy just isn't rigorous enough for our Julie, and so we moved her to a very prestigious and exclusive boarding school far, far away."

Julie sighed at the probable accuracy of her prediction.

Blueberry Hill had not been Julie's first stop, so her parents had a bit of time to spin just the right alibi.

She had spent three weeks in a more high-security facility after being released from the hospital. The doctors determined she had made enough progress to be transferred to a more palatable, less sterile facility. And apparently, the Blueberry Hill School for Troubled Youth was that upgrade.

At least there are no arm restraints here. So far.

She remained convinced the transfer made her parents feel better, less guilty. She just couldn't convince anyone, especially her parents, that she never intended to kill herself.

No one but Vickie, who seemed to know the truth without being told.

And with that confounding thought, she sank into sleep.

DAY 61 for Vickie
Room 402
2:22 a.m.

Annie awoke; her other two roommates were still sound asleep. But someone besides her was stirring. She could hear them.

She huddled against a large iron pipe that extended from the floor to the ceiling behind her bed, careful not to disturb the other inhabitants of the room.

Eyes wide, Annie pressed her ear against the pipe.

The sound of a female voice whispering, lilting, came through the pipes, and Annie hummed along with it.

The more we get together, together, together . . .

CHAPTER 13
Out of Sight, Out of Mind

The Cafeteria
10:20 a.m.

Tracy, Eagen, and Vickie stood chatting, holding their mops and broom, while Squirt put the finishing touches on the lunch menu chalkboard. The pine-scented cleaner wafted through the air, fighting the lingering smell of bacon for dominance. The wet tile glistened under the overhead lights as most of pod 1 surveyed their completed work. A look of contentment stretched across Vickie's face.

On the other side of the room, Julie made slow progress washing the tables, wearing big yellow gloves and crinkling her nose with every squeeze of the sponge. Vickie's expression dissolved into a scowl. "It's like she's never held a sponge before."

"Maybe she hasn't," Tracy said. "That doesn't make her a bad person."

"At least she's trying," Squirt said.

Vickie lowered her head, shooting a stabbing look in Squirt's direction. "Shut up, Squirt." She bobbled her head back over to Julie just as Julie struggled to scratch her face with her shoulder, hindered by the gloves. "And look at her. Who does she think she is? First, Linda's chair, then her bed, and now this. Linda always washed the tables."

"You can't blame her for not knowing what happened before she got here," Tracy said.

"Are you her lawyer or something? You can't just swap one blonde girl for another, like pound puppies. I do blame her and Blueberry Hill."

"At the end of the day, this place is just a business," Tracy said.

"They make money off our sadness. Like drug companies," Squirt said.

"No one asked you, Squirt," Vickie rebuked.

"She just fills a spot as far as they are concerned," Tracy continued.

"What about the missing four? What about Linda? Are we supposed to pretend they never existed?"

Tracy shrugged and Squirt looked down at the floor.

"Oh no!" Julie shouted as the pan of sudsy water spilled all over the floor. Squirt and Tracy ran over with mops, eager to help.

"She did that on purpose," Vickie said, with no one around to hear but Eagen.

Eagen picked up the chalkboard menu and drew on it. Vickie stared at him. "And what about you? You don't have anything to say? You were supposed to be Linda's friend."

"Linda. The missing four. They're all dead, rotting away somewhere. While we rot away in here. What's the difference?"

"Some friend you turned out to be," Vickie said.

Squirt and Tracy returned, with Julie close behind.

"My heroes," Julie said.

Squirt and Tracy nodded and fawned while Vickie rolled her eyes.

Eagen held the chalkboard up, admiring his work before placing it on the nail protruding from the wall. "There. That's better." The chalkboard now read: Chicken Salad Boat or Rice and Beans, French Fries, Sliced Peaches, Milk. And in bigger letters, Eagen's contribution, "Sanitation Grade Z."

"What are you doing? The lunch ladies will murder me!" Squirt exclaimed.

Eagen smirked. "That's the plan."

"Let's get out of here," Vickie added.

"But—" Squirt said.

"Come on, Squirt," Tracy said.

"But lunch is in a few minutes," Squirt added.

"I don't like to be first in line. The rice and beans taste better after they sit. Besides, I need to clear my head before our afternoon job," Vickie said.

"You mean the ridin—" Annie began.

"Don't say it. I don't want to think about it until I have to." Vickie huffed before walking away.

The Riding Ring
1:00 p.m.

The Blueberry Hill riding ring brought lots of joy to many residents and struck terror into others. Vickie wasn't sure which category she fell into and didn't intend to find out. She'd never entered the riding ring, preferring to watch from outside the fence. Today was no exception.

Tracy chewed on the end of one of the yellow hay strands, mimicking the cowboys in those old western movies. As some of pod 1 groomed the cross-tied horse and polished saddles, Vickie watched, sitting atop a couple bales of hay. The sweet smell of the prickly dried grass tickled its way into her nose.

The ring was on the left side of the manor, close to the lake, just under Vickie's side bedroom window. She scanned the exterior walls of the manor, up to the fourth floor, locating her window, and then noticed a large black bird sitting on the ledge. She knew that bird. It reminded her of . . .

"Come on, Vickie, give it a try?" Squirt offered.

"I'm good. We don't do horses in my neighborhood."

"You said neighborhood," Tracy said. "Na-a-a-a-yborhood. Get it?"

Squirt chuckled and Vickie glared.

"Like a horse. A horse says n-a-a-a-y," Squirt explained.

"Shut up, Squirt," Vickie said.

Snowflake the horse seemed accustomed to the attention, and not at all bothered by noise and activity. Julie brushed his fur, Annie whispered into his ear, and the boys prepared the water trough and feed buckets for Snowflake and the other horses still out to pasture.

"You don't have to be afraid of Snowflake. He's a special horse," Annie assured, gently stroking the horse's nose.

Special had many meanings. Sometimes it meant something you valued more than other things; sometimes it was that thing the parents told their kids, even though they had no talent or skill at a sport. *You're so special, my darling.* It was the honorable-mention ribbon of words. And sometimes it meant you were genuinely unique. None of these seemed to apply to Snowflake, the huge, snow-white beast glaring at Vickie, taunting her with its big, brown eyes. The deceptively cute name didn't fool her.

"He's an emotional support horse," Tracy said.

"I love horses. They're so free," Julie added, cozying up to Tracy.

Vickie scowled at Julie's intrusion. *Julie is probably one of those rich people who takes riding lessons for fun. She probably even has her own horse at home. Maybe even her own riding arena or whatever you call it.*

Vickie, on the other hand, didn't even like the creepy, dirty little hobby horses outside the 7-Eleven—the kind you put a quarter in to make them go. She remembered one of her mother's boyfriends had tried to put her on top of one when she was five. Little Vickie had punched him in the groin, and he never tried that again.

"They're so free? You mean that horse right there in that fence that you are about to ride, whether he likes it or not?" Vickie asked.

"She has a point. Maybe not so free," Tracy said.

Vickie stared at Tracy. *He's so pretty and smart. And pretty. So pretty.* She would have drooled if her mouth hadn't been closed.

"Ridiculous," Julie said, scrunching her face and turning away from everyone to brush the horse in short, quick strokes like she had been doing it her whole life.

Squirt stared into the distrance, then spoke. "Too much freedom is scary."

Tracy cocked his head to one side, "How can you possibly have too much freedom?"

"I think you need limits," Squirt answered.

Tracy winked. "Then that's not freedom."

"Unbridled freedom, pardon my pun, is like bungee jumping. Without the cord. Terrifying," Squirt said.

Eagen's ears pricked up before chiming in, never taking his eyes off the horse. "Jumping without the cord is called suicide."

"Even with the cord, who would jump off a bridge for fun in the first place?" Vickie said from atop her bale of hay.

"I did it. Once," Squirt said.

Julie flirted, "Aren't you full of surprises."

Squirt's face flooded with color. "The safety crew checked everything, twice. Made me feel good. Like someone cared."

"They don't care. They just don't want to get sued," Eagen said, still staring at the horse like it was some sort of alien.

"You're all so strange," Julie said.

"Sounds like you're in the right place, then," Tracy quipped, turning on the water hose and dropping it in a large bucket, filling it for Snowflake.

"Oh, yeah?" Julie giggled. She grabbed the hose from the bucket, turning it on Tracy.

They fought over the hose, soaking one another.

"Watch the shoes," Eagen said as they splashed by.

Meanwhile, from her bale of hay, as Vickie observed Tracy and Julie's interaction, her face contorted like she was watching a horror movie at 2 a.m. by herself. "Disgusting," she said under her breath.

The Nurse's Office
1:45 p.m.

Vickie sat at the nurses' station with her right pant leg pulled up over her knee, making herself comfortable in one of those fun rolling chairs. The room looked a lot like a pediatrician's examination room. There was an eye chart on the far wall, a tall scale that also extended to measure your height and an examination table with a roll of that tissue paper stretched across it. Only one thing seemed out of place and unexpected.

"The 'Flawless Rose,'" Vickie said, pointing to a single red rose in a delicate vase on the counter.

"Yes." Nurse Lilly smiled and sighinf out the word . "I found it withering in the sun. Someone plucked it before its time." Nurse Lilly cupped the bud in her hand, her eyes wide with adoration.

Vickie wondered what Nurse Lilly must have thought when she found it. *Was she hurt? Disappointed? Working at a place like this, disappointments must come with the territory.*

Nurse Lilly sprayed some ointment onto Vickie's wound. "Ow." Vickie involuntarily rolled her fist into a ball, but luckily for Nurse Lilly, she had the self-control to stop herself. Her body relaxed with an indrawn breath. She knew Nurse Lilly was only trying to help.

Nurse Lilly gently placed a Band-Aid on the angry scrape. "All better now?"

"Yeah. Yeah. Wow. That's amazing."

"Band-Aid power," Nurse Lilly said.

"Too bad there's nothing like that to cover up the cuts you can't see. You guys would be rich. I mean, more rich."

"There *is* something. A smile," Nurse Lilly said, a gorgeous grin splayed across her face. "You should try it sometime," she continued warmly.

"I'll put it on my bucket list."

Vickie couldn't take her eyes off Nurse Lilly's soothing expression. Beautiful. Mesmerizing.

She had such pretty teeth. Vickie always noticed them. She'd smile more if she had teeth like Nurse Lilly's. Who wouldn't?

Vickie couldn't even remember life before braces. She hadn't wanted them, but her mom had conveniently been dating a dentist for a couple of weeks, and he gave them a big discount. They broke up long before her mom made the last payment.

"What happened anyway? Did you fall off the horse?" Nurse Lilly asked.

"No, I fell off the bale of hay."

She knew Nurse Lilly must have seen it all during her ten years at Blueberry Hill, yet nothing seemed to faze her or bring her down. *Has she somehow learned the secret of unconditional happiness? Is there such a thing?*

Looking deeply into the two pools of cool water that were Nurse Lilly's eyes, Vickie didn't find any sign of the sadness she presumed was there. That pretend smile was surely covering a deep depression. But there was no trace of unhappiness. Either Nurse Lilly had learned to bury her sadness so deep no one could find it, or her signature smile was genuine.

Vickie's gut insisted Nurse Lilly was hiding something, and Vickie was determined to find out what. No one could be that pleasant and happy all the time.

"Vickie. Vickie?" When she got no response from Vickie, Nurse Lilly elevated her voice, still smiling. "Vickie!"

"Yeah?"

"You're staring again."

"Oh. I am?" Vickie continued staring. "Your teeth are so white they are hypnotic."

"Oh, why, thank you." Nurse Lilly laughed, adding a sun-yellow burst of light to the room that made her briefly glow.

Vickie groaned inwardly. She'd said out loud the quiet thing her brain had conjured up.

"All set."

Vickie stood, testing her bandaged knee.

"And Vickie, if you need anything, even if you just want to talk, I'm here."

Vickie headed toward the door, but before she exited, she paused with her hand on the knob to look back at Nurse Lilly, who was, of course, still radiant.

CHAPTER 14
Puzzles

The Lobby
2:00 p.m.

Vickie and Annie sat across from one another at a heavy oak clawfoot table that was so old the people who made it had carved their names underneath the tabletop: John, Amos, Irving, and Little Levi. Vickie had found the etchings when Nurse Fran gave her the job of checking underneath all the furniture for old wads of gum.

Vickie rubbed her hand slowly over the weathered, smooth surface each time she sat down. Sometimes she would give it a pat, like a trusty dog. She liked strong, sturdy, reliable things. Puzzle pieces lay strewn on the tabletop between Vickie and Annie. Vickie held a piece in her hand, tapping it on her chin and searching for a spot to place it.

"Do you think I need to smile more?" Vickie asked, still focused on the puzzle.

"On the inside or outside?" Annie asked.

Vickie twisted her lips to one side. "The outside. I guess."

Annie effortlessly placed her puzzle piece in just the right spot without any deliberation. "No. Hyenas smile a lot. Then they eat you. An outside smile can't always be trusted."

Vickie scratched her head, considering where the piece in her hand might belong, while Annie immediately positioned another piece in its place once again.

"How do you do that?" Vickie asked. "Without thinking about where it goes?"

"I think about it my way. With my heart."

Vickie raised her eyebrows. "Hmmmph."

Vickie found puzzles grounding, calming, safe even. Most of the puzzles at Blueberry Hill were no longer in their original boxes, but were kept in plastic canisters, so there was no way of knowing what the finished image might look like. Vickie liked the added challenge; it was a mystery to solve.

Having no picture to work from mirrored real life. In most situations, people didn't know what things would look like in the end, but they still had to keep going.

In many ways her time at Blueberry Hill felt like a box of disjoined puzzle pieces. Locations. Times. Activities. Conversations. Moments. Meds. Memories. The missing four. Linda. She longed to zoom out far enough to see the big picture and how each moment might fit together to form some sort of meaningful something.

But, for now all she could do was focus on the puzzle on the table in front of her. Atleast it was far enough along that she could discern a house with a white picket fence and a perfectly kept lawn.

No real people lived in a fairy-tale home like this as far as Vickie was concerned, and if they did, their life behind closed doors wasn't all roses. She was sure of it.

Anyone who believed perfection was at all attainable aroused Vickie's suspicions; there was no such thing as perfect. The sort of person inclined toward such ideals was a liar or a lunatic or the third option—both.

Vickie's gaze wandered while Annie placed her next piece.

Nurse Fran sat at the reception desk. Vickie noticed her uniform remained a little whiter and a little more starched than the other nurses, yet one strand of gray hair never stayed pinned back and always flopped its way to her face.

Vickie liked Nurse Fran. She was a sturdy and reliable woman who didn't seem to drink the Kool-Aid around here. Vickie could always count on her for a disdainful glare. Of course, it remained impossible to read Nurse Fran's expression without understanding her baseline. Her resting face was the exact opposite of Nurse Lilly's. She always looked like she had just taken a whiff of spoiled milk.

The desk phone rang, and Vickie jumped a little, making Annie giggle. Nurse Fran answered, sounding professional yet bored, mumbling into the receiver. There was some more back-and-forth Vickie couldn't make out, as she focused on a particularly tricky section of the roof. She tapped her chin with her puzzle piece again.

"Yes, it is the day. Hold please, and I'll patch you through." Then Nurse Fran's voice rose as if someone turned up her volume. "Vickie, you've got a call."

"Who is it?" Vickie asked.

"Your mother," Nurse Fran said in her no-nonsense, unaffected tone. "You can take phone number three."

Per the rules, Vickie's mom could only call once a week. But sometimes her mother would lose track of the days and miss a week or two. Vickie knew her mother loved her though, as best she could, and she missed her, but it was painful for her mother to accept it could still be a long time before they would see each other. Her mother preferred to believe she was out at the 7-Eleven and would be home anytime. She had told her as much.

7-Eleven. Mmmmm, yum. Vickie's mouth watered a little thinking about the wild cherry Slurpees with cotton-candy toppers.

She stood and walked to the phone bank in the alcove around the corner with a puzzle piece still in her left hand, looking for the label on the phone she'd been assigned.

Puzzles had become a pleasant distraction for Vickie growing up, especially on the late nights when she waited for her mother to return home from a date. As much as Vickie loved puzzles, her mother hated them. Rosemary Bartolucci didn't have the patience for them or much of anything.

As she approached phone number three, Vickie couldn't help but think back to a puzzle that she never got the chance to finish. It was probably still sitting there on the coffee table in their tiny house.

She remembered getting so lost in it as she had waited for her mother that she almost forgot to check the clock every hour—almost. Evening had turned into night and then into the wee hours of the morning. Vivid images of one of the last nights she had sat on her couch and worked on a puzzle of a hound dog mother and her pup flashed through Vickie's mind.

DAY 00 for Vickie

The Bartolucci Home

1:00 a.m.

Rosemary wore a short, bright, floral dress and lots of makeup as she stumbled in after a night out. She had pinned a fake white lily in her hair; its blood-red streaks matched her smudged crimson lipstick.

Vickie's mom waved jerkily toward the street at a car as it sped away while she swayed in the doorway of their home. She closed the door quietly, with practiced, deliberate movements. Startled, she realized she wasn't alone.

"What're you still doing up?" Rosemary asked, slurring her speech ever so slightly.

"You're late," Vickie said, not looking up from her puzzle.

"I told you not to wait up for me."

"Of course, I waited up. Anything could have happened to you out there."

Rosemary tumbled out of her shoes, almost following them to the floor. Vickie stabilized her mother and helped her out of her clothes. She wore a silky slip that peeked from underneath her cocktail dress.

"I can do this myself."

"Come on. Let's get you to bed."

"No, I'm just going to rest here tonight," Rosemary said as she plopped

onto the couch.

"That's not good for your back," Vickie said.

"I'm comfortable." Vickie covered her mother with a blanket, a brown and orange afghan they had picked up from Goodwill. Rosemary's long, brown hair spilled over the couch arm cushion. "You take such good care of me," Rosemary said, looking up at Vickie, a smile bleeding across her face.

"Did you have a nice time?" Vickie asked, helping her mother unpin the flower from her hair.

"It was real nice. We talked and danced. And danced. He actually reminded me of someone," Rosemary said.

"Who?" Vickie asked.

"Just someone."

"Someone who?"

"Your father."

"And that's a good thing?" Vickie asked.

"Your father and me, we had some special times. How do you think you were born?"

"That's gross."

"We were from two different worlds, but there was something about him. You remind me of him. He was kind like you. I was like a butterfly, and he was like a tree. He kept me grounded. But everything has its season. And its fruits." Rosemary looked up at her daughter from the couch, cupping Vickie's cheek in her hand. "My time with your father was short, but it brought me you."

Vickie tucked the corners of the blanket around her mother's body.

"I'm supposed to be the parent here," Rosemary said as she closed her eyes.

Vickie knitted her mouth together so tight her lips disappeared. "Good night, Ma." Vickie turned the lights off and walked to her own room, the puzzle forgotten.

The Lobby
12:01 p.m.

"Vickie, I'm transferring the call," Nurse Fran said.

Vickie shook her head once, coaxing herself back to the present, and looked at the puzzle piece still in her hand. Her fingers traced the rounded edges, caressing it for comfort.

"You know what to do. Just wait for the ring," Nurse Fran said.

She sat down on the tiny stool and put the phone receiver up to her ear, preparing herself. "Hi, Ma."

"Vix! I can't believe it. I got the right day."

"You did it, Ma."

"It feels like it's been so long."

"Three weeks."

"Sorry about that. How's that new friend of yours? What's her name?"

"Linda."

"Right. Linda."

Vickie turned the puzzle piece over in her hand. "She's not here anymore."

"Good for her. Well, that's going to be you soon."

Vickie rubbed the puzzle piece more vigorously. "Everything good with you, Ma?"

"Everything's fine. I'm not gonna fall apart just because you're away for a little while. I can take care of myself, you know? So, they treating you good there? Are you eating?" Rosemary asked.

"You know what, Ma? They give us breakfast, lunch, and dinner. And a snack."

"You're not putting on weight, are ya?"

Vickie flicked her eyes toward the phone receiver like a whip. "That's not really my biggest worry right now, I have to tell you."

129

"Sooo, you're liking it there?"

"I wouldn't say that. But it's all right. Are *you* eating?"

"I eat when I'm hungry, hun," Rosemary said.

"You've got to eat when I'm not there. Just get a bunch of the frozen things."

"I can't take those frozen dinners," Rosemary confessed.

"Then yogurt. You like the coffee yogurt."

"Oh yeah, but I get so overwhelmed at the grocery. So much to pick from, then I forget what I came there for."

"Write a list. And you can get canned soup."

"You can get botulism from cans."

"You've never had botulism. No one you know has ever had botulism."

"Well, I like my soup homemade, the way you make it."

"The soup I make is from a can."

"Nah! There's something special when you make it. It tastes different."

"I literally just open a can."

A silent breath passed between them. Vickie wound her hand up over and over in the phone cord.

"You doing all right, then? What do they have you doing all day?" Rosemary asked.

"They gave me a journal."

"One of those 'write your feelings' things?"

"Yeah," Vickie said.

"They make you do it every day?"

"Twice a day."

"Well, that could be a good thing? I always thought about doing something like that."

"And there's a barn where we can go brush a horse."

"A horse?"

"A real horse," Vickie said.

"That's something you don't see every day. Look at you," Rosemary said.

"He's got these big, creepy eyes, and he smells like crap. But he's beautiful. From a distance."

"They pay you for taking care of the horse?"

"It's supposed to be therapy."

"Well, I'm glad you're taking life by the tits. Ain't that what they say?"

"Nobody says that, Ma. I just want to be home on the couch."

"Awww. Vix. The couch ain't going nowhere. It's waiting for ya when you get back. Keep your mindset. Take a picture in your head. You know, like the pictures we used to take. See yourself on the other side, and that will give you a little something to look forward to. And, when you get back, we're going to have a party. A welcome back party. I'll make a punch," Rosemary said.

"Ma, I really miss you."

"Yeah. Well. I miss you too."

CHAPTER 15
Meaning

The Drama Classroom
3:00 p.m.

Students gathered behind their workstation desks, seated and waiting. The just-large-enough room was well-lit from the windows at the far end. Ten tabletop desks with accompanying chairs stood spaced evenly throughout the room.

The balance between dramatic play and therapy was a delicate one, and the doctor was quite adept at walking it. On the one hand, play could easily turn into chaos. Conversely, the type of restrictive structure that came with therapy could lead to the students shutting down, turning off, and tuning out. Dr. Cannon gathered her thoughts and summoned her muses, taking in a panoramic breath from one side of the room to the other.

Annie sat at a desk next to Vickie, whispering in a stage whisper that was louder than if she had just used her regular voice, "How's your mother?"

"The same. Always the same," Vickie said.

Dr. Cannon, of course, noticed the interaction. She stared at the chatty pair and waited. Dr. Cannon liked dramatic pauses, dramatic entrances, dramatic everything, and lived for silences and the discomfort they brought. You could learn a lot about someone in silence. Her head resumed its slow turn, gathering up each student by the eyes. *Showtime.*

"Objects," Dr. Cannon began with a wink. She liked to begin each of these play sessions with a wink. Then, the doctor stood so still, she looked like someone had pressed pause and forgot to restart her. Anticipation hung in the air like a wave sucked in from the shore before being spat back out by the sea. Vickie perched on the edge of her seat, with one eyebrow slowly rising as the space between Dr. Cannon's words expanded.

"Objects are neutral, but we give them meaning," Dr. Cannon continued, breaking the weighted silence.

Vickie leaned over to Annie. "Thank goodness. I thought she was having a mini stroke."

Dr. Cannon grinned as if her smile gave the words more energy so they might penetrate deeper into the skulls of the adolescents. "People and relationships are also neutral, but we give them meaning. I hate you! I love you! I don't even notice you. These expressions do not come from the object, but from the observer. The observer decides. You decide. That's power."

Dr. Cannon was so animated that a half-giggle, an involuntary "gig," escaped through Vickie's closed lips.

"Today, we remember our power to give meaning. Meaning is invisible, and yet it influences everything. Together, we will work on our relationship with objects. Now, in your imagination, pick up an object that's invisible to most, but real for you. Hold it in your hand."

Vickie's eyes widened. She steadied herself, bracing for the activity. Each student interacted with an invisible object of their creation, miming it as best they could, some with wide-open arms, moving around the room, others sitting, focused but exhibiting the tiniest of movements.

"Annie, would you like to share? What's your object?" Dr. Cannon asked.

Annie held her arms in front of her, carefully carrying her invisible item. "A giant, warm egg that will be my baby," Annie said.

Dr. Cannon's face softened at the maternal gesture before assessing the progress the other teens made. Julie's arms were lazily splayed out by her side, palms up. "Julie. Whatever you have there looks enormous. What could it be?" Dr. Cannon asked.

"Boredom," Julie said, cutting through Dr. Cannon with a stony stare.

Unfazed, the doctor continued. "And Eagen, what do you have?"

"A bat," Eagen said.

"Will you use it to hit a ball?" Dr. Cannon asked.

"I could try. But it bites," Eagen said.

"Ahhh. That kind of bat. And you, Tracy?" Dr. Cannon asked.

Tracy ran his hand along the head of an imaginary creature. "My pet," Tracy said.

"What's its name?" Dr. Cannon asked.

"Turtle," Tracy said.

"That's not a very original name for a turtle," Eagen said.

"He's a chimpanzee," Tracy said. Squirt laughed, beaming at Tracy in admiration.

Meanwhile, Vickie audibly grunted, her face contorting and her entire body stiffening with her creative effort.

"Vickie?" Dr. Cannon asked.

"I'm doing my best here Ms. . . . er, Dr. Cannon. But I got nothin'," Vickie said.

"That's okay. It's sometimes helpful to 'not know.' That's what we call beginner's mind."

"I hate beginner's mind," Vickie said.

"Often, it's through discomfort that we make breakthroughs. Discoveries. Surprises. Don't you like surprises, Vickie?"

"No. I hate surprises."

"That's so sad. What about presents under the Christmas tree?" Annie asked.

"If we had a Christmas tree, that would be a surprise. And I would hate it," Vickie said.

Tracy smiled at the comment, amused as always by Vickie.

CHAPTER 16
The Poltergeist

DAY 62 for Vickie

The Sunshine Room

7:30 a.m.

Some residents lined up outside the sunshine room for their morning medication. Nurse Dorothy called their names, giving them a small cup of water and a smaller cup with their pills in it. One by one, the groggy teens tossed back the tiny cup and the water, peeling away from the line and into the lobby area.

"Tim."

Gulp. Swig.

"Terrence."

Gulp. Swig.

"Todd."

Gulp. Swig.

"That's a lot of Ts in one pod. Rich people must really like that letter, huh, Tracy?" Vickie said to Tracy, nudging him with her elbow as she passed the line.

"It would seem so."

Inside the sunshine room, within earshot but out of view, a newscaster spoke from a small portable TV.

"Eagen." Nurse Dorothy read off the name from her clipboard as she shivered and clutched the collar of her sweater tighter. "It's freezing in here," she said under her breath but load enough to be heard.

"It's probably a poltergeist," Eagen said, expressionless, as he swallowed his pill and walked away.

Nurse Dorothy's face fell, and she clutched her sweater even tighter. "Julie."

Julie, seated in a chair by the fish tank waiting for her next activity, jerked in surprise when she heard her name called. "What? No. There must be some mistake."

Nurse Dorothy looked at the clipboard. "Julie Maxwell. No. No mistake. Your parents and your doctor signed off. So did you."

Julie rolled her eyes, stomped over to the office, grabbed the white cup holding the pills and the tiny cup of water, and turned to walk away.

"I need to see you take that."

Julie huffed and puffed, but defiantly faced the nurse, turning the cup of pills up, letting them fall in her mouth, then swallowed and opened her mouth wide.

"No water. Hardcore!" Squirt said, standing just behind Julie.

Julie made eye contact with Vickie, who raised her eyebrows with an "I told you so" face and looked off to one side.

Squirt stood near Nurse Dorothy despite having already received his meds. "Can I help you, Theodore?" she said, facing Squirt. One of the other teens in line giggled. Someone always giggled when they heard Squirt's real name.

"May I have extra water please?" Squirt said. Nurse Dorothy obliged.

A few minutes later, Julie sat down across from Vickie in a pink wingback chair with a small table between them. They stared at one another wordlessly. "Okay, you were right. They do stuff you up with drugs. But, like I said, I don't take meds." Julie opened her hand, revealing two pink pills, then stuffed them in the soil of a nearby potted plant.

"Hmmm," Vickie said involuntarily as she looked Julie up and down, before nodding her head in approval.

On the TV inside the nurses' station, a newscaster continued to drone: "Police are still investigating the tragic death of sixteen-year-old Linda Rossi. Officials believe a vehicle struck her during her attempt to run away from the Blueberry Hill Home for Troubled Youth. She's the fifth teenager to run away from the facility this year."

Vickie adjusted her head slightly so that she could see the TV. When a photo of Linda flashed across the screen, Vickie's face dropped downward.

Nurse Lilly entered the sunshine room, rushing over to the TV. "What are you doing? They can hear that!"

Nurse Dorothy flicked off the TV. "Sorry, it was just background noise."

Nurse Lilly rolled her eyes and shook her head as she turned back around, glancing in the direction of Vickie and Julie seated in the student lounge in front of the reception station. Vickie had indeed heard the report and couldn't help but remember sitting in that same seat just over two weeks earlier with Linda, poring over newspapers for information about the missing four. And now Julie was sitting where Linda should be, and Linda was in a morgue somewhere or in the ground, for all Vickie knew.

As if someone had snapped Vickie awake from a trance that had lasted since Linda's death, Vickie's mind turned. "Why would someone run away the night before their release? We talked about meeting up when I got out. We made plans. It doesn't make sense." Vickie was mostly thinking out loud, but part of her wanted Julie to hear, for someone to be included in her inner dialogue. Annie was a great sounding board and even sometimes insightful, but she wanted to disclose her thoughts to someone a little more grounded in reality and someone a little less optimistic. The new blonde girl seemed to fit the bill. But Julie didn't have time to respond before Vickie darted up and strode over to the reception desk.

"Where are you going?" Julie called after her.

Nurse Fran was sorting through some paperwork when Vickie approached her.

"Weren't you on duty the night Linda ran away?" Vickie asked.

"That's none of your concern."

"Why did you leave the desk?"

"You should discuss any feelings you are experiencing with your counselor," Nurse Fran said, not even bothering to look up at Vickie.

"The only thing I'm feeling is that something's not right here."

"Vickie, you're not a detective. Let it go." Nurse Lilly entered, smiling again.

"I'm a teenager. We don't let things go," she responded, her face devoid of any smile.

It was a threat, a promise, and a statement of fact, all rolled up into one, and no one could deny the truth in it.

CHAPTER 17
The Pen

Dr. Cannon's Office
10:00 a.m.

If this is what her brain is like, she must never get bored, Vickie thought. Filled with eccentricities and items of curiosity, Dr. Cannon's office wasn't a large space, but it packed a big punch. The Korean art, the tapestries hanging on the walls, and the shiny, patterned fabrics covering the pillows and the couch looked more like an exotic theatrical set than a place to conduct therapy.

Vickie's sessions with Dr. Cannon usually occurred every Wednesday at 2 p.m., in addition to "special" appointments. Generally, Vickie looked forward to them and was never late, but this time, after the incident in the lobby, she knew the doctor would have an agenda. She sat across from Dr. Cannon, biding her time until the "speaking game" began.

Dr. Cannon stared at an open folder labeled *Vickie Bartolucci;* a long, awkward, but familiar silence passed between them. It was like a game of chicken. Who would speak first?

Dr. Cannon broke the sustained silence. "This is your time to use however you'd like."

Yes! I won. Inwardly, Vickie fist-pumped and high-fived herself, even though she always won. Yet every once in a while, Dr. Cannon would let the silence linger past the painfully uncomfortable point, just to keep Vickie on her toes. Luckily, this wasn't one of those times.

"I can use it *however* I want?" Vickie asked.

Dr. Cannon nodded.

"Can I use it to leave?"

"No," Dr. Cannon said.

"I got nothing to say."

"You had a lot to say in our morning session a couple of days ago. About the chair. And Linda."

Oh, so this is going to be about the chair incident.

"Yeah, well, that was then, and this is now. I don't want to talk about that," Vickie said. She knew by avoiding the topic, she may have already revealed too much, but still stood her ground.

The interaction reminded her of classes at her mostly white public high school; when she didn't raise her hand to speak, the teacher inevitably called on her. So sadistic. And completely predictable. Now, the doctor would want to talk about the thing she said she didn't want to talk about even more. She also knew Dr. Cannon would write this down in her little folder. Sure enough, the doctor patted her jacket pockets, most likely searching for a pen.

"Have you thought about what you want to do in a few years? What kind of career you might want to pursue one day?" Dr. Cannon asked.

Wait. What prompted that change in the subject? Suspicious.

"You mean what do I want to be when I grow up?" Vickie asked.

"Where did I put my. . . I just had it," Dr. Cannon said.

Vickie held up a silver pen and smiled.

"Perhaps you'd like to be a magician. How did you do that?" Dr. Cannon asked with sincere curiosity.

"As you know, I'm very good at secretly procuring things," Vickie said. She handed Dr. Cannon back her pen.

"Evidently not good enough. That's why you're here, isn't it?" Dr.

141

Cannon smiled.

"Good point."

Vickie really did like this woman. She was the right mix of smarts and humor, but most of all, Dr. Cannon seemed to see right through the BS, not flinching, but smiling behind her eyes when something didn't ring true. Vickie respected that.

"You know, I was worried for a moment. I'm always losing things. And that's my favorite pen."

"Well, you didn't lose it. I took it from you."

"Same thing," Dr. Cannon said.

"No, it's not. They are two different things."

"How so?"

"One's your fault and one isn't," Vickie explained.

"And yet, the result is the same, isn't it?"

"Well, no. I mean, yes. True, you wouldn't have a pen either way. But how you feel about it is different."

"What do you mean?" Dr. Cannon asked

"It's worse if it's your fault. 'Cause you could have stopped it. If you had just paid more attention. I don't know."

"Why would that be worse?"

"'Cause it's my responsibility to stay on top of things. To keep up with my shit. Sorry. Pen."

"I thought we were talking about *my* pen?"

"We are. I mean. No, we're not."

Dr. Cannon raised her eyebrows.

"We're talking about Linda," Vickie said. *Geez, that woman's good!* "And I already said I don't want to talk about it."

"And yet you are?"

"So, what are you trying to say, that I feel guilty or something? That I should have known something was wrong? 'Cause I'm her best friend? That if I had found her just a few minutes sooner—"

"Is that what you think I'm saying?"

"No. No. But, you're saying, if I don't deal with this, then everything is going to be about Linda. Even your stupid pen. That I won't be able to move on."

Dr. Cannon shrugged.

"Well, I don't want to move on. And I will handle it. Not your way, but the way I want. 'Cause you don't tell me what to do or how to do it! I'm going to do this the Vickie Bartolucci way."

"What's the Vickie Bartolucci way?"

"I'm figuring it out." Vickie crossed her arms in a huff and swiveled her head and body slightly in her chair, away from the doctor. "And I wish I had kept your freakin' pen."

Dr. Cannon's eyes twinkled as she nodded ever so slightly.

CHAPTER 18
The Pencil

The Cafeteria
11:05 a.m.

His food barely eaten, mostly just rearranged on the plate, and his tray now pushed to the side, Eagen sat at a table by himself in the lunchroom. The afternoon light spilled through the windows, making the sketch pad in front of him shine brighter and brighter as he stared into the distance. He placed the point of his pencil on his sketch pad, his body tense, and his heartbeat quick and fluttery, but the pencil didn't seem to want to move in his tight grip.

Vickie set her tray down opposite him with a thud, the wooden legs of her chair scraping against the tiled cafeteria floor as she plopped in the seat. "Spill it," she demanded.

He ignored her.

"Do you know what they're saying? That she ran away?"

"So?" he said, still staring into space.

"We both know that's not true."

"Do we?" Eagen's icy stare and frozen expression teased a response from her.

"Linda hated her foster home, but it was better than here. Why would someone run away the night before they were going home?"

"Hmmmmph."

Vickie grabbed his pencil and stabbed it into the sketch pad between Eagen's fingers, leaving it standing by itself. Eagen didn't flinch, but a half laugh escaped his lips.

Color flooded Vickie's cheeks. "This is funny to you? Linda's dead."

"And you're *still* jealous."

Vickie furrowed her eyebrows. Air forced its way through her teeth in a mocking hiss. "Of what? You? What do I have to be jealous of? I'm her best friend."

Tim sat with a couple other members of pod 2 at a nearby table, taking notice of the interaction, but Vickie continued unfazed.

"Then why are you here? Asking me to tell *you* about *your* best friend," Eagen said.

"Unbelievable." Vickie shoved her chair back and got up in a huff. Just as she was about to walk away, Eagen's words stopped her.

"She wasn't going home."

"What are you talking about? She was leaving the next day."

"But not going home. Her foster parents refused to pay anymore, so she was being sent to a state facility."

"That's not true. Why wouldn't she tell me?"

Eagen shrugged. "She didn't want to upset you and have you throw something or someone out the window like my knife."

Vickie's entire face recoiled in disgust. "That's ridiculous."

Eagen looked at the pencil sticking up out of his pad and so did Vickie.

"So, you can't blame her for running away or — worse," he said.

Vickie scrunched up her face and shook her head back and forth. "What? You think she ran in front of that vehicle on purpose?"

Eagen shrugged again. "Or maybe she didn't have enough of a reason to get out of the way."

"She had a reason. A lot of reasons." Vickie stared at Eagen, then stood up and threw her chair into its place under the table.

Eagen returned his attention to the pad, plucking the pencil out of the paper like Excalibur from the stone as Vickie stomped away.

Tim offered an uncomfortable smile, watching Vickie leave. "What are you looking at?" Vickie asked dismissively.

CHAPTER 19
Neutral

DAY 63 for Vickie

The Drama Classroom

3:00 p.m.

Julie sat in front of her workstation in drama class.

All the desks were occupied except for the one next to her. Even the empty station had something on it covered by a cloth. Julie's station was the only one that had nothing in front of it yet.

A blank slate, a fresh start.

She smiled and ran her fingers around the desk. Then she cast her eyes around the room, observing the works in progress on the other desks.

Julie relaxed into the wooden chair as Dr. Cannon spoke, noticing she held a white, neutral, standard theater mask in one hand. The stark face was much different from the homemade, half-painted, not quite finished, papier-mâché masks in front of the other teens in the class.

Nothing seemed to escape Dr. Cannon's watchful eye while she stood at the front of the room, including Julie's curiosity. Julie found the doctor's attention strangely comforting.

Dr. Cannon winked as usual before beginning. "Since someone new has joined us, before we continue creating our own masks, we will review a few concepts."

Vickie bulged her eyes in frustration and leaned her face into her hands on her desk.

Julie smiled, until everyone turned and looked at her. There was such a thing as too much attention. She squirmed in the collared blouse she wore. Suddenly, the desk and chair felt smaller and more constricting as she shifted her weight from side to side, even though nothing had physically changed since the day before yesterday.

"We will start at the beginning." Dr. Cannon held up the plain white mask with the eyes and mouth cut out. "Neutral. Let's talk about what it is and what it isn't. Neutral is not nothing, neutral is actually the opposite; it's the presence of everything. Every possibility. Neutral is pure potential," Dr. Cannon said.

"I'm having a hard time understanding neutral," Annie blurted.

"Some people think neutral simply means relaxed," Dr. Cannon said in response. To illustrate, she allowed her body and face to go so limp it was comical, and the teens all laughed.

"Like a noodle? No!" she said, straightening up once again.

"Some think neutral is electric." Dr. Cannon's eyes darted around, and she moved in spasms. "Like too much Starbucks? No! Neutral is both relaxed and electric. At peace, but all your senses are awake. Neutral is living on the precipice."

She put the neutral mask on and embodied the emotion, pivoting her head from side to side, breathing deeply, then took the mask off again, shrinking back into her normal persona. She put it on, quickly removing it over and over to contrast the difference in the emotional energy neutrality, or hyper-alertness, brought. On. Off. On. Off.

"Come. Your turn," Dr. Cannon said.

The students meandered to the front of the class. Dr. Cannon drew back a curtain the color of coagulated blood to reveal a mirror covering the length of the wall. She distributed the plain, white masks; all were identically smooth, without any detail or distinguishing feature. "Neutral mask, no voice, only breath and your body. No expectation of who you are supposed to be. Anonymity."

"Now, hold the mask that I gave you up to your face. See how your face and the mask are similar and different. Then, when you're ready, put the mask on. Breathe life into the mask and become one with it as you exhale."

Slowly the teens slid into their masks, held securely by the elastic straps on the back.

"See yourself in the mask. Look in the mirror and look at yourself with no judgment. Your eyes and nose and mouth are just shapes," Dr. Cannon said.

"The mirror is pulling me inside. It's a tidal wave," Annie said, captivated.

"Yes. Continue being very aware of the feelings this exercise brings up for you," Dr. Cannon said.

Vickie strained hard to see something, anything, grunting with effort.

"You don't have to force anything, just observe," Dr. Cannon said.

"I just can't look at myself without being enraptured. I feel like I'm disappearing," Annie said, waving her hands and wiggling her body like an apparition.

More grunting escaped from Vickie's tightly pressed lips.

"What's going on for you, Vickie?" Dr. Cannon asked.

"This is stupid," Vickie said.

"Everyone's experience will be different. It always is. Now, everyone move throughout the room. Go around and look at each other."

Julie couldn't take her eyes off the desk that had remained empty since she joined the pod. She knew, even without asking, to whom that desk had belonged, which made her all the more curious. *After Vickie's reaction to Linda's chair, no wonder Dr. Cannon is hesitant to pack up Linda's workstation.*

"You're in a room of strangers now. You've never seen these people before because you are new humans. You are humans—being. Let's continue walking around the room as our new selves. It's not just faces that are different."

A new self. A new Identity.

Julie attempted to move around the room, but still stole glances at the desk and the cloth-covered mask atop it.

"Our bodies. Explore your new bodies," Dr. Cannon said.

Like a magnet, Julie moved toward the desk as if through water, wearing her own white mask, her head tilted to one side. All sound around her dulled; only the mask on the unoccupied desk existed. She extended her hand, touching the shimmering cloth, her heart racing, the sound of her own breath increasing. She grabbed a handful of the fabric in her fist and tensed her muscles to yank it off the misshapen lump it hid.

Out of nowhere, Vickie grabbed Julie's hand with so much force Julie's wrist popped.

"Keep your hands to yourself," Vickie said.

"Look who's talking? You're hurting me!" Julie said.

"That doesn't belong to you."

"Relax!"

"Everyone is just erasing her and moving on. Taking her things," Vickie said. Slowly, one by one, the teens stopped moving and watched, removing their masks.

"Linda didn't run away!" Vickie said for all to hear. Julie's right knee buckled as Vickie squeezed tighter.

"Vickie! Stop. Vickie." Dr. Cannon stepped toward the pair. "That's it! No Jell-O at dinner," she continued.

Vickie released Julie.

"That's all? That's her punishment?" Julie asked, rubbing her wrist, out of breath, still feeling Vickie's vice-like grip on her.

"She really loves Jell-O," Annie said.

"This is true," Vickie said. "It's my favorite."

Vickie turned away, her eyes the last thing to leave Julie. Dr. Cannon returned to the front of the class, running her hands down her waist on either side. "Now, where were we?"

CHAPTER 20
Catch

Room 402
6:00 p.m.

Up. Down. Toss. Catch.

Alone in room 402, lying on her bed, Vickie threw her baseball in the air. Engrossed in the rhythmic, meditative sound and movement of the ball hitting her palm, she didn't notice the door opening and Angelo poking his head inside.

"Hey," Angelo said.

"It's a little early for night checks," Vickie said, her focus still on the ball.

"I know. I thought I'd check on *you*."

Vickie rustled just a little, still lying flat on her back, but otherwise, offered no response. Angelo entered the room and quietly closed the door behind him. Vickie heard the click of the door and looked out of the corner of her eye to see if her silence had encouraged him to leave. Sadly, it hadn't.

Angelo took two sheepish steps forward. "I'm sure you miss her."

Vickie relented with an answer. "I'm all right."

Angelo looked at his feet, his whole body heavy with thought. "What was she like?"

"Why do you care?"

He looked from side to side, then to what used to be Linda's bed. "I--"

"She didn't have any real family. Just rich, do-gooder foster parents. They stuck her in here 'cause they didn't know how to handle the food thing. But, even with all that, she looked at the bright side."

Angelo's whole body seemed to exhale, making him look half his size. "I wish I could have known her better, but I'm glad I got to meet her. She was lucky to have you as a friend," Angelo said.

Vickie's face relaxed as she took a quick breath in and out. "She wasn't trying to run away, you know? No one believes me," Vickie said.

"I do. Hey, heads up," Angelo said.

Angelo threw Vickie a Jell-O cup, which she caught with her spare hand. She paused her ball toss.

"Skills," Angelo said.

Vickie looked at the Jell-O now in her hand. "Why are you being so nice to me?"

"'Cause I get the feeling you've been nice to a lot of people. You should get a little back."

"If you're trying to seduce me, I'm not interested."

The orderly offered that dazzling smile she had seen Nurse Dorothy fan herself over, revealing a dimple in his left cheek. He chuckled a little as he headed toward the door.

"But I'm keeping the Jell-O," Vickie quickly added.

Angelo put his pointer finger over his lips. "Shhhh," he whispered before slipping back through the cracked door as stealthily as he came, leaving Vickie alone once again.

"I don't trust that guy," she said aloud.

As Vickie situated herself and her Jell-O cup, the baseball rolled off from her side and under what once was Linda's bed.

With some effort, she shimmied off her mattress and got down on her knees, groaning a couple of times as she groped for the runaway ball. But to her surprise, her hand hit something solid and with corners, definitely not the ball. She withdrew her arm, her hand now holding a hardcover book with a dusty cover. The gold lettering of the title was worn, and some of the pages were tattered.

"*The Masque of the Red Death*," Vickie read. She felt the coolness of the abandoned book in her hands before absent-mindedly thumbing through it as if she were looking for something, though she hadn't a clue what it might be.

Vickie wasn't a reader. Not because she was uneducated or impatient; in fact, she was quite smart and was patient when she wanted to be, but she had never found a book that suited her sensibilities. She saw all books as fantasies of sorts. Even textbooks were told from unverifiable perspectives. Everyone had an angle. The teacher, the writer of the book, the historical figures the books were written about, their family members, the students reading the book. Everybody. And that's just what annoyed her about nonfiction.

When it came to fiction, well, that was just a waste of time. That stuff didn't happen, so what was the point? And if it wasn't happening to her, why should she care? She was a practical thinker, and fiction was anything but practical. At least, that's what she told herself.

But the deeper truth was that there was a part of Vickie that believed if she allowed herself to fantasize, to imagine, if she took a break from life's hard reality even for a moment, she would miss something; work would go undone, and people might get hurt. People like her mother, for instance. She was too responsible to dream.

In her mind, books didn't provide an escape. They were a scapegoat, a reason to delay taking action and getting down to business to change your situation. There was no escaping the cold, hard facts. Reality was reality was reality was reality. And so, she flipped through the dog-eared pages of the book quickly, spying the notes written in the margins by others who obviously read more carefully than herself.

She closed the book with a thud and smirked, happy she hadn't spent more time on it. Then something fell from between the pages, slowly spinning to the floor like a yellowed leaf in a fall breeze. Vickie reached down and picked up the photo of a younger Linda with her foster parents.

Vickie smiled, closing her eyes, and holding the photo against her heart, attempting to embrace the friend she missed so much. It was the first time in a long while that opening a book had made her feel something good.

The Lobby
6:15 p.m.

Julie respected antique things. They had survived against all odds, standing the ultimate test of time. Luckily for her, Blueberry Hill Manor was an odd mix of old and new, but mostly old. You got the impression that time had stopped and had picked up a few souvenirs across multiple decades, centuries, even. At the reception desk, Nurse Dorothy pressed a mint-green phone against her ear, a model and color no doubt discontinued decades ago.

"I told you she's not available. That's our policy. You too." Nurse Dorothy sighed.

"Who was that?" Nurse Fran asked.

"Rosemary."

"Who?"

"Rosemary Bartolucci, Vickie's mother. That's the third time she's called this week."

"Did you tell her about our policy?" Nurse Fran asked.

"Yes. One phone call a week."

"What did she say?"

"She wants to know when she can come visit."

"Good Lord. Did you tell her we don't allow‑‑"

"Yes. Every time she calls, I tell her."

Julie returned her attention to the lobby. Even in the makeshift lounge area, remnants of days gone by were sprinkled around the room like cupcake toppings. The opulent chandelier and high ceiling, mixed with a couple of midcentury couches and the squeaky, 1970s library carts, all rubbed shoulders without protest.

She enjoyed speculating about the objects' history, including their previous owners, preferring the company of objects to the members of her own pod, who busied themselves nearby. Eagen and Annie drew, Eagen with charcoal, Annie with crayon, and Squirt and Tracy, seated on either side of the large, clawfoot table, played a rousing game of tic-tac-toe by sliding a piece of paper back and forth between them. No sign of Vickie. Julie's chest tightened at the mere thought of her.

Angelo wheeled an additional metal cart into the lounge area. Julie was curious about the books crammed on its shelves. She enjoyed reading and loved writing even more. Mostly poetry, just for herself.

She looked through the books, letting her finger run across each spine. There was a thin layer of dust covering them. She liked the clean streak her finger left because it provided evidence she had been there, that she was real. Most of the books were hardcovers, but every now and then her finger would glide across a glossy paperback. Julie's finger paused periodically on the back of a classic title, lighting there like a butterfly suckling pollen from the center of a flower: *Wuthering Heights, Rebecca, The Hound of the Baskervilles*, all titles familiar to her. Her face lit up.

Gothic romances. My favorite.

She breathed in, gasping in delight, relishing in the simplicity of the vintage covers, the faded gold lettering hinting at what the reader might find inside. To her, modern covers gave everything away with their gouache colors and complex images, like watching a two-minute movie trailer and feeling like you've seen the whole movie.

That wasn't to say Julie didn't love the steamy Harlequins she found in her mother's bedside table, but she always finished those books hungrier than when she started them. A classic left her stimulated but satiated.

While still staring at the collection on the cart, Julie noticed someone beside her sliding a book into an empty slot in the top row of books. She read the words on the spine silently: *The Masque of the Red Death*. She smiled; the bright red cover reflected in her pupils.

Gothic horror. There's something romantic about death.

Her gaze moved from the book to the hand to the arm to the face of the person placing the book on the cart.

The corners of Julie's mouth drooped.

It was her.

Vickie.

Julie's heart suddenly beat faster, and words tumbled out of her. "I've never read that one," Julie said, stepping back a little. She immediately regretted sharing anything personal with Vickie, even something as harmless as her reading history.

"Me either," Vickie said.

Julie exhaled, her lips quivering into a smile. "Poe, right?"

Vickie shrugged. "Probably. Linda and Eagen loved that stuff. Not my thing."

"You sure, you don't mind?"

"It was Lind—I said no. All that makeup must be stopping up your ears," Vickie said, walking away.

Julie looked over at Eagen, who sat by the window, mostly so she didn't have to look at and wonder about Vickie any longer. Eagen's quiet sullenness and brooding energy made him an unlikely friend candidate, yet Vickie mentioned he had been Linda's friend. Once again, she wanted to know more about Linda, about what made her choose Eagen to confide in over everyone else. And now, to her surprise, she was curious as to what kind of friend Eagen could be.

Was Linda as strange as he was? Did they share an interest in dark things? In death?

More interested in her fellow pod members than she thought, Julie liked the fact that Eagen seemed to be one of those people that didn't pretend. He was who he was. And the fact that both Linda and Eagen liked this book made Julie even more curious about it. Holding it by the spine, she flipped it front to back to front again.

Then, Julie glanced over at Tracy. As usual, he perched on the sofa arm, strumming his guitar in that quiet way, watching his own fingers, occasionally closing his eyes. He acknowledged her with a quick nod. She could always tell when boys were interested in her, but to her dismay, Tracy gave no signals that he was.

"Hmmmm," she murmured to herself.

Maybe he's harder to read because he's English?

Julie turned the book over in her hand again, just as Angelo approached and grabbed the side of the cart to push it away.

"Didn't you just wheel this out?" Julie asked, smiling.

"I forgot I was supposed to switch the books out with some new ones that just came in," Angelo said, looking down at the book in Julie's hand, then back up at her. The color left his face, and his breath hitched with a hiss.

"What's wrong?" Julie asked.

Angelo forced a smile, color suffusing his cheeks once again.

"I thought we misplaced that book," Angelo said.

"Apparently not. You sure everything is OK?"

"Sure," Angelo said. He spun away from her and squeaked away, pushing the cart from behind.

By the time Julie found a comfy, overstuffed chair to sink into, Vickie and Annie were well into a round of Candyland. Julie casually flipped through the book, getting to know it, a small smile playing across her face as she ran her fingers over the elaborate inked illustrations. She hadn't noticed she had sat down across from Tracy.

"That was weird," Tracy said under his breath. "Angelo looked like he had seen a ghost." Julie gave in to the smile and nodded, staring at Angelo as he wheeled the cart down the hallway.

Room 402
10:10 p.m.

Vickie stole glances at Julie, befuddled that anyone would spend so much time getting ready to sleep. With every stroke of the brush through her long blonde hair, Julie's white satin nightgown swayed. She used the tiny oval mirror hanging by the light switch to help guide her strokes. Vickie smoothed her own hair with two quick swipes on each side when Julie wasn't looking, only to have it pop back into the same position.

Julie put her brush down gently on the dresser. Both girls walked to the head of their beds and turned back their covers. Julie was methodical, taking one corner at a time and folding them back into an even right triangle. Vickie, on the other hand, threw the covers back and slid under them in one fluid swoop. She immediately turned her body away from Julie and faced the wall.

"Hey, did Linda have a boyfriend here?" Julie asked.

"Who are you talking to?" Vickie asked, not bothering to turn over to look at Julie.

"There's no one else in here. So, you." Annie had excused herself to the communal restroom just before.

This was none of her business, and Vickie could have argued the point or refused to answer her altogether, but sometimes the fight wasn't worth it. "No," Vickie said dismissively.

"Are you sure?" Julie asked.

Vickie rolled over to face Julie and shut her down with a stare, but when she turned over, Julie handed her a book, *The Masque of the Red Death*, open to a page.

"There are messages back and forth in this book in two different handwritings. They talk about meeting," Julie said.

The message read: *Once you're out, we won't have to keep things a secret any longer.*

And the response in Linda's handwriting: *I can't wait.*

Vickie put the book down, staring at the floor, then picked it up again, reading the lines over and over, each time deflating just a little more.

How had she missed this? Secret messages?

A wave of heat rushed all over her, pulling her into the earth with the weight of the guilt squeezing her chest, as she realized she had overlooked something right in front of her. Again. She wasn't mad at Linda. How could she be mad at a dead girl? She was just confused, like a surprise tackle when you thought no one was anywhere near you.

A romance? With whom? Was this the secret Linda never divulged? Was it Eagen?

Her lip curled at the thought of it.

Her mind swirled like a slushie machine, but on the outside, she remained cold as steel. Vickie turned her back to Julie, pulling the covers up over her and staring at the wall.

CHAPTER 21
Apparition

The Fourth Floor
11:30 p.m.

A toilet flush echoed into the hallway from the communal bathroom on the fourth floor. Vickie undid the latch on the bathroom stall and slowly walked toward the sink to wash her hands, yawning. She opened both sides of the faucet, adjusting the hot and cold water until she had just the right mix.

Pumping the soap dispenser, she hummed a little song to ensure she washed long enough to get her hands clean. Vickie had learned the little rhyme from her kindergarten teacher in Queens, Ms. Gherkin, who, ironically, resembled a tiny pickle. Vickie's lips stretched into a small grin as she realized how hungry she was all of a sudden.

Pickles. Yum.

Vickie exited the bathroom, rubbing her eyes, stumbling into the hallway on her way back to her room. Even the ticking of clocks seemed muffled in the deserted and eerily quiet corridor. Piercing the silence, a creaking and clanging sound erupted from behind her, stopping Vickie in her tracks. It sounded like someone banging on the radiator pipes.

"Hello?" Vickie said.

No answer.

It's probably someone actually banging on the pipes. This is a home for troubled youths, after all.

The shenanigans of the residents didn't usually bother Vickie, but something about this noise made the hairs stand up on her arms and a chill run up her spine. She walked a little faster back to her room, but froze when she glimpsed a young woman in a long gown heading toward the door to the stairwell at the far end of the hall.

She squinted, not believing her eyes.

"Linda?"

Scarcely aware the name had escaped her lips, Vickie felt her heart swell. "Linda," she said again. The syllables felt good to say and even better to hear. She hadn't realized how long it had been since she had uttered the name of her best friend. It seemed silly now to avoid such sweet sounds. Her feet followed the young woman down the stairs.

Vickie spied the figure again and again as she rounded each flight, just missing the apparition at every turn. Her heartbeat drove her forward, exhilarated by the sudden burst of adrenaline brought by the anticipation of seeing her friend.

Vickie's pace slowed, her stomach in knots. The chase neared an end when she stood in front of the drama room on the first floor. She wasn't sure if the apparition had gone in, but something deep inside pulled her onward toward the entrance.

After six sure-footed steps, Vickie stood directly in the center of the doorway. And there she was, the girl in the nightgown, with her back to Vickie. Vickie moved through the door, continuing to place her feet carefully, not wanting to startle the girl, or worse, alert Angelo.

The young woman was standing in front of Linda's desk. Seemingly unaware Vickie was watching, the apparition in white reached out in slow motion to pull the cloth off Linda's mask. The blood drained from Vickie's face as her throat tightened, making it hard to squeeze out any words. But she did it anyway, this time loud enough to reach the figure.

"Linda?"

The young woman slowly turned, a blood-red mask covering her face, its mouth fixed into a permanent smile. The mask Linda had been working on so diligently in those weeks before Vickie found her lying lifeless in the middle of the highway seemed to have sprung to life.

For a moment they stood staring at one another, Vickie's hands trembling at her sides. Then, the white-clad figure gasped for air in three quick attempts at a breath and collapsed to the floor. Vickie rushed toward her and knelt down, her hands hovering over the figure's still body.

"Please don't be a ghost. Please don't be a ghost," Vickie said under her breath. A ring of perspiration erupted across her forehead and her breath puffed in little panting gasps as she reached out to remove the mask from the girl's face.

For a moment, Vickie saw Linda, her long hair, her peaceful, kind face. But the mirage only lasted until Vickie's eyes focused, and reality reclaimed her heart. She stared at the unconscious form of Julie, real and solid, most definitely not a ghost. She hadn't realized how similar the two girls looked until now, though they were nothing alike. She exhaled one long breath, pressing her ear close to Julie's mouth, making sure she could hear the rhythmic pattern of Julie's inhalations.

Room 402
11:58 p.m.

Twenty-eight minutes later, inside room 402, Julie lay in her bed with Annie and Vickie standing nearby.

"What is it with you and Linda's stuff?" Vickie asked.

"I was curious," Julie said. "I wanted to know what was under the cloth. And then, I wanted to see what it felt like."

"What it felt like?"

Julie paused for a moment as a flush crept across her cheeks, then she met Vickie's gaze. "To be her."

Vickie shifted her weight, and her shoulders relaxed. There was something vulnerable in Julie's admission and in the tone of her voice that made Vickie let things go, for now, but Annie's own curiosity stirred.

"And then what happened?" Annie asked.

"I don't know. I put on the mask, and I felt like I couldn't breathe, and I passed out. It was like I couldn't control my body," Julie said.

"It was Linda. She possessed you. Everything's all right now, though," Annie said.

Vickie felt her chest tighten as Annie held Julie's hand, rubbing it like she was comforting a pet. Before she even realized it, Vickie was sitting back on her own bed, looking off into the night beyond the window.

"You're not her," Vickie said.

"She couldn't help herself. She was compelled," Annie whispered.

"I had to know," Julie said again.

"Where is the mask now?" Annie asked.

"I put it back where it belongs. On Linda's desk," Vickie said. Vickie looked directly at Julie. "You're not her!"

Julie nodded and curled in on herself. There was nothing else to say. Vickie pulled her own legs into bed and flipped onto her side, turning her back to Julie.

CHAPTER 22
The Black Teardrop

DAY 64 for Vickie
The First Floor
7:59 a.m.

Vickie hurried toward the rec room through hallways littered with straggling teens. She hated being late. She bowled through the crowds, focused on her destination like a linebacker running a play. Her speed barely slowed when she felt the dull impact of another body against her own.

Tim.

"Watch where you're going!" Tim said.

"You bumped into me. Creep."

Vickie rushed into the rec room, grabbing just one chair. A week had passed since the group agreed to try new positions in the meeting circle. It had been easier than she thought to stop setting a chair out for her friend Linda.

Linda hated morning meeting anyway.

Vickie sank into her chair and took in the others in the room. Annie, quivering and bright-eyed, enjoyed sitting in what used to be Dr. Cannon's position in the morning meeting circle. Dr. Cannon now sat beside Annie. Squirt grinned ear to ear, relishing his new position next to Vickie. But not everyone was happy about the seating adjustments.

Vickie sat with her arms crossed, both corners of her mouth pointing downward. The more Squirt smiled, the more she rolled her eyes and wished she were anywhere else. She scooted her chair away from Squirt in the circle, moving closer to Eagen, who flanked her on her opposite side. Tracy watched them with those deep brown eyes that could wrap around her like a cloak. A black Sharpie teardrop adorned Eagen's right cheek. Leaning toward Eagen, Vickie whispered "Did you and Linda—"

"Did we what?" Eagen asked.

"Have a thing?" Vickie asked.

Eagen scrunched his face, his eyes darting from side to side. "No. Why?"

"No reason," Vickie said, leaning back into her seat, relieved, but still preoccupied by something.

Dr. Cannon settled herself, smoothing her hair with her left hand and readying her pen and pad. Julie entered the room and joined the circle, placing her chair in the space between Vickie and Squirt.

Under her breath, Vickie mumbled to Julie, "Eagen's hiding something."

"How do you know?"

"You read books. I read people."

Squirt tapped Julie on the shoulder. "Excuse me."

Julie turned to him.

"*I'm* supposed to sit beside Vickie."

Julie twirled her hair and looked away.

"Dr. Cannon. Excuse me. But we are not in the order we agreed on," Squirt said. His voice carried a petulant note that made Vickie grind her teeth.

"I never agreed," Vickie said.

"Julie, switch please," Dr. Cannon said, wiggling two of her fingers as if she were performing a magic spell to levitate them. Julie stomped her feet and sighed, but obliged, nudging her chair next to Tracy.

"For the record, this is how serial killers are made. By encouraging stalking behavior when they are prepubescent."

"I'm not prepubescent," Squirt argued, his voice cracking.

"But you admit you are a stalker?" Julie asked.

The teens of pod 1 snickered, with the exception of Squirt.

"Settle down. Moduleul hwan-yeonghabnida," Dr. Cannon began. "How's everyone feeling today?"

"Stalked," Vickie said.

"Same as last week and the week before. Ducky," Tracy said.

"I've been listening to that fake accent for weeks. Stop the charade," Eagen said.

"You mean the cha-ra-a-a-ahde," Tracy said, with the most British pronunciation he could muster.

"I'm going to strangle you," Eagen said, emphasizing one word at a time.

"Eagen, no threatening language. That's one of our ground rules. You know that," Dr. Cannon said.

"I am venting my frustrations. I thought that was what we're supposed to do," Eagen said.

"Let's keep this a safe space. For everyone," Dr. Cannon said. "Even when venting."

Tracy stared at the black tear on Eagen's face, his eyes brightening, eager to comment. He wasn't mean-spirited. Quite the opposite. He was kind in every way. Or at least, kinder than most. But from what Vickie could tell, he loved a good joke. His view of others was so positive that he assumed people were always laughing with him. Even when they got angry, surely, they weren't really angry but just play-fighting. He especially loved teasing Eagan. He seemed to think it was their special thing. Vickie knew he couldn't have been more wrong. She could tell Eagen hated Tracy. But it was a relative hate. Eagan operated on a different scale when it came to personal relationships. His scale started at moderate dislike and continued to homicidal inevitability.

"You've got a little something. Right here," Tracy said to Eagen, pointing to the location on his own cheek.

"What does that tear mean, anyway?" Julie asked.

"It means he fell asleep on a Sharpie," Tracy joked.

"In prison, I think it stands for how many people you've killed," Vickie said.

"More like how many people I want to kill, starting with someone in this group," Eagen said, glaring at Tracy. If looks could kill, Eagen's stare would have knocked Tracy through the wall.

Tracy scoffed.

"That's enough, Eagen. This is your second warning." Dr. Cannon let the command hang in the air until Eagen lowered his black-rimmed eyes. "How are other people feeling?" she asked.

"I'm however you want me to be," Annie said.

"I feel like *I'm* in prison," Julie said.

"Because we are," Eagen added.

"I'm worried. Not for me, but for everyone," Squirt said.

"You're always worried," Tracy said.

"We're not using this time productively to help each other," Squirt said.

"I really think you should speak for yourself," Vickie said.

"None of us chose to be here in this forced community," Eagen said.

"I did. There was a brochure," Squirt said.

"Shut up, Squirt," Vickie said.

"What? My dad gave me two options," Squirt said. Amid multiple eye rolls and sighs, the door to the rec room opened.

Not another new member, Vickie thought. *Julie was bad enough.*

All heads turned to see who it was.

Nurse Fran entered, accompanied by two stronger, disagreeable-looking orderlies, whose names Vickie didn't know. The room quieted quickly. Nurse Fran often had that effect on people.

"Nurse Fran? We are in the middle of a session," Dr. Cannon said.

"Sorry for the interruption, Dr. Cannon," Nurse Fran said.

"Whatever it is, can it wait?"

"I'm afraid it can't."

Curiosity flowed around the circle like a cold wave, hitting them one at a time in the face. Everyone's ears perked up.

Nurse Fran's still expression fixed on Vickie. "Vickie, come with us, please."

Vickie looked over at Dr. Cannon for direction, her heart beating faster. Even though she hadn't a clue what was going on, she sensed trouble.

"What's this about?" Dr. Cannon asked.

"Just leave your things and come with us, Vickie," Nurse Fran continued.

"Come with you where?" Vickie asked.

"Nurse Fran—" Before Dr. Cannon could finish, Nurse Fran handed Dr. Cannon a folded piece of paper as the orderlies positioned themselves behind Vickie's chair.

"Where did you get this?" Dr. Cannon asked.

"It was left anonymously on my desk."

Dr. Cannon looked up at Vickie, then at Nurse Fran, "Wait. There must be some mistake."

"Empty your pockets," Nurse Fran said, still boring holes into Vickie with her expressionless stare. In one quick, fluid movement, Vickie stuck her hands in both her pants pockets and turned them inside out.

Empty.

Vickie shrugged.

"Your sweater pockets," Nurse Fran continued.

Vickie reached into the left pocket of her sweater and pulled out a Saran-wrapped mini doughnut.

"I took an extra one at breakfast. Sorry. You didn't have to sic the doughnut Nazis on me," she said, motioning toward the orderlies.

"Vickie?"

Vickie reached into the same pocket and pulled out another mini doughnut.

"OK, two. But they are minis. So technically, they count as one."

"V—"

"Four, all right," she said, pulling two more out. "Since when are snacks a crime?"

"Nurse Fran—" Dr. Cannon began.

"The other pocket," Nurse Fran said, her voice stern.

Vickie reached into the right pocket of her sweater. Her eyes widened as she pulled something out and held it up. It was the homemade knife she had found on Eagen and thrown out the window weeks earlier.

She stepped toward Dr. Cannon, who involuntarily held her hands up as a buffer between the knife and herself.

"No. No. No," Vickie said, trying to wipe away the misunderstanding with her words.

Vickie put her hands in the air like she was surrendering and slowly knelt, placing the knife on the ground. Vickie surveyed the faces of the group, all ranging from shock to confusion, then zeroed in on Eagen.

"You did this. I know it was you." She turned toward Nurse Fran. "It was him!"

Nurse Fran nodded, and both orderlies lunged forward, reaching for Vickie. She evaded their clutches, ducking under their arms and running toward the window, bumping into the stack of folding chairs, sending them crashing to the floor. The two orderlies grabbed her, but had a tough time holding on to her. She punched one of them in the eye and kicked the other in the groin before they sufficiently subdued her.

"Vickie, stop, please. Just go with them. And we'll figure all this out," Dr. Cannon said. Nurse Fran moved over quickly, jabbing Vickie in the arm with a syringe.

"Dr. Cannon, it wasn't me." The medication worked through her body quickly, her muscles relaxing. As they dragged Vickie through the circle, Vickie screamed directly at Eagen. "I know it was you!" Eagen's eyes narrowed, his hands shaking. Faces blurred, but Vickie felt a comforting hand on her back. She thought it might be Tracy's, but could hear Squirt say, "I believe you." She even thought she heard Julie curse at the orderlies as they passed.

But it was one person's words that kept echoing in her mind. "We'll figure it out," Dr. Cannon had said. Only one person in that room could figure out what had happened, and it wasn't Dr. Cannon, even though her sincerity wasn't in question.

CHAPTER 23
The Reunion

The White Room
10:30 a.m.

Vickie grabbed her head, unable to lift it, not sure if the sedative had given her the headache or if she had hit it at some point when they subdued her. She cracked her eyes open for the first time since the incident and took the measure of her new surroundings, though everything was out of focus. The plastic-encased mattress crunched beneath her and the whiteness at the edges of her vision made her feel as if she were wrapped in a cloud.

The padded walls ensured she didn't injure herself, and the single door ensured nothing got in or got out. No windows. Her mattress lay on the floor, and a toilet and tiny sink occupied the back corner of the room. A stack of books lay next to the mattress untouched. She hated books!

She was only conscious long enough to see a tray of food by the door and then all the light drained from the room like dirty dishwater down the drain.

Light leaked out of the room, leaving only darkness.

And a sound.

Music.

The more we get together, together, together,

The more we get together . . .

Then she heard a familiar voice.

"I'm just going out for a bit. I won't be late."

"Ma? Don't go. Stay with me. Ma!" she said as her eyes fluttered open again, revealing the four walls of her small but cozy Maine bedroom. She lay in her bed, only her eyes moving.

"Don't worry, I'll stay with you," a voice said from the bedroom doorway.

Her eyes followed the voice to its source. "Linda!"

Linda glowed in the reflected light from the window.

"I thought you forgot about me," Vickie said, content to remain in bed if it meant Linda was with her.

"Best friends never forget about each other."

"But where have you been?" Vickie asked.

"Right here. I guess you couldn't see me."

"No. I couldn't. I'm sorry."

"But just because you don't see me doesn't mean I'm not there."

"Well, I'm glad I can see you now. I have so much to show you. This is my bedroom."

"I know," Linda said.

"And my bed," Vickie said, patting the covers. "And that's my desk. And my chair."

"It's just like I pictured it."

"And you're here," Vickie said, smiling, feeling her dry lips drag over the metal in her mouth.

Linda smiled briefly, but before the smile vanished, she looked down at the floor. "There were a lot of things I wanted to tell you. But I couldn't," Linda said, looking back up at Vickie again. "Are you mad at me?"

"I thought I was, but I think I'm more mad at myself. I should have known something was wrong. That last night I should have stayed up with you."

"Vickie."

A black bird flew into the open windowsill and watched, temporarily interrupting their conversation.

"There he is," Linda said, motioning toward the bird. "He watches over me. And he'll watch over you too. And so will I."

Footsteps echoed in the hallway outside.

"I've got to go, but Vickie —"

"What is it?"

"Be careful."

And just before the light drained from the room again, the distant pings of music returned.

The more we get together, together, together . . .

The notes drifted away into silence.

DAY 67 for Vickie
The White Room
11:30 a.m.

The door to the white room clanked open, jarring Vickie from sleep. Her eyelids cracked open, and she pried her tongue from the roof of her pasty mouth. Dr. Cannon pushed the large orderly aside and rushed toward Vickie, who lay motionless on the mattress.

"Vickie?"

"Are you real?" The words tumbled out in a scratchy rasp.

"Yes," Dr. Cannon said with an empathetic chuckle. "Are you all right?"

"Got to be honest, these haven't been some of my favorite moments, Doc."

"Have some water," Dr. Cannon offered, holding Vickie's head as she sipped from the plastic cup left on the tray by the door.

"Let's get you out of here," Dr. Cannon said. "It's still going to be a while before the drugs are out of your system. They had to sedate you several more times."

"Good," Vickie said. Even the effects of sedation couldn't hide the pride in her voice.

"We'll have the orderly take you to your own room."

"I wouldn't advise it. For his sake," Vickie said, staring at the large orderly in the doorway with the black eye.

The orderly shifted from side to side, nervously looking down at the floor. "Uhhhh, I think I'll wait outside. Let me know when you're ready, Dr. Cannon."

"Yeah! You better run!" Vickie said before drifting back onto the pillow and into the drug-induced slumber.

"There's that passion we all know and love," Dr. Cannon said. "You're getting quite a reputation around here."

"Good," Vickie mumbled, her eyes once again closed.

Room 402
2:00 p.m.

Vickie's eyes peeled open to find familiar faces looking down at her. Annie, Julie, Squirt, and Tracy gathered around her bed. Her groggy voice spat out the words, "What is this *Wizard of Oz* bullcrap? How long have you all been here, lurking by my bed?"

"Not long," Tracy said. "Julie came and got us."

"When you finally stopped snoring, I knew you were either waking up or dead," Julie said.

Vickie noticed a warmth around her hand that tingled all the way to her heart. For the first time, she realized Tracy's palm was in hers. She laughed nervously as he smiled back, blushing. They reluctantly released their hands at the same time.

"How long was I locked up?"

Her four companions glanced at each other, clearly unsure how they should respond. Julie made the decision first. "Three days. It would have been longer if he hadn't confessed."

"Look," Tracy said, opening the small window to the side of Vickie's bed. Vickie steadied herself, raising up to look over the ledge. She saw the stables four floors below and a boy covered in muck, shoveling manure. As her eyes focused, she recognized the boy to be Tim.

"Eagen figured it out and made him confess," Annie said.

Vickie collapsed back on her pillow, her mind whirling and physically tired from the exertion.

Dr. Cannon's Office
7:00 p.m.

Vickie sat across the desk from Dr. Cannon, who patted her pockets, presumably looking for something with which to write. Vickie stared out the nearby window.

"You're pensive today, Vickie."

"And you're pen-less."

"Yes, maybe you have a pen I can borrow?" Dr. Cannon hinted.

"Sure. It's probably yours, anyway." Vickie handed Dr. Cannon a pen from her pocket without looking at her.

"Considering everything that's happened, I wanted to speak with you."

"About anything?"

"Of course."

"Do you believe in ghosts?"

"What makes you ask that?"

"Is that what we're doing here, asking questions and never answering?"

Dr. Cannon smiled deeply, causing fine lines to appear in the far corners of her eyes. "I'll tell you a story if you like?"

"That's still a question. I thought we were done playing the questions game?"

"Very well. As you know, before I was a therapist, I was an actor. I took my first acting class with none other than Marcel Marceau himself. Have you heard of him?"

"That monkey on *Friends*?"

"No. The renowned French actor and mime. For ten years, I had a torrid love affair with him—in my own mind. I thought he was inspiration incarnate, and I still remember where I was when I received the news of his death in 2007. I was performing at the famed Théâtre du Marais in Paris."

Vickie yawned.

"Am I boring you?" Dr. Cannon asked.

"We can go back to the questions game."

"It gets better, I promise. I was in the middle of a monologue when I felt a gentle breeze blow across my skin, so soft that it raised the hairs on the back of my neck, and I heard a whisper in the voice of Le Maestro, "C'est bien de se taire parfois," which loosely translated means, "It's good to shut up sometimes. I almost giggled in the middle of my most dramatic, albeit wordy, monologue. Can you imagine?"

"I get like that sometimes at funerals."

"When I got off stage, I put my hand over my mouth and laughed into it, and that is when a fellow actor said to me, 'Have you heard? Marcelle is dead.' That is, the teacher, not the monkey."

"I hate seeing animals suffer. Like in those commercials. 'Every hour an animal is beaten or abused.' And then they play that music."

"Yes, well, this isn't about an animal."

"Good."

"But it hit me hard. I quickly went from laughter to the verge of tears, but the show had to go on. So, I pulled myself together, and after the show that night, instead of spending time with the cast at our favorite café, Divin' Art, I took a cab home and didn't say a word for the rest of the night, but simply opened the bottle of champagne I had been saving for the end of the show's run. At first, I lifted a real glass of champagne, then I had a better idea. I put the glass aside and lifted a mimed glass to the maestro, wherever he might be."

Vickie scrunched her face. "So, do you believe in ghosts?"

"That *was* my ghost story," Dr. Cannon said.

"That was your version of a ghost story? I guess it really is true, you can't be good at everything, like therapy and telling stories."

"I believe those we care about and those that care about us are with us forever. What's important is how their memory makes you feel. Comforted. Safe."

"Never thought about it that way."

"Do you have a safe place?" Dr. Cannon asked.

"You mean, like a panic room?" Vickie asked.

"A person, a place, an object, or even a memory that makes you feel safe, that you like to go to, not just when you are in distress. Maybe a place you can go to in your mind when you need to calm down," Dr. Cannon said.

"My house. It's not a big house, but we've got two bedrooms. And we have a little porch where we sit sometimes and a backyard with a kiddie pool we can put our feet in when it's summer. I don't want to leave there. That's the one thing that would rip me apart. If my mother sold that house I'd never talk to her again. Things can get messy outside. My life at home is messed up but perfect. My mom and I have a rhythm going," Vickie said.

"It sounds lovely."

"Yeah. And I'm sorry about your teacher."

"Thank you, Vickie."

"Ever thought of getting a monkey?"

"Oh, Vickie."

Vickie flashed a metal grin.

When Vickie left Dr. Cannon's office on the first floor, she headed directly toward the stairwell, climbing right past the fourth floor and all the way up to the sixth.

CHAPTER 24
Amends

Room 602
7:45 p.m.

E agen lay on his bed when the knock sounded on the door. "Go away." The door opened.

"That's your way of saying come in. Linda taught me that."

Vickie entered, noticeably better but still in her slippers and gown, shuffling her feet along the floor a little more than usual.

Eagen inhaled, his shoulders raising. "What do you want?"

"I heard what you did."

"Well, I told you I wasn't the one that planted the knife on you."

"I never thought you were."

Eagen's eyebrows rose.

"But I knew you would be the only person who would want to prove me wrong so bad, you might actually find out who did."

"I don't believe you. You're not that calculating."

"That knife fell outside the rec room window into the shrubs. You'd never take your shoes anywhere near that mucky mulch. It couldn't have been you."

Eagen grinned in reluctant agreement. "I still don't like you."

"The feeling is mutual."

"Good," Eagen said.

"Good."

"Good," Eagen said again.

"But Linda liked you." Vickie shifted her weight. "So, you can't be all that bad."

Eagen cut his eyes toward Vickie.

"Just, mostly bad," Vickie continued. Eagen snickered before he could help himself, and Vickie couldn't help but laugh as well. "Oh, that hurts," she said, grabbing her ribs.

"Did the orderlies punch you?"

"No, I pulled a muscle trying to body slam one of them."

"You know you're not a pro wrestler, right?"

"Hey, now. That might be one of the worst things you've ever said to me." A moment passed between them before Vickie continued, "So, how'd you do it?"

Eagen looked down at his pad and then back up at Vickie.

"You beat him with a notebook?"

"I drew something that unsettled him," Eagen said.

"Linda said you sketch fears or something, but that's BS, right?" Vickie asked.

"Tim didn't think so. He definitely didn't want anyone else to know what was on that paper I gave him. He heard us talking in the cafeteria about the knife and went looking for it. He slipped it in your pocket when he bumped into you in the hall."

Vickie's mouth gaped open. "What a snake."

As the smile melted off his face, Eagen picked at the black polish on his nails, his gaze back on the bed under him.

"So. What's mine? My fear?" Vickie asked, sticking her chest out a little as she spoke.

Eagen surged forward and grabbed his pad and charcoal from the nearby nightstand. His fingers flew back and forth as he whipped together a quick sketch, then handed it to Vickie.

She looked at it, turning it one way and then another.

"A spoon?" There was nothing else on the page.

"You're afraid they will run out of Jell-O," Eagen deadpanned. "I'm trying to be nice here? Come on."

"I was thinking. No matter the reason Linda wandered onto that road, she's not coming back," Vickie said.

"That's something we can agree on," Eagen answered.

"And people are just forgetting about her. Cleaning out her room, taking her chair. Nobody wants to talk about her. Friends don't forget each other. It's only been a month, and it's like she—"

Eagen stared at her with impassive eyes, waiting for the end of the sentence.

"Like she didn't just die. It's like she never existed," Vickie continued.

Eagen looked down, and this time, so did Vickie.

More than a moment passed as they shared the space, each drifting off into their own universe.

"Anyway, I owe you one."

Abruptly, Vickie took a quick breath in and out, and without another word, she walked toward the door.

Eagen's voice stopped her in her tracks. "You're wrong."

Vickie didn't turn, but waited to see what might come next.

"About what you said in the cafeteria; I am a good friend."

She never looked back at Eagen, but simply closed the door quietly behind her.

CHAPTER 25
Consequences

DAY 68 for Vickie

The Cafeteria

7:00 a.m.

The next morning, Vickie entered the cafeteria for breakfast, staring at the floor as she walked. When she rounded the corner and looked up, there was a crowd gathered in front of the brick wall. Surprisingly, all of pod 1 and pod 2 were there, along with a couple of other pods and a few staff members. Apparently, word was out about something, and it wasn't the oatmeal.

"What's going on?" she asked Squirt, coming to stand behind him. Although Vickie was only just above average height, she enjoyed looming like an evergreen tree over him. Squirt motioned with his head at the wall. Vickie followed his gaze and saw a giant, ten-foot-tall portrait of Linda's face painted in black, covering the entire brick wall. It looked a lot like her, eerily enough. There she was, smiling, hair down, not a care in the world, just like she had looked that morning in the wild blueberry field.

"Who did this?" Nurse Lilly asked, her voice devoid of its usual sunny cheer.

Vickie quickly looked around and saw Eagen's hands smudged in black paint. He put them behind his back, turning the palms to face inward. "He's a badass," Vickie said under her breath, then took a step forward.

"I did it," Vickie said.

Squirt's eyes widened, and his mouth dropped open. Before he had time to think it through, he stepped forward. "No, I did it."

Eagen's eyebrows shot up, and his face softened, his mouth parting slightly. Eagen was about to speak when Tracy looked at him, heading him off.

"It was me," Tracy and Julie chimed in simultaneously. They glanced at each other.

Nurse Lilly's eyes ping-ponged from person to person as the onlookers shifted their weight from leg to leg.

"Me too," Annie giggled.

Eagen stepped forward. "Stop it. I was the one."

Nurse Lilly surveyed the group once more, her eyes narrowing.

"All right, then," Nurse Lilly said. "If that's the way you want it." She clapped her hands together over her head. "Back to your tables."

Vickie and the others resumed their previous places in the cafeteria lines and at the long tables as a low, sustained murmur spread throughout the room.

"I think they'll all remember Linda for a while now. Don't you?" Eagen said. Vickie nodded, a bit impressed. She couldn't take her eyes off the giant sketch of Linda and could feel her watching over her, just like she said she would in the white room.

An hour later, the members of pod 1 stood shoulder to shoulder scrubbing the paint off the wall with small brushes and soap and water, working diligently and quietly.

Vickie saw Nurse Lilly, Mr. Fitch, and Dr. Cannon speaking in whispers off to the side. She tucked her hair behind her ear, tuning into their conversation as best she could, given the distance.

"Do you know how damaging this is?" Dr. Cannon said.

"To the premises?" Nurse Lilly asked.

"To those kids. They are being retraumatized," Dr. Cannon said. "They're already sensitive about Linda being forgotten. Now you're making them literally erase her."

"I agree. This is cruel," Mr. Fitch said, wringing his hands and speaking in a sheepish whisper, looking down, avoiding eye contact.

"It's not my idea. I'm just doing what I'm told," Nurse Lilly said. "But the image on the wall is disturbing for all the residents. It's got to be removed and Dr. Habsburg insisted the entire pod do it themselves. We've just got to move on."

Mr. Fitch fidgeted nervously.

"This isn't moving on," Dr. Cannon said. "Just deepening the wounds." She shook her head. "We've got to do something."

"I'm sorry. Dr. Habsburg was explicit in her instructions," Nurse Lilly said. "You know what she's like."

Dr. Cannon sighed. Mr. Fitch strode between the two women.

"Stop!" he shouted, then he paused and took a breath and spoke again in a more casual tone. "Stop, please."

The entire cafeteria fell suddenly silent, watching in amazed anticipation. Even Tim the bully, who was fond of tripping Mr. Fitch, paused with a spoon halfway to his mouth.

Mr. Fitch took the brush from Eagen's hand.

"I'll take care of it."

"Mr. Fitch," Nurse Lilly said.

"I'll take care of it." Speaking directly to Eagen, he said, "Go get your breakfast before they close the food lines."

The entire cafeteria erupted into whistled cheers. In contrast, Mr. Fitch's shoulders sank, and his face fell as he saw Nurse Lilly staring back at him. Not a trace of a smile graced her face.

Eagen and Vickie walked over to the food line together.

DAY 69 for Vickie
The Lobby
8:50 a.m.

The next day, several pods gathered in the lounge area before their first activity. They stole cautious glances at one another, unaccustomed to sharing extended periods of time in the same space.

Vickie and her fellow pod members sat closer together than usual. Annie was teaching Julie and Squirt how to make cup and saucer shapes from a string wrapped around her two inward-facing palms.

Tracy and Eagen reclined on a midcentury, tamarin-colored love seat together, though they busied themselves with independent activities. Tracy tapped a melody on his leg, while Eagen sketched, his focused intensity channeled through his charcoal pencil. His passionate strokes made Vickie curious. Finally, he tilted his pad in such a way that she caught a glimpse of a pair of piercing eyes on an otherwise blank page. Eagen outlined them over and over.

Vickie knew those eyes and the kind twinkle he captured.

Linda's watching.

Vickie sat on her usual wingback chair-throne. As usual, it provided her the perfect vantage point from which to see and hear everything and made her feel in control.

Newly formed pod 13, in contrast to her own group, remained as far from each other as possible, shooting suspicious, curiosity-laced stares at pod 1 and occasionally the rest of the room. Near the door, pod 2 sat together in the corner. Their leader, Tim, avoided Vickie's eyes several times. He had never approached her about framing her with the knife. No apology, no acknowledgment.

Vickie didn't need an apology from Tim or from anyone. She only wanted everyone to know the truth about the knife and what really happened. And thanks to Eagen, they did.

In the same way, all of pod 1 knew Eagen had painted Linda on the cafeteria wall. But he had only done what Vickie would have done herself if she had had the idea or his talent.

A few staff members gathered by the reception desk. Dr. Cannon, Nurse Dorothy, and Nurse Lilly talked in whispers, but the acoustics in the room funneled their voices right to where Vickie sat. She soaked up the words like a sponge.

Vickie pretended to read while she concentrated, noticing the book she'd chosen was upside down at one point. She righted the book, then glanced around to see if anyone else had seen.

"That's one brave man," Nurse Dorothy said.

"I didn't think he had it in him," Nurse Fran said.

"What do you think will happen to him?"

"He was in Dr. Habsburg's office when I came in this morning."

Vickie's posture straightened and the book slipped in her lap. She caught it before it went over her knees.

"That's never a good sign," Nurse Lilly said.

"I heard he spent the night scrubbing the wall after the kids went to sleep," Nurse Dorothy said.

Vickie felt her chest expand as her heart filled with warmth. She needed to find Mr. Fitch and say thank you.

"Well--" Dr. Cannon stopped midsentence when Mr. Fitch approached, carrying a cardboard box filled with personal belongings. "Oh, no," she said when their eyes met.

"I—Well, I . . ." Mr. Fitch trailed off as his chest caved. He lowered his head like a wilting flower.

"I'm sorry, Mr. Fitch," Nurse Lilly said sincerely. "I tried to warn you."

"Any idea what you'll do?" Nurse Dorothy asked.

He shrugged, eyes welling up. "Somebody had to do something. I had to say something."

All the residents in the lounge area had stopped conversing and stared at the cardboard box in Mr. Fitch's arms. Their faces said they knew the meaning of the box as well. Mr. Fitch turned to the doors, walking by Vickie and pod 1. As he passed, they each said goodbye, some with more feeling than others, but Vickie spoke the loudest.

"Bye, Mr. Fitch."

He nodded at them all in turn. Pausing in front of her, he said in a whisper, "Vickie. Don't forget." He stared at her so earnestly that Vickie's mouth opened slightly as if she were about to speak, but nothing came out. "And keep looking."

She nodded, still wordless.

As Mr. Fitch passed pod 2, Tim stuck his foot out as he had done countless times before. One of his cronies hit him in the head with a loud thwack. Tim withdrew his foot.

"Goodbye, Mr. Fitch," the other boy said, meeting the man's surprised glance. The rest of the boys followed suit, offering farewells.

Last but not least, Tim threw up his hand in a sort of wave. Mr. Fitch offered him a smile of resigned contentment as he took a deep breath and opened the french doors. He scrunched his eyelids closed when the sunlight hit them. "My, it's bright out here."

Mr. Fitch walked down the front steps in his telltale clumsy gait and disappeared out of Vickie's line of sight.

CHAPTER 26
Bonding

Room 602
11:30 p.m.

Well past the time for night checks, the darkness of the starless sky covered the manor like a heavy blanket until lightning flashed over the grounds, penetrating all the rooms.

Tracy plucked out a new song on his guitar on his bed. Squirt studied at his desk, thumbing through a coding book, and Eagen lay in his bed, arms folded, staring ahead, deathly still.

Tracy noticed Squirt shiver like a hairless cat, but pretended not to. Tracy noticed more than people gave him credit for.

"Lightning kills twenty people a year," Eagen said, still staring forward, expressionless, except for the twinkle in his eye.

The sound of rustling wind bled through the closed windows. What was that?" Squirt asked.

"I didn't hear anything," Tracy said.

"Probably a demon. Or ghosts. Or the ghost of a demon," Eagen teased.

"Stop. There's no such thing as ghosts. He's just taking the piss, Squirt," Tracy said.

"Actually, I've done the math. People could be like computer code. Code doesn't disappear completely, even when you delete it. It's always archived somewhere on your computer and can be retrieved with the right training. So, ghosts are scientifically plausible," Squirt said.

Another bright flash of lightning shot through the room. Eagen spoke aloud an Edgar Allan Poe poem from memory.

```
Back into the chamber, turning,
all my soul within me burning,
Soon again I heard a tapping somewhat louder than
before.
```

Tracy rolled his eyes and shook his head as Eagen continued unflustered.

```
Back into the chamber, turning,
all my soul within me burning,
Soon again I heard a tapping somewhat louder than
before.
```

```
Surely, said I, surely that is something at my
window lattice;
Let me see, then, what thereat is, and this mystery
explore—
Let my heart be still a moment and this mystery
explore;—
```

The lights in the room flickered. Squirt's eyes slowly panned from left to right to left again.

Tracy put down his guitar. "I've got an idea."

Room 402
11:30 p.m.

The darkness of the starless sky covered the manor like a heavy blanket. Lightning flashed in the sky over the grounds.

190

"One one thousand, two one thousand . . ." Julie mumbled under her breath, sitting in her bed, holding a book of Poe's poems. Annie rocked back and forth in her own bed, knees drawn up to her chest, while Vickie played a game of solitaire in the light of the tiny bedside lamp she shared with Julie.

Thunder boomed and crackled.

Annie jerked imperceptibly, although Vickie saw her flinch from the corner of her eye. Vickie missed little that went on around her.

"It'll be over soon. Storms never last long here," Vickie said, loud enough for Annie to hear.

A branch tapped against the window. The shadow of the tree outside seemed to come alive in the room, animated by the wind, writhing in all directions.

Julie read a Poe poem from her book as a bright flash from the lightning lit up the room.

```
Back into the chamber turning,
all my soul within me burning,
Soon again I heard a tapping somewhat louder than
before.

Surely, said I, surely that is something at my
window lattice;
Let me see, then, what thereat is, and this mystery
explore—
Let my heart be still a moment and this mystery
explore;—
```

The lights in the room flickered. Annie flopped over and curled up in a tight ball on her bed.

The tapping of the branch on the window grew louder and more insistent.

"Let my heart be still a moment and this mystery
explore ..."

Julie put her book down and walked slowly toward the window.
Annie whimpered.

"Stop it. You're scaring Annie," Vickie said, noticing Annie's reaction.

Tap. Tap. Tap.

As Julie got closer, she stared out the window with an exaggerated gesture and breathed a dramatic sigh of relief.

"'Tis the wind and nothing more!" Julie said, staring wide-eyed at Annie, who now stood beside her.

Suddenly, the window blew open, sending leaves into the room along with a large black bird fluttering its wings against the wind and coming to rest on the window ledge. Julie jumped in surprise. The bird stayed on the ledge, watching.

"Oh my God!" Julie exclaimed.

"Geez!" Vickie screamed.

"There's a pigeon in our room!" Julie said.

"It's Linda," Annie whispered.

Vickie climbed from her bed and approached the window, pulling the neck of her pajama top together to warm herself in the cool Maine night air.

"I know that bird. It's a crow or something. When Linda would have meals in the room and wouldn't eat, she'd feed most of her food to this bird," Vickie said. "Shoo, shoo! Linda's gone. No more handouts. Shoo!"

The bird obeyed, flapping its wings vigorously until it safely cleared the window.

"Don't go, Linda! Take me with you," Annie pleaded as she reached for the bird, who was no longer there.

Vickie closed the window with a *ka-thunk*.

Everyone was now quiet, not sure of what to make of the interruption.

Leaves were strewn all over the floor as the wind continued its eerie assault against the manor.

Thud.

The door slammed open.

This time, they all jumped.

"What the—Tracy!" Vickie exclaimed.

"Well, are you coming?" Tracy asked, poking his head through the open door. Had it been anyone else, Vickie would have had a few choice words for them.

"It's time we went on an adventure," Tracy said, raising a brow when he spied the scattered leaves on the floor.

"Yay!" Annie said.

"The wind is wild," Vickie said, explaining the leaves.

"We'll be wilder," Tracy said.

"Do you know how much trouble we could get into if we get caught?" Julie asked.

"So, we won't get caught," Tracy said.

Julie's eyes twinkled. "Where are we going?"

"Deep into the darkness," Tracy said, widening his eyes into his best crazy stare.

Vickie, Annie, and Julie didn't hesitate to follow Tracy.

Moments later, they moved as a cluster through the deserted hallway, dodging Angelo, who headed into the stairwell just as they were about to turn the corner.

"Check out that bloke's arms," Tracy whispered.

Angelo's short-sleeved white shirt was folded at the cuffs, making room for his bulging biceps.

"Massive," Squirt mouthed.

"Sun's out, guns out," Tracy said.

"There's no sun," Vickie said.

"When you look like that, the sun's always shining on you," Squirt said in awe.

"Yeah," Julie said, biting her lip, a dreamy, dazed look in her eyes.

"That doesn't even make sense." Vickie shoved Julie. "And someone please hose her down."

Annie giggled quietly, enraptured by the adventure.

The members of pod 1 finally arrived in the music classroom, where Squirt, Eagen, Tracy, Julie, Annie, and Vickie all stood in front of a locked closet. Vickie's hands fidgeted by her side, like she was solving two tiny Rubik's Cubes in each palm. Dr. Cannon called it cricketing and said it was a coping mechanism.

Julie stared at Tracy, widening her eyes as if she were poking him with her eyeballs.

"Poor Mr. Fitch," Annie said, rubbing the music room door like a cat.

"He's free," Tracy said.

"Now what?" Julie asked.

"We're stuck here at The Hill, so we might as well have a little fun," Tracy said, flashing his crooked grin.

"I'm down to have fun," Julie said, her spine melting like butter as she almost fell into Tracy. "But calling it 'The Hill' doesn't make it any cooler."

Squirt flicked on a floor lamp near the closet and Julie closed the door softly behind them, so as to minimize the light that spilled out. Tracy nodded to Vickie, who pulled a key ring from her pocket and fumbled until she found a small key, then used it to open the closet.

"I think Mr. Fitch would approve of a little breaking and entering," Vickie said.

Julie's entire face lit up underneath her china-white skin. "How'd you get that?"

"I took it. It's what I do," Vickie said, expressionless.

Tracy grabbed the guitar from the closet; the others grabbed miscellaneous instruments, like pulling toys from the treasure chest at the dentist's office — the prizes for enduring the pain. Eagen was the only one who abstained, preferring to sketch on his pad.

"Vickie's got a key to just about everywhere," Squirt said, beaming.

Eventually, they found their way into a circle of sorts, seated on the floor. They tinkered with their instruments. Tracy was the only one purposefully tuning, trying to bring the instrument back into some semblance of in-tune.

Vickie sat cross-legged next to Tracy, almost close enough for their knees to touch a couple times. Electricity shot through her body with every unintentional graze of his leg.

"So, is music a career path for you or a hobby?" Vickie asked, awkwardly making conversation.

"Option C. He uses it to get laid," Eagen said.

"Really? Think you could teach me? Maybe just some chords?" Squirt asked, perking up.

"You'll need more than a guitar, Squirt," Vickie said.

"I'm going to go with option D. I just feel like it and do it. Not so structured as a career or hobby. And definitely not for sex," Tracy said.

"Are you going to play something?" Julie asked.

"Don't encourage him," Eagen said.

"What do you want to hear?" Tracy asked.

"I like anything you play," Annie said.

"How about the Beatles? Favorite Beatles song?" Tracy asked.

"If you ever catch me listening to the Beatles voluntarily, shoot me," Eagen said.

"Vickie? Favorite?" Tracy asked.

"I don't know many of their songs," Vickie said. "Just the ones on the two albums my mother had and played over and over."

"Well, we'll have to change that. Your Beatles education begins now," Tracy said.

"All You Need Is Love," Julie said.

Tracy sang the first verse.

"How about you, Squirt?" Tracy asked.

"I Saw Her Standing There," Squirt said.

Again, Tracy happily obliged with a verse.

"Someone make it stop," Eagen said.

"You're funny, mate," Tracy said.

"I think you could be a rock star if you wanted," Annie said.

"You've got just the right kind of sob story for it, that's for sure," Eagen said.

"And the hair," Julie said.

"I don't want my hair to define me. I'm not a consequence of my hair; my hair is a consequence of me. You know?" Tracy said, tussling his hair a little and winking.

"You have a favorite Beatles song?" Vickie asked quietly, as if just for him.

Tracy strummed.

"I'd have to go album by album, but if we're just saying one? This one. I like this one a lot. It's sad and lighthearted at the same time," Tracy said.

"Like you," Vickie said, whispering to him.

Tracy smiled. He sang a lyric or two in a slower version of "Blackbird" that seemed sadder than the original.

Still strumming, he paused to speak again. "This one's for Mr. Fitch."

"And for Linda," Annie added.

As Tracy continued singing, one by one, the teens raised an instrument and joined in. Julie played the tambourine. Annie was on the triangle, Squirt played bongos. Vickie pulled out her instrument, the cowbell.

"Cowbell. Yes!" Tracy said.

Eagen sketched, but even he began tapping his pencil to their somewhat harmonious rendition.

DAY 70 for Vickie
Room 402
3:33 a.m.

Early that morning, after everyone had tucked themselves into their respective beds, they all fell asleep with contented smiles spread across their faces, except for the most jovial of the group, Annie. She sat close to the pipe that ran up the wall beside her bed, cradling it, giggling softly. Just above her head was a window.

Annie placed one of her hands on one of the panes.

"Linda, are you there?" Annie whispered.

She removed her hand from the window and her handprint slowly disappeared, fading like the embers of a campfire.

Annie slid back down the wall just after the outline of two other handprints appeared, then disappeared, as if they had never been there.

SCAN ME

PART THREE

My Friends
Are Your Friends

Assessment and Plan

Provider: Blueberry Hill Home for Troubled Youth, LLC   **Client Name:** Tracy Hunter
Group Assignment: Pod #1   **Session Number:** #1

Diagnosis: Mild PTSD

Treatment

Intake Protocol: Clinical Assessment   **Medications:** Fluoxetine 20 mg/day,
                    Self-Assessment Questionnaire   *as per* Dr. Mariska Habsburg, M.D.

Short-Term Goals for Client (2 Weeks):
1. Encourage physical and creative outlets, like swimming and private music lessons.
2. Form positive pod relationships.
3. Journal feelings around death.

Long-Term Goals (3 Months):
1. Openly discuss feelings around mother's death.
2. Display ability to dialogue about father's romantic interests without aggression.

Session Notes

Body Language, Facial Patterns: Frequent eye contact, presents as open and even charming. Too early to know if he uses charm as a form of manipulation.

Summary:
1. Reluctant to discuss recent death of mother. Posture stiffened, jaw clenched when topic was introduced. Possibly avoided grief and other affect related to her death.
2. Tapped a rhythm with the pencil on the desk, presumably to self-soothe.
3. No visible remorse for violent attempted assault that resulted in injury of a pet.
4. Defends against negative affect with jokes and deflection. When asked if he exercised regularly, his response was, "I exorcise daily. But only my own demons." When pressed further, he reported a consistent regimen of cardio and weight training.
5. When asked how he identifies, race for instance, he replied, "relay," as in relay race.

Other Observations/Comments:
- Father reports violent outbursts that led to physical harm of father's girlfriend. More information needed.
- Father also cites rebelliousness, challenging authority, attempted assault of father's girlfriend with an automobile.
- Unsure if violence is isolated to father's girlfriend.

Client Signature: *Tracy Hunter*   **Primary Caregiver 1:** *Mark Hunter*
(Age 14 and up)   Tracy Hunter   Mark Hunter
                                                                (Father)
Primary Caregiver 2: _____   **Therapist Signature:** *Ara Cannon*
                    N/A   Dr. Ara Cannon, Ph.D.

CHAPTER 27
The Bored and The Board

The First Floor
8:50 a.m.

A cognitive haze clung to many of the residents most mornings, likely the residual effects from the prior day's medication. Vickie preferred the morning for that reason; everyone was more subdued.

Just after the morning meeting, Vickie and Julie made their way toward the lobby. Vickie's mouth stretched into an unrestrained, wide-mouthed yawn that she refused to hide. Hiding things required energy. She figured it didn't make sense to expend resources covering something up if you were already tired to begin with.

Julie sighed. "I didn't think that session would ever end."

"How do you think I felt? I had to sit next to you," Vickie said.

"And if I eat one more bowl of oatmeal, I'm going to throw up," Julie said. "I don't even know why I got up for it this morning."

"Try it with raisins. They let you sprinkle on as many as you want."

"This place is so boring," Julie said.

Vickie plodded ahead, eyes forward. Tiredness sunk into her shuffling feet, making them heavier than usual. "How could anyone get bored here? The days are packed with activities."

"The same activities. Same everything. Same food. Same schedule.

Same people." Julie glanced in Vickie's direction. "No offense. Every day. Same. Same. Same."

"It's nice to know what's in store day to day. And you mean to tell me sneaking into the music room wasn't different enough for you?" Vickie asked.

Julie shrugged.

Vickie spoke with an elevated tone. "Four kids disappeared, my best friend died, I was framed and locked in a padded room. A teacher just got fired for standing up for us. What kind of life are you used to? I'd like a little less excitement, myself."

Vickie glared at Julie, and Julie reciprocated with a mocking stare, twisting her head back and forth, drilling her eyes into Vickie.

A laugh broke through Vickie's icy façade, and Julie joined in until it petered into silence.

"That was weird," Julie said.

"Yeah."

"I think we just shared a moment."

"Don't let it go to your head."

The pair continued their stroll right by Nurse Lilly at the reception desk. Vickie paused abruptly, her body stiffening.

"What's wrong?" Julie asked.

"Something's different. Very different," Vickie said, all senses firing on yellow alert.

"What?"

"Nurse Lilly. She didn't say hello."

"Maybe she's busy," Julie said.

"She always says hello to me in the morning. And this next thing is bad. Very bad."

Julie waited in anticipation for the next words from Vickie's mouth.

Vickie continued, "She's not smiling."

"Maybe she's on her period."

"Nothing fazes that woman. Not even cramps," Vickie said.

"That's inhuman."

"Worse than inhuman. It's optimism."

Julie nodded in agreement.

"She's always smiling and upbeat," Vickie continued, processing things, her hands by her sides, fingers wiggling like she played an invisible piano. Vickie spied something that made her eyes widen. "Yep, this is serious. I thought that hair of hers was a helmet. It's never out of place."

A sprig of hair hung in Nurse Lilly's face as she spoke to two men wearing shirts monogrammed with the name of a catering company. They carried what looked like trays of food. Nurse Lilly directed them with a few words and a pointed finger until they disappeared around the corner.

Vickie noticed the other nurses also seemed more frantic than usual, moving quickly from task to task, barely stopping to chat with one another or gossip.

Vickie watched as the grandmother clock ticked out the seconds. Ten minutes passed.

The rest of the pod joined Vickie and Julie in the lounge, waiting to traipse out to the gardens for scheduled pruning. They were only allowed to head into the garden after Nurse Lilly gave the green light.

"She's two minutes late," Vickie whispered.

Julie rolled her eyes. "It's two minutes."

"She's never late."

When Nurse Lilly finally appeared again from around the corner, she jerked to a halt in front of the assembled teens, her entire manner unfocused and distracted. All of them perched or reclined in various relaxed positions on the furniture and the floor, in sharp contrast to the bustle and frenzy taking place across the room. Vickie took a deep breath and exhaled, her shoulders relaxing in anticipation of the quiet the gardens would provide, despite it being 'yardwork.' She placed her hands on the chair arms to give herself a push out of the comfy seat, ready to thankfully resume her routine.

"No horticulture today," Nurse Lilly said.

"Yes!" Squirt exclaimed, fist-pumping the air.

Nurse Lilly pursed her lips and wriggled her mouth to one side. "Make yourselves comfortable, read a book, find a puzzle, something until your next activity."

A shaky grin spread across Vickie's face as the muscles under her right eye jumped. Julie sank deeper into the overstuffed chair, audibly delighting in the change.

"Different is yummy," Julie said, touching her tongue to her lips in mock ecstasy.

"Stop," Vickie said.

"What?"

"Never lick your lips like that again. Gross," Vickie said.

An old, beat-up car pulled around the circle drive, stopping in front of the manor. The driver steadied himself before getting out of the vehicle. Through the french doors, Vickie recognized the man by his walk, a sort of forward stumble, like the old pony in the stables that no one rode anymore because he was literally on his last leg.

"What does he want? And what's he driving? They'll be arriving any minute," Nurse Lilly said. "Angelo!"

Angelo's whole body tensed, ready to spring into action, when Nurse Lilly called his name.

"Help me get rid of him and that car!" Nurse Lilly barked.

In contrast, Nurse Fran didn't seem as bothered as the other members of the staff. She craned her neck so she could get a better look at the car in question that dared disgrace the driveway with its puttering. "I used to have a car like that. Lots of good memories in that back seat," Nurse Fran said to Nurse Dorothy as Angelo dutifully followed Nurse Lilly out the french doors onto the front porch. Nurse Dorothy's eyes widened at Nurse Fran's nostalgic comment, and a surprised giggle slipped from her lips.

"Nurse Fran!" Nurse Dorothy exclaimed.

"What? We were all young and foolish once."

Vickie continued watching the confrontation through the glass doors. Nurse Lilly did most of the talking to the old reporter, who stared off into the distance. For a moment, the rumpled man turned his head toward the french doors and stared right at Vickie. She wasn't sure if he really saw her, but in any case, she stared right back at him through the glass. She excelled at staring contests.

It was only a matter of minutes before the old reporter was back in his car, rattling around the circle drive in a cloud of black smoke, leaving the smell of gas fumes behind. Nurse Lilly and Angelo entered the manor victorious and closed the glass doors behind them.

"Thank God," Nurse Lilly said. No sooner had Nurse Lilly breathed a sigh of relief than a large limousine pulled up, then another, and another.

"It's a whole herd," Vickie thought aloud.

Julie's eyes widened and she moved to get a better view of the procession.

"Sit up, everyone," Nurse Lilly said, the forced enthusiasm in her voice pushing the words out, "and just pretend to be—happy!" No movement met her request beyond a sea of eye rolls. It was in their DNA to do the opposite of whatever an adult asked. If anything, their faces became even more sour.

Nurse Lilly motioned for nearby staff members to stand by her side at the lobby entrance, as if they were the wedding party greeting guests in a reception line. She reached up with a shaky hand to smooth the stray curl back into place, only to have it pop right back to its original position.

Two women and three men, all expensively dressed, entered. They were so comfortable in their tailored business suits they moved in them like second skins.

"Welcome back to Blueberry Hill," Nurse Lilly said, a bright, but nervous pitch coloring her voice.

Vickie and the rest of the pod watched intently. This was the next best thing to TV — unexpected visitors! Vickie only recognized one of the men, who appeared friendlier than the rest. Kent Johnson, the Korean American man from the paper she snatched from Mr. Fitch, who was running for re-election as mayor, vigorously shook the hands of the staff lined up in front him.

"Where's Dr. Habsburg?" one of the fancy ladies asked.

"She'll be along shortly. In the meantime, may I escort you into the sunroom for some refreshments?" Nurse Lilly said.

"I don't have a great deal of time to wait," said the other woman, stuffed so tightly into her business suit she looked as if the buttons might fly off at any second.

"Understood. We are still expecting one more arrival. Angelo, do you mind letting Dr. Habsburg know our guests are here?"

"Do I have to?" sighed Angelo, now standing next to Nurse Fran.

Nurse Lilly laughed nervously, then whipped around, flaying Angelo with her stare.

"Better you than me," Nurse Fran said under her breath, just before Angelo departed.

Kent Johnson looked at Vickie and flashed his overly whitened teeth. *I hate the way Koreans are always staring at me, like they don't know what to make of me.* At least in Queens, people came in all flavors, but in Maine, anything that wasn't vanilla stood out.

Vickie stared back so aggressively it made Kent's eyes flutter as his smile melted from his face, dripping onto the floor. Julie noticed, a laugh bubbling out of her.

"Hey, that's my 'screw you' face. Get your own!" Julie joked.

Vickie drilled the 'screw you' glare into Julie. Julie shot it back. After several rounds back and forth, Tracy intervened. "So, is this a rumble? 'Cause it's worse than a *Westside Story* dance-off."

"It's a face-off," Squirt snort-giggled, eliciting an eye roll from both

Julie and Vickie.

"Who are the suits?" Vickie whispered to Tracy, seated next to her.

"That is a board of directors," Tracy answered. "I'd recognize the type anywhere. Rich and powerful and important, at least in their own minds. But really, they're just munchkins come to pay tribute to the Wicked Witch of the East."

Vickie nodded knowingly. She knew who the witch of the manor was. "I hate munchkins," she said.

"What? But they are so peppy," Tracy said.

"Exactly, I hate peppy."

"And they like lollipops and flowers," Tracy said.

Vickie whipped her eyes toward Tracy.

"Let me guess. You hate lollipops and flowers," Tracy continued.

"I love lollipops. Who doesn't like lollipops? I'm not a monster," Vickie snapped back.

"Good. I hate monsters." Tracy cocked his sideways grin at her.

CHAPTER 28
Outrunning the Sun

The Cafeteria
11:40 a.m.

Having just finished lunch in the cafeteria, the members of pod 1 were both figuratively and literally shaken when the entire room vibrated. Even the rectangle folding tables trembled. Vickie held on to her Jell-O cup to keep it in place on the table.

"Earthquake!" Squirt said, nervously half joking.

"I'll bet you didn't have that on your Blueberry Hill bingo card," Tracy joked.

"Seriously, what was that?" Squirt asked. They all inched toward the window.

"That, my friends, is the Wicked Witch of the West. And she's much worse than the other one," Tracy said.

They stared out the window beside their table as a helicopter landed on a stretch of pavement in front of the stables. An exotic, middle-aged woman alighted, wearing dark glasses and a flowing scarf that trailed her neck like smoke. The figure moved as if she were wind herself, undulating sensually, lapping up every sensory thing around her. Julie clasped her hands together, eyes sparkling and fixed on the woman's every move.

"Hubba-hubba," Squirt uttered, mouth open.

"I want to be her when I grow up," Julie added, gobsmacked.

"Be careful what you wish for," Tracy responded. "It takes the blood of many virgins and newborn lambs to keep her looking that way."

The Rec Room
1:00 p.m.

Chaos. Madness. Heartburn. Vickie was fine with free time. But this was unexpected free time. In other words, it didn't appear on the schedule — anywhere! A wave of nausea wafted over her like an unpleasant smell. She closed her eyes for a moment and breathed.

Dr. Cannon would be proud.

Tracy, Squirt, Annie, and Julie played pool in teams, giggling and high-fiving after each shot. Pods garnered more freedoms if their collective behavior improved or remained positive. Pod 1 had earned the privilege of playing pool unsupervised. Vickie played solitaire with a deck of well-worn cards, and as usual, Eagen sketched in an artist pad. Tracy spoke to Vickie in between shots.

"I rarely see you playing cards," Tracy remarked to Vickie.

"Only solitaire," Vickie said.

"The misanthropists' game," Tracy said.

"If that means I hate group games. That's me. Just call me Ms. Anne Thorough."

"And always pissed," Eagen said.

"Ha. Ms. Anne. Thoroughly. Pissed," Squirt laughed. "That does sound like you."

Vickie stared Squirt down and he immediately stopped laughing. Tracy looked out the window, watching the limousines exit round the drive, one by one.

"There goes my something different," Julie said under her breath, her face falling. "Why are they leaving so soon?"

Tracy handed Julie the stick to take her turn. She poked at the white ball ineffectually, sending it banging forward without regard.

"I say good riddance," Tracy said.

Just then, Nurse Dorothy entered the room. "You have a visitor, Tracy. Such a captivating woman."

Julie perked up again.

"Captivating woman? Oooooh. Go Tracy!" Squirt said.

Various oooohs and ahhhhs echoed throughout the rec room in the relentless way teenagers teased one another. Tracy froze.

"It's your mother," Nurse Dorothy added, smiling. In fact, everyone but Tracy giggled. But their laughter dropped off as if falling over the side of a cliff once they registered the look on Tracy's face.

"I didn't think they allowed parents to visit. Good to be rich, I guess," Vickie said.

"She's on the board here," Tracy said between clenched teeth.

"The woman from the helicopter? Hubba-hubba," Squirt said.

"She said she was my mother? Nurse Dorothy, that woman is not my mother or anything close to it. My real mother's been dead for eight months. Can I deny the visit?" Tracy asked.

"Come on. Let's go, Tracy. It'll be over before you know it," Nurse Dorothy replied.

"Save me! Someone? Anyone?" Tracy joked dryly, tugging at an imaginary noose around his neck and sticking his tongue out to one side, trailing behind Nurse Dorothy.

Vickie's body tensed. She knew a joke usually sprang from some truth. Her friend needed her help.

The First Floor
1:25 p.m.

Just past the reception area there were a couple of unused office spaces left to house stuffed cabinets that bulged with office supplies and other miscellaneous items. A large, midcentury wooden desk took up most of one of the rooms, flanked by a high-backed swivel chair.

Beatrice sat, staring out the window behind the desk with her back to Tracy as he entered. Nurse Dorothy knocked lightly before escorting Tracy inside, then closing the heavy door softly behind her.

Tracy stood quietly, unmoving, defiant, and ready for a fight. After a moment, Beatrice swiveled around to face him, smiling, taking Tracy's measure in one long, sweeping glance.

"Why are you turning around like that? Oh, you're an evil villain. I get it. Congratulations on landing that role," Tracy said.

"Hello, Tracy, darling," Beatrice said in a muddled European and Brazilian accent.

"What brings you to the neighborhood?" Tracy asked.

"You, my sweetie. How are you doing?"

"Just ducky."

"That's wonderful news. Your father will be so happy to hear that."

"Well, if he called, he would hear it for himself."

"I can see you're blossoming."

"Mmmm. What do you really want, Beatrice?"

Beatrice fiddled with the antique pen and ink set on the desk, tickling her arm with the feathered pen. "We're going to Europe for a special trip, and I didn't want you to hear it from someone else."

"What do I care? Bon voyage."

"And things will be different when we return. Adjustments will be necessary when you are released from this facility. So, I wondered when

211

that might be?"

"I'd really love to speak to my father directly. Because, well, it's my life, and he's the one paying for this—facility. I'm not sure why you're involved at all in this conversation."

"Because. I'm family."

"No. You're not."

"Your father and I are going to Europe for our honeymoon."

Tracy's face fell as all the air seemed to vacate his lungs at once. His knees quivered.

"Are you all right, dear? Shall I call one of the nurses?"

Tracy looked away toward the doorway and saw the shadow of someone's legs through the crack at the bottom of the closed door. The door opened and Vickie entered. He thanked Vickie for interrupting with his eyes.

"Knock, knock. Coming through. Don't mind me. Just needed a journal. They make us journal twice a day, and I write big. Don't know why they keep the extras in here. Ah, found it. Tracy, don't forget we've got that thing to do. So. Chop, chop."

Tracy smiled, his face more relaxed now, even chuckling a little. "Thanks. This shouldn't take long."

Turning toward Beatrice, Vickie continued, "You *are* kind of hot. As you were." She bowed as she exited.

"Charming." Beatrice reapplied her lipstick as she continued talking. "Your father would've come, but it's hard for him. Seeing you makes him feel bad about himself. Like he's failed."

"Can I go now?" Tracy asked.

Beatrice's face contorted.

"Let me tell you something. Some people are born into families. Some are chosen to be a part of a family. Your father loves me very much. He chose me. We have a long history together, as you well know. And I have a profound influence over him. Embrace this family. All of us. When

212

you're ready to embrace us all, then you're welcome, always welcome, to live with us at the estate."

"Does that mean I can come back home?" Tracy asked.

"Hmmm." Beatrice looked Tracy up and down, then leaned forward. "Tell me three things you admire. About me."

Tracy inhaled deeply.

"Seriously?" Tracy stood up straighter. "I think you're a brilliant actress."

"Thank you, darling."

"Very intelligent. Very organized. You—"

"That's three. No need to go on."

"You put them all together and you get a manipulative sociopath," Tracy continued.

"I see. It was lovely visiting." Beatrice stood, walking around the desk. "Well, I'm off to pack for Europe. Come, give your stepmother a kiss on the cheek."

"I'd rather not."

Beatrice kissed her pointer finger and placed it on Tracy's cheek.

"Well, that's going to leave a rash," Tracy said.

"Tracy, I'll either see you at home when we return or we'll visit you at a nice boarding school far, far, far, far away. Ciao."

Beatrice threw her scarf around her neck and put her sunglasses on, adjusting them with a wiggle before exiting, leaving Tracy alone. Tracy heard Beatrice and Nurse Lilly speaking through the open door, their voices trailing down the hallway.

"Do tell Mariska I send my regrets that I can't stay longer. Next time," Beatrice said.

"It's Dr. Habsburg. You know she hates it when you call her by her first name."

"You'd think she'd be used to it by now. This place never changes. Good to see you, Lillian. You look great. You must finally be moisturizing."

Beatrice's retreating footsteps faded after a few seconds. Tracy slumped a little, deflated.

"You doing all right?" Vickie asked as she entered once again, peeping around the doorway.

"I don't want to talk about it."

"You've come to the right place. I hate chitchat. Sit down."

Vickie replaced Beatrice in the desk chair nearest the window and pulled out a deck of cards, shuffling them like a pro. She now faced Tracy, who sat on the opposite side of the enormous desk.

"I thought you only played solitaire?"

"I'm over that game. Don't tell anyone, but I think the dealer is cheating."

Tracy laughed. "That doesn't surprise me."

"New game? What's your pleasure?" Vickie asked.

"Doesn't matter."

"Spoken like a real fifteen-year-old," Vickie said.

"Sixteen-year-old, thank you very much."

"I stand corrected. And gin rummy it is."

An hour went by, but it felt like only minutes to Vickie. The duo lost track of time laughing and drawing cards, talking about everything but Tracy's new family member. Tracy's shoulders relaxed the more they talked and played. These unscheduled moments with Tracy were surprisingly enjoyable for Vickie. Her chest didn't tighten once. She had just recognized her level of comfort when Tracy stood up, but he wasn't moving toward the door. Something was wrong. He just looked at her. She stood and looked back at him in awkward silence for a moment, until he finally spoke.

"Thanks," he said.

"For what?"

"For making me feel better."

"Uhhh, well," Vickie said.

"You're good at that."

"Nah. I'm only good at one thing. Being Vickie Bartolucci."

They continued looking at each other, nodding to mask their self-consciousness.

"I feel like we should—"

"Get going?"

"Yeah."

"Yeah."

As they left, they paused to look at the wall outside the office lined with framed photos spanning decades. Dr. Habsburg appeared in most of the photos, cutting ribbons, shaking hands, speaking from lecterns. Tracy's hand grazed Vickie's as they both pointed at the same picture. A fluttery tingle welled up from deep within her and danced along her skin, leaving goose bumps behind, like she had touched something electric.

Quick, make a joke.

"I didn't know Dr. Habsburg ever got out. I always imagined she slept in a coffin in her office."

"A place like this doesn't run on kindness."

"Tell me about it," Vickie agreed.

"You need rich friends to kick in dollars and powerful friends to look the other way," Tracy said.

"You know a lot about being rich," Vickie said.

"They drown you in it from the time you're born. You sink or swim."

"You seem to be doing all right."

"I hang on to the side of the pool blowing bubbles."

Tracy peered closer at a photo hanging on the wall of Beatrice with Dr. Habsburg.

"So, what are you going to do when you get out of here?"

"I'd like to head west. You know, drive until the sun sets on me. 'Cause I'm sixteen now. I can get my license soon." He smirked and glanced at her.

"Don't rub it in," Vickie said.

"I'd drive and drive, make the day last as long as I can. Outrun the sun."

Vickie looked at him admiringly. "Outrun the sun?"

"Try to. Gotta live through this first. How about you?"

"Well, I'm fifteen, so I take the bus. Public transportation has never outrun anybody or anything. I don't know, I'll probably just go back to doing what I was doing before. Back to my house. My mom."

"The simple life."

"Yeah. But I wouldn't mind a ride to work now and then. Saves on bus fare. When, you know, you're not outrunning shit, how about swinging by and giving me a lift?" Vickie punched Tracy on the shoulder.

"You got it. And ow-w-w-w!" Tracy grabbed his arm.

Vickie turned back to the wall and picked out a recent photo of some of the nurses, including Nurses Lilly, Dorothy, and Fran, standing behind Dr. Habsburg, who held her arms outstretched in front of the Blueberry Hill sign.

"But, before I leave this place, I've got some things to figure out," Vickie said.

"Don't we all?"

"Not about myself. About them." Vickie nodded toward the photo. "And this place."

CHAPTER 29
Crouching Tiger

```
The First Floor
6:00 p.m.
```

Vickie knelt with her ear to a pipe near the staff lounge as Julie approached. "What are you doi—"

"Shhh," Vickie said, with her finger pressed to her lips. Julie crouched beside her. "Staff lounge. How do you think I stay two steps ahead?" she whispered.

"That's not the lounge, that's a pipe," Julie said sarcastically.

"Don't question my methods."

Julie leaned her ear to the pipe, her mouth falling open; the voices drifted up, crystal clear, through the metal casing.

"Told you," Vickie said.

They both tuned to the conversation carried by the conduits. Vickie easily made out who was talking through the reverberations of the bowels of the manor. "Let me see the paper after you," Nurse Dorothy said from the other side of the door. She continued, reading out loud judging from the plodding rhythm of her words, "Five runaways may be linked, says an insider close to the situation." Almost immediately, she continued more conversationally, "Insider? Who do you think it is?"

"They're grasping at straws," Nurse Lilly said, dismissing the traitorous thought.

"Whoever it is has guts," Nurse Fran added.

Nurse Lilly responded quickly, "Oh, they just make that stuff up. Insider! Yeah, right."

"I wonder if the board saw this?" Nurse Dorothy added.

"Hard to miss," Nurse Fran said.

Cheek still pressed to the pipe, Vickie whispered to Julie, "There's an article in the paper about Linda and the others. They say they are all connected and that they all ran away." Vickie's mouth tightened. "So ridiculous. They are still saying Linda was trying to run away."

"Who cares what they say in a newspaper?" Julie huddled closer to Vickie. "At least they are talking about it again. That means there's a chance someone might find the truth."

Vickie nodded. It was a good point.

"Maybe it's that reporter?" Julie offered.

Vickie shrugged, then snuggled more tightly against the pipe, unsure if she was ready to acknowledge Julie might have made two good points in a row.

"On to other topics . . . how's that young, handsome cousin of yours working out? Liking the job?" Nurse Dorothy asked.

"He'll get the hang of things," Nurse Lilly said.

Nurse Dorothy cut in, "I couldn't work with family."

Nurse Fran added, "She's used to it."

"Well, he's really cute." Nurse Dorothy inquired, "Single?"

"He's surprisingly shy," Nurse Lilly said.

"That's not what I asked," Nurse Dorothy reiterated.

Nurse Fran mumbled, "You know what they say about the shy ones."

Vickie's mouth dropped open. She turned to Julie in horror. "Oh my God. Angelo and Meth-head Lilly are related. They're cousins."

"She's not on meth, she's just naturally happy," Julie whispered back. "And I'm listening to the same pipe you are. You don't have to keep recapping."

The conversation continued on the other side of the door.

"This is sexual harassment. Leave him alone," Nurse Lilly said.

"We're not harassing him."

"Yeah, we're harassing you," Nurse Fran added.

"On to more important matters. Costumes and props keep disappearing and some old masks. I can't imagine what the teens are doing with them," Dr. Cannon said.

"What on earth?" Nurse Lilly commented.

"And I'm not sure how to stop them," Dr. Cannon said.

"You've got to outsmart them. I have padlocked the instrument closet," the new music teacher said, in a thick Eastern European accent.

Vickie pulled the key ring from her pocket and jiggled the keys. Vickie and Julie giggled. "She's so smart," Vickie said, imitating the accent. Julie cupped her hand over her mouth to quiet herself and to keep from laughing louder.

"Well, break's over. Back to work," Nurse Fran said.

"All work and no play . . ." Nurse Lilly said.

"Are you quoting *The Shining*?" Nurse Dorothy asked.

"Every day in here is like a Jack Nicholson movie," Nurse Fran said.

The nurses laughed in agreement.

The faculty exited the lounge, and Vickie and Julie scrambled to stand, acting casual. As soon as the staff cleared out, Vickie grabbed Julie, and they covertly entered the lounge.

"What are you doing?" Julie asked.

"You mean, what are *we* doing. *We* are seizing the moment."

Vickie walked over to the staff sign-in log. She opened the large book and flipped through the pages.

"There were five teens that 'ran away' over the last three months, including Linda. Nurse Fran was on duty on the night the missing four disappeared and the night Linda—" Vickie didn't finish her words.

Vickie flipped through pages, stopping, lost in thought.

"What is it?" Julie asked.

"I'm just remembering Angelo was there too. He's the one that helped me inside after I found her," Vickie said. She flipped backward in the log. "And he was also on duty the night the missing four vanished."

"I'm sure a lot of people here were on duty both nights," Julie said.

"Are you defending Angelo?"

"No," Julie said, casting her eyes to the left.

"Good-looking people can be homicidal maniacs, too, you know."

Footsteps echoed through the hallway as someone approached. Julie and Vickie darted under a nearby table, the long tablecloth shielding most of their bodies from sight. Angelo entered, put his things in a locker, then walked over to the sign-in log.

"It's him," Julie said, mouthing her words.

Angelo searched for the pen that was normally sitting next to the log. Vickie held up the pen, still in her hand, her eyes as big as saucers, mouthing a couple curse words. Julie grabbed it, rolling it a couple of feet in front of the table.

Angelo looked down and, spying the pen, knelt to pick it up. He promptly signed the log and exited. The duo breathed a simultaneous sigh of relief. They waited a couple minutes, then opened the door and squeezed out, but were immediately stopped in their tracks by Angelo. Leaning against the wall with his massive arms crossed, he cleared his throat.

"What were you ladies doing in the staff lounge?" Angelo asked.

Julie pointed toward herself. "Who, us?"

Angelo nodded.

"We were looking for Nurse Fran's jam," Vickie said, pointing at Julie. "She wanted to try it."

"I love that jam," Julie said, rubbing her belly, licking her lips in that way Vickie hated. Vickie grimaced.

"Looking for jam under the table?" Angelo asked.

"You saw us?" Julie asked.

Angelo smirked.

"Gotta go," Vickie said, grabbing Julie by the collar.

Angelo shook his head, snickering.

CHAPTER 30
Dance Steps

DAY 71 for Vickie

The Sunshine Room

7:30 a.m.

Vickie yawned big like a cat, waiting in the meds line just outside the sunshine room. Her chest warmed at the sight of Nurse Lilly's hair and smile firmly back in place. Vickie's world had officially returned to order.

Nurse Dorothy distributed medication from the window, while Nurse Lilly stood nearby, calling each teen by name. Vickie's pod members lined up one right after the other. Both Vickie's and Julie's posture straightened as Tracy moved in close behind them. "Good morning, ladies."

"What's good about it?" Vickie asked.

"Tonight, after night checks, we all take our relationship to the next level."

Julie flashed a slow smile, while Vickie's body remained at a disinterested angle, though her eyes brightened.

"Vickie, we might need your help with a few things. I'll be in touch." Tracy slipped back into his position further back in line.

"What was that about?" Julie whispered to Vickie.

"I guess we'll find out."

Nurse Lilly surveyed the list on her clipboard. "Vickie." Nurse Lilly's eyes met Vickie's. "Good morning."

"Good morning, Nurse Lilly." Vickie tossed back the little white cup of pills along with a paper mouthwash cup full of water and took her seat in her throne-chair. When her name was called, Julie followed the same routine and sat in the chair across from Vickie.

Julie clandestinely took the pills she had pretended to swallow from her hands and stuffed them into a nearby potted plant. Vickie covertly coughed her own pills into her hand, then slipped them under the table to Julie.

"This is going to be one happy plant," Julie said, taking Vickie's pills and stuffing them into the dirt.

"You don't mind they've been in my mouth?"

"I'm cleaning my fingers in the dirt." Julie leaned closer to Vickie. "So, do you think Angelo will say anything? About yesterday in the lounge?"

"What are they going to do? Drug me and throw me in isolation for three days? Been there, done that."

Julie considered for a moment, looking to the left, then staring straight at Vickie. "What if that's not the worst thing they can do?"

Vickie's eyebrows pulled toward one another, her gaze falling to the floor, turning the thought over in her head. The sound of Nurse Lilly, Nurse Dorothy, and Nurse Fran's nearby conversation rose above Vickie's considerations, reaching her ears to win her attention.

"You must be so relieved the board is gone," Nurse Dorothy said.

"Yes. I feel free! Don't have to worry about that again until next year," Nurse Lilly said.

"Aren't they coming back sometime before then to plan the centennial celebration?" Nurse Fran said.

Nurse Lilly scowled. "Don't be a Debbie Downer."

"My name's not Debbie," Nurse Fran said with a full frown.

"Did you just make a joke, Nurse Fran?" Nurse Lilly asked, giggling.

Nurse Lilly returned her attention to her clipboard. "Tracy."

Tracy swallowed his pill, then tapped his chest, forming a rhythmic beat. Other kids in the line joined in, until he continued breaking the monotony of pill distribution with a song.

"I found my pills, on Blueberry Hill," Tracy sang.

As if temporarily released from a trance, one by one, each of the residents in line sang along to the improvised tune. Nurse Lilly even joined, smiling.

"I'll have what he's having," Nurse Fran said under her breath to Nurse Dorothy. Squirt, now standing near Vickie and Julie, clapped off-beat, grinning ear to ear.

Vickie squinted, not trusting her eyes, when she noticed someone new entering the lounge area. She was the first to recognize her.

Dr. Habsburg.

The bronze bust was more lifelike than the real-life version in Vickie's estimation. The doctor wore a tight skirt and jacket with a frilly mauve blouse. A large brooch pinned to the lapel of her jacket seemed out of place, like something a predator might use to distract its prey. The doctor lowered her head, her face tightening. The veins in her neck bulged. Nurse Dorothy saw Dr. Habsburg and immediately stopped dancing, standing up straight and still.

"Oh my God," Nurse Dorothy said. "Shhhh. Shhhh."

"Is that—" Julie began.

"Yep. I wonder if she'll see her shadow," Vickie whispered.

"Ha, like the groundhog," Squirt said, explaining the joke. "'Cause she never comes out."

Julie rolled her eyes. Simultaneously, both Vickie and Julie said, "Shut up, Squirt." They cast an amazed look at one another.

"Dr. Habsburg?" Nurse Fran said, loud enough for everyone to hear.

Nurse Lilly danced on with abandon, surrounded by laughing teens, until her eyes swung up and met the doctor's disapproving, stony gaze.

All movement and joy in the room ceased, now replaced with a painful, expectant silence.

Dr. Habsburg cleared her throat. "I just wanted to congratulate everyone on another successful board meeting."

"Thank you, Dr. Habsburg," Nurse Fran said.

"Thank you," Nurse Dorothy said.

Nurse Lilly began, "That's very kind of —"

"Lillian, in my office. Now," Dr. Habsburg uttered in her commanding German accent.

Dr. Habsburg's Office
8:15 a.m.

Dr. Mariska Habsburg's sixth-floor office at Blueberry Hill was palatial, fit for a queen. The room had an old-world feel. She had filled the space with methodically curated antiques and just the right amount of tasteful extravagance and gold finish. Several display cabinets against the walls housed china, commemorative plates, candelabras, music boxes, and other priceless trinkets. It was the type of family collection procured over several lifetimes. The elegant furniture, though welcoming, encouraged you to sit up straight and not get too comfortable. Kerosene lamps and candles appeared throughout, with burned wicks that illustrated they were often utilized and not just for decoration.

Nurse Lilly sipped her tea, the cup trembling in her hand, smiling at the doctor seated across from her.

"Pinky up, dear," Dr. Habsburg said, offering a disparaging smile.

Nurse Lilly lifted her pinky obediently as she took another tentative sip.

"I run a tight ship," Dr. Habsburg said.

"Yes," Nurse Lilly agreed.

"The ship has gone off course, it appears."

"Yes, I just thought . . ."

"You thought?"

"I decided it would . . ."

"You decided?"

"Yes," Nurse Lilly said.

"Let me understand this, you thought, and then you decided," Dr. Habsburg said.

"Yes."

"We won't fail here just because you couldn't do as you were told. Am I clear?" Dr. Habsburg asked.

"Was there a problem with how I handled the meeting preparations?"

"If you weren't so busy dancing with teenagers, maybe you would have seen this." Dr. Habsburg placed a newspaper folded neatly to page five in front of Nurse Lilly, who glimpsed it.

"It's the second article this week. Did you know that?"

"I saw the first one. I–It's that reporter," Nurse Lilly stammered.

"I convinced the editor there was no story weeks ago. Someone is stoking the fire again. Go on, read it." Nurse Lilly's eyes moved across the article line by line. "Out loud," Dr. Habsburg suggested with increased volume.

"Neglect, lack of oversight, staffing issues . . . said an inside source," Nurse Lilly relayed softly.

"Take care of it. I don't want to see another article in print, or the consequences will be most unpleasant."

Nurse Lilly nodded dutifully. Dr. Habsburg sipped her tea, savoring it a bit more than usual. "Mmmmm. Perfect. I can always count on you to get things done. Eventually."

"Will that be all?" Nurse Lilly asked.

"For now."

Nurse Lilly stood up, offering a quivering smile.

"Oh, and one more thing. Have the staff change the locks on my office. One of my music boxes is missing."

Nurse Lilly looked over at the antique display case and scanned the shelves. Second row from the top, she spied an empty space.

"And fire whomever is handling the cleaning in here."

"Ms. Templeton? You don't think she—"

"Of course not. But it will send a message."

Nurse Lilly's face drooped. She turned quickly to hide her expression and hurried away.

CHAPTER 31
Busted

DAY 72 for Vickie

The Music Room

12:30 a.m.

E agen cast his eyes toward Vickie. "Do you have the stuff Tracy asked you to get?" They had only turned on a couple of lamps in the music room and not the overhead, so as not to alert the staff of their late-night escapade with light leaking around the closed door. The muted glow was just enough to illuminate the space.

Vickie pulled a package from her waistband and dropped it in front of Eagen like a sack of drugs. Eagen unwrapped the paper, revealing six sterilized and packaged needles, a six-inch dried reed, and some twine. Squirt's eyes stretched as wide as saucers at the sight of the paraphernalia. Eagen pulled a small vial of ink from his pocket, gently placing it beside the rest of the contraband. "And you're sure you want, er, *we* want to do this? The same tattoo?" Eagen asked, looking around at the group.

"This is what you meant by take our relationship to a new level?" Julie asked, eyes fixed on Tracy.

Tracy nodded and flashed that sideways grin. "Wilder than the wind, people!"

Julie rolled her eyes. "Okay. I'm in."

"I want one," Annie said.

"Why not?" Squirt asked, his lip quivering and his eyes darting.

"I've only got black ink, so keep that in mind. What'll it be?" Eagen asked. "A tarantula? Skull? Dagger?" Eagen removed the first needle from the package, placing it inside the reed and then wrapping the twine around it, creating a makeshift handle.

"How about a bird?" Annie suggested. "Like a phoenix."

"Or a hummingbird. Something small," Squirt said.

"A crow could be cool," Tracy said.

"Any black bird as long as it's small," Squirt said.

"All right, then." Eagen knew no matter what kind of bird they had settled on, they were just going to get a nondescript black bird anyway. And given his limited experience in tattooing, the chances of all the birds matching were slim.

"Well, understanding that I'll probably get better as we go along, who wants to go first?"

"I'll go first," Julie said.

"OK. Where?" he asked.

Julie pulled up her sleeve and turned over her wrist, showing her scars to the group for the first time.

"Cool," Eagen said without looking up at her. He dipped the needle into the bottle and then pressed it into Julie's wrist. He watched for a reaction from her, but her eyes only narrowed the harder he pricked.

"My parents are going to hate this," Julie said with a devilish grin on her face.

An hour later, Squirt admired his tattoo, touching it over and over.

"Stop that," Vickie said, slapping his hands. "It's going to get infected."

"All right, I've got just enough ink left for the last victim." Eagen glared at Vickie.

"My turn already, huh?"

Eagen nodded.

Vickie looked around at her pod all admiring Eagen's work on each other.

He beamed, pleased with his efforts so far.

Vickie pulled the sleeve of her sweatshirt up in one fast jerk, then thrust her arm in front of Eagen. "Do it."

Squirt smiled sweetly. "I can hold your hand if—"

"Come near me and I'll break your fingers," Vickie growled at Squirt.

Squirt smiled and turned his attention back to his own tattoo, admiring it again. Vickie bit her lip and turned her head to the left, away from Eagen and the imminent first stab of the needle, and her eyes met Tracy's, who had sat down beside her.

"Hi," he said. "Might help take your mind off things to talk to someone."

"I'm fine. Ow! Son of a—" Vickie glared at Eagen.

"I'm poking a needle in your arm. Did you think it would tickle?" Eagen asked sarcastically. "You'll get used to it. Just keep looking at pretty boy."

Vickie relaxed a little, letting out a breath, then focused on Tracy.

"You heard him. Look at pretty boy," Tracy said.

Vickie winced as Eagen continued poking.

"See? Not so bad," Tracy said. "So where were we?"

"Talking, to take my mind off things," Vickie said.

"Right."

"So, how are you doing? You know, after your visit from the hot lady in the helicopter? Hela-mom."

"Don't be fooled. The helicopter is just an upgraded broomstick. All the witches have them now."

Vickie snort-laughed, shaking her arm. Eagen glared and tightened his grip in displeasure.

"Sorry," Vickie said, briefly turning to Eagen.

"I'm fine," Tracy said. "It's not all her fault. If my father wanted to do something about it, he could. If I were going to be mad at someone, it would be him. But I'm not mad."

"Not even a little? How do you do that?"

"I have a high tolerance for pain, I guess," Tracy said.

Vickie nodded, then twitched her lips to one side. "I'm not sure if that's a good thing or a bad thing."

"It is what it is. And I'm in good company." Tracy elevated his voice, looking around at everyone in the group. "How many other people here have daddy issues?"

Everyone except Vickie put up their hand. Tracy raised a waiting eyebrow at her.

"I don't have a dad. So, I don't have a lot to contribute to this conversation," Vickie said.

"Lucky you," Tracy said. The rest of the pod migrated back over and joined in the conversation.

"Everyone has a dad," Julie said.

Expressionless, Vickie responded, "Yeah, well, mine wasn't around. I used to tell people he was dead."

"I'd say that qualifies as a daddy issue," Tracy said.

"Would it make you feel better if he was?" Eagen asked.

"Yeah. If I'm being honest, yeah. Hope hurts," Vickie said.

"Yeah," Squirt said.

"Yeah," Julie and Tracy said in unison.

Annie smiled in agreement, nodding.

Silence cut through their hearts, bonding them together, then a piercing creak shattered the moment. Nurse Fran lurched through the doorway, peering into the dim light. Her voice whipped at them, shrill and incredulous. "What's going on? How did you get in here?"

Room 602

2:00 a.m.

From inside their bedroom, the boys heard keys jingle and then the door lock thunked. "We'll deal with you in the morning," Nurse Fran said through the door. The muffled sound of her angry footsteps dissolved into silence.

"Morning can't come fast enough," Eagen said, bringing out his sketch pad.

"It's not so bad. We can get to know each other more," Squirt said.

Eagen scowled. "We've been trapped together for months."

Squirt smiled. "But how much do we really know about each other?"

"Leave me alone."

"You sound very grumpy. Maybe you need to try a new hobby, Eagen?" Tracy suggested, strumming his guitar.

"Good idea. How about noose making?" Eagen asked.

"A noose? Don't say that. We'd miss you," Squirt said.

"The noose is not for me." Eagen glared at Tracy.

"Awww. That just means he likes us. Death is his love language," Tracy said to Squirt.

"Maybe you can teach me some chords, and, you know . . ." Squirt asked.

"How to pick up girls?" Tracy added.

Squirt shrugged.

"Just be yourself," Tracy said.

"That's easy to say when yourself is you," Squirt said.

"It's a numbers game, really. Just a numbers game. Scratch enough cards and eventually you'll win—" Tracy said.

"The jackpot?" Squirt asked.

"Or at least a couple bucks," Tracy said.

Room 402
7:00 a.m.

Nurse Fran placed a tray of unappetizing food on the foot of each

232

girl's bed.

"You can't keep us locked in here," Julie said.

"I didn't make the rules or break the rules," Nurse Fran said.

"But you don't have any trouble enforcing them," Vickie said.

"That's what I'm paid to do," Nurse Fran said, closing the door after herself and locking it with the large set of keys.

Julie picked up one of the food items and let it fall back onto her tray as Vickie proceeded to eat. "This is the worst summer ever!" Julie said.

"What would you be doing if you weren't here?" Annie asked.

"I was supposed to go to Paris again for the summer. You?" Julie asked.

"My mom and I used to go to our house in the Hamptons every summer. It's just the two of us now. But my mom's in the hospital," Annie said.

"I'm sorry. Is she all right?" Julie asked.

Annie shook her head back and forth. "It's OK. My new family is coming for me soon."

Julie resumed pushing food around her tray.

"How about you, Vickie? What would you be doing this summer if you weren't here?" Annie asked.

"I'd be working at the 7-Eleven. Making some spending money," Vickie said.

"Sounds awful," Julie said.

"It may not be the same as frolicking around France or a Hamptons holiday, but it's got its own beauty. I like watching the slushie machine churn. It's colorful, and the assortment of snacks is mind-blowing. And the people that come in there are even nuttier than the candy bars. It keeps me entertained. Plus, it's not far from my house. All in all, I can't complain," Vickie said.

"I take it back, then. Sounds absolutely horrific," Julie said.

A key rattled in the lock, and Nurse Lilly opened the door. "Vickie?"

"I'm in the middle of breakfast here," Vickie said.

"She doesn't like to be kept waiting."

Vickie stood up. The girls knew exactly who "she" was.

"Why me? Send Julie." Vickie said.

"Something about missing supplies, missing keys . . ."

"How about some concern about the missing kids? No one wants to talk about that."

"Dead woman walking," Julie said.

"Good luck," Annie said, waving like Vickie was leaving forever.

"Say hello to the missing four. And good-bye number five, I mean, Vickie."

Vickie flashed her middle finger to Julie.

Nurse Lilly shook her head. "That's enough, girls."

CHAPTER 32
Teacups and Shot Glasses

```
Dr. Habsburg's Office
7:10 a.m.
```

Vickie entered Dr. Habsburg's office, vigorously chewing her gum, and stopped in the middle of the room to take it all in. Dr. Habsburg stood behind her large antique desk, then slowly crossed the room to sit on the Victorian wingback couch.

"Don't be shy." Dr. Habsburg patted the seat next to her.

"I'll stay toward the middle of the room. Everything in here is kind of delicate," Vickie said. "I don't do delicate."

Dr. Habsburg offered a napkin.

"Here you are, dear. For your gum," Dr. Habsburg said.

"Sorry, I chew gum when I'm nervous," Vickie said, then she swallowed it in one big gulp. "It's gone now."

"May I offer you some tea?" Dr. Habsburg asked.

"I normally drink coffee. Sanka, if you got it?"

Vickie lowered herself slowly onto a fancy chair that had no back.

Why are fancy things so uncomfortable?

Dr. Habsburg poured tea into a dainty teacup, ignoring Vickie's preference. The sound of the deep brown liquid hitting the bottom of the porcelain made Vickie want to urinate. She pressed her knees together.

"Allow me," Dr. Habsburg said, rising to pour for Vickie, who held out her tiny teacup.

"Could you pour a little faster? I really have to pee, and that dribbling sound isn't helping."

Dr. Habsburg looked at Vickie with a blank expression.

"Sorry. I also pee when I'm nervous," Vickie said.

"No need to be nervous. The saucer goes under your cup," the doctor said, pouring the tea and watching Vickie.

"Why do you need a plate under a beverage?"

"To catch the spills, dear."

"That's just more dishes to wash. Have you thought of using a high-quality paper product?" Vickie asked.

Dr. Habsburg answered with a condescending smile. A folded cloth napkin with a ring around it rested on the table in front of Vickie. She picked the bundle up and examined it.

"Napkin in your lap. The napkin ring may be placed in front of your tea setting," Dr. Habsburg directed.

"You know, instant coffee's a lot quicker. And a lot fewer rules. You just plop it in and stir. You sure you don't have any Sanka?" Vickie asked.

"Shortcuts, darling, will get you nowhere fast," Dr. Habsburg said.

"Isn't that why they call it a shortcut, 'cause it gets you there faster?"

Dr. Habsburg feigned another smile.

"I like the design on your china. What are those, tomatoes?" Vickie asked.

"Elderberries."

"I have to say, this is a pretty cup all right."

"I'm glad you like it. Look how delicate the cup is, how fragile it appears, yet it holds scalding liquid with ease. It doesn't crack under the intense heat, not even a chip. And it remains just as beautiful all the while on the outside, even though it is boiling on the inside. Strength. Discipline. Control."

236

"I'm going to put this down now, because I'm nervous holding something so important."

"Have you ever owned something truly beautiful? Jewelry, or perhaps a dress?"

"I'm not really a clothes person. But we have a really nice couch in our living room. It's green. I don't know what you call it. It's kind of like velvet, but fake. And there's a permanent ass print. Sorry, butt print, actually two, one for me and one for Ma, or would that be four? What's the correct way to say that? You sit down and you know you're home. Is that what you mean?"

"I'm talking about the finer things. I would like you to develop an appreciation for them. Do you know why?"

"I surely do not."

"It's about honoring yourself. The way you treat the things you gather around you is how you train others, through your example, to treat you." Dr. Habsburg straightened her back and leaned closer, looking Vickie over. "And it's about control. There's nothing to be gained by indulging in your negative emotions. I've heard you are prone to outbursts. And to taking things that are not yours, like keys. Is this true?" The rising arch of her eyebrow taunted a response.

"This is sometimes true. Yes."

"I'm afraid that is not acceptable behavior. You must rise above. Control your emotions. My daughter was like you. But not anymore. Smiling is control; remember that. Smiling lifts the face and the emotions. Smile and it will be all better."

Dr. Habsburg smiled again, one eyebrow waiting to rise until Vickie returned the smile.

"How lovely. How easy. And then simply say, 'All better now.' Go on," Dr. Habsburg invited.

"You really want me to repeat that?"

Dr. Habsburg nodded.

"OK," Vickie said.

Dr. Habsburg smiled. Vickie forced a smile back.

"All better now," Vickie grunted through her teeth.

"I need you to be a teacup, Victoria," Dr. Habsburg said.

"Actually, it's just Vickie. Says Vickie right on my birth certificate. And I got to tell you, I'm not as complicated as your fine china here. If we're gonna be dishes, I'm kinda like a shot glass. What you see is what you get."

Dr. Habsburg smiled. Vickie smiled back.

"Not for nothing, but can we take a break from smiling? My cheeks are feeling fatigued. The cheeks on my face, that is," Vickie said. "Although this pretty seat of yours isn't doing anything to relax my other cheeks."

"All right. That will be all for now. Vickie, if we see each other again, we won't be having tea. Understood?" Dr. Habsburg warned.

"Yeah. It was nice to try it. But Sanka's so much quicker," Vickie said, chugging the remainder of her tea.

Vickie rose from the antique chair and exited the room without a backward glance.

Dr. Habsburg forced a smile and looked down to where Vickie had put down the teacup. It was gone. Her eyebrows crinkled.

Room 402
7:45 a.m.

Minutes later, Vickie was back in her room, staring contently out the window, stirring her instant Sanka into her tiny, new teacup, sipping, and enjoying it much more than the posh tea.

"Something's not right about that lady."

CHAPTER 33
Healing

The Drama Classroom
3:00 p.m.

D r. Cannon stood in front of the class, gathering her materials around her, lost in her preparations. Vickie sat at her desk in between Annie and Julie.

"I'm so over this," Julie said, not caring who heard her.

Vickie, growing more accustomed to Julie's complaints, countered, "At least we're out of our rooms."

"So, we should celebrate because we have a bigger cage? I've got to get out of here," Julie said in barely a whisper.

"There's nothing you can do about it. So . . ."

Julie weighed Vickie's comment, a sly smile spreading from one side of her face to another. "Watch me."

Vickie rolled her eyes at Julie's comment. Dr. Cannon winked to signal the beginning of class. Vickie's face and her body relaxed into her seat.

"Why is storytelling important?" Dr. Cannon asked.

"So, you can go nighty-night," Tracy said. A couple of giggles followed his comment. Squirt laughed the loudest.

"That's one reason," Dr. Cannon said.

"Because we have magical things inside us that want to get out,"

Annie said.

"Absolutely," Dr. Cannon said. "Anyone else?"

"So, we can pretend reality is not real," Vickie said. "Which sort of makes it a waste of time," she added.

Julie observed Dr. Cannon's reaction to Vickie's comments closely. Dr. Cannon didn't reveal a significant amount of emotional intel, but when someone answered in a way that pleased her, her eyes grew subtly brighter. "Storytelling moves us forward. Helps us to heal by not looking back."

"Excellent, Julie," Dr. Cannon said.

And there it is. That dull twinkle. Jackpot.

"I think facing the truth is crucial to the healing process," Vickie said.

"There's a lot of truth in stories, even if they're made up," Dr. Cannon said.

Vickie twisted her lips, looking to one side. "I hadn't thought of that. You're pretty smart, Ms. — Dr. Cannon."

Julie imagined Dr. Cannon would have blushed if she were the type. When you got a compliment from Vickie, you could rest assured it was genuine. Julie wouldn't describe herself as genuine. She figured in order to be genuine, you had to have a pretty good idea who you were. She knew who people wanted her to be. Her father wanted her to be his obedient princess. Her mother wanted her to be seen and not heard, and her friends at school wanted her to think just like them about everything! But what did she want? All she knew was she didn't want to be at Blueberry Hill any longer. And so, she decided in that moment to be what she thought Dr. Cannon might like her to be.

"Oh Vickie, God bless you," Dr. Cannon said.

"I don't believe in God, but thank you."

Annie's hand shot up into the air, waving emphatically.

"Yes, Annie."

"I see a web right now, among us. A web of stories like veins."

"I think what Annie is saying is that we're all connected," Dr. Cannon said.

"More like we are pretty, giant spiders. And I do believe in God if you want to bless me."

Dr. Cannon nodded. "God bless you."

Annie made the sign of the cross in the air like the Pope.

Dr. Cannon closed her eyes briefly, acknowledging and accepting Annie's blessing before continuing. "Regardless of your opinions on God, stories help us heal."

"They can also hurt," Vickie said.

"Absolutely."

"Like when the stories are lies. About someone you care about," Vickie said.

"It's up to each person to find out their truth for themselves and then share that truth with everyone who cares to listen." Vickie looked directly at Dr. Cannon, leaning in just a little. "The stories we tell about ourselves, our experiences, the people we care about. They matter," Dr. Cannon added.

Vickie whispered to Julie, "You know what else helps us heal? Justice."

"What do you mean?" Julie asked. Julie could tell something specific had clicked for Vickie as well during the class session, but she wasn't sure what. She was sure Vickie had no intention of being what someone else wanted her to be.

"Ladies?" Dr. Cannon stared at the whispering girls. "Anything you'd like to share with the class?"

"No," Vickie was quick to respond. "Not yet." Vickie cast an assertive glance over at Julie, then back at Dr. Cannon.

"Well, I love a good teaser, so I look forward to hearing what has you both so captivated, but until then, let's table the side conversation. And Julie, you're making great progress, let's continue in that direction."

Vickie and Julie turned to face forward.

"And now it is time. We've worked diligently to create a version of ourselves we'd like to show to the world. These versions do not always make those around us comfortable, but what matters is it is our choice what we show, to whom and when. Displaying these aspects of ourselves is as easy as putting a mask on or taking it off. Shall we have a look at your creations?"

Each student pulled the scintillating, glistening cloth from their mask, including Julie, all the masks now complete.

"Let's appreciate what we've created. Let's see all the ways this mask represents you and how it represents 'the other.' It's not just a tool for theater, but a tool for discovering yourself. Follow me to the mirrors, holding your mask up to the side of your face. Look into the mirror and just see yourself. What do you see when you look at the mask?" Dr. Cannon asked.

"Am I the other or is the mask the other?" Annie asked.

"You are you and the mask is the other," Dr. Cannon answered.

"I see that there is something really exaggerated in each of our others," Eagen said.

Eagen was right. Each of the masks had an exaggerated feature, like a large nose, elongated forehead, etc.

"How are you different? Julie?" Dr. Cannon asked.

Julie turned her head to the left, thinking for a moment. "I think we're the same," Julie said.

"Go on," Dr. Cannon said.

"Isn't that why we're all here? There's just one part of us a little more exaggerated than everyone else out there, and they can't handle it. Tone it down and we get out. Right?" Julie asked. Julie realized she had gone too far in her honesty. Giving Dr. Cannon what she wanted might prove more difficult than she thought.

"I don't think it's quite that simple," Dr. Cannon said.

"We'll see," Julie said under her breath, but just loud enough for Vickie to hear. Vickie cut her eyes to Julie, tightening her eyebrows together.

242

The First Floor
3:50 p.m.

Vickie and Julie walked swiftly down the hallway from drama class toward the lobby.

"Stop getting me in trouble," Julie said.

"Stop sticking your nose up Dr. Cannon's ass."

"Don't you want to get out of here? Didn't you hear what she said to me? I'm making progress."

"She said the same thing to Linda."

"What's that supposed to mean? And what were you talking about in there, anyway? Justice?" Julie asked.

"I'm going to find out the truth and make sure Linda gets justice," Vickie said.

"What?"

"Make sure people know her story. The real story."

"Vickie, if the police and the reporters can't figure out what happened to Linda or even the missing four, what are you going to do?"

"They can't figure it out because all they see are five screwed-up kids, which makes writing them all off as runaways easy, convenient."

"What if they did run—"

"Linda didn't run away. And if she didn't, maybe the others didn't either," Vickie said.

"Vickie—"

"I may never know who killed Linda. Maybe just a drunk driver. But the missing four, Linda, it's all related, like that paper said. Even Mr. Fitch knew something wasn't right."

"Vickie—" Julie began again.

"It's like a puzzle. And I'm good at puzzles. I'm just missing a few pieces, but I'll find them. I just have to be patient. And find my strategy."

"Vickie—"

"And don't tell me I should drop it," Vickie interrupted. "That's pissing me off."

"I was going to say, maybe you need someone to help you find the other puzzle pieces, instead of trying to do it all by yourself."

"Like who?"

Julie shrugged.

"You?"

"Yes. And someone smarter than me."

Assessment and Plan

Provider: Blueberry Hill Home for Troubled Youth, LLC   **Client Name: Theodore K. Moses**
Group Assignment: Pod #1   **Session Number:** #1

Diagnosis: ADHD, Generalized Anxiety

Treatment

Intake Protocol: Clinical Assessment   **Medications:** Adderall 10 mg/day,
                    Anxiety Questionnaire   Fluoxetine 20 mg/day,
                                              as per Dr. Mariska Habsburg, M.D.

Short-Term Goals for Client (2 Weeks):
  1. Foster relationships within pod.
  2. Assign increased responsibility with jobs program.
  3. Introduce coping mechanisms that will aid with focus.

Long-Term Goals (3 Months):
  1. Self-reported increase in social confidence.
  2. Increased ability to recognize social cues and ability to build a social vocabulary.
  3. Construct a plan for his ten-year goals, with action steps on how to achieve.
  4. Verbalize remorse for past actions involving computer hacking and an understanding of the harmful consequences.

Session Notes

Body Language, Facial Patterns: Fidgeting, excessive talking, darting eyes.

Summary:
  1. Client completed his patient information sheet quietly and presented as pleasant during the session.
  2. Client very politely pointed out several grammar mistakes on the intake form.
  3. Possible that he has not been stimulated enough intellectually, which led to deviant behavior, like computer hacking.

Other Observations/Comments:
  - School records indicate client has a tested IQ of 197, which supports theory that his exceptional intelligence might make it more difficult for the mundane to hold his interest.

Client Signature: _Theodore K. Moses_   **Primary Caregiver 1:** _Ralph Moses_
(Age 14 and up)   Theodore K. Moses   Ralph Moses
                                                                   (Father)
Primary Caregiver 2: _Minka Moses_   **Therapist Signature:** _Ara Cannon_
                   Minka Moses   Dr. Ara Cannon, Ph.D.
                   (Mother)

245

CHAPTER 34
Comics

The Sixth Floor
7:00 p.m.

Squirt sat at a desk alone in his room, flipping through a comic book. He landed on a page depicting a male superhero surrounded by adoring women. His eyes gleamed. This particular hero sported an unusual hairstyle. The sides flared out, a bit like Wolverine's, and there was a Superman-like curl that hung down his forehead.

Squirt stood so he could see himself in the tiny mirror above the desk and adjusted his hair to look like the character in the comic. Gazing into the mirror, he admired himself and struck a hero-esque pose, pointing his chin down and raising one eyebrow.

He spoke to the reflection in the mirror.

"Don't worry—" Squirt said, his voice cracking. He adjusted his stance and cleared his throat, speaking again.

"Don't worry, I'm here now. Everything will be—"

A knock at the door interrupted him. Startled, Squirt shoved the comic into the desk drawer and walked over to the door to open it.

His eyes expanded at the sight of Julie and Vickie standing at his threshold. Squirt slammed the door in their faces, popping his slobbery retainer out before slipping it into his pocket. After taking a deep breath, he opened the door again, leaning casually against the door frame.

"Hello, ladies."

"Squirt, we need you," Julie said.

Squirt gasped. "You. Need. What?" he said, his voice cracking again.

"Come on!" Vickie insisted.

Squirt immediately followed them down the hallway.

"What's up with your hair?" Julie asked.

Squirt reached up and touched his super-do as all the color drained from his face, the pretense of coyness and confidence gone.

"Oh, I-I was working out."

"Oh, 'cause I was going to say I like it," Julie said.

"You do?"

"It's very manly," Julie said.

Squirt laughed nervously and blushed red to the tips of his ears. Vickie rolled her eyes. The trio paused outside a familiar door on the sixth floor.

"Wait. This is Dr. Habsburg's office."

"Now I see why they say you're a genius," Vickie quipped.

"We can't go in there," Squirt added.

Vickie tried the handle, and it held fast, as expected.

"Oh well," Squirt said, his shoulders relaxing as he turned to leave. Vickie reached into her pocket and pulled out something jingly.

"You've got a key?" Squirt asked.

"Does that club for geniuses know about you?" Vickie said.

"Mensa? Not yet. But they will. How'd you get another set?" Squirt asked.

"Same way I got the first one."

Squirt's voice shook as he spoke. "We are so getting locked up again."

The door opened easily with the key, and they stepped inside, Vickie closing the door quietly behind them. Julie and Squirt gaped as they took in the lavish decor.

"So, this is the monster's lair," Julie said. She approached the fancy tea set, running her fingers over it. "The monster drinks tea. She's a refined beast. Wait, I've seen these cups before. We have one in our room. No. You didn't?" Julie stared at Vickie, grinning.

"I might give it back. Worst coffee cup I've ever had. My fingers barely fit in the little handle. And it only holds two sips."

"That's because it's a *tea* cup."

"What's the difference? It's a cup for drinking, and who wants to keep filling it up?" Vickie walked over to the doctor's desk.

"I don't really think you should touch anything," Squirt said, his eyes shooting to her fingers.

Multiple pages of what looked like some sort of design proof for a catalog lay strewn on her desk. Printed at the top of each page in a bold font was: "Blueberry Hill: Home for Troubled Youth, Centennial Celebration." Photos of all the staff over the years filled the pages, with the number of years of employment underneath.

"Look, there's Nurse Fran. Wow, she's been here for thirty-five years. No wonder she's so crabby all the time," Vickie said.

"Can we go now?" Squirt asked.

"Not until we've done what we came here to do," Vickie said.

"I don't even know what that is," Squirt said.

Vickie pointed Squirt to an antiquated computer.

"Can you get into that?"

Squirt smirked. "With my eyes closed. Then can we go?"

Vickie nodded.

Squirt sat in front of the computer, his fingers gliding over the keys, Vickie and Julie standing behind him. In a matter of seconds, Squirt spoke. "I'm in. Now what?"

Julie rubbed Squirt's back, making him quiver. "You're good."

"Would you stop that? You'll give him a heart attack and we still need him. Stay focused There's got to be something that connects everyone that's gone missing," Vickie said. "Can you pull up their files?"

"What were their names again?" Squirt asked.

"One of them was Nartanka or something like that," Vickie offered.

"What?" Julie smirked. "No. That's not even a name. Nartanka? There was a Sarah. A Justin."

"And Tika and Nathalie," Squirt added.

"Nathalie." Vickie nodded.

"Nartanka?" Julie shook her head.

"And Linda. Pull her up too," Vickie interjected.

Vickie and Squirt exchanged glances as Squirt continued typing.

A few moments later, Squirt provided an update. "I've cross-checked the notes in all their files."

"And?" Vickie asked.

"Nothing."

"No. That can't be right. There's got to be something."

"What if the only thing that connects them is that they didn't want to be here anymore? Maybe they did run away?" Squirt said. "It's not that hard to believe."

"Try cross-checking some of the standard fields," Vickie said. "Like address, age, parent's name."

Squirt typed and waited.

"Nope. Nothing. Oh, wait. The only thing that is similar across all files is that the primary caregiver is shown as SW."

"What does that mean?" Squirt hovered over the abbreviation with the mouse. 'State Ward' blinked up on the screen.

"And here's something else. They are all listed as discharged. And it looks like the date was prior to when they went missing. The day before."

"Linda too?" Vickie moved in closer to Squirt.

Squirt nodded. "Sorry, Vickie. Wish I had found something more."

"That's plenty. Don't you see? We're just teenagers and we're locked up, but if something happened to most of us, someone, somewhere, would care, would notice. There was nobody out there to fight for the missing four or Linda," Vickie said.

"Except you," Julie said.

"Except us," Vickie corrected.

"So, what does this all mean?" Squirt asked.

"It means we keep digging," Vickie said.

Dr. Cannon sat with two files open on her desk. One manila folder was labeled Julie Maxwell, the other Vickie Bartolucci. She rapped her fingers on the espresso-colored desk in concentration, remembering her recent private sessions with each girl and how different their responses to the same questions had been.

Do you have any affirmations that you like?

JULIE: So many. My favorite is, "Everything's working out for me."

VICKIE: I believe more in reality.

Do you find affirmations helpful?

JULIE: Ultimately, it's another tool. Action's still needed, but they make things so much easier.

VICKIE: No.

How are affirmations related to reality?

JULIE: It's all about perception.

VICKIE: They are the way you wish your life was. I don't like fake things or lying to myself.

Total waste of time.

How are you feeling about things?

JULIE: Happy. Positive.

Vickie, how are you feeling?

VICKIE: Hungry.

Dr. Cannon wrote something in one of the folders, closed the other, and buried her head in her hands, exhaling deeply.

CHAPTER 35
The Jeweled Dagger

DAY 73 for Vickie

The Grounds

12:00 p.m.

The summer sun at high noon cast harsh shadows around the edges of the sloped, manicured grounds. Uncle Aldo's cop car came to a stop in the circular drive outside the Blueberry Hill Home for Troubled Youth.

Rosemary rode shotgun, ready for battle, or so she thought. Her face fell slack as she took in the enormity and grandeur of the manor. She felt herself shrinking at its feet.

Uncle Aldo paused for a moment, staring straight ahead before looking at his sister. "You sure you don't want me to come in?" he asked.

Rosemary's response was quick, as if she were defending against the thought. "No. I'm going to do this."

Uncle Aldo's eyes sparkled, smiling, before the rest of his face followed. "I'll be right here if you need me."

Rosemary flipped the sun visor down, revealing a mirror on the other side. She twisted open her fancy purse, the one she reserved for weddings and funerals. This was a big event, too, making sure her baby was really all right, because she couldn't get the answers she wanted on the phone. Taking out her lipstick, she puckered and quickly covered her lips with a deep red. She smacked her lips together and fluffed her hair.

Rosemary opened the car door, walking carefully up the steps in her heels. A nurse sitting behind a reception desk did a double take when she glimpsed Rosemary approaching the french doors. Rosemary registered the stolen look as a compliment. "You got this, Rosemary," she said to herself before flinging the door open and charging inside.

Across the room, Angelo glanced up from where he sorted books on the library cart. The woman's bold entrance drew his attention, and he angled his body away to listen less obviously.

Clip, clop, clip, clop. Rosemary had loved the sound high heels made on a tiled floor since she was a girl. They made people pay attention.

"May I help you?" Nurse Dorothy asked.

"I'm Rosemary Bartolucci. Vickie's mom."

Angelo quirked a tiny smile hearing the woman introduce herself. He shifted around to the other side of the cart for a better view of the desk and continued arranging the books.

"Do you have an appointment?" Nurse Dorothy added..

"To see my own daughter?"

"We don't allow parent visitations unless they've been scheduled and approved."

"I've been calling, and you tell me I can't speak to her."

"Our policy is clear, only on—"

"I called on my day. I put it on my calendar. And they still wouldn't let me speak to her. Now I'm here in person and I can't see her? A parent has rights. Who's in charge here?" Rosemary asked, surprising herself with the forcefulness of her own voice. She thrust her shoulders back a little and settled into this new persona.

"I'm the nurse on duty."

"I want to see the head of this place," Rosemary said, casting her eyes around the surroundings.

"That will not be possible."

"Call the person in charge. Now. Please. She's my daughter."

Nurse Dorothy dialed the phone, tilting her head to the side, speaking in a hushed tone. "Sorry to bother you. Ms. Bartolucci is here. Vickie's mother. She wants to see you. She insists. OK."

Nurse Dorothy hung up the phone. "Right this way," she said, standing and leading the way to the staircase.

The Sixth Floor
12:05 p.m.

The door to Dr. Habsburg's office was closed. The nurse, having escorted Rosemary to the entrance, waited for her to knock before she rounded the corner of the dark-paneled corridor and headed back toward the staircase. Rosemary steadied herself, catching her breath after climbing six flights. She straightened her clothes and cleared her throat, then knocked more forcefully.

"Enter," Dr. Habsburg said.

Rosemary's initial impulse had been to burst into the room, guns blazing, and pull Vickie out of this place immediately, but having taken the time to calm herself, she decided a couple of pleasantries couldn't hurt. She opened the door, walking into the large and overwhelmingly opulent space. A severe-looking woman sat behind a spotless desk opening mail with a jeweled, dagger-like letter opener.

"Hi. How are ya?" Rosemary asked.

"Yes? Mrs. —" Dr. Habsburg began.

"Ms. Bartolucci. Nice to meet you, Mrs. —"

"Dr. Habsburg," she corrected, not bothering to look up from the letter she held.

"Dr. Habsburg. Ohhhhh," Rosemary said. Annoyance crept up the back of her neck. Expensive things didn't mean this woman could be rude to her. And she was being rude.

"This is very unusual, having a parent come unannounced."

"Yeah," Rosemary responded.

"I'm afraid I have limited time so . . ."

"I'm sorry I'm taking your valuable time here. I just haven't been able to get in touch with my daughter."

"We are having some challenges with Vickie and feel it's best if we minimize her interactions with—"

"With family? You're saying I'm part of the problem or something?" Rosemary asked, her voice louder and her face reddening.

"Vickie is uncooperative, disruptive, and impolite," Dr. Habsburg said.

"Sounds like a teenager to me."

"Which is a kind way of saying she is on thin ice. We weren't sure, but now, after having met you, I can see this is a learned behavior."

"What are you trying to say? That I'm not a good mother?"

"I'm saying that until we can break Vickie of these habits, she is better off without your influence."

"Ms. Habsburg—"

"Dr. Habsburg, please."

"In my opinion, life is a two-way street, and if you're telling me Vickie is difficult, it makes me wonder what kind of care she's under. Maybe she should leave this place."

"By all means."

Dr. Habsburg pressed the intercom button on her phone.

"Yes, Lillian, could you bring her in please? Thank you."

Nurse Lilly escorted Vickie in and promptly left.

"Vix?" Rosemary said.

"Ma, what are you doing here?" Vickie asked.

Rosemary surmised the staff had collected Vickie preemptively just in case she was needed, but hadn't informed her as to her mother's presence. "I came to help you out. I was worried. They wouldn't let me speak to you," Rosemary said. "Uncle Aldo's downstairs. If he drives fast, we'll be home before lunch."

"I'm afraid, if you leave with her, she won't be going home," Dr. Habsburg said.

"What are you talking about? Where else would she go? Vickie, just talk straight with me. What is going on, baby?" Rosemary asked.

"Ma, the judge explained all this to us. If I leave before they say so, they'll send me to juvie. That's like prison for kids," Vickie said.

"Isn't that what this is?"

"This is like a bad vacation with all the people you normally try to go on vacation to get away from. No offense," Vickie said, flicking a glance at Dr. Habsburg.

"What are you saying?"

"I've got to stay, Ma. For a lot of reasons. I've got to stay. I'm working on stuff here."

"Are we done?" Dr. Habsburg asked.

"I just thought . . . I wanted to help," Rosemary said.

"Ma, look at me. I got this. I'll be home soon," Vickie said, strength and resiliency shining bright in her eyes. She held her mother's unsteady gaze and conjured a smile. Rosemary's head dipped toward the floor, her eyes drifting back and forth.

Vickie reached out, steadying her mother, placing a hand on each of her shoulders. Rosemary reveled in the familiar, comforting touch of her daughter, allowing it to flood through her. She grabbed one of Vickie's hands and held it between her own. Rosemary smiled at Vickie and breathed in deeply.

The First Floor
12:35 p.m.

Leaving the manor was much more of a blur than her entrance had been. Rosemary remembered the staircases that never seemed to end, the sound of her shoes on the shiny, expensively tiled floor near reception, and remembered speaking to a muscular young man, dressed in a white uniform.

"Your daughter is a great girl. Don't worry, I'll keep an eye on her," the young man said, smiling brightly as he walked her to Aldo's car. He looked to be a few years older than Vickie. *What is his position here?* He reminded her of the bouncers she had to charm to get into her favorite establishments at home. But he did appear to be familiar with and even like Vickie, which gave her some comfort.

Before she knew it, the sound of the car door slamming reverberated through her chest, making her heart flutter.

After a moment of silence passed between Aldo and Rosemary, he spoke. "Sorry you came?"

"No. Not at all. It helped me to come here. I think I'm the one that needed to grow up a little and start taking charge. I'm the mother. That's my daughter they're holding in there. Something's wrong in that place. I can feel it."

"So, what do you want to do?"

"I trust Vix. I just want to be there for her when she needs me. Like she is for me."

Uncle Aldo drove away as Rosemary stared out the rearview mirror, Blueberry Hill disappearing in the distance.

CHAPTER 36
Spirits

The First Floor
12:40 p.m.

Vickie's eyes scanned the lobby for her mother, but she had already departed. She exhaled, her body relaxing. She was glad to see her mother, but the added responsibility of having her there added an additional weight to the task at hand, assembling the puzzle pieces into a picture of what really happened to Linda.

She soaked in the now familiar surroundings with a new determination.

Her gaze wandered to the fish tank and stuck there. *The fish are kind of fascinating,* she thought, watching them swim back and forth in their watery confines. She wondered if they knew they were trapped, that the hand that fed them, which they had grown dependent on, was also their jailer.

Her ears perked up as the two nurses at the reception desk launched into conversation, but her eyes never left the fish.

Nurse Fran held a newspaper, her attention fixed on it. "Another article."

"That's the third in less than a week. *She* thinks it was me," Nurse Dorothy said.

"Well, was it you?"

Nurse Dorothy paused before she spoke. "What if it was? Is there anything in there that's not true?"

Nurse Fran raised both eyebrows and sighed. "We signed a non-disclosure agreement."

"Maybe I should just quit. I'm getting married in a couple months anyway."

"Just what every man dreams of, an unemployed bride."

Nurse Dorothy laughed short and sharp. "You're not funny."

"Not trying to be. I do know what will take your mind off things, though," Nurse Fran said.

"What?"

She handed Nurse Dorothy a stack of folders for filing. "Focus on these."

Nurse Dorothy rolled her eyes and walked away. "Still not funny," she said over her shoulder.

"Still not trying to be." Nurse Fran threw the newspaper in the tiny trash can next to reception. It peeked above the rim just enough that Vickie could clearly see it from across the room.

Vickie walked over to reception, propping herself on the lip of the waist-high circular desk, and leaned over conspiratorially.

"May I help you?" Nurse Fran asked, looking over the top of her glasses.

"No. It's me that can help you."

"I don't need any help, my dear."

"The centennial is coming up."

"And?"

"You've been here a long time."

"And?"

"People like you and me, we've seen a lot of shit. Right, Fran? May I call you Fran?"

"No."

"You and I are a lot alike."

Nurse Fran stared at Vickie suspiciously.

"We don't like BS," Vickie whispered, leaning in closer.

"You mean like what you're saying right now?"

"Exactly. A woman like yourself, close to retirement. Probably angry, real angry by now. At work. At life. At everything. You might even lash out at a resident or two or four. Maybe five."

"I don't need to be angry to lash out at all of you. I do it because I enjoy it. Now, get off my desk and go do something."

"Which brings me to how I might be of service. I need something to do, and you need to get rid of me. Win-win. Why don't I sharpen some pencils or polish this lovely? What is this?" Vickie knocked on the desk. "Pine veneer. Beautiful. Or—"

Vickie paused before looking directly at Nurse Fran. "I could take out the trash."

"Of the three options, do whichever will take you the farthest away."

"Roger that, my captain!"

Vickie pulled the trash bag out of the wastebasket, saluted Nurse Fran, and walked around the corner through the cafeteria. She casually pulled the paper out, reading it as she walked. "Dark Cloud Over Blueberry Hill," the headline read. The tagline underneath continued, "No answers in mysterious disappearances and tragic death."

Vickie walked through the double doors leading to the back of the facility and onto the loading dock where two dumpsters sat.

"Oh, hi, Vickie." Vickie looked up to see Angelo holding a cigarette and leaning against the loading dock wall, making a halfhearted attempt to hide the smoldering carcinogen death stick.

"Angelo. I didn't know you smoked."

"Yeah. Picked it up in one of the group homes I lived in."

"You're a lot more like us than I thought."

His body relaxed, still leaning against the wall. "More than you know."

He blew out a cloud of smoke that drifted toward the sky.

"Mind if I have one?" Vickie asked, holding out her hand.

"I'd get in big trouble for giving you one."

"I won't tell," she said, hand still extended.

He pulled out a pack of American Spirits and shook a cigarette out for her. Vickie's eyes widened, recognizing it as the brand Linda tried smoking the day before she died.

Her heart beat faster. "Is that a common brand?"

"American Spirits? Nah. I don't know anyone else who smokes them."

"I gotta go," Vickie said without taking the cigarette.

"Don't you want—"

"I'm trying to quit. Oh, right."

Vickie spun and threw the trash bag and newspaper inside the dumpster, then shuffled back inside. "Oh my God. Oh my God," she whispered under her breath as she walked. "Oh my God."

```
The Stables
2:30 p.m.
```

Later that day, as pod 1 cleaned the horses' stalls, Vickie pulled Julie aside to share her revelation.

"The newspaper printed a third article. Maybe someone's finally on our side. And when I went to throw it out, I saw Angelo in the back by the dumpster, and he offered me cigarettes! American Spirits!"

"Was he flirting?"

"No. Didn't you hear me? He offered me cigarettes," Vickie whispered.

"So?" Julie commented.

"And no one else smokes that brand. Get it?"

"Yeah, I get it, you're a smoker. I've always thought you looked like one," Julie said. "Where are the cigarettes now?"

"Why does that matter?"

"Because I want one. I'm going to ask him to give me one," Julie said, attempting to stand, but Vickie pulled her back into the empty stall.

"You can't. Because then he'll know that I know. That I'm suspicious."

Julie stepped back, scrunching up her left eye and shrugging her shoulders.

"Don't you get it?" Vickie asked. "He gave Linda the cigarettes she was smoking. They were the same brand."

"And?"

"Cigarettes. He's a boy. Maybe he was *the* boy. I thought it was Eagen. Maybe it still is, but I'm going to find out."

"Just ask Angelo. Like you asked Eagen. Ask if he and Linda—"

"I can't. If Eagen had a thing with Linda, he would have jumped at the opportunity to rub it in my face. So, I know he told me the truth. Angelo's not going to admit to it. I'm pretty sure staff aren't supposed to canoodle with the residents."

"He's only like eighteen."

"He's nineteen," Vickie corrected.

"I've dated boys twice his age."

"Linda wasn't like that. And I'm not surprised. And gross!"

"How do you know Linda wasn't like that, anyway? Seems like there was a lot about her you didn't know."

Vickie's mouth pulled tight against her teeth, and she turned to stomp away.

"Wait. I know you'll figure things out. What did you say? You just need patience and a strategy."

"*We* will figure things out. We're doing this together right?"

Julie hesitated in a way that made Vickie uneasy, before she nodded her head.

CHAPTER 37
V is for Vickie

DAY 74 for Vickie

The Rec Room

8:40 a.m.

D r. Cannon facilitated the morning group discussion for pod 1 in the rec room as usual. As usual, the highlights included: moments of contention, more than a few snarky comments and, of course, multiple eye rolls.

The only notably different thing about the meeting was Julie, who wore a pink smiley face T-shirt and was herself all smiles. Vickie had noticed Julie making an extra effort to smile whenever Dr. Cannon and the rest of the staff were around. She knew the game she was playing, and Julie was good at it, but Vickie refused to do tricks for anyone, no matter what the reward. It went against her nature.

"We're almost out of time for today's session, but before we go, I want you to join me in congratulating a member of our group who will leave us to return home tomorrow. Julie, would you like to say anything?" Dr. Cannon asked.

Vickie coughed.

"Wow. Um, well, when I walked through those doors a few weeks ago, I wasn't in the best of shape. But I'm leaving hopeful and ready for whatever's out there. I owe a lot to Dr. Cannon."

Julie's eyes landed on Vickie. "And to all of you."

Vickie's heart beat unsteadily, and she could feel perspiration forming on her hairline. But for some reason her cheeks quivered into a lackluster smile.

DAY 75 for Vickie
Room 402
10:00 a.m.

Julie packed her suitcase as Vickie sat on her own bed eating popcorn. She threw a kernel at Julie, then another, and another, until Julie finally spoke. "What?"

"You did it. Played the game and won."

"Told you I would only be here a few weeks."

"Congratulations."

"But the prize is, I have to go back to my family. Not exactly what I call winning. Still better than here, though."

"So, are you just telling Dr. Cannon what she wants to hear, or do you believe all the crap you're saying?" Vickie asked.

"I'm telling her what I want to hear. I just want to move on. Leave this place."

"You should have tried the oatmeal with the raisins. Would have made a big difference in your opinion of this place."

Julie allowed herself a half-hearted chuckle. "Shouldn't you be journaling right now? And isn't it a little early for popcorn?"

"Number one, I'm making sure you don't take anything of mine."

"Not likely."

"Number two, who made you the queen of snack etiquette? And number three . . ."

"How many numbers are there?"

Vickie rolled her eyes. "Number three, I get that you want to leave, we all do, except for maybe Squirt, but you can't just stuff all the stuff you feel down."

Julie picked up one of the pieces of popcorn that had landed in her suitcase and ate it. "Watch me," she said.

"It's going to leak out one way or another. Or eventually you're going to explode," Vickie said. "You may fool other people, but it's like Dr. Cannon said, you can't run away from you. You take yourself with you wherever you go."

"What do you care?"

"I'm a loyal friend."

Julie shifted her weight and cocked her head to one side. "Wait, are you saying I'm your friend?"

"No, I'm saying you're not loyal. You were supposed to help me find out what's going on at this place."

"You're right. I'm not like you, Vickie."

"You know, I'll never forget when we first met," Vickie said.

"Me either."

"When I first saw you, it was automatic hate."

"Ditto. But I thought we were past all that."

"Do you want to know what I didn't like about you?" Vickie asked.

"No."

"You expected to be liked. It looked like you didn't need to earn us, and that pissed me off. You've got to earn us."

"That's ridiculous."

"And another thing—"

"I've had enough of this."

"You grew on me."

"You are so—What did you say?" Julie said.

"Like a fungus. I just learned to accept you."

"Are you trying to give me a compliment?"

"I'm trying to say yes."

"Yes, what?"

"Well, we got matching tattoos, right? If that don't say friend, what does? Yes. Yes, I'm your friend," Vickie said.

Julie sat on the side of her bed, facing Vickie. "Thank you. I wish I were friend material."

"Well, when I get out maybe the two of us can—"

"I tend to let people down, you know? So, I think this is goodbye. For good. I think that would be for the best. But I'm glad I met you."

"I'm glad I met you too. Refraining from punching you in the face on a daily basis has made me a better human," Vickie said, a small smile bending her lips upward.

Julie laughed.

"So, why do you wear your initial on your clothes?"

"It's not my initial. Stands for the Vikings. As in the Koreatown Vikings. As in Koreatown, Queens. As in a high school mascot. I found it at the Salvation Army and grabbed it 'cause it was warm. Or the V can just stand for Vickie."

Julie nodded, stuffing her hairbrush in the side of her suitcase, "Don't worry. You'll be out of here soon."

"Over my dead body. I'm not leaving until I know what happened to Linda."

Julie smiled. "You *are* a good friend. Linda was lucky to have you. Take care, Vickie."

Vickie threw a piece of popcorn and hit Julie in the face.

Just a few minutes later, Vickie watched from the fourth-floor window as a stretch limo pulled up, and Julie descended the front stairs of the manor.

This time Vickie was the girl trapped behind the glass. She wondered if she looked as sad in that moment as Linda did on the day Vickie arrived. Julie turned back one last time, and Vickie tossed her hand up with a tiny wave goodbye. Julie nodded her head and climbed into the car.

"Good luck, Julie," Vickie whispered.

PART FOUR

The
Happier We'll Be

CHAPTER 38
Wishes

The First Floor
8:30 p.m.

Seated in her usual chair, Vickie pretended to read a book, careful to make sure it was right side up this time. Thankfully, residents were allowed to study anywhere in the facility, including their rooms or the sunroom or the lobby. It was one of the teens' few savored freedoms. Vickie watched Nurse Lilly from across the room without raising her head. The lobby was empty except for the two of them and the occasional passerby.

Moments later, when Nurse Lilly exited to a back office, Vickie cast a look to the left and then the right before stuffing her book under the seat cushion and shuffling over to the french doors. In the blink of an eye, she slid out the entrance.

She would have gone through the back, but there would have been too much activity with the cafeteria workers preparing for the next morning and residents meandering through the adjacent sunroom. Vickie also wanted to exit the front door because Linda most likely used it that night. Retracing Linda's steps was the entire point of this evening field trip.

The clean scent of the outdoors hit her in the face immediately. The air had a nip in it that she found refreshing. Bullfrogs and crickets competed for dominance in the orchestra of the night, but most surprising was the smell of the roses. Nurse Lilly had taught her that the favored bloom cycle for some varieties was mid-October. She never knew something could smell so sweet for so long.

Vickie didn't need to go on a special adventure to think of Linda. When others departed and you stayed behind, you were left with all the memory ghosts. Everything about Blueberry Hill still reminded Vickie of her best friend. Even this garden. Vickie remembered Linda's giddy face when she grabbed Vickie's hand and whisked her off on their forbidden trek to eat wild blueberries and smoke cigarettes. She seemed so alive and happy that day. What had happened in the hours that followed?

Despite the ghosts of memories past, Vickie decided to use the fact that she still had access to the crime scene to do her best reenactment of the event and perhaps find a clue as to what really happened that evening.

Linda would have walked by Nurse Lilly's rose garden that night. She would have smelled these smells, heard these sounds. But what would have made her get up in the middle of the night in the first place? Something she wanted? What was out here at night that she couldn't wait until the morning to get? Linda liked flowers, but not enough to get out of bed for them.

Vickie passed the garden and the tree-lined lake and moved beyond the Blueberry Hill stone marquee until she finally found herself standing at the edge of the road.

Linda wouldn't have traipsed this far in a nightgown. Vickie was more certain than ever that Linda didn't intend to leave forever. *But why venture so far?*

Vickie took a deep breath to fortify herself for the barrage of memories she expected would overtake her the moment her feet stepped onto the pavement. She placed her toe and then her entire foot onto the hard surface as if it were made of lava. Before she knew it, her unsteady legs gave way and she knelt on the road. Though there remained no blood-stained trace of where Linda had fallen, Vickie sensed in her bones that this was the spot.

"Come on, Linda, help me figure this out. You said you'd be watching. What am I missing? I don't get it," Vickie said, talking to the air around her.

In the dark distance, two pinpricks of light grew steadily. The whirling of the air against the car's metal body pierced the night long before she saw a vehicle. Vickie stood, covering her eyes with her elbow as the lights got closer, stumbling to the side of the highway as the car whooshed past and disappeared down the long road.

Vickie lowered her elbow from her eyes with a newfound realization. *She had plenty of time.*

Unless she was injured, there was no way Linda didn't notice the vehicle approaching. And there was no way she walked in front of that vehicle on purpose.

What am I missing?

The Linda I knew wouldn't have run away, or killed herself.

There was another possibility. That Vickie didn't know Linda at all. She shook away the thought.

What Vickie could accept was that Linda must not have been thinking rationally to have missed the warning signs of an oncoming vehicle.

Was she running from something? Running to something?

A chill ran up Vickie's spine.

That's enough for tonight.

Vickie meandered back toward the manor with more questions than answers. But she knew in her heart that Linda hadn't intentionally thrown herself in front of that car. Someone or something else had directly caused her death. And there were still more answers to be found here at Blueberry Hill.

The First Floor
9:40 p.m.

Vickie didn't dare sneak back in through the front door at this hour. Instead, she walked around to the back, entering through the loading dock door. The kitchen staff had left for the night and most residents were showering, which made it the better option. Once safely indoors, she made her way down the side hallway, then strolled past reception triumphantly.

"It's almost time for night checks," Nurse Lilly said to Vickie, straightening the desk, plopping a pen into a jar with dozens of others. Nurse Fran and Nurse Dorothy busied themselves nearby with tidying up for the night.

Vickie saluted them all matter-of-factly, acknowledging Nurse Lilly's comment as she continued her stroll past.

The nurses resumed with their own conversation.

"I'm so happy to be getting out of here," Nurse Dorothy said. "Didn't you think the day dragged on?"

"Just another day," Nurse Fran responded.

"And it's freezing," Nurse Dorothy said. "It's not winter yet, for goodness' sake."

"They probably damaged the duct work for the furnace when they moved it to the attic last spring," Nurse Fran said.

"Why did they move it anyway?"

"It's supposed to be quieter," Nurse Fran said.

"Shouldn't we call someone to repair it before it gets really cold out?" Nurse Dorothy asked.

"No." Nurse Lilly's mouth shriveled into a fine point. "I'll ask maintenance to have a look," Nurse Lilly said.

Nurse Dorothy stepped over to the thermostat behind the desk, paused, then banged the side of it with her hand. "That's odd. It says it's 78 degrees."

"So, what are you complaining about?" Nurse Fran said.

"Does it feel like 78 to you? This place has cold spots," Nurse Dorothy added.

Nurse Lilly explained, "It's drafty, that's all."

Nurse Dorothy closed a file cabinet, the sound underlining her comment. "Or haunted."

Vickie didn't pay much attention to their exchange as she continued down the hallway and up the stairs to room 402, even though she always listened to what went on around her. It was a special skill she could never completely turn off.

She opened the door and entered, after having avoided returning to her room most of the day. She had grown accustomed to having two roommates. Now, with only one again, she'd have to readjust.

Annie was there and met Vickie with a warm smile, but the first thing Vickie saw was Julie's empty bed.

A small suitcase lay open on Annie's mattress.

"What's going on?" Vickie asked.

Annie carefully folded each clothing item as she hummed happily, her ever-present smile animating her lips. "Packing."

"Why?"

"My new family is coming to get me."

Vickie dropped onto her bed.

"No one is coming, Annie." Vickie threw one of her shoes to the floor with unexpected force.

"They told me so. You'll see."

"Who's they?"

"The people in the pipes want me to come live with them," Annie said.

"You've been packing and unpacking since you got here. No one's coming."

"This time's different."

"Then tell them to hurry up already? I'd love to have this room completely to myself and get some peace and quiet for a change."

Annie stopped folding her shirt for a moment, lip quivering, then she continued packing. "They are already here," she said under her breath, but Vickie heard every word. "Haven't you heard the music?"

"In the pipes?"

Annie nodded.

"Pipes clang. That's not music. And people don't live in pipes, Annie."

"Maybe they aren't alive in the way you think."

"Ghosts? Not you too." Vickie rolled her eyes and fell back on her bed, staring at the ceiling.

"There are lots of ways to be alive." Annie folded another item and placed it in the suitcase. "And lots of ways to be dead."

Vickie's eyes glazed over for a moment as she retreated into her thoughts, exhaling softly, and smiling in acknowledgment. There was some truth to what Annie was saying. There always was, but Vickie thought it best to leave it for another day. After sliding into her pajamas with her back to Annie, Vickie pulled back her covers and climbed into bed. Less than a half hour later, both Vickie and Annie were asleep. Annie's tiny suitcase sat next to her nightstand, full of her meager belongings.

DAY 76 for Vickie
Room 402
12:50 a.m.

"Annie," the female voice whispered so sweetly it sounded like a song. "A-a-a-annie."

Annie rustled from her sleep, sitting up in her bed, rubbing her eyes. She looked in Vickie's direction and, although it was dark, she could see the bed was occupied. The light snores coming from the other side of the room provided further confirmation that Vickie hadn't called out to her.

"A-a-a-a-nie."

"Hello?" Annie whispered back. Her eyes brightened quickly, excited to play whatever game this might be. She made her way over to the door and opened it, leaning out to the left and then to the right.

Nobody in sight.

Then she spied it, shimmering in the moonlight. The mask she'd been working on in drama class hung on the doorknob along with a pair of colorful fairy wings, glittering in the sparse moonlight that shone through the window behind her.

Her homemade papier-mâché creation looked elfin, the cheekbones high, and the ears enormously out of proportion. She couldn't resist strapping on the sparkly wings. One shoulder at a time, she slid her arm through the elastic, gasping in delight with every movement until finally, she clasped her hands together and bounced in her version of a happy dance. She plucked off a note attached to the wings and read it:

Come play. Meet us on the sixth floor. Bring your suitcase. — Your New Family.

Annie looked over at Vickie, who was still snoring. She giggled out a "told you so," her face radiating happiness.

Vickie stirred in her sleep, and Annie shushed her laugh, bringing her finger to her mouth. Grinning from ear to ear, she carried her suitcase out of the room and into the quiet hallway, barely noticing the faint sound of music that followed her like a nudge forward, underscoring the moment.

The more we get together . . .

Assessment and Plan

Provider: Blueberry Hill Home for Troubled Youth, LLC **Client Name: Annie Meadows**
Group Assignment: Pod #1   **Session Number:** #1

Diagnosis: Symptoms of Schizophrenia. Further monitoring needed for diagnosis.

Treatment

Intake Protocol: Clinical Assessment   **Medications:** Chlorpromazine 50 mg/day,
                     Schizophrenia and   Fluoxetine 20 mg/day,
                     Anxiety Questionnaires   *as per* Dr. Mariska Habsburg, M.D.

Short-Term Goals for Client (2 Weeks):
1. Form peer relationships.
2. Begin reality testing in clinical conversations.
3. Introduce coping strategies to mitigate auditory hallucinations: humming or singing a song several times, listening to music, reading (forward and backward), talking with others, exercise, ignoring the voices, medication.
4. Adjust medication levels as needed.
5. Educate about triggers such as anxiety.

Long-Term Goals (3 Months):
1. Client consistently employs coping strategies.
2. Self-reports ability to distinguish reality from imagination.

Session Notes

Body Language, Facial Patterns: Easily distracted, constant movement, manic affect.

Summary:
1. Client stated that she feels "energized" and "happy."
2. Client spoke of "magic powers" and other topics illustrative of magical thinking.
3. Evidence of auditory and visual hallucinations presented, such as voices in her head that tell her what to do.

Other Observations/Comments:
- Her speech was normal in rate/pitch and flowed easily.
- Her thoughts were coherent, and her conversation was appropriate.
- Though magical thinking is present, it does not seem to be correlated with any sort of obsessive behavior.

Client Signature: _Annie Meadows_   **Primary Caregiver 1:** _James Barrows_
(Age 14 and up)   Annie Meadows   James Barrows for Margarette Meadows
                                                          (Power of Attorney)

Primary Caregiver 2: _____   **Therapist Signature:** _Ara Cannon_
                    N/A   Dr. Ara Cannon, Ph.D.

CHAPTER 39
Paper Clips

Room 402
6:30 a.m.

When Vickie woke, she pawed the covers off in a big cat-stretch, grunting audibly before slowly opening her eyes. It took a moment for the room to come into focus.

Her contented, early morning smile disappeared when her gaze landed on Julie's empty bed, the covers still neatly made. She had said she wanted the room to herself the previous night, but even then, she knew she didn't mean it.

She sighed, then looked over to Annie's bed to reassure herself, expecting to be met with Annie's warm smile and sleepy eyes. The covers were tousled, but Annie was nowhere to be found.

Vickie's eyebrows crinkled and her face tensed.

I must have overslept, was her first thought. *But I never oversleep.*

She got out of the bed and peeked out of the window. The sun hadn't yet reached the top of the trees outside. That meant Vickie wasn't late.

Maybe Annie got up early?

Her chest tightened as her body acknowledged other possible explanations her head was not prepared to explore.

At breakfast, the entire pod sat at the same table, except for Annie,

276

who did not appear. Everyone ate in apprehensive silence. The occasional scraping of a fork against the cafeteria tray penetrated the quiet. Each of them took turns glancing toward Annie's seat until Vickie aggressively slid back her chair, marching out of the cafeteria and toward reception.

As she rounded the corner of the tiny hallway connecting the lobby to the cafeteria, Vickie noticed something new: A uniformed security guard stood in front of the french doors.

He wasn't there the night before. What's changed?

Vickie overheard Nurse Lilly speaking to the guard as she approached. "Not in here! You'll upset the kids. Stand outside."

Vickie now stood in front of the reception desk and spoke directly to Nurse Fran and Nurse Dorothy. "Where's Annie?"

Nurse Fran and Nurse Dorothy looked at one another, then glanced at Vickie, and finally stared at Nurse Lilly, who was making her way over to Vickie from the french doors.

Standing a little straighter, Vickie puffed out her chest. "Well?"

Nurse Lilly didn't speak until she was close enough to touch Vickie.

"Vickie," she began in a hushed tone.

Something in the way she spoke made Vickie's stomach flutter. Vickie crossed her arms and stared at Nurse Lilly.

"I'm afraid Annie is missing."

Nurse Fran and Nurse Dorothy pretended to file things, but moved in slow motion, listening to the conversation.

"What?" The sound was more like a breath than a word. She didn't even realize she had spoken. Vickie's chest was expanding and contracting, but no air filled her lungs. She felt lightheaded. Nurse Lilly put her hand on Vickie's shoulder, but Vickie shook off the gesture.

"Have you noticed any odd behavior from her?" asked Nurse Lilly.

"Of course, I have. She's Annie."

"What do you remember about the last time you saw her?"

"I came in and she was packing."

"Packing?"

"She packed and unpacked every other night."

"We think—"

"You think?" Vickie responded with increased volume.

"We think she may have run away." Nurse Lilly's words pounded into the temples of Vickie's head with an echoing thud.

"Doesn't anyone see what's happening here?" Vickie looked at Nurse Fran, poinrinf her words at her. "*You* see everything." Then, Vickie looked at Nurse Lilly. "You just—lost another one?" Vickie picked up a box of paper clips and threw them on the floor, scattering the thin, silver pieces everywhere.

"Vickie," Nurse Lilly spoke with a measured tone.

"*They* may just be teenagers to you, but they are still human beings. They're not your office supplies! Oh, I misplaced my stapler! Oh well. There's plenty more where they came from. They matter!"

By now, the rest of her pod had gathered, listening nearby. Residents from another pod were close as well, sitting in the lobby, waiting for their first activity of the day, all attentive to Vickie's impassioned words.

Vickie gestured at the security guard, who had moved onto the porch as requested, oblivious to the interaction, raising her voice even more so all the bystanders could hear. "Doesn't anyone care? Can't you see? Something is not right here!"

Nurse Lilly nodded her head, signaling a couple of strong, white-clad orderlies, who had appeared in the staff room doorway, to come nearer. They happened to be the same two that had escorted Vickie to the white room.

The orderlies approached Vickie, but dare not touch her. Yet.

Nurse Lilly spoke again, her lovely smile not reaching her eyes this time. "Why don't you take the day off? Go and rest. In your room."

"So you can disappear me too?"

The orderlies inched closer to Vickie, one of them reaching cautiously for her shoulder.

"You like that hand? Better keep it to yourself," Vickie warned.

The orderlies hesitated, one of them still nursing a black eye from his last encounter with Vickie and the other unconsciously covering his crotch, remembering the kick to the groin she had given him.

"I'll walk with her," Tracy intervened. The two orderlies relaxed their shoulders, exhaling in relief.

"I'll go by myself."

"Vickie, we are on your side," Nurse Lilly said.

"Like you were on Linda's side? And those other four, now five? Were you on their side? I don't know whose side all of you are on, but I like my chances more if I'm on the other team."

The orderlies reached out for her again, but she wriggled out of their grip.

Vickie held up her hands in front of her, palms outward facing. "I'm going."

"We'll keep you posted," Nurse Lilly said.

As Vickie walked away, she was pleased to hear Nurse Lilly shriek as she slipped and almost fell on the scattered paper clips.

"Someone clean this up, please, before Dr. Habsburg sees it," Nurse Lilly said, trying to stand.

The tall, thin janitor, his dark, stringy hair tucked messily under his cap, rushed over with a dustpan and broom.

He must have just been finishing up his rounds. He normally works the night shift.

CHAPTER 40
Quiet Doors

Room 402
8:00 a.m.

For the first time since coming to Blueberry Hill, Vickie was roommate-free. She canvassed the room, checking in Annie's nightstand and then her section of the chest of drawers, only to pull out one empty drawer after another.

Then she knelt, looking under Annie's bed.

Nothing.

No clothes.

No luggage.

Nothing.

"Annie," Vickie sighed, collapsing into a seated position on the floor.

Room 402
11:45 p.m.

Vickie spent the entire day in her room. Two untouched trays of food, lunch and dinner, lay on the top of the chest of drawers. She lay on her bed, tossing her baseball in the air and catching it, over and over.

Sometime around the one hundred fifty-third throw, everything seemed to slow down. She felt the muscles in her right hand tense around the cool, smooth leather casing of the ball before bending her wrist back slightly, then snapping it forward, releasing it into the air. Vickie watched as it flew up, up, up, until it slowed and stopped for a moment in mid-air, then fell back into her open palm.

An empty mind. She could almost hear Dr. Cannon speaking the words.

Flashes of memories seeped into her head, lingering, and then floating away with every toss of the ball.

The first time she saw Linda through the fourth-floor window.

Linda chatting the night away while Vickie tried her best to go to sleep.

Their foray through the woods.

The quick mud.

The blueberries.

The cigarettes.

Full heart. Vickie smiled.

Vickie heard Dr. Cannon's words echo again remembering her friend Linda, her eyes twinkling as she read *The Masque of the Red Death* in the lobby.

Vickie caught the ball again, then paused, looking over at the nightstand she had shared with Julie, and Linda before her.

The Masque of the Red Death lay there, left behind by Julie when she departed.

Objects. Objects are neutral, but we give them meaning.

Dr. Cannon's words compelled Vickie to pick up the book and flip through its pages. This time she treated each page differently, like it mattered.

When she got to the pages containing the handwritten messages in the margins, she paused. The messages were clearly written by two different people, one neater than the other, the way a teacher might write; it was Linda's handwriting. And the other was, well, barely legible. But this book and these messages meant something. Vickie acknowledged that rising certainty in her heart.

On the top of one of the pages, she noticed one message stood out more; the ink was brighter, like it was newer.

GARDEN. DURING MY BREAK AT MIDNIGHT. SO MUCH TO CATCH UP ON.

What?

Vickie read it again, not believing her eyes.

So, the boy Linda was interested in did work here. How else would he have access to this book? Angelo. It's got to be Angelo.

Vickie put down the novel and sat up on the edge of the bed.

Her shoulders shot up and she clamped her elbows tight to her sides, staring straight ahead. The tension bubbled and raged within her, threatening to explode out the top of her head. Before she knew it, she was on her feet, pacing back and forth across the room. The faster the thoughts came and went, the faster she paced. She could almost see the memories fluttering around the room, finding their place like 3D puzzle pieces.

Annie's words surfaced in her mind. She saw Annie in her bed saying them right now. *The people in the pipes want me to come live with them.* The memory was so vivid that Vickie walked over to the pipe and placed her ear near it, listening. She heard nothing at first, but then she emptied her mind and listened closer, latching on to every tiny sound and following it. That's when she heard the whispers threading through the metal casing.

She stood up on Annie's bed and, with her hands, followed the pipe up to the ceiling.

Another memory overtook her as she felt her way up the pipe.

She recalled watching the other members of her pod grooming Snowflake while she perched on a bale of hay outside the fence, just before she had fallen off and scraped her knee. Linda's black bird had been sitting on the ledge of a window at the very top of Blueberry Manor. In her mind's eye, she counted the floors, one through six, and the bird was higher still, on a seventh-floor ledge.

"Seven floors," she mouthed.

They probably damaged the duct work for the furnace when they moved it to the attic last spring, she remembered Nurse Fran saying.

Vickie's eyes stretched wider, then she bolted to the door, but halted with her hand on the knob. She looked back over her shoulder, thinking for a moment. Then, she rushed back over to the chest of drawers she had shared with Annie, Linda, and Julie.

Vickie slid open the top drawer that belonged to her and shuffled through a couple of her sweatshirts, revealing the picture of Linda with her foster parents and something shiny beside it. The glare from the tiny lamp on the dresser bounced off the metal object into her eyes. Vickie lifted Nurse Lilly's golden garden shears out of her drawer, turning them over in the dim light.

She studied the photo of Linda and then the shears, finally placing the photo back in its spot and tucking the shears into the elastic band of her sweatpants. She gave the photo one last affectionate pat before sliding the drawer back into place.

Vickie returned to the door, easing it open. Luckily, the whining hinges were no longer an issue since the cleaners had oiled them. It was late, and she knew she'd be late returning, too, but with no roommates to wake, it didn't really matter anymore. And getting caught was worth the risk. Her mouth tensed and drew up tight as she slipped through the gap.

She shuffled quickly down the still hallway, then descended the staircase to the first floor. The hired security guard snored near the front door.

He must've moved inside after we were all in bed. This is going to be easier than I thought.

Vickie snuck up to him and grabbed the heavy, black flashlight propped next to his chair. She steadied herself before moving forward, trying her best not to make a sound, yet, despite her efforts, the wooden floor creaked in betrayal and the guard stirred. Vickie scrunched up her face and held her breath as if that would somehow make her invisible.

Luckily, the guard resumed his slumber, and Vickie shuffled past the unmanned reception area. She noticed something familiar next to the desk, the pair of white nurse shoes Nurse Dorothy changed into and out of every day. Thinking they might be useful, Vickie picked them both up with one hand by the laces, tying them around her belt, and continued on her way as quickly as possible.

She climbed five flights of stairs until she reached the sixth floor, then scanned the hallway, looking for a room that wasn't a residence. Halfway down, she found a door not marked with a room number.

Why didn't I notice this before?

She made her way toward it, one creaky footstep at a time, until her feet were squarely planted in front of the threshold. It was smaller than the rest of the doors, older looking, and worn, not shiny and polished like the rest of the surrounding paneling.

Vickie placed her free hand on the knob, which was much newer than the other handles she was accustomed to at Blueberry Hill, and with a swift turn discovered—it was locked. She blew out her long-held breath, turning over the possibilities of what to do next in her head. Within seconds, she decided to return to her room and regroup.

No shame in retreating, right? I gained some ground tonight, and now I know what to focus on next.

As she turned away from the unmarked entrance back toward the stairs, she bumped into someone blocking her way. Her eyelids fluttered as she gasped.

"What are you doing here?" Vickie asked.

"Night checks. Why aren't you in your room?" Angelo asked, grabbing her by the arm.

"Hey." Vickie shook free of his grasp.

"I'm trying to help you," Angelo whispered.

Vickie surprised herself with the words that blurted out. "Why were you always asking about Linda?"

"What?"

"And the book. The book Julie was reading. It was you, wasn't it? Meeting with Linda?" Vickie had so many questions; her mind was moving lightning quick.

"Come on," Angelo said, avoiding eye contact and grabbing for her arm again. He missed.

"Was it you?"

"Yes. But you can't say anything." He looked Vickie directly in the eyes.

"What? Do you know what really happened to her? She didn't run away. Or run out in front of that car on purpose. What was she doing out there in the middle of the night?" Vickie asked. "Meeting you?"

"Shhhh! Come with me, let's go somewhere to talk," Angelo suggested.

This time, when Angelo grabbed Vickie's arm, more forcefully than before, she struggled with the kind of determination a rush of adrenaline brought. He was strong. But Vickie was by no means weak, and her reflexes were unmatched.

Before Angelo could react, Vickie hit him in the head with the flashlight, so quickly and forcefully all he could do was collapse.

That was for you, Linda.

With Angelo out cold, Vickie sprang into action, unfastening his key ring from his belt. Rifling through the antique keys, none of them seemed anywhere close to what the new-looking lock on the small door required. She paused for a moment, glancing up and down the hallway before looking back down at Angelo, flat on his back, head tilted to the side, mouth open, drooling.

With some effort, she rolled Angelo to his side long enough to fish in his back pocket for his wallet. It was warm in her hands. The second she opened it the blood drained from her face. Everything seemed jammed up inside Vickie; even her thoughts froze for a moment. Inside Angelo's wallet was a photo of Linda. Judging by the normal-looking clothes she was wearing, and the shorter hair, it was taken before she entered the care of her current foster parents. The image looked like a school photo, the kind a case worker might staple to a file.

Angelo's hand flinched as he regained consciousness. Vickie's pupils dilated. In one fluid motion, she cracked him in the head again with the flashlight, with all the care and regard that would be given to an annoying fly.

"Hmmmph," she said under her breath, unloading a disapproving grunt for good measure.

Vickie removed two credit cards from Angelo's wallet and walked over to the door, sliding the two cards in and out between the frame and door until it clicked open.

"Cha-ching." She placed the two credit cards in her bra just in case she needed them again.

Vickie opened the door and then returned to the still unconscious Angelo, dragging him through the small doorway and into a utility closet on the other side of it, immediately to her left.

After stuffing his body inside, she slammed the door hard a time or two, but it didn't latch. She looked down and saw Angelo's left arm had slipped out of the door, keeping it from closing. Her nostrils flared as she slammed the door even harder on his limb, deliberately this time, before kicking his arm inside and leaning on the door to close it.

Vickie had kept Nurse Dorothy's shoes with her this entire time; now she untied the laces from her belt. She sat on the first step of the long, narrow staircase and slid into them. Standing, she shifted her weight back and forth, wiggling her toes inside the supple leather, her eyes gleaming. "Woah. Sweet." She relished the two inches the shoes added to her height.

As she placed her foot on the first step, she waited for the sound of creaking wood, tensing her face in anticipation. Only silence followed, in part because of the shoes and mostly because of the new construction of the staircase.

"Stealth," she said to herself as she continued climbing.

Light spilled from under the door at the top of the stairs and her flashlight helped ensure no more missteps. Oddly, she heard the faint sound of music.

The more we get together, together, together . . .

Her eyebrows raised and her lips puckered in concentration as she ascended the staircase. She wasn't sure if the tightening in her chest, the lump in her throat, and her quickening heartbeat meant she was going to pass out or that she was more hyper-aware than usual, that she was ready for whatever lay ahead. Regardless, Vickie continued climbing, step by step, more determined than ever to keep moving forward.

For Annie.

And dare she think it—*for Linda.*

She hadn't been able to protect Linda, but hopefully there was still time to help Annie. Her desire to find any kind of clue grew as she approached the attic door. She didn't expect to find Annie greeting her on the other side of the threshold, but maybe she'd find some sort of sign that would offer direction.

As she reached the top, she was both surprised and relieved to discover the door cracked slightly open. When the music abruptly stopped playing her throat constricted. Vickie placed her hand on the door and, thankfully, it opened without any warning squeaks. She peeked inside, like a mouse in a cave.

CHAPTER 41
Shifting Shadows

DAY 77 for Vickie

The Attic

12:30 a.m.

Vickie cast her eyes from one side of the space to the other, taking notice of every shifting shadow that slid along the walls. Refusing to be intimidated by the large, dimly lit attic, she steeled herself to fight from inside the belly of the nightmarish beast of a room.

Vickie began by collecting the visual details of her surroundings. Her mind turned cartwheels, taking in the specifics. She recognized a nail gun as well as other tools scattered throughout the space. Ladders. Sawhorses. Together, these were the telltale signs of recent construction.

"What the . . ."

Sheets of plastic hung from the rafters of the high ceiling, swaying gently from the type of drafts that snuck in through the cracks in old buildings. She pulled the collar of her sweater tighter around her neck, shivering.

Vickie laid her flashlight next to the door, finding the ambient light sufficient. Although she was relieved to free her hands, without something to hold, each step away from the flashlight and the door left her feeling more vulnerable and exposed.

Only a few steps past the threshold, she encountered her first sheet of hanging plastic, and then another, and another. She pushed each dangling, cold panel to the side one at a time. She continued her progression, despite the plastic sheeting making a heavy crackkling sound each time she touched it.

Vickie heard her own heartbeat as it thundered in her eardrums, feeling the perspiration squeeze through her pores and each hair on her arms raise on its end. For a moment, she thought she might never find a way out, doomed to stay trapped in this shifting plastic maze forever. These cloudy barriers reminded her of the ten-foot hedges beside the manor. She felt her chest tighten with no exit in sight. She loved puzzles, but mazes were another story. The insistent fluttering in her stomach grew stronger as the air suctioned from her lungs. She thought the fear might overtake her, swallow her, bury her alive when, at last, she neared a larger opening.

Something told her whatever was on the other side of that filmy barrier would change things forever. Yet another impulse deep within invited her to stop now and retrace her steps back to the attic entrance, through the sixth-floor hallway, down the staircases, and into the safe confines of room 402. It would have been easy enough. She hadn't crossed any lines yet that she couldn't explain away.

Even if she physically left and went back, the morning would still bring consequences for having come this far and for what she had done to Angelo.

But what about Linda? And now, Annie?

If answers lay ahead, she deemed the risk worthwhile.

"No going back. Only forward," she bargained with herself.

Through the final sheets of plastic, she could make out five shadowy figures. Her hand trembled as she pushed the last thick sheath to the side. Vickie's eyes went wide, and she drew in a sharp breath as she stepped through.

Eight chairs sat around a large makeshift table, a piece of plywood held up with sawhorses under each side for support. Five of the seats were occupied. Vickie focused her attention on the four seated individuals nearest her first. She knew these kids. Three girls and a boy, all around her age. *What are their names? Think. Think. Think.* She still couldn't recall them easily. *Why can't I remember? I've heard them several times now.* Slowly, the jumble of thoughts seemed to disappear as she concluded, regardless of their names, together they were the missing four.

Still processing, turning things over more quickly now in her head, she noticed their odd dress—the extravagant outfits, feather boas, costume jewelry; they looked like dolls. Masks covered their faces, each with an exaggerated feature of some kind: a grotesque nose, a large forehead, protruding eyes, or rotund cheeks.

She moved closer until she stood near enough to see their eyes through the masks. No one greeted her or looked her way. It was as if they were frozen or fixed in place, even though Vickie observed their chests rise and fall with their breaths.

Still alive. But dazed.

And then Vickie noticed a fifth figure at the table. She recognized the familiar mask.

"Annie?" Vickie whispered.

Annie wore shimmery wings and the elfin-faced mask she had created in drama class. Her eyes still held her signature magic sparkle; Vickie could see them through the mask, but they were muted just a bit, like those of a child who'd just learned there wasn't a Santa Claus.

Vickie rushed over, removing the mask from the girl's face. "Annie? Annie?"

Annie's head bobbed toward Vickie, now close by her side.

"Vickie?" she croaked in a voice coated with sleep.

"Yes. What happened?"

"My family didn't come," Annie whispered, her eyes overflowing with disappointment.

"It's all right, I'm going to get you out of here. Come on."

"Vickie," Annie whispered.

Something about the helpless and feeble tone in Annie's voice made Vickie pay closer attention to the table. Each of the teenagers held their left hand on the table, palm down, including Annie.

That's odd.

Then, looking closer at Annie's left hand, Vickie noticed a trickle of dried blood down the side and something shiny on top of it. A nail, burrowing straight through her flesh and into the plywood on the other side. The pinched skin around the nail head was bruised to an angry red and purple.

Annie looked deep into Vickie's eyes now and whispered, "Hide."

Vickie heard the rhythmic sound of the plastic sheets being pushed out of the way, one after the other. And through what must have only been five layers of remaining plastic, she saw a figure in white approaching.

Quickly scanning the room, Vickie saw a nearby closet. "I'll be back. I promise," she said. She hurried to the closet and shimmied inside, leaving the door cracked slightly so she could see from within her hiding spot.

"We have a special guest joining us for our party, so it's important everyone be on their best behavior," a woman said in a voice Vickie thought she recognized, though it took a moment to retrieve the memory from her fear-addled brain. She finally placed the vocalization just before the woman moved the last piece of plastic out of the way and stepped quickly toward the table. "Sit up straight and remember to smile," Nurse Lilly continued.

An antique music box sat on a bench just behind the makeshift table. A male and female figurine in eighteenth-century formal garments began to rotate atop the antique pedestal as Nurse Lilly twisted the tiny knob. Heating and cooling pipes lined the wall just behind the music box, stretching from the ceiling and extending below, connecting one floor to the next. The hauntingly familiar tune it eked out reverberated through the attic and into the metal casings of the pipes.

The more we get together, together, together . . .

As Nurse Lilly walked toward the teens, her eyes tracked toward Annie's mask, lying on the plywood in front of her. "What's this?" Nurse Lilly pulled a shaker from her pocket and sprinkled something into the mask before placing it back on Annie's face. "Breathe. That's it. That's a good girl."

Watching from the closet, Vickie's mind raced as the pieces fell into place. Quick flashes, like daydreams on speed, combined memories with Vickie's own imagination.

Flash.

Nurse Lilly shaking powder into Linda's red mask.

Flash.

Linda waking up at the table with the other four teens, dazed, confused, then walking away from the table, stumbling through the plastic and down the steps.

Flash.

Linda hit by a vehicle and left dead in the road.

Linda.

Now Annie.

Drugs.

Control.

Vickie froze in place, reminding herself to breathe like Dr. Cannon taught her.

That's it. In and out.

Nurse Lilly watched as Annie's eyes, peering through the mask, shifted to the other side of the room toward the closet. "What has your attention over there?"

Just then, a bird, Linda's crow, landed on the windowsill next to the closet, looking in from outside. The flapping of its urgent wings as it steadied itself was loud and relentless. "I hate those birds. They ruin a garden. Shoo!" Nurse Lilly cocked her head to the side, staring at the closet that stood partly open.

From Vickie's vantage point inside the closet, Nurse Lilly appeared to be staring directly at her. Vickie shrank back into the darkness. She held the breath she had worked so hard to control, nearly choking on the trapped air, when something else drew Nurse Lilly's attention away. Vickie could hear it too.

Footsteps. Someone else is coming.

"Lillian?" Vickie recognized that awful, pinched German voice as well.

Dr. Habsburg.

Thank God, Vickie exhaled. *Dr. Habsburg will take care of this, whatever this is.*

Vickie craned her neck around a broom handle and saw Dr. Habsburg holding a fancy envelope tightly in one of her hands.

"What's going on here?" Dr. Habsburg asked. She planted her feet and crossed her arms as she surveyed the gruesome scene.

Nurse Lilly clapped her excited hands in rapid succession. "You came! And you got our invitation," she said, walking over to the musical contraption and cranking the tiny silver knob a few more times.

"My music box," Dr. Habsburg said. "You know better."

Nurse Lillian waltzed in a circle holding the music box, more like a child spinning to ring-around-the-rosy than a grown woman dancing. "Remember how we used to dance round and round listening to it?"

Dr. Habsburg uncrossed her arms, holding her hands loosely by her sides. Vickie knew this stance. She found herself posturing much this same way when a physical fight was imminent. Dr. Habsburg grabbed the music box as Nurse Lilly spun past and placed it on the table with a thud.

Vickie urged the doctor on with her thoughts. *Get her, Dr. Habsburg! Come on!*

In a voice even higher than usual, almost childlike, Nurse Lilly spoke. "Why did you do that?"

"What have you done?" Dr. Habsburg asked as she surveyed the children at the table.

Vickie could almost hear the veins in the doctor's neck protrude through her words.

"Look how happy they are to see you." Nurse Lilly grabbed the head of one of the masked teens and angled it toward Dr. Habsburg. "I've always wanted four girls and a boy of my very own." Nurse Lilly gasped. "I just realized something. This makes you a grandmother. We're one big, happy family."

Vickie's mouth dropped open. *These two are related? Dr. Habsburg is Nurse Lilly's mother?*

The Attic
1:00 a.m.

Nurse Lilly's eyes sparkled, and her heart overflowed at the sight of so many of her favorite things in one space. The sound of the music box unwinding its notes, her mother witnessing all her work, and her new family, rescued from their unwanted loneliness.

Could anything be more perfect?

"Lillian," Dr. Habsburg said, her tone firm and even.

"Don't worry, no one is going to get away again. I made sure of that this time," Nurse Lilly said, holding up a nail gun. "Not after Linda. Poor Linda. She got away. I didn't mean to let her get away. You understand."

Nurse Lilly's eyes glazed like she was in two places at once. She cocked her head to one side, her body swaying, her mind stuck somewhere in time, remembering.

DAY 45 for Vickie

Dr. Habsburg's Office

10:25 a.m.

17 Hours, 8 Minutes Until Linda's Death

Dr. Habsburg sat at her desk with Nurse Lilly standing nearby.

"As I mentioned this morning, we are discharging Linda. Take care of the paperwork," Dr. Habsburg said as she sorted the mail, not bothering to look up at Nurse Lilly standing in front of her desk.

Nurse Lilly smiled. "I love seeing families reunited."

"Her foster parents don't want her back. She's going to a state facility."

"We can't just send her away."

"Her foster family relinquished her placement, and they no longer want to pay. This isn't a charity. At least she has somewhere to go."

"Poor girl. No family." Nurse Lilly shook her head.

The Sixth Floor

10:29 a.m.

17 Hours, 4 Minutes Until Linda's Death

Nurse Lilly exited Dr. Habsburg's office, straightening her uniform and sighing. She stopped just before rounding the corner to the sixth floor's main hallway when she heard voices. Sensing she had stumbled on a private moment, she peeked around the corner, careful not to be seen.

Angelo caught Linda by the arm as she left Eagen's room.

"I got your note. I'll be there," Linda said, a soft grin playing on her face.

"We're going to get through this," he said, gently rubbing her arm.

"I believe you. I just feel bad about keeping things from Vickie."

"Only for a little longer. Until we can be together."

Linda nodded. "See you in the garden at midnight."

Angelo nodded. "I'm so glad I found you. After all these years." Linda and Angelo parted and walked off in opposite directions.

Nurse Lilly pressed her back against the wall of the side hallway, still out of sight, her eyes darting back and forth, processing what she had heard before taking a determined step forward.

The First Floor
11:30 p.m.
4 Hours, 3 Minutes Until Linda's Death

Nurse Fran worked at the reception desk as usual, methodically filing away the day's business. Nurse Lilly approached and stood next to her.

"Why don't you go on home early? I'll cover the rest of your shift," Nurse Lilly said, smiling in her usual sunny way.

"Again? Well, I'm not one to look a gift horse in the mouth," Nurse Fran said.

"What did you call me?" Nurse Lilly joked.

Nurse Fran filed one last folder, then walked toward the staff lounge to collect her things. "I'm getting out of her before you change your mind."

DAY 46 for Vickie
The First Floor
12:01 a.m.
3 Hours, 32 Minutes Until Linda's Death

Angelo left the staff lounge hurriedly, throwing his arms through his leather jacket one at a time. Nurse Lilly watched from the window of the sunshine room. Angelo exited through the french doors and into the night. She moved out into the corridor as he left the stairs. Moments later, Linda

296

tiptoed down the stairwell and into the lobby.

Nurse Lilly sat in a chair near the door and cleared her throat.

Linda jumped. "Nurse Lilly. I didn't see you."

"Relax. I'm not going to get you in trouble on your last night."

Linda's shoulders dropped. "Thank you."

"I heard where they are sending you. I'm so sorry. It's all just so wrong."

"Yeah, well. I drew the short straw when it comes to families."

Linda cast a glance toward the closed french doors that led to the garden. "But maybe that will change one day, and I'll find someone who wants me and a place I belong."

Nurse Lilly stood and grabbed both Linda's hands in hers. "Life can change in a heartbeat."

Linda smiled, warming in Nurse Lilly's glow.

"Where were you heading?"

Linda looked back at the doors again. "Nowhere. Just couldn't sleep."

"Well, since you're here, there's something waiting for you in the drama classroom. I figured you'd want to take it with you. Why don't you go and grab it?"

Linda kissed Nurse Lilly gently on the cheek. "I don't know what to say. You've been so good to me."

Linda walked down the hallway toward the drama classroom. Nurse Lilly touched the cheek that Linda kissed, her heart melting.

```
The Drama Classroom
12:05 a.m.
3 Hours, 28 Minutes Until Linda's Death
```

Nurse Lilly watched from around the corner as Linda entered and

297

immediately caught sight of her blood-red mask, carefully placed on the desk nearest the door. Touched by the gesture, she took hold of it with both hands and spun around to look at herself wearing it in the mirror.

She moved closer, admiring the mask on her, took a deep breath in, and collapsed.

The Drama Classroom
12:07 a.m.
3 Hours, 26 Minutes Until Linda's Death

Linda lay on the floor, the mask half on, half off her face. Someone entered behind her, gathered Linda in their arms, ignoring the mask as it fell to the floor, and whisked her away.

The Lobby
12:35 a.m.
2 Hours, 58 Minutes Until Linda's Death

Angelo re-entered the manor through the french doors, startled at finding Nurse Lilly sitting at reception.

"Back so soon," Nurse Lilly commented.

"Yes, just needed some air. You didn't see anyone come by, did you?" Angelo asked.

"No."

"Just checking. Usually, I'm the only one in the lobby at this time, but I like to make sure no one else is out and about who shouldn't be."

"How diligent of you. Well, I'm leaving soon myself. Paperwork." She held up a stack of papers and files as proof.

They exchanged a knowing smile as Angelo headed down the hallway, casting a last look over his shoulder at Nurse Lilly.

Day 77 for Vickie
The Attic
1:00 a.m.

The ghosts of Nurse Lilly's memory haze lifted as quickly as they descended. Only seconds had passed, yet so much had occupied her mind. She righted her tilted head, her finger accidentally hitting the nail gun's trigger, sending a projectile shooting out, which embedded itself in the closet door.

"Oooops," Nurse Lilly giggled. "I'd better stick to garden tools." She laid the nail gun down.

"I didn't raise you this way," Dr. Habsburg said.

"This is exactly how you raised me."

The doctor slowly inched backward toward the sheets of plastic, not breaking eye contact with Nurse Lilly.

"Mother. What's wrong?" The corners of Nurse Lilly's lips turned downward, her rosy cheeks losing their color. "You're not going already, are you? Let's make sure," Nurse Lilly said.

Lightning quick, Nurse Lilly took a syringe from her pocket, jabbing it into her mother's neck. Dr. Habsburg went limp immediately, collapsing onto the floor.

The Attic
1:05 a.m.

Seeing Dr. Habsburg collapse, Vickie gasped, and in her distress, knocked something over in the dark closet, making a loud thud.

With a swift hop and a step, Nurse Lilly stood at the closet. Before Vickie could register what was happening, Nurse Lilly yanked her out by the arm, and with three quick jerks, spoke. "Does anyone else know you're here? Don't lie to me! I'll know."

Vickie's heart leaped into her throat, making it hard for her to conjure words. She looked Nurse Lilly in the eyes for an eternal moment.

The crow at the window jabbed at the glass, over and over, until it began to crack, bloodying the bird's beak.

"Just your cousin," Vickie said.

"That's okay, then. I couldn't have carried our new family here without him," Nurse Lilly said.

"Mother, it looks like we'll have another guest for tea," Nurse Lilly said, in a sweet, singsong voice. "Vickie, their parents didn't care about them. You have to understand, no one wanted any of them but me. That's why I chose them, and they chose me. I am their only hope."

Nurse Lilly grabbed the nearby nail gun and sat Vickie down at the plywood table, smiling calmly as Vickie struggled. Vickie was strong. But Nurse Lilly had the strength of a crazed person, her eyes so intent that Vickie felt the weight of her stare squeezing the life out of her.

"Guess we'll have to make sure you stay put too," Nurse Lilly said, her voice still sugary sweet. Vickie struggled even more to no avail.

"This was supposed to be Linda's seat," Nurse Lilly said.

The crow hammered even more fervently on the glass.

"Go away!" Nurse Lilly screamed over her shoulder at the determined bird. Her finger squeezed and a nail shot toward the window, shattering the glass. The crow flapped away into the night.

Taking advantage of the distraction, Vickie pulled the golden garden shears from her pocket with her free hand and stabbed them into Nurse Lilly's shoulder, pushing away from her and rolling out of the chair.

"My shears. You found them." Nurse Lilly expelled a forced laugh, mechanically ignoring the pain.

Vickie ran through the sheets of plastic, pushing and shoving them out of the way, but hadn't gotten far when Nurse Lilly called, "Oh, Vickie. You're not going to leave Annie here all by herself, are you?"

Vickie paused, then turned back to face Nurse Lilly's bright, white form through the plastic. Nurse Lilly had pulled the shears from her shoulder and stood behind Annie, holding the sharp shears open, one blade next to Annie's neck, pressing into her flesh.

"Come back, and I'll make sure no accidents happen. I don't want anyone to get hurt. I want them all to be happy. We had no choice with Linda. Once she got out, she would have ruined everything. I will do anything to protect my family. Anything." Nurse Lilly pressed the shears even further into Annie's neck, until a trickle of blood ran from the fresh wound, staining the white collar of Annie's gown.

"Stop!" Vickie slowly inched back toward the table, shaking. "You won't hurt Annie if I stay?"

"You can trust me. I'm a nurse," Nurse Lilly said, smiling sweetly.

When Vickie was within arm's reach, Nurse Lilly seized her, pushing her into the seat again, and then forced Vickie's open palm down on the table.

She watched in horror as Nurse Lilly's finger hovered above the nail gun's trigger, then slowly made contact with it. Vickie squinted, preparing for the pain, when someone grabbed Nurse Lilly's other arm.

Angelo stood unsteadily behind her, a stream of blood running down his cheek and his left arm bruised. He did his best to hold Nurse Lilly and pull her away from Vickie, despite being unable to use his left hand.

Nurse Lilly, caught by surprise and still clutching the nail gun, whipped around and squeezed the trigger. With a loud pop the nail gun spat a piece of metal into Angelo's leg, sending him to his knees, howling in pain. He managed to grab the nurse from behind, taking her down to the floor with him. The gun fell from Nurse Lilly's hands as she hit the floor.

Angelo writhed in pain as Nurse Lilly crawled away, freeing herself from Angelo's grip. He quickly grabbed her by the hair, pulling her to the floor again, until they were eye to eye. She stared at him for a moment, scrunching her nose and snarling through her teeth. Then with one quick thrust, she head-butted Angelo, knocking him unconscious.

Nurse Lilly stumbled to her feet, with a bloodied bull's-eye circle marring her forehead.

Vickie, now ten feet away, grabbed the nail gun and held it up, pointing it at Nurse Lilly in a standoff. Nurse Lilly smiled. "Vickie," she said, taking a step forward.

"Stop." Vickie squeezed the trigger.

Click.

Then squeezed again.

Click. Click. Click.

Vickie and Nurse Lilly stared at one another. Then, in a sudden move, Vickie threw the nail gun at Nurse Lilly's head. She successfully dodged it, but it gave Vickie just enough time to get into the plastic sheeting and hide.

Nurse Lilly walked through the plastic, wielding her garden shears like a machete, clearing the way in front of her, grunting with each swipe.

"It doesn't have to be this way, Vickie. Come out."

Slash. Rip.

"Come out."

Slash. Rip.

"Wherever you are."

Nurse Lilly heard a sound come from behind a four-foot-high stack of Sheetrock. She smiled, holding the shears in front of her as she walked over to the building materials, peeking behind them.

"You can't hide from—"

Linda's crow furiously flapped its feathers in Nurse Lilly's face, startling her. She screamed and shielded her eyes, attempting to block the assault.

By the time she recovered, Vickie stood behind her, relaxed and poised to strike. Before the nurse could react, Vickie hooked a piece of stretch plastic wrap around her face, covering her mouth, nose, and eyes, squeezing it tight, making it impossible for her to breathe. Nurse Lilly swiped blindly at Vickie like a caged animal, cutting Vickie's shoulder.

Vickie winced as they both fell to the floor, but she maintained her grip on the plastic wrap until Nurse Lilly finally stopped flailing and passed out, the shears sliding out of her now open palm as she lay still on the floor.

Vickie, breathing heavily, jumped at the sound of Angelo limping over.

"Are you all right?" Angelo asked.

"Yeah. You?" Vickie relaxed her grip just a little on the plastic.

"Yeah. But my arm is killing me."

"Yeah, uh, sorry about that. The closet door wouldn't close."

Angelo smiled in confusion, attempting to make sense of her comment. "Help me tie her up, and then we can get help."

They grabbed a nearby spool of electrical wire and secured Nurse Lilly to a chair, removing the plastic from around her face. Angelo helped as best he could with his one good arm. Vickie wound the wire around Nurse Lilly's feet, then her hands. "I don't understand. Why did you help me and not your cousin?" she asked, still stunned and out of breath.

"My cousin? Her? She's not my cousing. I mean, my family is screwed up, but not Nurse Lilly screwed up," he said, his voice shaking with pain.

Exhausted, Vickie didn't acknowledge his attempt at a joke. She simply willed her trembling hands to tighten the wire around Nurse Lilly's ankles with one final tug.

CHAPTER 42
'Til Death Do Us Part

The Grounds
5:45 a.m.

The early morning sun beamed, signaling a new day, but remnants from the night before remained fully present. The lights atop police cars and ambulances rotated quietly, the vehicles parked haphazardly on the finely manicured grass, crushing it into the dark earth.

Like frenetic bees, paramedics cluttered the circle driveway in front of Blueberry Hill. Tents had sprung up to provide shade while they treated Annie and the other missing teens for their injuries.

The remaining residents of the manor clustered in groups, talking, hugging, and saying goodbye. Rumors circulated about who was being released and who was being transferred to another temporary facility. Although this was the moment many had prayed for, the way in which it had happened was abrupt and disconcerting. Not everyone was taking it well.

Dr. Cannon did her best to talk the confused teens through the turmoil, at points placing her hands on their shoulders to help steady their emotions.

Vickie walked down the steps into the sun, chewing gum to calm her nerves. She carried a plastic bag half full of water and the seven goldfish from the tank in the lobby. The fish sparkled in the sunlight, flashing orange hues like signal flares. She paused at the back of an ambulance, catching sight of a shirtless Angelo being treated on a gurney. His hairy chest glistened in the sunlight, almost as bright as the fish. His sad, tired eyes lassoed her toward him. She set the fish down on his gurney as he turned and spoke to her.

"Vickie, I'm sorry I didn't tell you. When I found out about Linda, that I had a sister, I couldn't believe it. I grew up in the foster system, and I didn't even know our mother had had another baby. I had to do anything I could to find her and get to know her, so I got a job here. It was the only way I could meet her. And when she died, I wanted to stay and figure out what happened to her. I wanted to at least give her that. I never would have guessed — if I had had any idea about Nurse Lilly — I should have told you sooner."

Vickie placed her hand on top of Angelo's open palm, and he exhaled, his muscles relaxing, and his eyes fluttering closed until she spoke.

"It's OK."

Angelo peeled his eyelids open. Whatever sedative the EMTs had given him was clearly having an effect. "I'd like to make it up to you. I hope you'll stay in touch."

As Vickie looked deep into his hazel eyes, she knew they would always be connected, even if they never saw each other again. They both loved and had been loved by Linda. "Goodbye, Angelo." Vickie slipped her hand out of his. "Oh, yeah, one more thing." She dug her hand inside her bra, retrieving the two credit cards she had taken from him, placing them on his chest, and patting them. They bore no evidence of their rough treatment in the doorjamb.

Angelo knitted his eyebrows in confusion as Vickie grabbed the fish, and the EMTs wheeled him away. She continued walking down to the lake where Squirt, Eagen, and Tracy stood. Annie joined a few minutes later and seemed to be recovering quickly, at least, physically. Vickie stumbled a bit, bleary-eyed and exhausted, but caught herself, then steadied her footing as she continued toward the water's edge. The teens watched as she walked past.

She lifted the plastic bag, speaking to the goldfish as if they could understand her. "Well, you made it. We made it. I hope you grow as big as you want to. Oh, and if you see a delicious worm, just dangling there, and wonder if it's too good to be true, it is! Humans are pretty devious. Tricky. For your sake, I hope mine is the last human face you ever see."

Vickie ceremoniously emptied the seven goldfish into the lake, exhaling as they swam away.

She sensed someone move into the space behind her.

"So, you're going home?" Squirt asked.

"Yes. Apparently, I'm rehabilitated. Which just means they ran out of room at the other place they're sending everyone else to," Vickie said.

Just then, a police car, different from the rest, approached the police line, honking its horn. Uncle Aldo and Rosemary waved out the windows. "Looks like my ride's already here."

"Vickie!" Rosemary yelled.

"I'll be right there, Ma!" Vickie smiled and waved. "From one crazy house back to another. But they're my favorite flavor of crazy. Extra nutty, with all those toppings that are bad for you but make life worth living."

What remained of pod 1 gathered around Vickie in a loose circle, all staring at the ground like they did most days during their morning session in the rec room.

"Don't forget me, er, us, Vickie," Squirt said.

"How could I ever forget any of you? Especially you, Squirt," Vickie said, smiling at him. Squirt blushed red all the way to the ends of his ears.

Vickie pulled back her shirt sleeve, revealing her tattoo. "After all, I'm stuck with this birdlike blob for the rest of my life."

They all laughed, then one by one, stuck their arms into the circle, revealing their tattoos. Except for Eagen.

"Just missing a couple of people," Vickie said.

"Julie?" Tracy remarked.

"And Linda," Eagen added.

Annie looked at each member of the circle. "For life," Annie said, her arm still outstretched.

"For life," Tracy said.

"For life," Squirt quickly added.

They all looked at Eagen.

He stuck his arm into the center, finally revealing his own tattoo.

"'Til death do us part," Eagen said.

An older gentleman dressed in an expensive, tailored suit stepped out of a blue sports car behind the police line. His voice boomed across the lawn in a Liverpuddlian accent. "Tracy!"

"Dad?" Tracy said. He held his hand up to the man, waving, before turning back to the group.

"I don't believe it. His accent is real," Eagen said.

Squirt and Vickie chuckled.

Vickie's eyes tracked toward an ambulance where the missing teens each lay on their own gurney. Justin stood next to Tim, cradling his hands, their foreheads touching one another, nose to nose, eyes closed.

Vickie looked at Tim, then back at Eagen. "So, his fear was that people would find out he likes boys?"

"No, his fear was that he had lost the only person he's ever loved who loved him back."

"Guess being in love's not good for a bully's street cred," Vickie added.

"Apparently, some things are more important than street cred," Eagen said.

Vickie nodded. "And more powerful than fear."

"Hmmm," Eagen said as they both stared at Tim and Justin, who were still engaged in a gentle embrace.

"What happened?" Tracy asked.

Vickie watched as officers escorted a handcuffed Nurse Lilly to the back of a police car. "I may never know who drove the car that hit Linda or why they didn't stay to help her. But, at least I can tell part of Linda's story. She didn't run into the road because she wanted to die. She was drugged, not in her right mind, and trying to save herself from Nurse Lilly, from this place. Linda wanted to live."

The members of pod 1 stood in silence, staring at the ground and off into the distance, until each of the teens peeled off one by one, after saying good-bye in their own way.

The first was Annie.

Vickie hugged Annie the tightest, careful to avoid her bandaged hand. "I hope you get that new family."

"I like this one," she said, looking at the faces of everyone in her pod.

"Take care, roomie," Vickie said. Annie walked back toward the medical teams, zigzagging her way up the hill. Her meander would have been worrisome if it had been anyone but Annie. Instead, it was simply the way she walked.

Squirt put out his hand to shake Vickie's. "Well, nice knowing you."

Vickie shook it then pulled him in for an embrace, his eyes bugging out of his head in surprise. He seemed to float along the grass when he walked away shortly after.

Eagen and Vickie stood opposite one another for a moment. Vickie ran through all the possible ways they could part: hug, handshake, high-five. None seemed appropriate, until Eagen simply nodded his head and, in the simplest of gestures, spoke volumes. Vickie received, then volleyed back the movement.

"So, you never said — what's your fear?"

"You're right. I didn't, did I?"

And then, like a dark storm cloud that was appreciated and even respected for its foreshadowing, he was gone.

With the other members of pod 1 having left, Vickie and Tracy faced each other as the last to depart.

"My ride's here too. I probably shouldn't keep him waiting any longer." Tracy pointed with a grin back at his dad.

"Let's not let this be the last time we see each other," Vickie said.

"I'm really glad you're safe. Stay wilder than the wind, Vickie," Tracy said.

"I'm still not sure what that means, but will do." Vickie's breath left her in a rush, sweeping the last words out of her mouth, as Tracy moved closer and rested his hands on her arms.

Tracy winked, then kissed Vickie on the cheek and walked away. Vickie, still chewing her gum, was momentarily stunned; then she made a decision and called after him.

"Hey, Trace!" Vickie said.

He stopped and turned back to face her.

With her signature swagger, wind blowing through their hair now, Vickie strode over to Tracy and bent him back in her arms, kissing him on the lips. She slid her mouth back and forth over his like he was a Sour Charms lollipop from the 7-Eleven. When she had had enough, she righted him back on his feet, then walked away without saying another word.

Tracy stared after her, equally stunned and smiling, chewing the gum Vickie once had in her mouth.

"So hot," Squirt exhaled, fanning himself, observing them from the garden path. "A number's game. Hmmm," he said to himself, remembering Tracy's dating advice. He made his way to the front steps of the manor and stood by the french doors as some of the female residents exited the mansion toward a transportation van.

As each girl passed, Squirt addressed them in his most suave voice, which cracked occasionally despite his best efforts. He stood on his tippy toes so he could look them in the eye.

The first girl passed.

"Stay wilder than the wind," Squirt said.

A second girl passed.

"Stay wilder than the wind," he said again.

A third girl passed.

"Stay wilder than the wind."

The third girl paused, then turned and smiled at Squirt, the wind picking up again as if just for him, before she continued to walk toward the van.

Squirt's face lit up like a Christmas tree and he breathed deep, puffing out his chest in accomplishment. "He was right!" Squirt said, pumping his fist in the air. "Yes!"

Vickie watched him from a distance, amused, as she walked toward Uncle Aldo's car. Emotion welled up inside the pit of her stomach, but she knew the car was so close and yet so far. There were still other goodbyes to make.

She passed the old reporter, who tipped his hat in greeting. And there was someone familiar beside him. Mr. Fitch.

Insight dawned on her. *He must have been the informant. I guess I kind of knew that.* Vickie high-fived him as she passed.

Outside one of the ambulances, Dr. Habsburg reclined on a gurney, undergoing an evaluation by an EMT. "How are you feeling?" the EMT asked.

Dr. Habsburg smiled with some effort, then slowly repeated her mantra. "All better now," she said.

Vickie's heart twisted in knots as if someone were kneading it like bread. She felt anger. Sadness. Relief. And now, the most surprising emotion of all, she felt compassion for the doctor as their eyes met.

She continued walking, not smiling, because sometimes you didn't feel like smiling, and that was okay. A thought gnawed at her, but she tried not to listen to it.

This won't be the last time you see Dr. Habsburg.

She preferred to think of other things, like Uncle Aldo's gentle smile as he greeted her, hugging Vickie when she reached the car, which was now parked on the front lawn. He had inadvertently driven over some of Nurse Lilly's ivy. Vickie bubbled with pleasure, noticing the act.

Finally, the wave of emotion reached her throat and spilled out of her in words, her head on Uncle Aldo's shoulder. "You know, Uncle Aldo, I thought I didn't have a dad. But I do," Vickie said, her voice trembling.

"Yes, you do, kid." Uncle Aldo tapped the side of his head with his pointer finger and dragged it down to his heart. "And don't you forget it."

Vickie looked up at him and smiled and then turned to hug her mom, who was bursting with tears next to him. She breathed in the scent of her shampoo, Wella Balsam. Familiar, comforting, like home. Rosemary gave in to the hug, surrendered so completely that Vickie could feel their hearts beat in unison.

As they climbed into the car, Vickie looked back toward the manor through the rear window. She watched Eagen break off a colorful rose in full bloom as he passed the garden, sending it falling to the ground. Then he paused and picked the blossom up, putting it into the buttonhole on the lapel of his black jacket.

The bright color contrasted sharply with his perpetually dark apparel, and she thought she saw the ghost of a smile cross his face as he followed Annie toward the manor. With everything she had seen today, this was one of the most surprising things. A smile spread over her own face.

At the fourth-floor window of her old room, Vickie could have sworn she saw the curtains part and a frail, young woman waving to her, just as she had done on that very first day. "Goodbye, Linda," she whispered.

A solitary crow sat atop the ledge in front of the attic window. Flapping its wings in a triumphant flutter before rising into the air, it rode the wind, the morning sun on its back, following Vickie's car as it wound its way down the country road and back toward home.

Home, Vickie thought as she settled into the back seat, before the word fell out of her lips. "Home."

SCAN ME

CHAPTER 43
The Couch

DAY 01 for Vickie
Bartolucci Residence, Queens, NY
11:30 a.m.

Vickie stuffed her excitement down, still unsure if she could trust that it wouldn't all be snatched from her like a blissful morning dream.

The car crawled to a stop, Uncle Aldo effortlessly parking so close to the curb you couldn't have slid a piece of paper between the side of the right tires and the concrete.

Vickie took a deep breath before she allowed herself to look up through the car window. The house seemed so much smaller, but still just right, with its chipped yellow paint and shrubbery in various stages of life.

Uncle Aldo opened the rear door for Vickie. Perps usually rode where she sat, but, judging by his teary-eyed smile and outstretched hand, the kind gesture was especially for Vickie and not just out of habit.

Vickie reached across the back seat for the canvas bag full of her belongings, but Rosemary put her hand on her shoulder.

"I've got it," Rosemary said.

"You sure, Ma?"

"Today is your day. Just relax. Here's my keys, why don't you just open up, and we'll be right behind you," Rosemary said, winking at Uncle Aldo.

"You all right, Ma?"

"Just excited to have you home."

Vickie took the keys and savored every step she took on the cracked concrete walkway until she finally stood at the door. The key slid into the lock with ease, welcoming her inside as she pushed the faded green, wooden door open.

"Surprise!" A few neighbors and Bartolucci relatives sprang from their hiding places into the hallway.

Vickie's heart jumped in her chest. She wrapped her fingers in between the keys like they were brass knuckles, ready to fight.

Rosemary appeared close behind her. "I wish it could be under different circumstances, but I still wanted to show 'ya how happy I am you are home. I can cancel it if it's too much."

Vickie scanned the room and the smiling faces of neighbors and family that had no clue about what she had been through. With the help of family members, her mother had even gotten balloons in every color of the rainbow and a cake for the occasion.

"It's perfect. And you even made a punch."

Rosemary blushed.

"You outdid yourself," Vickie said, kissing her mother on the cheek.

Rosemary smiled, and a giggle rose inside her and out of her lips. "And I have another surprise."

"Ma? You've done enou—" Vickie said.

Vickie heard the sound of high-heeled shoes walking across the wood veneer floors.

From a nearby room, Julie entered.

"What? Get outta here. Julie Maxwell? In my house?" Vickie commented, her mouth gaping open.

Julie approached Vickie and flashed a grin. "I've never been good at being a friend. But I figured if I was going to learn, why not learn from the best?" she said.

313

"Well, here's rule number one of friendship. Friends never let a good couch go to waste," Vickie said.

The small crowd of guests laughed.

"Just like you left it," Rosemary said, motioning toward the couch like one of those models on *The Price is Right,* and shooing a Bartolucci cousin away who sat there, his mouth full of chips.

"Get up already!" Rosemary said sternly.

Vickie stopped herself from flopping down on the couch's familiar softness, then turned toward her friend. "Yeah, but you know what? I've been thinking. I want to get out more," Vickie said.

"Oh, yeah?" Rosemary asked, surprised, lifting her voice even higher than usual.

Moments later, the green-and-yellow floral-print couch rested outside in the tiny backyard, and Vickie and Julie sat together, drinking punch in small, faux-crystal cups with handles.

Rosemary approached them, grinning from ear to ear. "Here's that thing you wanted me to pick up. Uncle Aldo drove me to get it last weekend." Rosemary gently placed a crumpled brown paper bag with a peel-and-stick red Christmas bow on it between Vickie and Julie.

Vickie picked up the bag and offered it to her couch mate.

"For me?"

Vickie shrugged. Moisture gathered in Julie's eyes.

"What? You're crying?"

Julie nodded.

"You think this is a Hallmark movie or something?"

Julie opened the bag and removed a sweater similar to Vickie's monogrammed cardigan, only with a *J* on it.

"I love it. *J* for — ?"

"Jamaica Jaguars. As in Jamaica, Queens." Vickie raised her left shoulder to her ear and pursed her lips to the side. "Or Julie. Take your pick."

Julie grinned and put on the sweater, snuggling into it.

Vickie's face softened from the still, warm feeling that emanated from inside her. She looked at Julie as if pulling her into her thoughts.

"You know, I've been thinking," Vickie said. "We were all at Blueberry Hill for different reasons, but turns out, we had more than just being there in common. We were all also growing and changing. Sometimes in big leaps and sometimes in ways so small we didn't even notice."

They each picked up their punch cups.

"We didn't need to manage our lives. We needed to live them a little more," Vickie said.

Vickie and Julie clinked their cups together.

Vickie took one long slurp. "What? I'm living a little more by enjoying my punch with a slurp."

Julie grinned, then tried to outdo Vickie with her slurp. "Me too."

They both giggled, with dueling slurps back and forth.

"I've never met anyone like you," Julie said.

"What do you mean?"

"You are so good at so many things."

"Me? Like what?"

"Deep thoughts. Figuring stuff out. Puzzles. People. You're like a superhero."

Vickie could feel the heat rise from around the collar of her sweatshirt and color rush into her face. "Nah, I'm just good at one thing."

Julie looked at her intently, her posture stiffening as she leaned in a bit more.

"I'm just good at being me."

Julie smiled and nodded in agreement and admiration.

"There is one thing I haven't figured out, though. If Angelo wasn't Nurse Lilly's cousin who was?" Vickie asked. "And where is he now?"

A Gas Station
12:15 p.m.

The sun was high overhead as a man exited the deserted gas station. The tall, thin figure got into a red pickup truck, the same vehicle that prematurely ended Linda's life.

He wore a Blueberry Hill janitor's uniform, his face obscured by his hat and dark, stringy hair. Starting the engine, the truck only moved forward a few feet before something tumbled from the seat to the floorboards. The janitor slammed on the brakes and reached down to retrieve the object.

An antique music box.

He held it gently in his hands, tracing the gold detailing with his pointer finger as his memories turned over in his head like an engine firing.

DAY 45 for Vickie
The Lobby
3:10 a.m.
23 Minutes Until Linda's Death

The descending moon penetrated the french doors. The lobby still smelled of pine cleaner. All remained quiet except for rustling movement coming from the open janitor's closet.

His face obscured by his hat, his gaunt features barely visible because of his downcast eyes, the night janitor put away the last of his supplies; only the rolling yellow mop bucket remained. He turned to grab the bucket, when he realized someone had joined him.

"Lillian?"

"I need your help, cousin."

"Whenever you call me cousin, it's serious."

"She got away."

"Who?"

"Little Linda."

"How's that possible? I just carried her up a few hours ago."

"Maybe I didn't use enough powder. I don't know what to do. Please help me."

Nurse Lilly's shoulders sank under the weight of her pleading eyes.

"I'll take care of it. That's what family's for."

The janitor left everything, and in a blur, disappeared down the hallway, past the cafeteria, and out the rear door that led to the kitchen loading dock.

The old, red pickup truck sat, cool from the night air, already slumbering for the evening. The janitor climbed inside its cab and started the engine with one turn. Quick as lightning, he barreled down the dirt service road that ran around the estate.

The thick line of trees that lined the dirt drive spat him onto the highway. There he stopped, then sighed in relief that he had found her so quickly.

Linda.

She drifted through the grass and onto the highway without noticing him, likely still under the influence of the powder or whatever else his cousin might have given her.

Linda gathered her arms around herself. The janitor watched her moon dance before placing his foot firmly on the gas. The truck accelerated quickly. Within seconds, Linda's white nightdress reflected the beams of the headlights so intensely, the janitor squinted.

No turning back.

"That's what family's for," he mumbled to himself.

Crash.

The passenger-side tires rose up and then down, leaving Linda's lifeless body in the rearview mirror.

A Gas Station
12:15 p.m.

The janitor still held the music box and cranked the knob in three quick turns. Its sounds tickled the air with its faint, whispered notes.

He hummed along as he drove into the distance.

The more we get together, together, together.

The more we get together . . .

"The happier we'll be," he sang out loud to only himself.

The Bartolucci Backyard
12:15 p.m.

"I just got goose bumps," Julie said, shivering a little.

"Hmmmph. I'm sure whoever the cousin is will come to me. I'll figure it out," Vickie said.

They both drank their beverages, staring at the backyard fence.

Vickie paused, peering into the distance as a yellow leaf fell from the large tree that hung over their heads from the neighbor's yard on the other side of the fence. She picked up the leaf and twirled it between two fingers.

"Yep. Things are changing. And if everything's changing, that means everything is temporary. So, you got to enjoy things while you can. 'Cause who knows what's waiting around the corner," Vickie said.

Julie joined Vickie in her stare into the horizon and beyond.

"I like you, Vickie Bartolucci."

"As much as I know I might regret saying this, I don't hate you so much anymore either."

The pair shared a genuine, friend-worthy smile, cementing their unlikely bond.

The End
For Now

AMAZON REVIEW

If you enjoyed your experience of, *The Vickie Chronicles*, would you take a moment to review, *Dark Masks*, on Amazon? We'd love to hear what you think.

IN THE MEANTIME...

Turn the page for a sneak preview of the next book in the series, *Dark Chains*.

DARK CHAINS
Sneak Preview

The wind rustled the hedges outside Vickie's cracked bedroom window, fluttering the Dollar Store lace curtains.

Julie lay in Vickie's bed as the gentle breeze licked her awake like a puppy. Her eyes drifted open, and she smiled as the room came into focus, remembering where she was. She propped herself up with her arm and rubbed her eyes.

"Vickie," she whispered.

Julie looked down at the mattress on the floor where Vickie slept when she stayed over, but it was empty. She always tried to talk Vickie out of giving up her bed, but Vickie insisted.

Julie peered through sleep-hazed eyes at the window. Moonlight poured in, giving the room an ethereal glow. She shimmied over to the end of the bed, where she slid her feet into the pair of slippers they had bought at the Dollar Store. Julie loved that place. It was a treasure chest of absolute necessities that you didn't need one bit. The first time Vickie had taken her there, Julie had spent $157, which was roughly 157 items. It was thrilling to dig through the bins and find just what you didn't know you were looking for, like these fuzzy slippers.

Julie shuffled toward the door, stopping when she caught sight of herself in the mirror. She took a moment to examine herself further.

Julie hadn't yet grown accustomed to her new haircut. The Parisian stylist called it a collarbone bob because it stopped at the clavicles. "This timeless French cut is in between a long and short hair length and features soft, textured layers, exuding a nonchalant, French-girl look," Frederick enticed. "And it's a very easy-to-manage cut. You can refresh your length without sacrificing a ponytail or bun."

Julie had never had bangs, so the adjustment would take a while. She had hated it at first, but after spending time with Vickie these past few days, she was reminded that it was just hair. Julie surveyed the rest of the room.

She liked the coziness of Vickie's room; it was just the right size for two girls having a sleepover.

The bulletin board over Vickie's desk made Julie smile. It was covered in every postcard Julie had sent during her summer trip to France. She imagined Vickie reading each word with the same joy she read the correspondences she received from Vickie when they were apart.

The desk underneath was littered with all the signs of a sleepover: empty Twizzlers and Sour Charms wrappers and two bowls stained with the remnants of the cherry Jell-O they had made together the day before.

She shuddered to think what her life would have been like without 7-Eleven Slurpees, dollar stores, and cheap press-on nails. But mostly she couldn't imagine her life without Vickie as her friend.

Julie stacked the bowls and spoons, deciding she would carry them to the kitchen. That was another thing she would have never thought of before her stays at Vickie house, where there was no maid to tidy up twice a day.

She had spent the night several times over the past year. Strangely, she felt more at home here than just about anywhere in the world.

Julie walked toward the door, bowls in hand. Vickie's mom always kept a little nightlight on in the hallway in case of late-night bathroom breaks. Julie paused, looking at the photos of Vickie through the years in simple frames on the wall. In Julie's estimation, Vickie and her mother didn't have a lot, but they had everything. A smile played across her face as she touched a picture of baby Vickie, mouth covered in chocolate.

On her way to the kitchen, Julie saw Vickie standing in the living room with her back to her.

"Vic —" Julie said.

Vickie swung at Julie with a baseball bat. Julie ducked, but dropped the dishes. Luckily, they were plastic, from the Dollar Store.

"You scared me," Vickie said, loosening her death-grip on the bat.

"I scared you?" Julie said, picking up the dishes and spoons.

"I thought I heard something. Shhhh. Listen," Vickie said.

They listened so intently that when the landline attached to the wall rang, they both jumped.

"Who's calling at this hour?"

"You sound like you're eighty-five," Julie said.

Vickie picked up the phone. "Hello? Hello? Who is this?" Vickie's face dropped as the color ran from her cheeks. Vickie slowly hung up the phone.

"Who was it?"

"It sounded like Squirt."

"Squirt? How'd he get your number?"

"The kid's a genius. He can look up a phone number."

"What's he doing calling at this hour? Pervert," Julie said.

"I don't know. He sounded like he's in trouble." Vickie picked up the phone again.

"What are you doing?"

"I'm star-sixty-nine-ing him." Vickie waited for a few rings and was close to hanging up when someone answered.

"Hello? Blueberry Hill Home for Troubled Youth," the voice said on the other end. The words hung in the air and hit both their hearts with dull thuds.

Vickie stumbled through her response. "Ahhhh. We're calling about your car's extended warranty."

The night nurse hung up.

"Squirt's at Blueberry Hill," Vickie said.

"Why would he be there?"

"I don't know, but he called me by name. And then the phone went dead. He sounded scared."

"What do we do?"

"Let's go to his house in the morning. I know where he lives."

The two girls stared at one another in a concerned silence until ssomething outside caught both their attention.

Outside the living room window the girls spied a black bird peeking indoors, its wings shining in the moonlight.

Available on Amazon.

SCAN ME

WANT TO HELP SPREAD THE WORD?

If you loved, *The Vickie Chronicles,* half as much as we did and want to help us spread the word, consider the following:

1. As mentioned, leave a **review** on Amazon.
2. **Subscribe** to our newsletter at: bit.ly/TheSavageBooksNews
3. **Recommend** the book to a friend.
4. Ask your **local bookstore** to stock it.

CONNECT WITH THE AUTHOR

Got something you'd like to say to I. Savage? You'll either find him in a local coffee shop writing his next book or connect with him here:

@thesavagebooks

https://thesavagebooks.com/

COFFEE SHOPS

A special thanks to the coffee shops that provided an extra-vibey backdrop for the writing of, *Dark Masks*.

Please support those who so generously caffeinate creatives.

Café Cluny

284 W. 12th St., New York, NY 10014

Common Good Harlem

2801 Frederick Douglass Blvd., New York, NY 10039

Lucille's Coffee and Cocktails

26 Macombs Pl., New York, NY 10039

Sadie's Coffee

324 S. Garnett St., Henderson, NC 27536

Think Coffee

208 W. 13th St., New York, NY 10011

PLAYLISTS ON SPOTIFY

Have a listen to the music that inspired I. Savage as he penned the series and check out our character playlists.

ACKNOWLEDGMENTS

Thanks to every member of the IN Studios Family, past, present, and future. May we continue to inspire the creative best in each other.

I'm so appreciative of the beautiful minds of my editors, Kylie Maron-Vallorani, Aime Sund, and Cassie Newell, as well as my proofreader Joanne Lui. Thanks for ensuring it all made sense.

To all who added visuals to the book, thank you: our illustrators Katerina Prenda and J. Fern, blueprint designer Oleg Stepanov, and photographer Ismael Fernandez. You made everything pretty, including me.

Thanks to those who participated in readings and improvisation workshops, or purchased the book, or simply sent well wishes.

So many went above and beyond, offering input on various drafts of this book. Thank you. A special acknowledgment of my beta readers: Gabriele Schafer, Mindy Kaplan, Caren Skibell, Ellen Ko, Richard Johnson, Vaveria Etheredge, Kylie Maron-Vallorani, Toren Savage, and Gitana Savage.

Special appreciation goes out to our members who stoked each other's creative flames during the pandemic with this particular project: Annika Andersson, Timothy Coleman, Don Comas, Adrian Danila, George Davis, Vavaria Etheredge, Armando Guzmán, George Hider, Travis Himebaugh, Richard Johnson, Gloria Jung, Mindy Kaplan, Ellen Ko, James Lacey, Kylie Maron-Vallaroni, Elizabeth Parish, Zoe Parker, James Phinizy, Agustin Rodriguez, Kenya Sophia, Sheilah "Starlight" Smiley, Gabriele Schafer, Caren Skibell, and Rodney Umble, to name a few.